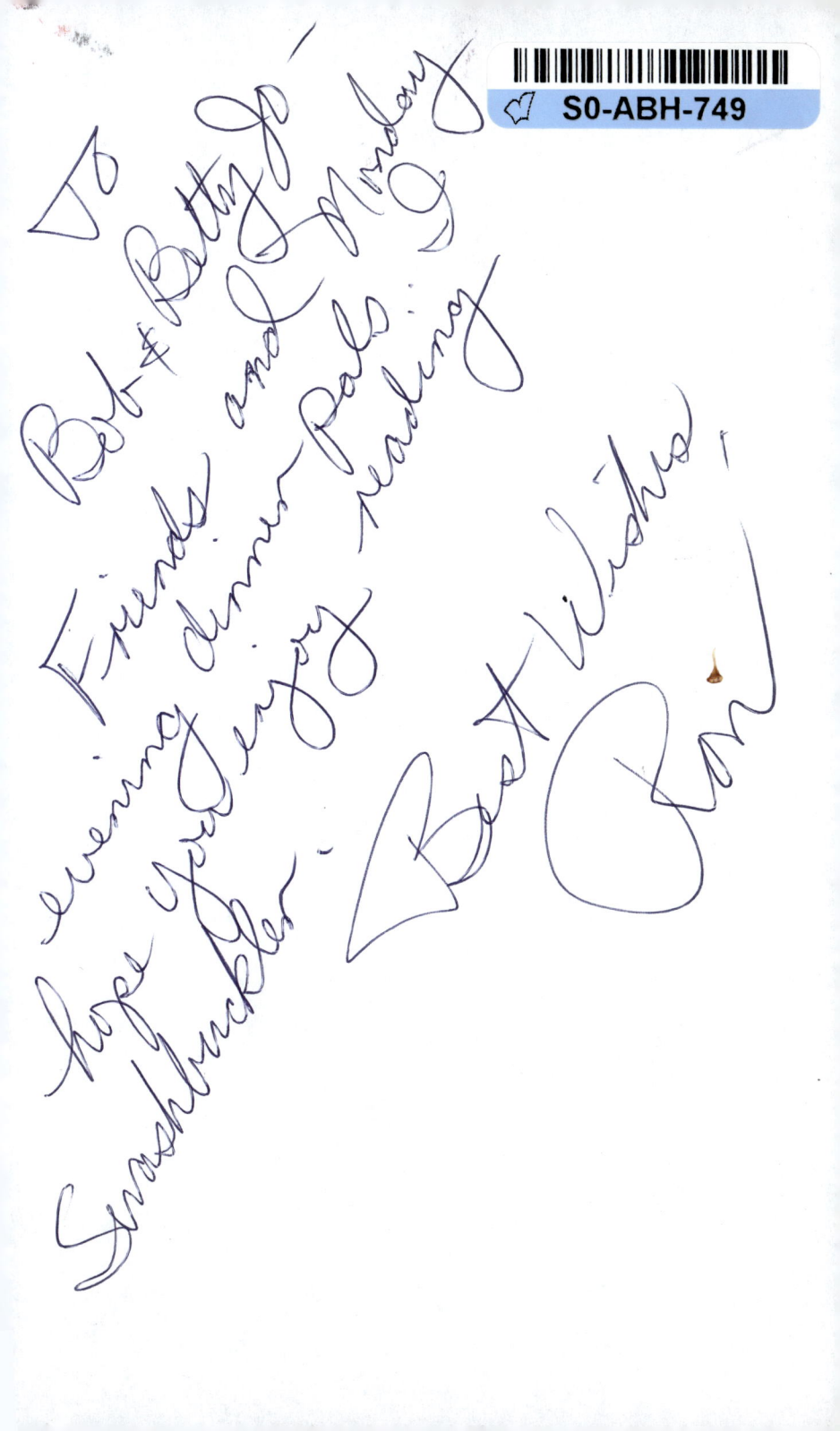

To
Bob & Betty Jo —
Friends and Monday
evening dinner pals —
hope you enjoy reading
Swashbuckler — Best Wishes,
[signature]

SWASHBUCKLER

An **FBI** International Thriller

Ron Cleaver

Copyright © 2008 by Ronald Cleaver

All rights reserved. No part of this book shall be reproduced or transmitted in any form or by any means, electronic, mechanical, magnetic, photographic including photocopying, recording or by any information storage and retrieval system, without prior written permission of the publisher. No patent liability is assumed with respect to the use of the information contained herein. Although every precaution has been taken in the preparation of this book, the publisher and author assume no responsibility for errors or omissions. Neither is any liability assumed for damages resulting from the use of the information contained herein.

This is a work of fiction. Names, characters, places, and incidents either are the product of the author's imagination or are used fictitiously. Any resemblance to actual events or locales or persons, living or dead, is entirely coincidental.

ISBN 0-7414-4633-2

Published by:

INFINITY
PUBLISHING.COM

1094 New DeHaven Street, Suite 100
West Conshohocken, PA 19428-2713
Info@buybooksontheweb.com
www.buybooksontheweb.com
Toll-free (877) BUY BOOK
Local Phone (610) 941-9999
Fax (610) 941-9959

Printed in the United States of America

Printed on Recycled Paper

Published August 2008

ACKNOWLEDGMENTS

Thanks to all of you who have continued to give me encouragement in my writing. I have very much appreciated the kind comments received regarding my first novel "**TRAP DOORS**" and hope that you enjoy reading "**SWASHBUCKLER**."

Cover Photo: Palau / Ron Cleaver

CHAPTER ONE

The faint sound of foghorns could be heard in the distance and quick flickers of dim light emanating from the moon and stars appeared from time to time as a dark cover of heavy clouds briefly parted overhead.

Although disconcerting, this eerie night with its ghost-like conditions was not unlike many others on the high seas for two solemn-faced crewmembers assigned to stand watch on the lonely deck of the *Hafa Adai*, as their Guam based cargo vessel cautiously made its way through the Makassar Strait.

From his position on the bridge, Captain Cruz was also keeping a watchful eye out into the thick mist for any signs of peril that may lie ahead. For over a year, the ship's skipper had been receiving warnings about menacing pirate attacks in the shipping lanes throughout the Indonesian waters. Crews had been assaulted and killed, and ships commandeered, never to be seen again. Now, with his attention focused into this uneasy darkness, the captain slowed the cargo ship's speed for an upcoming treacherous passageway.

Unknown to the captain and the crew aboard the *Hafa Adai*, however, a series of events were about to unfold that could prove life changing for all. Several miles into this murk of thick fog and darkness, modern-day swashbucklers were completing final preparations for an impending assault.

These perilous conditions were ideal for what pirate Captain Buruk had in mind. Continuing to monitor the sophisticated electronic tracking devices installed aboard his ship, the *Fantom*, Buruk had been searching for vulnerable cargo ships, freighters, and luxury yachts on which to launch an attack. Now, having identified what appeared to be an exposed target, the captain decided it was time to take action.

When the alarm sounded, hoists lifted specially constructed outer shells from what otherwise appeared to be a collection of standard containers, the type found lining ports, carried on trailers of eighteen-wheelers, and sitting onboard vessels. Underneath each of these exposed shells, however, was something very special – a modern, sleek, black, open-hulled, high-speed fastboat. These boats were similar in design to those frequently encountered by law enforcement when interdicting smugglers of illicit drugs, as they made runs between traffickers' mother ships and nearby stash houses.

With the containers' outer shells removed and stacked on the deck, the crewmembers attached overhead hooks to the boats. Crewmen climbed into the boats and they were carefully lowered into the daunting sea.

Shortly thereafter, the captain flashed a signal to the crew and the high-powered engines began to rumble. On his radio command, all of the men and their crafts charged simultaneously into the darkness.

As the heavily armed pirate crews raced their sleek crafts toward the vulnerable *Hafa Adai*, pent-up excitement began building inside each of these thrill-seeking renegades. After all, this was the kind of action they lived for. Nothing beat seeing the look of sheer terror spread across the faces of those they engaged. That was the ultimate high for this collection of contemporary swashbucklers.

Dressed in camouflage fatigues and jungle boots, each pirate strapped a blowgun across his chest, and carried either an AK-47 or a grenade launcher. From their belts hung a collection of knives, flash grenades, loaded magazine/clips of ammunition, and holstered pistols.

Upon catching glimpses of blurred light emanating from the *Hafa Adai*, the fastboats' engines were cut, and the mates began to paddle into the dense fog.

As the pirates came along side the stern of the cargo ship, they pulled black masks over their faces and put up grappling hooks. When all of the hooks were secured, Buruk issued a hushed signal to board, and the pirates climbed silently up the ropes.

One of the two shipmates standing watch suddenly heard a noise and started cautiously moving in that direction. Spotting what looked like a grappling hook attached to a rope hanging over the side, he quickly summoned the other mate, but before help could arrive, one of the pirates had already assembled a three-piece blowgun.

The swashbuckler aimed the loaded blowgun at the neck of the crewman and blew through the mouthpiece. The poison dart dropped the mate in his tracks. Seeing his shipmate's body slumped on the deck, the other mate sounded a cry for help, but he was quickly silenced by the blade of another buccaneer and left for dead.

Captain Cruz ordered the doors to the decks of the *Hafa Adai* secured, but it was too late. Additional masked pirates had already boarded from the other side of the stern and were storming through doors leading to decks, interior passageways, and the engine room.

As the ship's crewmen were confronted by the heavily armed intruders, they immediately threw up their hands and were herded into an interior storage room. There, the door was secured from the outside with a steel bar being forced into an opening and wedged through the handle.

Meanwhile, pirate Captain Buruk and several others from his renegade crew quickly made their way up to the bridge, where they engaged the *Hafa Adai's* captain and one mate who were attempting to send an emergency SOS. After a brief struggle, the mate was knocked to the deck with a powerful blow to the head from the butt of an AK-47, and Captain Cruz was brutally pistol-whipped until he dropped. Both men now lay bloodied and motionless on the deck of the bridge.

"Are they dead, Captain?" asked one of the pirates.

Buruk plunged a knife into the chest of the mate just to make certain. He then strutted over to where Captain Cruz was lying and gave a bone jarring kick to the skipper's bloodied face and head with his boot. There was no reaction.

"Yeah, they're dead," grunted the pirate captain.

Now, in total control of the *Hafa Adai*, Buruk began pondering his next series of decisions.

Who would live?

Who would die?

Does he dare return the *Hafa Adai* to its crew, leaving enough pirates onboard to insure its arrival at a secluded port where the cargo would be offloaded and black-marketed, and the ship sold as yet another phantom?

Or, would they offload part of the cargo onto the pirate ship, *Fantom*, and then make their escape? If that were the choice and the crew was to remain locked up and the ship set to sea without guidance; well, that would be a sure formula for disaster.

Yes, these were all decisions Captain Buruk would soon make as he once again had the opportunity to act like some kind of a god. A role he had grown to relish.

Suddenly Buruk's radio beeped. When he picked up the receiver, the excited voice on the other end was that of his First Mate, Tomy. He had been left behind in charge of the *Fantom*, while Buruk led the pirate crew on the raid.

"Radar shows boats coming your way, Captain," reported the first mate. "They are probably navy or police patrols."

"How many, Tomy?" asked Buruk.

"Looks like three, Captain. Approaching from two directions!"

"Maggots!" Buruk yelled. "Maggots everywhere!"

"Blow the Master's safe!" shouted one pirate to another standing nearby.

There was a loud pop, followed by a puff of smoke, and the mate quickly opened the safe's door.

"Take all of the cash and valuables!" bellowed Buruk.

"Aye, aye, Sir," responded the mate.

"Time to go," commanded Captain Buruk. "All hands to the boats!"

"What about the ship's crew?" asked a pirate mate.

"Keep them locked in the storage room," ordered the captain.

"But. . . what about?"

"No buts!" interrupted Buruk. "As soon as our men are off, I will set the ship to sea."

"Without guidance?" questioned another buccaneer.

"Without guidance!" Buruk smugly replied. "That will teach those maggots!"

While scrambling along the deck to make their escape, one of the pirates stopped to take a trophy. Lopping off an ear of one of the two crewmen who had been standing watch on deck, this grizzly swashbuckler then raised the bloody ear high into the air before running to the grappling hook, where, after letting out with a piercing shriek, he slid down the rope and dropped into the last of the waiting fastboats.

In the meantime, the approaching patrol boats had received a call for assistance from the captain of a nearby freighter that was taking on water. That plea from the distressed freighter, coupled with the *Hafa Adai's* continued movement ahead, and Captain Cruz's failed effort in his attempt to transmit a call for help, had now resulted in those patrol boats changing course.

With all of the buccaneers now onboard their fastboats, and the engines rumbling, the black masks were removed and the spirited cutthroat chase back to the *Fantom* was about to begin.

"On my signal!" the pirate captain yelled over his radio.

Next came a blip of light, and the sleek craft charged into the darkness. The race to the mother ship went without incident, and within minutes of their return, the pirate crews had the fastboats out of the water and back into their cradles aboard the *Fantom*.

Captain Buruk bellowed, "Are the boats secured and all of the mates accounted for?"

"Yes, Sir," replied First Mate Tomy.

"Lower the container covers and bring Besar forward," ordered the captain.

The crew jumped into action. The container covers were carefully guided back into position around the fastboats and locked down, and the cage containing Buruk's pet Komodo dragon, Besar, was rolled onto the bridge beside him.

"After a stopover on Flores, we will go to Jakarta to fill the order," the captain told Tomy.

The sleazy first mate responded with a sinister snicker, "Girls again, Captain?"

"Girls again," Buruk assured his first mate. "These will be going to the U.S."

A creepy, evil smile now slowly spread across Tomy's face as he gave an approving nod.

"Prepare to make way for the Java Sea," shouted Captain Buruk. "Full speed ahead!"

As the powerful engines roared and the captain and his pirate crew aboard the *Fantom* quickly disappeared into a deepening fog, those remaining aboard the *Hafa Adai* sailed dangerously out of control toward an unknown destiny.

CHAPTER TWO

The dense fog did not subside, and as the *Hafa Adai* continued its blind and perilous charge through the Makasar Strait, the unimaginable was about to unfold.

"Captain!" yelled a panicked young merchant marine officer as he sat nearby on the bridge.

"What is it?" the skipper responded.

"Radar shows us on a collision course with an oncoming vessel!"

The captain rushed to the screen and peered downward, his eyes studying every blip. Should their filled to capacity, single-hulled, oil tanker collide with another ship, the potential for loss of life would be disastrous, and the massive spill created in these Indonesian waters bordering Borneo and Sulawesi would be devastating for years to come.

The tanker captain immediately ordered warning blasts.

As the cautionary sound from the ship's horns resonated through the thick mist, the radar screen showed no wavering on the part of the approaching vessel.

"What in the hell is going on?" the captain yelled in frustration. "Why wasn't I told sooner?"

The young officer responded defensively, "Captain, w-w-e-e-e thought the ship would slow or change direction, but nothing has happened. It is as if they cannot see us. The ship just keeps coming!"

The captain seethed as he barked out orders.

"Slow the speed to one-third, and change our direction to due north!"

The adjustments in speed and direction were hastily made. At the same time, an announcement went out over the loudspeaker for all crewmembers to put on their life vests in preparation for a possible collision.

Lying on the bridge deck of the *Hafa Adai*, Captain Cruz was slowly beginning to stir. The blasts emanating from the huge horns aboard the oil tanker caused him to come around.

Groggily, the cargo vessel captain shook his head. The pain was excruciating. As he attempted to focus his eyes, everything was a blur. He tried wiping them with his hand and fingers. That seemed to help a little. As he continued running his fingers along the side of his face, however, several of the cuts reopened and started bleeding.

Reaching up for a nearby support, he slipped back to the floor. The blood covering the fingers on one hand had caused him to lose his grip when he grasped the metal bar. He wiped his hand on the front of his shirt and tried again. This time that hand did not slip away, and he began to slowly pull himself to his feet.

His eyes now focusing, Cruz glanced at the radar screen.

"This can't be!" the terror stuck skipper said to himself.

The cause for the horns blowing became instantly apparent.

Although in great pain, the *Hafa Adai's* captain had the presence of mind to recognize that he must do something, and quickly, or a high seas collision was inevitable.

Captain Cruz grabbed the wheel and frantically began turning the cargo ship in another direction.

As the single tower oil tanker and the *Hafa Adai* drew closer to one another, the radar screens on both ships were being watched intently. Indications that their paths were beginning to alter came as a welcome sign, but because of their close proximity, it was still an uncertainty as to whether a collision would be avoided.

Suddenly, several crewmembers aboard the oil tanker reported seeing lights, and the next thing they saw was a ship about 150 feet away. Fortunately, the cargo ship was now running nearly parallel with the oil tanker, but the venturi effect was causing the ships to draw even closer together.

Both captains continued steering their vessels away from one another. As they moved ahead, the two ships finally began separating until at last, the cargo ship disappeared into the heavy fog.

Radar aboard the oil tanker showed the cargo ship now moving on a northeasterly course while the oil tanker stayed the strict northern route. Both were heading toward the Celebes Sea.

The oil tanker captain wiped his brow with the back of his hand and gave a giant sigh of relief. The threat of an at sea disaster had been diffused. An announcement went out over the loudspeaker that the emergency had passed and the crew could now stand down.

Aboard the *Hafa Adai,* Captain Cruz held tightly to the support bar and gazed upward giving thanks before slowly slumping to his knees. As he knelt on the deck of the bridge trying to gain strength, he noticed one of his men lying across the way with a blood crusted knife handle extending from his chest.

The captain crawled to the crewman and took hold of his wrist. There was no pulse. Struggling to his feet, the captain stumbled back over to the ship's controls where he checked the radar and saw no ships or other danger approaching. With that, he left the *Hafa Adai* on its northeasterly course and slowed its speed to a safe minimum of two knots.

Staggering down a nearby stairway Captain Cruz cried out for his men, but there was no reply. Out on the main deck he spotted one of them. He walked unsteadily over to where the mate was lying face up in a pool of blood. The man's eyes were open, his throat slit, and an ear had been lopped off. There was no question he was dead. Tears came to the captain's eyes as knelt down and closed his shipmate's eyes with his fingers.

Further back, another of his men was lying on the deck. The captain crawled back to him on his hands and knees. There was not much blood, but neither was there any sign of life. Then, he spotted an object protruding from the crewman's neck. It was a dart from a blowgun. The dart was most likely poisonous and his death instantaneous.

Captain Cruz buried his face in his hands.

As he got up and weaved his way along the deck, he cried out repeatedly for anyone to respond.

No answer was forthcoming.

Nearing another stairway, he suddenly heard the faint sound of voices. He yelled an encouraging response, and as he moved forward, those faint voices became clearer and grew increasingly louder.

Approaching the door leading into an interior storage room, he noticed a steel bar wedged through the handle. He pounded on the door and yelled excitedly. The response came with multiple fists pounding on the door and cries of exhilaration from within for him to get it open.

Captain Cruz tried to move the steel bar with his hands. First, he pushed down on it to no avail, and then after falling to his knees, attempted to pull it. Since he could barely stand and walk without support, he knew it would be almost impossible to gather enough strength to remove this wedged bar without assistance.

Spotting a fire axe on a nearby wall, the captain had an idea. He pulled himself up and using the wall for support, slowly moved toward where the axe hung. He loosened the supports and grabbed the handle, before again sliding to the deck. Dragging the axe with him, he crawled back to the door separating him from his crew.

After getting to his feet, he lifted the axe and with the blunt end hit the wedged steel bar. Other than a slight jarring of his hands and arms, and a loud clang resonating as steel met steel, there seemed to be little else to note. The bar remained firmly wedged in place. After several more hits, with the bar moving a little farther down each time, he raised the axe higher than he had on any previous attempt, and with all of the force he could muster, came down on it. As he dropped to his knees, the bar gave way and tumbled down beside him onto the deck.

Captain Cruz reached up with both hands and pulled down on the handle, sliding it out of the way. The men confined inside the storage room quickly pushed the door open and rushed out.

"Captain Cruz!" yelled a crewmember as he glanced to the side and saw his captain lying on the deck.

A broad smile spread across Cruz's face, "You don't know how good it is to see you men."

"Almost as good as it is to see you, Captain," replied the mate. "We thought we were going to die in that storage room. There was no way out!"

Several more crewmembers gathered around and helped to get Captain Cruz to his cabin. There, the captain began issuing instructions to Jesse Lujan, his next in command, while an onboard medic gathered a physician's bag and began treating his wounds.

Lujan dispatched the crew in all directions, with orders to get an accurate accounting of all now aboard the *Hafa Adai*, and to secure any bodies found.

In the meantime, he made his way to the bridge. There, per the captain's instructions, Lujan was to remain and monitor the ship's progress.

The cargo vessel continued sustaining the minimum two-knot rate of speed and same northeasterly course Captain Cruz had turned it to just prior to the near collision. Lujan was not to make any changes in either the direction or the speed of the ship unless he saw something on the radarscope dictating adjustments were required. Otherwise, the captain would make the necessary corrections when he re-joined Lujan on the bridge.

Wanting to get back to the helm as soon as possible, Captain Cruz pressed the medic to hurry, and with the final bandage now in place; he got off his bunk and limped out the door.

"Everything OK?" Captain Cruz asked Jesse Lujan upon his return to the bridge.

"Just as you ordered, Captain," Lujan replied with a note of relief in his voice.

"Good," the captain nodded. "Now, get Guam on the radio for me."

"Yes, Sir," Lujan answered.

After the shipping company's security officer received Captain Cruz's grizzly recount of the pirate attack and the near miss at sea, he contacted the FBI Resident Agency in Guam with the details. Instructions relayed back were for Captain Cruz and the crew of the *Hafa Adai* to proceed directly to Manila. Upon their arrival, the captain was to go to the American Embassy and contact the FBI legal attaché (LEGAT).

CHAPTER THREE

The *Fantom* made port on the island of Flores shortly after dusk. There, Buruk would link up with the captain of a renegade coaster ship moving between ports to take on additional cargo. This cargo, a hijacked steel container holding a new, armor plated luxury SUV, originally destined for an Asian head of state, was now being rerouted to an island in the southern Philippines. There, the specially built SUV would soon be protecting and transporting a major trafficker in the style to which he had become accustomed.

Flores, known for its giant Komodo dragons, was the place where nearly a decade before Buruk had saved Besar, his then very young dragon, from jaws of a giant Komodo. *Besar*, which means "mighty" in *Bahasa Indonesian*, had since grown to a length of nearly ten feet and two hundred pounds, and as a giant Komodo dragon was even more intimidating to the crew and others than was his rogue master.

His scaly broad head, thick muscular neck, and powerful tail that extended nearly as long as his flattened trunk made him frightening to anyone. On his feet were strong, sharp claws used when he attacked and rose up on his hind legs to fight. And, in his mouth, he had serrated teeth designed for ripping and tearing, and a poisonous bacteria and toxic drool that would eventually kill most prey. Also, protruding from his mouth was a darting, forked yellow tongue he used for sensing.

While in the Flores port, crews from the two ships joined other old salts in a drunken bash that continued throughout the night and well into the following day. After all had sobered up, and the container holding the luxury SUV was offloaded from the coaster and onto Buruk's freighter, it was time for the *Fantom* to move on.

Entering the Java Sea from the Flores Sea, Buruk and his men took their ship along the coastline of the Island of Java, and into the old port at Jakarta, where they would make their next stop and pick up.

Java, one of the nearly fourteen thousand islands making up an Indonesian archipelago that forms a natural barrier between the Pacific and Indian Oceans is also the location of Jakarta, the capital city for this, the fourth most populous country in the world. A port city, Jakarta is home to some nine million people and paints a vivid portrait of the world's haves and the have-nots.

The capital's hazy skyline sports opulence with a collection of towering skyscrapers housing business suites, high-rise penthouses, and luxury apartments for the wealthy. These signs of prosperity, however, are in stark contrast to the squalor in which millions of poor reside in small boarded-up, unpainted shanties covered with rusting metal roofs, and all crammed one on top of another.

As the old port of Jakarta came into full view, the crew of renegade pirates became increasingly anxious. Most would soon be rushing off the *Fantom* in an effort to get first pick from the stables of alluring women housed at those enticing dens of iniquity and wild nightlife.

As Buruk and his first mate walked along a dock in the old port area of Sunda Kelapa, Tomy made light of the differences between the *Fantom* and this fleet of graceful old Bugis schooners as they sat majestically in their berths. The *Fantom*, after all, was state of the art, and these old schooners, well. . . .

Renamed the *Fantom* in honor of its status as a captured "phantom ship," their retrofitted freighter was the newest addition to Buruk's small fleet. The captain and his crew of modern-day swashbucklers placed the ship into service following the execution of a daring nighttime attack carried out only a few months earlier in the Strait of Malacca. That Strait, a major passageway for ships traveling between the South China Sea and the Indian Ocean, has long been a center for vicious pirate attacks and assaults, and a regular haunt for Buruk.

Threatening first, to put any captive who did not comply into a dark, empty steel container alone with Besar, and later forcing its skipper to walk the plank, as the crew stood by silently watching, Buruk made his point for all present to never tell anything, or else. They would be killed anytime, anywhere.

Such actions were typical for this infamous pirate captain, and it was no stretch for one to understand how the *Bahasa Indonesian* word "*buruk*," meaning "nasty," "rotten," or "bad," and the captain had become inseparably linked. That loathsome moniker had initially attached following the vicious beating and stabbing of a merchant seaman during a knife wielding bar fight that had taken place more than a decade earlier.

"Captain Buruk!" the dying man had cried out with disdain.

The sadistic captain reportedly responded with a grunt and deep belly laugh. The nickname immediately stuck and "Captain Buruk" is all that he had been known by in the years since.

With the captured freighter and its crew under his command, Captain Buruk had ordered them to transport the ship from the Strait of Malacca to an obscure, little out-of-the-way port located in the southern Philippines. Once there, the captive crew was released, and the cargo sold to a scruffy, gray bearded, middle-aged fugitive. This American ex-pat, who for years had been making a living as an arms dealer, was now also profiting from the brokering of pirated goods.

While in the Philippine port, a comprehensive refurbishing and retrofitting of the *Fantom* took place. So as to not attract any undue attention, however, the vessel still sported the chipped paint and rust spots similar to that seen on most any other freighters moving between ports up and down the Asian coastline. And, the freshly painted *Fantom* name was made to appear old and weathered, but that was where the similarity between the old and new ended. Everything else under that dark, rough exterior was state of the art.

Inside, the engines had been reworked, the quarters refurbished, and the electronics equipped with some of the most sophisticated radar, global positioning, and other high tech tracking devices and equipment found around the world today. Much of this equipment was either stripped from other ships during high seas attacks carried out by Buruk and his pirate crew or purchased from brokers engaged in the cannibalizing of other captured vessels.

As Buruk and Tomy continued their walk along the dock, scores of barefooted men with leathered skin and weathered faces revealing the toil and struggle that made them appear well beyond their years, balanced themselves as they walked along narrow boards spanning the gaps between the decks of the schooners and the dock. Their backs were bent and shoulders hunched as each carried heavy loads of mahogany and teak to nearby storage piles.

"Those suckers," remarked Tomy, shaking his head. "Working that hard for a *rupiah* pittance each day and smiling like they do. They are stupid," he scoffed. "There are easier ways to make money."

"You mean like we do?" Buruk laughed.

"Yeah," nodded Tomy, "just like we do."

Catching a pedi-cab at the dockside, Buruk directed the driver to a local bar. This was the meeting place where they would have drinks and link up with some OC guys who had been getting everything together for the party to be held later that evening at one of the local clubs controlled by organized crime.

Anxious to get to the bar, Tomy repeatedly kicked the seat of the driver in an attempt to get him to hurry along. The driver glanced back with a look of disdain. Tomy gave him a steely-eyed stare and gripped the handle of a dagger shoved into the waist of his pants. The driver quickly returned his head to the roadway in front of him and began pedaling much faster. When they arrived a short time later, Buruk threw some *rupiah* in the direction of the driver while Tomy hurried into the bar.

Grabbing a beer from the bartender's hand as he rushed by, Tomy quickly made his way to the side rooms. Accessed through a single doorway and entered off a long hallway, each of these side rooms had mixes of solid and multi-colored string beads hanging from the passageways. Inside the small cubicles were collections of seductive posters hanging from the walls, a single bed, and of course a prostitute whose services were negotiated for, and payment made as mutually agreed upon with the john.

Stopping at the first string of beads and flinging them aside, Tomy peered in on an experienced, young woman as she posed seductively on the bed. Although still only in her early twenties, she looked hard and well beyond her years. It was obvious that turning tricks for a living had certainly taken its toll.

She was slight in build and had long, thin, smooth legs, and combed, straight black hair that extended halfway down her back. A thick layer of caked make-up covered blemishes on her scared face, and with nothing more than a scanty g-string and baby-doll see-through negligee covering her body, there was little left to the imagination.

Giving an alluring smile, the young woman wiggled her finger in Tomy's direction for him to come to her.

When he stepped into her dimly lit space to take a closer look at what she had to offer, Tomy got a strong whiff of the cheap perfume she was wearing, and closed his eyes as he sucked in a deep breath from the pot she had been smoking.

"How much?" the first mate mouthed, as he repeatedly ran his thumb across his fingertips.

The young woman held up fingers indicating an amount.

Tomy emphatically shook his head "no," mumbling "too much, too much," under his breath, and walked toward another strung bead opening.

There, he once again stuck in his head and mouthed, "How much?"

This girl, who was somewhat younger and less experienced than the other was, signaled a lower amount.

Tomy offered less.

She sheepishly shook her head "no."

He offered her a little more.

Once again, the girl shook her head "no."

Finally, Tomy reluctantly agreed to the price and gave her a belligerent nod.

It was not that Tomy did not have enough *rupiah* to pay any of them whatever they wanted. No, it was an ego thing. After all, he was Tomy, the ship's first mate, the big man, and because of who he was, they should want to satisfy his sexual fantasies and do him for nothing.

CHAPTER FOUR

In addition to being renegade pirates carrying out lone raids on vulnerable ships and luxury yachts, Captain Buruk and his band of ruthless swashbucklers also transported cargos for international organized crime syndicates. This time their destination was Jakarta, and to pick up a load of unsuspecting Indonesian girls, but it could just as easily have been females from a coastal village of Thailand, Cambodia, Korea, or another human trafficking location thousands of miles away.

One such place was an out of the way port in the Adriatic Sea, where Buruk, tasked by a Balkan mafia organization, loaded onto his ship a group of young women trafficked from Moldova. He took them along with others from throughout that region to brothel centers in the West.

It didn't matter to Buruk where he went or what he did. Money was money. And, as for all of these women, well. . . they were just something to be used.

Buruk and his pirate crew also regularly transported marijuana, heroin, hashish, gold, jewelry, diamonds, and even stolen luxury cars between various ports for OC syndicates and drug traffickers. In fact, the Asian syndicate he was now working for had developed into a family affair.

While Buruk and other pirate crews carried out acts of violence and smuggling on the high seas, his younger, college educated MBA, half-brother avoided getting his hands dirty, working on the financial side of the house as a money mover and launderer for the mob. Wanting to keep his true name and identity secret, this half-brother had followed the instructions to the letter in one of those old underground books describing how to create an alias, and had successfully created a new, fully documented name and identity that he had used since shortly after arriving in the United States.

In preparation for a night of action at their Jakarta stop, Buruk and his band of carousing buccaneers were already getting into the mood. Busy drinking and partying with local bar prostitutes, the pirates continued having a great time, while members of the local syndicate fanned out.

Word quickly spread that there would be a party tonight at a nearby upscale club. Sought were those interested in "international travel and making big money as models, dancers, hostesses, and waitresses. Any girl wanting to attend must show her passport at the door and be willing to leave the city immediately."

With an overabundance of vulnerable teenage girls and young women wanting to escape the throes of poverty and despair, there was no problem getting attendees. Jakarta had proved to be a prime source for Buruk's OC associates when carrying out recruiting efforts in the past, and things were the same this time around.

By the time Captain Buruk, Tomy, and the guys from the crew arrived at the dance club, girls were already standing outside, puffing away on cigarettes, and giggling with one another, while they anxiously awaited the time for the doors to open. The dress of the day appeared to be a combination of low cut midriffs or only partially buttoned blouses, mini-skirts, and stiletto heels.

Most of the girls were wearing bright red lip-gloss and a couple of them displayed small tattoos. Only a couple wore stockings on their thin, smooth legs, and with the exception of hoop earrings, a few ankle bracelets, and a ring or necklace here and there, they did not show off much jewelry. This was to be expected though, as most of these young women had little in the way of wealth.

The girls also knew that the more sexually alluring they could make themselves, the better their chances of being selected were, so it was the intention of each girl to appear as provocative as possible.

Buruk and the other men were all wearing expensive woven *batik* shirts, hanging loosely outside their dark slacks, and sandals on their feet. Concealed under most of those colorful *batik* shirts were chrome-plated pistols tucked into the waistbands. Tomy, however bucked the trend, and rather than packing a gun, had instead slid his dagger into a sheath and strapped it to the calf of his leg, under his pants.

When the doors opened, a group of the syndicate's men escorted the girls into the floorshow room. For many, this was the first time they had ever been treated to a production by professional entertainers of this caliber, and especially in the elegance of a clubroom such as this with its crystal chandeliers, highly polished floors, and mahogany walls trimmed in red velvet tapestry with pearl and gold decor.

As the girls looked around the room in awe, one of the syndicate's men said, "This is the kind of place you will be working in, that is, if you are selected for one of our international positions."

Several of the girls simultaneously drew deep breaths and swallowed as they expressed their amazement.

Once each girl had received her drink and was seated at one of the linen covered tables surrounding a center stage, the gongs sounded and the drums started beating. As the lights dimmed, a troupe of Indonesian dancers, wearing traditional dress, followed one another onto the stage. Their faces were caked with make-up and the costumes worn by each of the barefoot entertainers were made from beautiful satin and embroidered fabric. On the head of each dancer was either a glittering band or a traditional ornate golden crown.

Beautifully choreographed, this troupe of graceful dancers mirrored one another as they moved in unison to the rhythm provided by an ensemble of bamboo instruments, drums, and a xylophone. During one number, two female performers mesmerized the entire audience as their big, brown eyes remained wide open, and they moved in total concert with one another while dancing.

Near the conclusion of the show, some of the girls in the audience were invited to join the entertainers on stage in singing and dancing, and it was obvious several of them were taking full advantage of this opportunity to try to make an impression on their hosts.

As the floorshow wound down, the girls were led out of that room and into a less formal part of the club. This scene was a bit more familiar to most of them. There were multi-colored strobe lights flashing brightly over a darkened dance floor and giant speakers blasting a reverberating beat from every corner.

Now it was time for the crew from the *Fantom* to fan-out alongside their syndicate counterparts and start dancing and making it with the girls. This was not the first time most of them had been through this routine and all certainly hoped it would not be their last.

Along with all of the booze, came the ecstasy and ketamine. It was whatever you want. Most of the pirates and syndicate associates stuck to the hard stuff, but the younger crowd seemed more eager to try an MDMA tablet or experiment with the "K." Having heard about the popularity of ketamine in some Hong Kong dance clubs, several of the girls wanted to try it, and did, but most stuck with either the booze or the ecstasy. Those few girls, who opted to stay with only juice or soft drinks, and said "no" to the drugs, were quickly eliminated from the prospect pool by their hosts and sent on their way. "Goody-goodies are not wanted for these positions," they were told.

Before long, out came the glow sticks, lollipops, and pacifiers for the ecstasy huggers taking an e-trip as they caressed and hung onto the men, as well as one another, in euphoric states. Their sex drives were also causing them to want to touch and be touched. These actions were in stark contrast, however, with those sampling the "K," who after inhaling an initial dose began to wobble and hallucinate, before eventually falling prostrate onto the cushions littering the perimeter of the dance floor.

While the girls remained in contrasting euphoric and hallucinogenic states, depending on the drug taken, the pirates and thugs took every advantage of them that they dared, especially those who had unwittingly opted to try the "date rape" drug.

As the late evening grew into early morning, Buruk announced to those girls who had remained, "You have been selected!"

A shrill went up from those girls still enough in touch with reality to understand, and they grabbed and hugged every guy in sight.

"You must bring me your passports for safekeeping," Buruk told them.

Several ran toward him waving their passports.

Buruk collected the passports from all those still able to walk and directed them to nearby crewmembers. From there, the girls were escorted to waiting vans. The passports of those girls unable to walk or who had passed out from the booze and drugs were then taken from them before they were carried to the vans.

Fires burning in trashcans lit up the darkened streets as the loaded vans sped toward the dock. Once there, the pirates quickly herded and dragged the girls into empty containers aboard the *Fantom*. These hot and steamy steel boxes would be home to the girls while they were at sea. Air holes located near the top of the containers provided nominal ventilation, and each was equipped with a couple of small battery-powered lights, bottles of water, a chemical toilet, stacked bunks, and woven mats strewn across the metal floor.

By the time the morning sun peered over the horizon, Captain Buruk and his *Fantom* pirate crew had already cleared the port and made their way back into the Java Sea. Soon, crewmembers began unlocking the doors leading into the girls cramped container quarters so that the ship's cook could distribute pots of cold rice, fish, and bread. Several of the girls were having trouble eating due to having bitten their cheeks. Swollen cheeks, and sore jaws, teeth, and gums resulting from grinding were not unusual consequences for e-trips.

Later, it would be time for the pirate fun and games to begin aboard ship, and for any girl unwilling to participate, or creating problems for the crew, there loomed the ominous threat of being thrown into an empty steel container with Besar, or tossed overboard and fed to the sharks in that deep, dark, and lonely sea.

CHAPTER FIVE

With a single line feeding nearly a dozen teller cages, Bridgette Tomas wondered what the odds were that this mysterious man might make it back to her window again tomorrow. Normally, she would not have given it a second thought, but that was a lot of cash. For the past three days, this same guy had come to her window, opened a foam padded, aluminum briefcase, and handed her between nine and ten thousand dollars in cash for deposit.

With this business day now over and the lobby closed, she was becoming increasingly curious about what had been going on and decided it was time to give the bank's director of compliance and security a call.

"Mr. Moore's office," answered his assistant.

"Is he in?" Bridgette asked.

"May I ask who is calling?"

"Bridgette Tomas. I'm one of the tellers downstairs."

"Just a moment, please."

"Hello. This is Harold Moore."

"Mr. Moore, my name is Bridgette Tomas. I've been a teller here for only a short time, and am still learning about the banking business, but I attended your recent briefing for new tellers and some things you said there make me think there's something kind of funny going on."

"Would you mind coming up to my office and talking about it?" asked Moore.

"No, that would be fine, I just have to finish closing out for the day. As soon as I'm done, I'll be right up."

"We're on the fifth floor, room 502," he told her.

"Okay. I should be there within about a half hour," she replied.

Bridgette quickly finished what she was doing and jotted down information from the suspicious customer's account deposit slip before taking the elevator to the executive suites located on the fifth floor.

The raised, gold, letters on the impressive dark stained door read "Director of Compliance and Security."

Bridgette tapped on the door.

"Come in," invited a voice from inside the room.

Bridgette cautiously opened the door and looked in. Upon seeing a woman sitting behind a desk, she quickly responded, "My name is Bridgette Tomas. I'm here to see Mr. Moore."

Harold's assistant smiled and escorted her into his office, closing the door behind her, as she left.

"Please be seated Ms. Tomas. Would you like a cup of coffee or tea?" Moore asked.

"No, I'm fine. Thank you."

"You mentioned on the phone that something funny was going on?"

"Yes," she hesitated. "It's probably nothing, and maybe I shouldn't even be bothering you. But, well, there's just something about it that just doesn't seem right."

"Why don't you go ahead and tell me, and let me be the judge as to whether it's anything," Harold replied.

"Okay," answered Bridgette, and she started telling him of her suspicions. "For three days in a row this same man has come to my window and taken thousands of dollars in cash out of a briefcase for deposit. Some customers will bring in a couple of thousand in cash, but this man has brought in a little less than ten thousand dollars each time."

"Interesting," Harold leaned back in his chair and began stroking his chin. "Did you bring the account information with you?"

"Yes, it's all right here." Bridgette handed him the sheet of paper with the account information she had copied from the deposit slip.

Harold typed the account number into his computer, bringing up an account activity summary for the past thirty days. The three deposits made with Bridgette went into a grocery store account, and they were not the only large cash deposits made to that account. Scrolling down, he spotted no less than a dozen similar transactions. None of them were made on the same day and most were deposited at different branches. He also noted a wire transfer out of the account for a little more than $100,000.

"It's ironic that he got your window three days in a row," commented Harold.

"That was my thought," Bridgette replied. "I think he was surprised, too."

"Why do you say that?"

Shaking her head, she said, "He was paying attention to something else going on in the bank as he walked up to my window. I don't think he noticed who was behind the counter until he opened his briefcase and took out the cash.

When he saw me, he gave a surprised look. You know the kind, 'Oh. . . , its not you, again.' I'm sure I reacted similarly and we quickly completed the transaction, and he was on his way out the door. After all, what are the odds of the same man waiting in a single line at the bank and randomly getting my window three days in a row."

Harold smiled and shook his head in agreement, "Especially, considering the fact that the same line feeds nearly a dozen different tellers during the busy times."

Before he could say anything more, there was a tap on the door and his assistant stuck her head in. "Sorry about the interruption Mr. Moore, but there's been a robbery at the Valley branch."

"Tell them I'm on my way."

"I will," she responded.

Looking back to Bridgette, Harold said, "Sorry about the interruption, but duty calls."

They stood up simultaneously, and Harold grabbed his suit coat.

As the two of them left his office and walked toward the elevator, Harold mentioned to her, "I would like you to take a few minutes this evening and jot down anything that comes to mind about that customer. Anything he said, was there an accent, what he looked like, his age, how he dressed, was anyone with him, and if so, what did he or she look like. Anything you can remember that stood out or was unusual about him. Also, the denominations of the bills, how they were sorted or bound, and what his briefcase looked like would be helpful. Just anything that comes to mind."

"I don't know how much help I'll be, but I'll give it a try," Bridgette responded.

"That's all I can ask for, and in the meantime, I'll take a look at the digital recording of the line and see what it shows," Harold replied, adding, "Thanks for coming by, Ms. Tomas. I'll be in touch."

CHAPTER SIX

On his way to the bank the following morning, Harold Moore stopped by the Los Angeles FBI Headquarters, located on Wilshire Boulevard, to learn if there was anything new from the previous day's robbery of the Valley branch.

With his reading glasses hanging halfway down his nose, Supervisory Special Agent (SSA) Mike Mathis looked up from the stacks of papers covering his desk and saw Moore standing outside the door.

"Don't be a stranger, Harold. Come on in," Mathis told Moore.

"Swamped under, huh?" commented Harold.

"That's an understatement," noted Mathis. "Many more days like yesterday and we'll be back on pace with that record set back in '92."

"That's why they call LA the bank robbery capital of the world, Mike. Just think of it as job security. By the way, what is the BR record for a year in the Division?"

"2,641," answered Mathis.

"And how many BR's did you have in LA yesterday?"

"Sixteen," replied Mathis, with a note of exasperation in his voice.

"That must have been close to a record for a single day, huh?"

"A ways away," replied the long-time LA bank robbery supervisor. "Twenty-four is the record and that was a few years ago, but sixteen tops the daily score for this year."

"And I'll bet most of those sixteen weren't like the one at our Valley branch, either," answered Moore.

"Not hardly. In fact, most of 'em were takeovers. Guns out, customers put down on the floor, the whole nine yards. We're seeing more and more of those these days."

"That's what I understand," Harold agreed. "Speaking of the Valley job. Did you manage to get our guy?"

"Was there any question in your mind," replied Mathis.

"Well, you never know," responded Harold, showing a sly grin. "I've seen some crazy note jobs in my time, but scribbling the stick-up demand on the back of a deposit slip. That's about as bizarre as it gets."

"Especially when it was his own deposit slip," Mathis added. "Yeah, we sat on his place and ended up getting him a little after midnight."

"How was he?" asked Harold.

"High as a kite. He was sure on something. Put up a real fight."

"Pretty crazy, huh. I remember those PCP days back in the '70's and '80's. We would be arresting some guy and he would start biting us, gouging at our eyes, and trying to throw us off balconies. I couldn't believe how strong and crazy some of 'em could get on that stuff."

"Yeah, I remember those days, too," agreed Mathis.

"Anybody get hurt last night? Harold asked.

"Nothing serious, but he did try to gouge the eyes of one of my guys," Mathis replied.

"Where did they take him?" asked Harold.

"County. Two agents left just a few minutes ago to pick him up and take him over to the Marshals. He should be arraigned sometime this afternoon."

"Another stat for the Bu," commented Harold.

"We'll take all we can get. I just wish they were all this quick."

"Yeah. Well Mike, I've got what I stopped by for so I guess I'd better let you get back to all of that important paperwork you've got stacked up," Harold smirked. "If you need anything, let me know."

As Moore was walking out the door, Mathis quipped, "Thanks Harold, and remember. . . ," but before he could finish getting out what he was going to say.

Harold interrupted, "I know. Call me when you can help me," he laughed.

"You've got it," Mathis replied.

"Good to see things haven't changed around here," Harold shot back . "I'll be in touch."

Back at his office, Moore noticed that the sheet of paper with the account information Bridgette Tomas had given him the previous afternoon was still lying on the blotter on his desktop. Once again, pulling up the account on his computer screen, and this time asking for the past three statements, he noticed similar activity. Each statement reflected numerous large cash deposits made to the account, followed by a wire transfer being sent out whenever the balance reached six figures. Where the money was transferred to, he could not tell from the statement, but that information could be retrieved from the bank's records.

Harold also noticed that all of those daily cash deposits made to the grocery store account had skirted the Currency Transaction Reporting (CTR) law. That's the law requiring financial institutions to file a CTR with the Treasury Department whenever a cash deposit, exchange, or withdrawal is made in excess of $10,000. There were exceptions, such as businesses placed on the bank's "Exempt List," but since none of these deposits exceeded the $10,000 threshold, and the grocery store was not on the list, anyway, that did not matter.

Based on his meeting with Bridgette Tomas, and what he had noted in his review of the account, Moore decided he had seen and heard enough. It was time to complete a Suspicious Activity Report (SAR) and send it into Treasury.

Once the SAR was filed, Harold called Mike Mathis to let him know what he had discovered.

Mathis queried Treasury's Financial Database for any related reports, but located nothing. He then ran the names Harold had given him through the FBI indices. That check came up with one informant file reference. The case agent for that file was Special Agent (SA) Jack Stacy, who had until recently been assigned to Mathis' Bank Robbery Squad.

Special Agent John "Jack" Stacy, was a cigar smoking, hard-charging, hard-playing, twenty-plus year FBI veteran who had spent most of a somewhat checkered career, assigned to LA's reactive squads. There, Stacy did what he regarded as the "heavy" work of the Bureau – chasing fugitives, kicking in doors, and solving high stakes kidnappings and takedown bank robberies.

However, as FBI priorities changed to terrorism and other areas, so did the squads for some of those "old-time" reactive agents. Now, Stacy was assigned to the newest of several recently created Organized Crime and Gang Task Force Squads. His first major case there had placed him in the unenviable position of having to chase more paper than fugitives, and a resultant frustration was slowly settling in.

"OC-2," answered the squad secretary.

"Teri, is Tim in? This is Mike Mathis."

"Just a moment Mr. Mathis. He is on the other line."

There was a short pause, then, "Sullivan," responded the voice from the other end of the line.

"Tim, its Mathis."

"Mike. How are things on the BR Squad?"

"About the same. At least the front office hasn't transferred any more agents off the squad."

"That's good. I don't think Stacy was too happy about having to come over here, but you know I didn't have anything to do with that."

"I know. 'Priorities of the Bureau,' and all that...," he responded somewhat sarcastically.

"Hey, did you get that guy in the Valley last night? I heard the radio traffic as I was driving home."

"Yeah, we got him early this morning."

"Was that one of Harold Moore's branches?" asked Sullivan.

"Sure was. In fact, my calling you has to do with a call I just received from him."

"How's that?"

"He filed a SAR and wanted to let the Bu know about it. I did a database check and got nothing more, but when I ran the name through indices, a reference came up from one of Jack's informant files. The name was a grocery store, with an address down south. I thought he might be interested."

"Yeah, I'm sure he will," responded Sullivan. "I'll leave a 'stop' for him to drop by your office when he gets back in. You can fill him in on what Harold had to say, then."

"Will do."

CHAPTER SEVEN

There was a tap on the painted metal doorframe. Mike Mathis looked up from an FD-302 Report Form he was reading regarding the robbery at the Valley bank.

"Hey, Jack. Come on in," Mathis told him.

Stacy nodded, and walked over to the lone chair sitting directly in front of Mathis's desk.

"I got a 'stop' that you wanted to see me," Stacy said.

"Yeah, it has to do with one of your informants, Jack."

Stacy gave him a questioning look.

"You remember Harold Moore, don't you?"

"Sure, I knew him when he was here, and then after he left, I used to give some of those 'this is what to do if you're robbed' talks to tellers at his branches. What does he have to do with this?"

"Well, he filed a Suspicious Activity Report and called over with some details regarding it. I ran indices and came up with a recent reference from an informant file assigned to you. Some grocery store down south."

"Yeah, I just got that the other day. There's something about it being used for money laundering. I haven't had a chance to check it out yet, though."

"That would seem to fit," Mathis responded. "From what Harold said, I gather there have been a number of, as he put it, 'unusually large cash deposits' made to the account of that grocery store over the past couple of months."

Swashbuckler

"H-m-m-m-m," Stacy nodded.

"I guess a teller brought it to his attention. It seems that this guy ended up at the same teller's window several days in a row. She got suspicious and reported it to Harold. The deposits were all in cash and just under $10,000."

"Were those all of the deposits he found?"

"Not from what I gather. Those were the most recent ones, but I think he also found more deposits made at several of the other branches, too."

Stacy shook his head. "On the BR squad, we used to chase robbers for making large 'withdrawals' from the tellers. Now, on the OC squad we chase guys for making large 'deposits.' Does there seem to be something funny about this picture to you, or is just me?"

Mathis smiled and nodded in agreement. "I guess it depends on whether they're trying to rob or launder. And, remember, Jack. If the dye pack goes off, the stick-up guy may be into both."

"Literal money laundering," chuckled Stacy, with a smile. He then went on to explain that this reminded him of one case in particular where a bait dye-pack had led to literal laundering. The dye pack was put into the bank robber's bag along with the other bills from the teller's drawer. As the robber was making his getaway, the dye pack exploded, sending red dye over everything in the bag. When agents raided the suspect's apartment early the next morning, they found clothespins holding rows of red dye blotched pink colored bills hanging from lines throughout the apartment.

Upon questioning, Stacy learned that the currency had managed to survive the cycles of the washing machine okay, but getting all of the dye out proved to be another story. What had once been "greenbacks" were now "pinkbacks," and when Stacy asked the guy how he planned to dispose of his new supply of pink colored bills the bandit just shrugged.

Mathis smiled, adding, "I remember a couple of other cases where there wasn't any washing involved, but the bandits did take the red dye stained bills just as they were and tried depositing them into accounts at other banks."

"Like that wouldn't be suspicious," laughed Stacy.

Mathis smiled, and then shoved a sheet of paper across the desktop toward Stacy to look at.

"Here's a copy of the SAR Harold filed," he said.

Stacy quickly read over the Suspicious Activity Report.

"Since yours was informant info, I didn't say anything to Harold, but you might want to stop by and see him."

Jack nodded that he would. "I'll also talk to the teller," he said.

Upon his return to the squad bay, Stacy stopped by Tim Sullivan's office to let him know what he had learned from Mike Mathis. He also reminded Sullivan what his source had said about the grocery store having ties to Asian OC.

Sullivan nodded that he remembered seeing the informant report before initialing it into the file.

"I'll O&A a PI," Sullivan told Stacy.

Before Stacy left for the day, he had already received the newly Opened and Assigned Preliminary Investigation and had called over to the United States Attorney's Office to request that a Federal Grand Jury Subpoena be issued for the bank records for the grocery store account.

CHAPTER EIGHT

By the time Jack Stacy got to the United States Courthouse in downtown LA to pick up the Federal Grand Jury Subpoena for the bank account records, it was already mid-morning, and he still hadn't gotten a chance to check out the grocery store. That would be his next stop.

The address was in a south LA neighborhood and turned out to be a small, two-story, tan colored, stucco building, with the word "grocery" scrawled on a hand painted sign above the doorway. The place looked to be in disrepair. Torn screens and cracked panes of glass stood behind the bars on the windows, and the dark brown trim had not seen a new coat of paint in years.

Parking across the street, Jack Stacy took a long and careful look around before getting out of his car and walking toward the single door entrance. He could not imagine how this little run-down grocery store could have ever made enough money to keep the door open, much less generate the large amounts of cash that were currently being deposited into its account at the bank.

As Stacy gripped the handle and pushed the door, it opened, and a small bell rang above his head. There was no sign of customers, or anyone else, for that matter. He slowly approached a dimly lit aisle, and noticed that several of the bulbs hanging from the extended cords were burned out. A closer look around revealed dirty, sticky floors, dead flies hanging from several yellow tacky strips, and shelves with mice droppings spread here and there.

Also, scattered across the half-empty shelves were rows of dusty cans. Some were partially crushed and stuck to the shelves with seeping food caked around the outer bottom edges. First picking up a box and then a can he noticed the dates imprinted on the labels of both showed they were expired, and it all made Jack wonder if LA's health inspectors had ever been near the place, much less in it.

As he moved to another aisle, Stacy spotted two guys standing near the rear of the store. They briefly glanced in his direction, but showed little interest and continued to talk. Jack assumed they were either the owners or employees, and since he was not interested in talking to either now, decided not to linger any longer and returned to his car.

While sitting there waiting to see if any customers went into the small grocery, one of the two men he had seen standing in the rear came out. He was carrying an aluminum briefcase and walking toward a black Mercedes parked on a side street near the corner. The man unlocked the car door, crushed his cigarette butt out on the pavement, got into his car, started the engine, and slowly eased around the corner and into the traffic flow. Stacy waited until several cars passed, then did a U-turn in the intersection and began his tail.

He ran the license plate on the black Mercedes. It came back to a luxury car rental agency located near the Los Angeles International Airport (LAX). Stacy would check that out, later. Now, he needed to see where this guy was headed.

Onto the 405 freeway, and then off a few minutes later, his first stop was at an old strip mall restaurant. As was the case with the small grocery store, this restaurant with its peeling paint, cracked asphalt, vacant building on one side, and second hand clothing store on the other, appeared to have seen better days.

Stacy pulled over and waited, watching as his yet to be identified subject got out of his car, and carrying the aluminum briefcase, headed into the restaurant. Since it was lunchtime, Stacy briefly considered following him in and getting a cup of coffee or something to eat, but after taking a second look at the place, decided he was not very hungry after all. Besides, his surveillance would be blown if by chance he were recognized from his earlier visit to the grocery store.

After waiting several minutes, Jack then did a slow drive-by to see if he could spot any activity going on in the restaurant. A reflective glare from the sun and a series of uneven hanging blinds stretching across the large tinted windows made it nearly impossible to see in, but from what he could tell there was nothing going on inside, anyway.

Now parked half-a-block in front of the black Mercedes, Stacy waited and watched his rear view mirror for any sign of movement. Minutes later, the subject emerged from the restaurant, still carrying the briefcase. He lit up a cigarette, and took a couple of quick puffs, while looking around. Apparently noting nothing of interest, he crushed out the cigarette on the pavement with his foot, got into the car, and left.

Stacy waited for a couple of more cars to pass before falling in behind and resuming his tail.

As the black Mercedes entered a 405 ramp and headed North, Jack followed, continuing to keep his guy in sight, but at a distance. The next stop was an LA branch bank located just off a freeway exit. While on the BR squad, Stacy had responded to countless "91-new" bank robbery cases at these hit and run branches over the years. They were prime targets for stick-up artists seeking quick getaways.

He followed the subject into the bank and watched as he waited in a short line for the next available teller. Stacy's man went to the open teller window and laid the briefcase on the counter. After greeting the teller, he opened the aluminum case, pulled out stacks of bills and pushed them toward the teller before closing the lid.

When she finished with those, the guy again opened the case and set several more stacks on the counter. The teller then counted those bills and smiled as she handed him his deposit receipt.

His man nodded approval, and once again opened the briefcase, this time dropping the deposit receipt in, and walked out the door.

Stacy couldn't tell if the briefcase was empty when it was closed for the last time, but he certainly had seen more than enough to convince him that something was not right with that little rundown grocery store.

When he returned to his car, Stacy again picked up the tail on the black Mercedes, which led him directly back to where he had first spotted it parked, on the side street, beside the small grocery.

CHAPTER NINE

"Well, hello, Mr. Stacy," Harold Moore's sexy-voiced, eye-catching assistant said, as she greeted Jack.

"As always, it's great to see you, Monica," smiled Stacy. "Is he in?"

"He was on the phone but I think he just got off. Let me check."

From the second she got up and leaned over to brush a piece of lint from her perfectly fitting tight straight, short skirt, Jack's eyes remained fixated on that incredible body and those long, shapely legs as she walked to Harold's door.

"Mr. Moore, Mr. Stacy is here to see you," she said.

"Send him in," Harold told her.

Jack waited, and watched Monica walk back to her desk, before entering Harold's office and giving the bank's director of compliance and security a look that said, "Wow!"

"I know, I know," smiled Harold, adding, "and, she's bright and very competent, too."

Stacy stood shaking his head in disbelief, "I think I'm in love," he quietly mouthed to Moore.

"Don't think I can help you there," Harold laughed, "but, how about a cold shower or a cup of coffee?"

"No, I think I'll pass on both for now, but thanks, anyway," smiled Stacy.

"Well, how have you been Jack? We haven't seen your smiling face in a while."

"Since they moved me off the BR Squad I don't get to see much of you guys anymore."

"Well, we'll just have to make it a point for you to come to one of the bank security luncheons. For old time sake," Harold told him.

"Yeah, that would be good."

"In fact, I'll breakdown and buy," offered Harold.

"That would make it even better," Jack agreed.

"Well, not to wanting to change the subject, but I know you're here for something, Jack. So, what is it I can help the FBI with today?" Harold asked.

"It's about that SAR you forwarded to Treasury. Sullivan opened a PI and I've got the ticket. In fact, here's a subpoena for the account records."

"Okay," replied Harold. "I should be able to get it processed in the next couple of days."

"Sounds good."

"Did you talk with Mathis?" asked Harold.

"Yeah, I talked with him the same day you two met in his office."

"Those deposits just don't look right, Jack."

"That's what I understand," responded Stacy. "In fact, after what I saw yesterday. . . ."

Harold gave him a quizzical look.

Jack continued, "I went to the address you had for that grocery store. You wouldn't have believed it. A small, dirty, rundown store with half-stocked shelves of outdated goods, and no customers."

"Sounds like a thriving business to me. Makes me wonder where all that cash comes from," responded Moore.

"Me, too," Jack agreed. "In fact, yesterday, I followed one of two guys I spotted standing in the back of the grocery to one of your branches over off the 405, and guess what?"

"He made another large cash deposit," chuckled Harold.

Stacy smiled, "You've got it."

"You said yesterday, Jack?" Harold asked.

"Yeah," Stacy answered.

As Jack Stacy sat there, Harold Moore took the account information that Bridgette Tomas had given him and typed it into his computer. A puzzled look came over his face.

Stacy asked, "What's the matter?"

"That account number shows no deposits made into it, yesterday."

"No, it wasn't here," Stacy replied.

"No Jack, I mean nowhere in our system."

"That can't be," Stacy responded. "I was standing there in the lobby watching him. I saw the guy take stacks of bills out of an aluminum briefcase and give them to the teller."

Harold shook his head, "I don't know what to say, Jack. Nothing comes up."

Stacy added, "In fact, he opened the case a second time and took out even more bills. You're sure that's the right account number, Harold?"

"I'm sure," nodded Moore. "There's nothing, Jack."

"Does the grocery store have another account with the bank?"

"Not that I can tell, but I'll go back into the paperwork and see."

"Another thought," cautioned Stacy. "Could the teller be dirty?"

"Anything's possible, Jack, but. . . ," shaking his head, Harold said, "I don't recall any particular problems with the tellers at that branch."

Stacy shrugged.

"Did he go anywhere else?" Moore asked.

"A restaurant, on his way to the bank," Stacy chuckled. "It looked to be about as prosperous as the grocery store we were talking about. You might see if you have an account for that place."

"What's the name?" Harold asked.

"I didn't see any name," answered Stacy. "But, I did get the address."

As Stacy was jotting down the street and number, Harold heard a tap on the door panel and looked up. It was Monica.

"Mr. Moore, they're waiting for you in the conference room," she told him.

"Is it that time already?" he asked.

She nodded.

"Okay, tell 'em I'm on my way."

He then looked back at Stacy, "Sorry, Jack, weekly staff meeting."

"No problem," Stacy replied. "Here's the address."

"Okay. I'll run it through our system as soon as I get back from the meeting. That should tell us if there's an account."

Stacy stood up and extended his hand. "Thanks, Harold. I'll plan to see you when I pick up the document return for the subpoena, if not before."

"Right. I'll call you when it's all together, Jack."

Stacy nodded, and as the two of them walked out of Harold's office and into Monica's reception area, Jack added, "I should be back in the office in a couple of hours, so if you find out anything on that address, just give me a call."

"Will do," Harold assured him as he hurried out the door to the meeting.

"Don't be such a stranger, Jack," Monica said in that tempting tone of voice that had turned more than one guy into putty.

"I'll try not to be," Stacy replied with a big smile. "In fact, you should be seeing me in the next few days. Remember, I have to pick up those subpoenaed records."

"So I will see you then," she smiled.

"Yeah," Jack nodded.

She gave him a wink.

"Later," he waved, and walked out the door.

Rounding the corner leading from the hallway to the elevator, Jack stopped and shook his head as a broad grin spread across his face.

"If I was just fifteen years younger," he thought.

CHAPTER TEN

When Jack Stacy returned to the squad bay, there was a message waiting for him.

"Call Harold Moore at the bank."

From the time noted, the call had come in only minutes earlier.

Stacy dialed Moore's number, "Harold, this is Jack. I got a message that you had called. Were you able to come up with anything on that address?"

"You're not going to believe this, Jack, but we have an account for a restaurant at that address."

"With a deposit made yesterday?" Stacy asked.

"You've got it. $8,500."

"Well, I guess that clears any suspicions we might have had regarding the teller being dirty."

"Looks like it, Jack."

"Were there any other big deposits made to that account recently?"

"None like this one," answered Harold. "That account's only a couple of months old, and the monitoring period we put on new accounts went off just last week."

"Sounds like they might have known how long that period was, doesn't it?"

"Surprise, surprise," replied Harold. "We have certainly seen customers waiting until the monitoring period was over to start kiting checks, and now it appears we also have them waiting until it's over before starting to make big cash deposits."

"Yeah, it looks like that was the case this time. What were the earlier deposits like?" asked Jack.

"Nominal."

"Nothing that would attract any attention, huh?"

"Right," Harold agreed.

"I'll need to get that account information for a subpoena."

"No problem. I'll send you a fax."

"Thanks, Harold."

"Oh, Jack, one other thing you need to know before we hang up. I still need to do a little more checking, but it looks like both the grocery store and restaurant accounts might be related to at least one other business account here at the bank."

"And, what kind of business is that account engaged in," chuckled Stacy, "a launderette?"

"Wouldn't that be ironic," Harold laughed. "No. It's some kind of entertainment business."

"Ok-a-a-ay?" responded Stacy questioningly. "Well, let me know what you find out."

"Will do," Moore assured him.

CHAPTER ELEVEN

While checking out a report of possible minor damage sustained to one of the *Fantom's* fastboats during the nighttime attack on the *Hafa Adai*, Tomy heard a pounding coming from the inside walls of an adjacent metal cargo container.

"Stop, you whores!" he shouted. "I'm just one guy and can only service one of you at a time." Then, snickering to himself, the sinister first mate added, "Well, I could maybe handle two of you at a time if you need me that bad."

The pounding from the inside continued.

Tomy again shouted for them to stop, and this time when they did not, he unlocked and slowly cracked open the heavy metal door.

The sea was rolling, and the putrid conditions inside the confined quarters of the steamy, hot container had become intolerable. Several of the girls had already gotten seasick, which had in-turn caused others to also throw-up. With the gagging and coughing from the stench of vomit now permeating everything inside, the girls were desperate, and they started to push.

"I'll beat you!" he threatened, trying to get them to stop.

But, with the door now cracked even more widely open from their sudden surge, and a state of panic rapidly setting in, Tomy's threat went unheeded. The desire to get to fresh air was so strong that these girls weren't going to let anything stop them.

After getting a whiff of the repulsive smell himself, Tomy gave a queasy laugh and slowly released his hold. When he did, they all charged onto the deck. Some of the girls braced themselves against the container coughing and gagging, while others rushed to hang over the rail as they continued to vomit.

Tomy said with disgust, "You all owe me now for letting you out. You can be sure I will collect, and soon."

Dragging a hose lying nearby on the deck, and opening the water valve, Tomy turned the hard spray onto the girls.

As they squatted down and covered their faces with their hands in an attempt to protect themselves from the force, he laughed and yelled, "Get up, you bitches! Get up!"

Pulling one of the girls to him by her hair, he handed her the hose and pointed to the container, "Start washing down the inside. And the rest of you, don't just sit there, get your pussies in there, and help her."

The hose was heavy and the pressure made it hard to handle, but with two or three of them holding on at a time, the girls did get the container washed out and the surrounding deck sprayed off.

Once that was completed, Tomy herded them all back into the container and yelled, "Time for me to start collecting. Who wants to be first?" he snickered.

Squatting on the wet mats, all of the girls lowered their heads, not wanting to respond or establish any eye contact with their captor.

"You," Tomy growled, as he grabbed the hair of the nearest girl and yanked her head back. "You are coming with me," he said.

The girl did not immediately react.

Tomy jerked her up and yelled, "Do you understand me, bitch?"

With tears streaming down her cheeks and trembling, his young victim nodded timidly.

After securing the container, Tomy dragged his captive to the first mate's quarters, where he quickly locked the door behind him and threw her onto the bunk. Ripping her clothes off, he began forcing himself upon her.

She squirmed and screamed as she tried to escape, but he was too big, too strong.

"Stop, you bitch!" he yelled. "If you don't do what I want and the way I want you to do it, I will kill you. Understand!"

The girl cried out in excruciating pain for help as he continued his vicious attack, but there was no one to hear her plea, and furthermore, no one who cared.

Finally, her eyes closed and she went limp.

Tomy started cursing and shaking her vigorously.

"Look at me, you bitch," he yelled, "Look at me!"

There was no response.

CHAPTER TWELVE

The *Hafa Adai* arrived safely in Manila, and while her crew was busy making their rounds of local establishments and putting that near death experience behind them, the skipper went to the American Embassy to meet with the FBI legal attaché.

"Before we finish with this interview, there is one last thing I need to do," LEGAT Bill Robinson told Captain Cruz.

Robinson removed a group of photos and sketches from a large envelope and spread them out across the desktop.

"Do any of these guys look familiar?" the FBI agent asked the captain.

"That's the bastard!" shouted Cruz.

Jumping up and pointing, the captain placed his visibly shaking finger on an artist's sketch located toward the far end. "That sketch does not really give a true feeling for the face, those eyes, that look, but that is him. I will never forget that bastard!" he yelled. "Who is he, anyway?"

"We believe his name is Buruk," answered LEGAT Robinson.

Still visibly shaken and quivering, Captain Cruz snarled, "Buruk, huh."

"Yeah," Robinson answered. "And, from what we've been told, he's one of the worst of his type in the region."

The captain nodded, "I've heard of him, and that name says it all." Then, with vengeance in his eyes, Cruz added, "Somebody's got to get him."

"It will happen," Robinson assured him.

"But when, and how many more will have to die?" the captain replied.

Robinson acknowledged that he understood, but could obviously not give the captain a definitive answer.

With the questions asked and the photos shown, their interview was finished. "I think that will do it for now," Robinson told the captain. "Do you have any questions?"

Captain Cruz just shook his head in disbelief regarding this madness that had nearly caused a disaster of unimaginable proportion on the high seas, and left three of his men dead.

The LEGAT's face and his solemn nod told the captain that he understood. Privately, however, Robinson knew that it was going to take time.

Although small strides were being made to combat these renegade pirate attacks, reports coming out of the recent conference held there for the Pacific Rim LEGATS were not encouraging. The FBI Headquarters' Terrorism and Asian Organized Crime Unit chiefs told them that no one should expect things to improve dramatically in the near future, as this menace remained out of control.

Returning to his Old Manila office, Robinson took time to pause for a few moments and reflect on the day's events. This was the first free moment he had since returning to the city early that morning. An American missionary was being held captive on a southern Philippine island and he had been attempting to secure her release.

Having served as the FBI legal attaché and living in Manila for nearly three years now, Bill Robinson was unfortunately becoming all too accustomed to hearing dreadful accounts of hostage taking, ransom demands, and atrocities like those carried out aboard the *Hafa Adai*.

Now peering out through the large barred and bullet-proof window located near his desk, Robinson's gaze across the Bay drew his attention to a string of large ships as they rested majestically on the horizon. Behind them lay a scattered array of colorful clouds, which served to supply yet one more brilliant Philippine Islands sunset.

As he watched, Robinson could not help but wonder how many of those vessels might eventually fall victim to more unwarranted and vicious pirate attacks like the one that had been recounted to him that afternoon. As if the stealing of goods and wares was not bad enough, the killing of crewmembers with knives and blowguns, cutting off the ear of a dead mate for a souvenir, and finally leaving a ship with no one at the helm in a heavy shipping channel where it nearly collided with a loaded oil tanker were unconscionable.

Shaking his head, the LEGAT asked himself, "What kind of minds are these who would carry out such despicable acts?"

CHAPTER THIRTEEN

Approaching the main entrance to the LAX terminal, Jack Stacy spotted his cross street and turned right. It was obvious that this was rental car row, with line after line of nearly new cars sitting behind high chain link fences, and protected from illegal removal by sharp, tire damaging spikes, protruding from long metal bars located at the entrances and exits of each of the lots. At last, spotting the agency he was looking for, Jack turned into an empty parking space located near the front of the building and went inside.

"Is the manager in?" Stacy asked.

"That's him, over there," an attendant standing behind the counter replied, as he pointed. "See the guy sitting behind the desk, talking on the phone."

Stacy nodded and walked in that direction. This had to be him. He was wearing a dark colored, knit shirt with the agency logo, and the word "Manager" embroidered above the pocket. Jack waited until the manager completed his conversation before approaching.

"May I help you?" asked the manager.

"Agent Stacy, FBI," Jack replied, pulling a worn black leather FBI credential case and gold badge from the inside front, breast pocket of his blazer.

"Please be seated, Agent Stacy," the manager responded. "Does the FBI need some cars? We've got some great extended lease deals and rental option plans."

"Not today. But, I'll keep that in mind," Stacy answered, handing the manager a piece of paper, with a California license plate number written on it.

"Can you tell me if this is one of your cars?"

The manager took the sheet and turned to his computer, typing in the letters and numbers.

"It's one of ours, all right. A black Mercedes."

"Who's it rented to?" asked Stacy.

"The name on the agreement is Luis Ayala."

"You check driver's licenses when you rent the cars, don't you?"

"Sure, always. Our records show him having a California license."

The manager then showed Stacy a piece of paper with the words "Rental Agreement" printed in bold letters across the top.

Jack quickly jotted down the pertinent information – name, date of birth, driver's license number, rental data, address and the like. When he returned to the field office he would run what he had through FBI Indices, NCIC, and Criminal History Checks to see if anything came up.

Why, is anything wrong?" asked the manager. "Our car hasn't been stolen has it?"

"As far as I know it hasn't been stolen," Stacy answered. "The car has come up in an investigation, and I'm just doing some checking to see who has been driving it.

"The black Mercedes?" clarified the manager.

Stacy nodded that was correct.

Noting the way the manager specified "The black Mercedes," Stacy asked, "Has Mr. Ayala rented other cars from you?"

"Oh, yes," the manager said somewhat hesitatingly. "Why do you ask?"

"Just curious," responded Stacy. "Can you pull up his other rentals on your computer?"

"I should be able to. Let's see. Yeah, he's been renting cars from us for quite a while now. It appears that he must like to try out different makes and models."

"Why do you say that?" asked Stacy.

"Well, initially it was a Mustang Cobra convertible, then a JAG sport coupe, and now the black Mercedes sedan."

"Any reasons given as to why he changed cars?"

"None that I know regarding the Mustang, but the JAG had some damage to the front end. He said it was hit while parked and there were no witnesses."

"Was it still drivable?"

"Oh, yes. Nothing serious. A broken headlight, and some minor fender, hood and grill damage, but it was still drivable. In fact, as I recall, he said this occurred while he was away on an out of town trip, so he didn't know exactly when it happened. He did say it was a hit and run, though, and whoever did it, didn't bother to leave a note or anything."

"Was a police report filed?"

"We told him to, but since he didn't know exactly when it happened and there were no injuries, there was nothing done as far as I know, except for possibly the report being completed."

"What about insurance and repairs?"

"He carries the maximum coverage with us, so we immediately sent the car in and had it repaired. The JAG looks like new and has been rented to other customers since then."

"Have you had any problems with Mr. Ayala making his payments?"

"None at all," responded the manager with a smile. "In fact, as I remember, it's always been in cash, and we require that in advance."

"That's unusual, isn't it?" asked Stacy.

"Yeah, most people pay with a credit card."

"That's what I thought. I know they always tell me they want a credit card before renting me a car."

"That's true, even with us," the manager told him. "We do on rare occasions, however, rent vehicles to customers who either don't have a credit card or for one reason or another are opposed to using them. In cases like those, we require a VERY large cash deposit."

Jack smiled to himself. It was obvious that Luis Ayala was well aware of the paper trail left by credit cards, and as a result wasn't about to use them.

The manager continued, "Most of our competitors won't do it at all, but our feeling is that if the customer has the kind of money we're talking about to leave on deposit, and is willing carry all of our maximum coverages, and pay everything up front, we don't want to turn that business away."

"Can you tell me anything else about him?" Jack asked.

"No, not really. The only times I've seen him is when he's come in to return a car or pay his bill."

"When he's been in, have you two discussed anything else?"

"Nothing in particular that I can recall. He doesn't seem to want to talk much."

"Has there been anyone else with him?" Stacy asked.

The manager hesitated before answering, "Only once. It was when he returned the JAG."

"The car with the front-end damage," Stacy confirmed.

"That's the one," responded the manager. "I remember, because when I started questioning Mr. Ayala about what had happened, the guy with him gave me one of those looks."

"One of those looks?" questioned Stacy.

"Yeah, kind of an intimidating scowl. It's hard to put into words, but you know, the type that makes you feel very uneasy. There was just something about the look he gave me, and that stare."

Stacy nodded that he understood.

"Did this guy say anything?"

"No, not a word, and he never cracked a smile, either."

"Do you remember what he looked like?"

"Not much other than his face was really pockmarked, and he wore his hair in a ponytail.

"Age, height, weight?"

The manager shrugged and shook his head. "I seem to recall him being somewhere around the age of our customer, and 'average' is about all I can say about his height and weight. He wasn't way overweight or something like that."

"Was there anything else that stood out about him that you can remember?" Stacy asked.

"Nothing I can think of," answered the manager.

Stacy rose from his chair, "Thanks for your time, and here's my card. If Luis Ayala switches cars again, or should there be anything else that comes to mind, please give me a call."

"Will do," the manager assured him.

"And, please, don't mention our conversation to Mr. Ayala," added Stacy.

The manager nodded, "No problem," and the two shook hands.

As Jack was driving back to the office, his cell phone rang.

"Stacy," he answered.

"Jack, its Harold Moore. Just want to let you know that it turns out the other account I mentioned is also related. It's a movie theater."

"Ah-h-h, okay. When you said entertainment business, Harold, I was thinking strip joint."

"Sorry to disappoint you, Jack, but. . . ."

Stacy laughed, "Well, I guess that means I'll be going to the movies, instead. . . ."

Harold interrupted, "Instead of seeing the action live, huh."

Smiling to himself, Stacy responded, "Yeah, that's what I was about to say. By the way, are you going to be in your office for the next hour or so?"

"Sure. Come on over. I'll try to have the info you'll need for a subpoena when you get here. If for some reason, I'm away from my desk when you come in, just ask Monica and she will get it for you. I'll leave any info on the corner of my desk with a note that it's for you."

"What about the address for the movie theater?"

"I'll get that for you, too, Jack."

"And, Harold. . . ."

"Yes, Jack"

"I've also got another name for you to check on for a personal account."

"Okay, why don't you give it to me now."

"It's Luis Ayala, that's A-Y-A-L-A, and the address on his driver's license is the same as that little grocery."

"I'll see if we have anything, and if we do I'll have it with the other account info when you get here."

"Thanks, Harold. I should be there before long."

CHAPTER FOURTEEN

The first feature at the movie triplex did not start until 7:00 P.M., and the other two movies followed at ten-minute intervals. That gave Jack Stacy a little over an hour to find something to eat and get back.

Since the movie theater was located in the same vicinity as the restaurant where he had followed the guy in the black Mercedes, Stacy decided it was time to take a chance on the food and see if he could grab a bite to eat there.

No one was in sight when Jack pulled up to the restaurant and got out of his car to look around. There were no cars parked nearby and the blinds covering the restaurant's large plate glass windows were pulled.

He did notice, however, a plastic, sun-bleached, sign sitting on the windowsill, between the glass and the blinds. Stacy squinted as he tried to read the faded hand printing under the words, "Hours of Operation," and as best he could tell, today was the day of the week they were closed. He then tried the door. It was locked, but there was a partially broken blind near eye level through which he could get a peek inside.

Peering through the opening, he could see rows of booths on both sides, with tables and chairs in the center, and a bar lined with stools near the front. The floor was black and white checkerboard patterned linoleum, and the stools and benches were red, white, and black shiny vinyl. The rest of the décor appeared to be mostly chrome, plastic, or some combination thereof. Since the only light seemed to be emanating from single security lights located high in the four corners, there was little more for him to see.

Still hungry, Stacy decided to try another restaurant on his way back to the cinema. It also had a fifties motif. This one was open and rocking, and there to greet him at the door was an energetic, young, bubble gum popping waitress, wearing pink lipstick, a fitted blouse, poodle skirt, big-rolled bobby socks, and saddle oxfords. She led Jack over to a nearby table. When he was seated, she slid onto the bench across the table from him to take his order.

"What can I git ya?" she asked, popping her bubble gum.

"How about a half-pound burger with LTM, a thick slice of onion, crisp, cheesy fries, and a large chocolate malt."

Smiling, the waitress giggled, "Would you like to add a salad with lo-cal dressing and some steamed vegetables to go along with that?"

"I didn't see that on the menu," laughed Jack, "but no, this should be enough."

"Just checking. You never know," she cackled.

Healthy eating was fine with Jack Stacy and he did generally watch how much he ate, but on occasion. . . .

When he was finished, the waitress brought the check and asked, "How was it?"

"Great," replied Jack. "There was just the right mix of grease and cholesterol to make it the way I like."

She once again, cackled, "We always try to please."

After paying the bill and returning good-bye waves to a group of '50's dressed waiters and waitresses standing near the counter, Jack made his way back to the movie theaters.

Upon entering the triplex, Stacy found no lines at the concession stands, so before heading down the entryway leading into all three theaters, he decided that there would be no turning back. This evening of fat and calorie packed decadence would not be complete without a bucket of hot buttered popcorn and a giant soft drink. He did realize that indigestion would be a consequence when he went to bed, but so be it. There was a bottle of antacid tablets sitting on his nightstand, and that greasy burger and those cheese-topped fries had tasted so-o-o-o good.

Since none of the features showing in any of the three theaters were current hits, Jack didn't anticipate having trouble getting a seat for any of them, especially considering this was a week night. He would check out all three of them at the start of their showings, and as the evening progressed would continue to stick his head into each from time to time, but most of his interest was in watching the action sequel in theater number three that was scheduled to start at 7:20 P.M.

Standing in the rear of theater number one, as the feature was about to begin, Jack gave his eyes a chance to adjust, and then began counting seats and rows. As best he could determine there were about 220. That was 220 seats, but there were at most only twenty people sitting in them. Theater number two looked to be configured exactly the same as number one, and shortly after the movie started there, he counted twenty-five heads. Theater number three was a little different. It had stadium seating, but still seated only approximately 220. Again, about 10 percent of those seats were occupied.

Later checks into each theater showed no late arrivals, and thus it was safe to assume that the total number of patrons in all three theaters combined had not exceeded seventy-five.

CHAPTER FIFTEEN

There was a knock on the door.

"Got a minute, Boss?" Jack Stacy asked Tim Sullivan.

"Sure, come on in, Jack," his squad supervisor replied, What's up?"

"It has to do with the referral from Harold Moore that I'm doing the PI on. I just got back from serving the bank with a third subpoena for records."

"Okay," Sullivan responded, nodding for Stacy to take a seat and continue.

"Things have been moving pretty fast. In addition to the mom and pop grocery store, we now have separate, but related bank accounts for a restaurant and a group of movie theaters."

"Sounds like a real conglomerate to me," Sullivan said with a chuckle.

"But not a very flourishing one, from what I can tell," responded Stacy. "I told you what I found when I went into the grocery."

Sullivan nodded that he remembered, "Pretty dirty, huh."

"Yeah, dirty might be an understatement," Stacy remarked. "Well, anyway, last night I took in a movie at the theaters and also drove by the restaurant. I've been to that restaurant twice, now, and didn't see any business going on either time, but they must be doing something, because I watched our guy deposit stacks of bills into the bank account for that restaurant at one of the branches."

"Ok-a-a-ay. Any ideas?" his boss asked.

"None, yet," answered Stacy.

"What about the movie theaters?"

"There are three of them in one complex. Each of them seats about 220."

"How do they look?"

"Okay. The carpets are showing wear, marks on the walls, and a broken seat here and there, but certainly nothing like what I saw at the little grocery store."

"Lots of people at the movies?"

"When I counted heads, there were at a max, maybe seventy-five, there."

"Seventy-five in the movie you watched?"

"No, seventy-five in total. That's counting all three of the theaters, combined."

"So, close to 600 of those 660 seats were left empty," summed Sullivan.

"You've got it," confirmed Stacy.

"It doesn't appear then that any of their businesses are doing very well," Sullivan concluded.

"Not from what I've seen," agreed Stacy, "But from that SAR and the deposit I saw being made, they sure seem to be generating cash."

"Sounds like it."

"So, let me get this straight," Sullivan said. "We've got a dumpy little grocery store with virtually no customers, a restaurant that hasn't been open whenever you have stopped by, and a movie theater that was 10 percent full when you checked it out."

"That's about the size of it," Stacy confirmed.

Sullivan added, "And, to top it all off, we have bank accounts overflowing with suspicious cash deposits."

"That's also true," Jack agreed.

"Laundering's about the only explanation I can see," Sullivan concluded.

"Uh-huh," nodded Stacy.

Sullivan added, "Nick Costigan was talking about money laundering at an in-service I went to last year, and during it he gave several examples of how high-cash businesses can be used to launder. One of 'em he used was a movie theater. Nick pointed out how we have all been to theaters when there is a hit movie and most, or all of the tickets for that feature and maybe the next few showings are gone. In those instances, the theater owner is making close to all he can from the 'legit' ticket sales, so laundering is pretty much out of the question, except for possibly adding 'dirty cash' to gross-up some phony sales at the concession counter."

"Makes sense to me," Stacy responded.

Sullivan continued, "So, although there's not much laundering available when a hit movie plays to a sold out crowd, it was also pointed out that sold out movie theaters are, of course, not the norm. In fact, just like you saw, Jack, sometimes there may be only 10 percent of the seats filled. And, when that happens the theater could very easily be used to launder. All the bad guys need to do is claim that instead of there being seventy-five people in those three theaters like you saw, there were 375 people. They already have legitimate receipts for the seventy-five tickets sold and plenty of 'dirty cash' to pay for the 300 additional ticket sales needed to be commingled, so that the receipts can now be grossed up to the 375 level, and a little more of that 'dirty money' they have becomes washed and 'legitimate.' "

"They need to keep changing those numbers, though," Stacy added.

"Sure," Sullivan agreed. "Nick mentioned that they'll mix it up to show half of the tickets sold this time, 2/3rds at the next showings, then 1/4th, 3/4ths, and so on. Also, if they're smart, they likely won't ever show all of the seats taken, except when they really are sold out, because that might create suspicion."

"That's probably what they're doing all right," Stacy said, giving a nod and a slight smile, before adding, "And, by continuing to mix that 'dirty cash' in with the other, day in and day out, they can make a lot of it appear 'legitimate.' "

"Yeah," Sullivan agreed, "And, the same probably goes for that grocery store, the restaurant, and who knows whatever else they're into. They'll inflate phony sales with 'dirty-cash,' and claim those high gross receipts reported as 'legitimate' income."

"On at least one set of books, anyway," Stacy chuckled, adding, "And also, in order to avoid questions from the man, they might even decide to pay taxes on the 'profits.' "

Sullivan smiled at the thought of the guys paying taxes on those "dirty money profits," but. . . . "It wouldn't be the first time," he told Jack. Sullivan then asked Stacy, "Any ideas as to the source of the 'dirty-cash?' "

"Nothing yet, but I have a feeling we're going to find out something before long," Stacy answered.

"Yeah, me too," Sullivan agreed.

"You mentioned their talking about money laundering at that in-service you went to at the Academy. Why don't you give your buddy back at Quantico a call and ask him if the white-collar or OC guys can take a look at what we have," Stacy suggested.

"Good idea. I'll talk to Will Crane. Maybe we can get one of them to come out here for a few days. Besides, it's good for those academics at the Academy to get away from 'Club Fed,' and back onto the street every once in a while," smirked Sullivan.

CHAPTER SIXTEEN

"FBI, come out with your hands up," the amplified voice of the FBI agent resonated through the bullhorn.

Within seconds, a pair of bulletproof glass doors cracked slightly open and the profiles of two middle-aged women slowly emerged. Their heads and shoulders tilted back in strained, unnatural positions, and looks of sheer terror spread across their faces. As the doors opened wider, a pair of ski-masked gunmen were seen in the background shadowing every move of each woman. The two gunmen maintained tight grips on the back of each woman's collar, and held pistols to their heads.

With the two female hostages now serving as human shields, the ski-masked gunmen slowly made their way down the walkway leading to the corner phone booth. Suddenly, one of the masked gunmen spotted a man in his early thirties, wearing khaki pants and a dark blue blazer, crouching beside a brick wall across the street.

On a second glance, he saw a pistol in his hand.

The gunman fired once in the direction of the man, and as he did, he pulled the hostage closer for protection.

No shots were returned.

The gunman popped off two more rounds, again in the same direction.

His gun jammed.

Trying to clear the chamber, he temporarily lost his grip on the hostage and she fled toward the man in the blue blazer. No time to give chase, the gunman stepped back next to his accomplice and the two of them forced their remaining hostage across the street and into the offices of the Dogwood Inn motel.

The gunmen, who were still inside the Bank of Hogan, now closed the heavy, reflective doors, and directed their remaining hostages to move back away from the windows and squat behind the counter.

"Arms up, and hands and fingers laced behind your heads," the hostages were told.

"Can you get some more help over here?" requested an agent over the radio.

"What's your 20?" responded another, using the standard ten-code.

"I'm at the back of the motel with the woman who was being held hostage."

"Is she okay?"

"A little shaken up, but she seems to be okay."

"10-4, stay with her and hold your position for now. We don't know how many 91 subjects are still in the bank," responded the agent, not knowing how many of the bank robbers still remained inside.

The microphone was tapped, "click, click," as the agent acknowledged he understood.

Another call quickly followed, "I saw a guy that looked like he might be the getaway driver."

"Where?"

"Up here, at the other end of the block. He ducked back around the corner."

"By the drug store and the rooming house?"

"10-4"

"Try to stay on him."

Another double click came over the radio, indicating that was "affirmative."

The distinctive thumping of an approaching low-flying helicopter could be heard getting louder and louder in the background. As the chopper's blades pounded, those agents on the ground crouched even closer to their bureau cars (Bucars) and shielded their eyes from the grit and debris being blown about. Several were already preparing to make their move in the direction of the Dogwood Inn, but they would have to await the supervisor's final nod.

Now hovering near the Biograph Theater, the chopper pilots kept the helicopter steady as men carrying scoped MP-5 submachine guns, and dressed in olive drab uniforms, helmets with goggles, boots, and black ballistic protective vests, prepared to step off the skids.

Word came over their headsets to go, and the fast roping to the ground by the operators began. A half-block away from where they dropped, the nod was given and agents concealed behind cover began to fan out around the motel. When one agent was spotted, several more shots rang out from one of the gunmen hiding behind the office doorway.

Meanwhile, the hostage negotiators got calls stiffed into both the bank and the motel in an effort to get some kind of dialog going, and hopefully keep anyone from getting killed or hurt.

Swashbuckler

To the rear of the perimeter, agent operators went over with Supervisory Special Agent Matt Kelly the final details for their anticipated assault.

Another call came over the radio. "There's a white Mercedes parked beside the pawn shop. It's facing the opposite direction."

"Is anybody in it?" came back the response.

"I can't tell. The glass is too dark. I'll try to get a closer look."

As a female agent crept past the three-story rooming house and stood up along the outer wall of the restaurant next door, she took a quick glance around the corner of the building. There was an image barely visible inside the car.

Trying to get a closer look, the agent was suddenly surprised when the door opened, and out popped a guy who easily might have been mistaken for the doughboy. He had what appeared to be a gun tucked in his waistband.

"Halt, FBI!" the agent yelled, as he started to run.

The doughboy glanced back in her direction before resuming his lumbering run down the walkway.

With a standard issue .40 caliber red handle pistol in her hand, the agent gave chase.

Passing a billiard hall and reaching the corner, the doughboy stopped to catch a breath as he looked down the side street. To his right were a group of brick row houses. Several of them had lower stairwell entrances that he might duck into, and near the end of the block was another two-story building with a large wooden balcony overhang. From there he could get a good view of the entire street, and maybe even get a shot off in the direction of anyone following him.

The FBI agent stopped before reaching the cross street. Maintaining a low profile, she peered around the corner. There was no sign of the heavyweight. She knew he had to be around there, though. At the pace he was moving, there was no way he could have made it much past the end of the block before she was able to get a look.

"This guy is one giant rabbit," she said over the radio. "I'll need a back-up. Maybe another team can come up from the other end of the street."

"Behind the bank?" questioned the supervisor.

"10-4" answered the female agent.

"We'll get somebody over there. Hold your position for now."

Next door to the bank was the post office, and beyond that the All Med Drug Store and rooming house. Agent Matt Kelly and several of the operators from the team brought in by the chopper were now assembled along the glass front of the drug store, out of sight of the robbers. From there they would await further instructions.

Suddenly, an agent from the Practical Applications Unit appeared in front of the doorway to the bank.

Bullhorn in hand, the agent instructor announced, "This phase of the practical exercise is completed. Actors, return to the Hogan's Alley role player center. New Agents, holster your red handle training pistols. I want to see all of you in the classroom. It's critique time."

With that, Supervisory Special Agent Nick Costigan gathered up his clipboard and walked over to see Matt Kelly.

"How many robberies does that make for the Bank of Hogan so far this month?" asked Matt.

"Two, three, who knows?" Nick laughed. "However many it is, I'm sure this is still the most robbed bank in the entire United States."

"Probably the world," Matt added.

"Thanks for not embarrassing the Investigative Training Unit with that little drop you made from the chopper," cracked Costigan.

"I appreciate that Nick. Next time we'll see if you can have a turn."

"That's all right, the last time I jumped off a skid like that was in Vietnam," Nick replied.

"And you didn't hurt yourself?" Matt quipped.

"No, but we were only about five feet off the ground."

Matt laughed, "Did they give you a ladder?"

"No ladders."

"But you were a lot younger then, too," Matt responded sarcastically.

"Okay, keep it up, wise ass," Nick smiled. "We'll be watching you jump out of helicopters in fifteen years."

Agents Matt Kelly and Nick Costigan were originally scheduled to be out of the United States teaching an international money laundering program in Central Asia during this time, but the FBI legal attaché for that region called the Academy at the last minute and requested their program be put on hold. There was some kind of serious internal strife going on in the country, with civil disorder and riots anticipated, and the ambassador didn't believe it was wise for the U.S. to conduct the planned training. Besides, their classroom might very well be empty since the selected attendees would likely be in the streets attempting to quell any disturbances.

As a result, these two well-traveled, international agents now had a couple of weeks to work with other units around Quantico.

Having been a SWAT team leader in the field, Matt jumped at any opportunity to train with the Hostage Rescue Team (HRT), and the Practical Applications Unit in Hogan's Alley had contacted Nick to assist them as a New Agent evaluator.

With the exercise completed, windows in the Bank of Hogan, the Biograph Theater, and other buildings in the area were once again rattling as the HRT helicopter returned and set down in the space vacated by the New Agents.

Shielding his eyes and trying to make sure Nick could hear him over the loud roar coming from the engine and blades, Matt shouted, "Time to go. See you back at the office when we get done today."

As Matt jogged over toward the chopper, Nick gave him the high sign, indicating he understood. Clipboard in hand, Nick headed off in the opposite direction toward the Hogan's Alley classroom where the critique for this first phase of the bank robbery practical problem was about to begin.

When all were back onboard the chopper, it lifted out of Hogan's Alley and headed toward nearby Lake Lunga. Looking out over the water, Matt saw HRT agent operators conducting water training below. Wearing black wet suits, masks, fins, and tanks, several were already slipping into the water from their gray and black IBS inflatable rafts. Matt and the agent operators with whom he had been working at practical applications complex would be joining them shortly.

Setting down near the shoreline, they jumped from the chopper and quickly changed into their diving gear.

Earlier that morning they had pre-positioned their equipment. After they changed and got back onboard, the pilots headed out over the water to the area where these agents would practice entering the water from the air.

As he looked down, Matt Kelly could not help wondering what it would be like to do this jumping from several thousand feet by parachute. While a cadet at the United States Air Force Academy, at Colorado Springs, he had done some sky diving and made his share of standard jumps, but none ever into a lake. Even more awesome, he thought, might have been an ocean jump.

As they dropped in from the low flying chopper, everything went without a hitch, and since Matt kept his scuba certification up, this portion of the training was no obstacle.

In the meantime, several more of the IBS inflatable rafts had been brought out to where they were diving. As Matt pulled himself over the bulging side of one of them, Cole Dawson, the HRT commander gave him a hand.

"A little different out here than across the street in the hallowed halls at the seat of knowledge, huh, Matt?" chuckled Dawson.

Cole Dawson was a twenty-eight year Bureau veteran and former Army Green Beret in Vietnam who had come to HRT from FBI Headquarters a year earlier.

"A little different," laughed Matt. "It's good to know we can call on you guys to come rescue us though."

Dawson smiled.

"By the way, what's your cell number?" Matt asked.

"For you, it's unlisted," Dawson sarcastically shot back.

"That's what I was afraid of," replied Matt.

"Seriously, how have you liked training with us these past two weeks, Matt?"

"It's been great. I just wish I could do it more often."

"You can always apply to test for the team," Dawson told him.

"Now, I didn't say full-time," Matt answered. "Just more often."

"Okay," replied Cole. "We'll see what we can do."

"Thanks."

"By the way, in the coming days we'll be down on the James River conducting tactical ship boarding practice. Maybe you can come with us."

"Sounds good to me. I'll check with Will."

"Oh, yeah, that reminds me, Matt. Crane called over and wanted me to tell you to be sure to stop by his office before you leave today. He said it was important."

"I just hope he hasn't volunteered me for another OPR (Office of Professional Responsibility) investigation," sighed Matt.

Dawson nodded, knowing that most FBI supervisors did not like having to conduct internal affairs investigations.

CHAPTER SEVENTEEN

On the way back to his 1970's bomb shelter office located in building nine of the bowels of the FBI Academy, Matt stuck his head into the Investigative Training Unit (ITU) chief's office. "You wanted to see me, Boss?"

"Come on in and have a seat, Matt," responded Will Crane.

The two had known each other since the days when Crane was a field supervisor in Matt's first field office, and Matt had endured more than one of Will's dreaded sixty-day file reviews.

"You and Nick have the Pacific Training Initiative (PTI) in Guam coming up, right?"

Matt nodded that was correct.

"Do you see any problem with your leaving a few days early and stopping over in LA on your way?"

"Nothing I know of. Why? What's up?"

"I was talking with Tim Sullivan. He's an OC supervisor out there that I've known for years. One of the agents on his squad has a new case that is not making a lot of sense, and he asked if somebody from our unit could go out there and take a look. Since you were already heading that direction on a trip, anyway, I thought a stopover might fit into your schedule. Besides, it'll get you back on the street for a few days."

"That sounds fine, but when do I need to leave?" Matt responded somewhat hesitatingly.

"How does tomorrow morning sound?"

"Good to see you're in no hurry," Matt responded, tongue in cheek. "I'll have to give Terry a call to make sure he can take care of Buddy while I'm gone."

"You and that yellow dog," chuckled Crane. "Terry's the retired Marine Colonel who lives next door, right?"

"Yeah, that's him, Terry Draw, and he's almost as close to Buddy as I am."

"With all of your travel, it's good he's around."

Matt nodded in total agreement.

"Back to this thing in LA, Will. What's the case about?"

"As best I could determine, they've opened a PI on a case involving lots of cash being deposited to the accounts of different businesses. A retired agent out there is in charge of compliance at the bank where the deposits are being made. He filed a SAR and then contacted the Bureau."

"Is Nick going, too?"

"No, he reminded me that he'll be giving a presentation to the Legislature in Palau on his way to the PTI."

"What's that thing in Palau about anyway?" Matt asked.

"A request came in to HQ from their justice people for AML (anti-money laundering) assistance. I guess there's some of that old 'any money is good money' syndrome going on around there and they want to get it addressed before it festers and Palau becomes the next haven."

"Okay," Matt replied, adding with a sly smile, "Sounds like tough duty though, huh?"

Crane smiled and nodded in agreement.

"Well, I guess that leaves me. I'll call over to Cole and tell him that my days to train with the HRT have once again been put on hold."

"Glad to see you've got the picture," replied Crane. "By the way, the case agent out in LA is a guy named Jack Stacy. He can fill you in on the details."

"I'll give him a call as soon as I get back to my office," Matt told his boss.

"Oh, before I forget, Matt, here's your new GPS watch. It came in today."

Matt grinned, "Still trying to keep track of me, huh, Boss."

"Yeah, that, and keep you from getting lost," he smiled. "As many countries as you and Nick are in, it can get tough for a unit chief to keep up."

"Look at it this way, Will, when we're half-way around the world, it makes it hard for them to blame you when we violate some innocuous Bureau policy," replied Matt.

"You're right, but they still try, and then if something should happen to you there's all of that messy paperwork I have to deal with," moaned his unit chief.

"I always knew you cared," smirked Matt.

"Sure, I had to put up with you in Chicago and now here at Quantico. It's beginning to look a little like 'til death do us part,' " wisecracked Crane.

Kelly laughed, "After all of those stats I got you in Chicago, and now everything that I've done for you here. You should be so lucky."

"If I could work for a guy like me, I'd stay on the job for fifty years," replied Crane, with a sly smile, before adding, "And remember all of that other stuff you mentioned is past tense. In the BU, it's 'what have you done for me today.' "

"I know, I know," groaned Matt, cracking a smile and shaking his head at hearing, one more time, Will's fifty year quip about how great he thought it was to work for him. And, also being reminded of that old Bureau management mentality that he had been exposed to since day one on the job of "what you've done in the past is history;" what we're concerned with is "what have you done for me today!"

"On a more serious note," his unit chief then added, "This new GPS watch has a special feature. Should there be an emergency and you need immediate help, there is button you can press that will transmit an alert to HQ that you are in trouble and give your exact location anywhere in the world."

"Well, that's certainly something I hope I never have to use, but . . . ," replied Matt.

"Me, too," Will Crane agreed. "It's good for you to have though, just in case. Considering some of those places you and Nick go to, you never know."

"Right," Matt gestured, as he put the watch on and shook his wrist to test the fit. "By the way, does Nick have his new watch, too?" he asked.

"Yeah, I gave it to him earlier today," answered Crane.

As Matt was getting up to leave, Will told him, "Be sure to say 'hello' to your dad for me when you're out in LA."

"For sure," answered Matt.

On his way down the hall, Matt noticed the door to Nick's office partially open and a light on.

"Tap, Tap."

Nick looked up. "Come on in. I see you survived your drop into Lunga."

"This time anyway," Matt replied.

"Did you stop by and see the boss?" Nick asked.

"Yeah, I just got out of there. Did he tell you what it was about?"

"A little bit, and I would have gone, but . . . ," responded Nick, with a coy smile.

"I know," sighed Matt. "You were already committed to do duty for God and Country way out in the Pacific."

"Somebody had to go," laughed Nick.

Matt responded with a humorous moan. "Yeah, I get sent to the streets of LA while you're off getting rays on some pacific island paradise. Now, does that sound fair?"

"Does to me," answered Nick, in a less than convincing tone. "Remember, 'needs of the Bureau,' Matt. And, who knows, it could be tough duty out there."

"Sure, keep telling yourself that, Nick. Remember who you're talking to."

"Okay. Well, at least you'll get to see Guam."

"You mean, again," responded Matt.

"Again?" Nick looked puzzled.

"Yeah, remember my telling you about being assigned to Andersen Air Force Base for a while when I was an intel officer. We were there working with OSI and DEA monitoring some traffickers coming out of Thailand."

"I forgot about that. How did you like it there?"

"Other than getting a little island fever and the fact that the area seems to be magnet for natural disasters, I thought it was great."

"A magnet for natural disasters?" Nick gave a curious look and smile.

"Yeah. Typhoons, hurricanes, whatever you want to call those things with two hundred mile an hour winds, and earthquakes, too. Guam seems to attract 'em all."

"And what about all of those brown snakes I've heard about?" added Nick.

"Yeah, those too. And, not many birds, either."

"Because of the snakes?"

"Right, because of the snakes. But, I still thought Guam was great, anyway."

"I'm looking forward to seeing it," Nick replied.

"Well, I'd better get back to my office if I'm going to get out of here and on my way to LA by O-dark tomorrow morning. I don't even have airline reservations yet. By the way, when are you leaving, Nick?"

"Not exactly sure, travel is still working on the Pohnpei segment of my trip."

Matt gave Nick a puzzled look.

"Oh, I guess I forgot to tell you that I'll be meeting up with Laynie West, I mean Steele, on my way. I keep forgetting that she changed her last name when she got married. Well, anyway, Laynie asked if I could stop by Pohnpei with her for a couple of days on the way to Palau. She's the Pacific Liaison Agent, and the government of Micronesia wants to give us an award for assistance the

Bureau gave in connection with a massive fraud investigation there."

"Us?" Matt responded with a somewhat surprised expression. "And what part did Nick Costigan play in all of this to wangle an invitation to paradise? I don't remember your telling me about being in Micronesia."

"I've never been there. This all happened when I was uptown. I was the headquarters supervisor for the case."

"Okay," Matt said with a sly smile.

"No, seriously," Nick replied somewhat defensively. "The case was assigned to me at HQ. Laynie did the real legwork on the case in the islands, but I managed to get her the help and support she needed. And, since both of us were already going to Palau for the presentation to the Legislature, there, Laynie thought it would be nice for me to also attend the ceremony in Micronesia. They invited both of us, and Will thought I should go, too."

"Sure," Matt smugly replied. "You don't have to convince me, Nick. Just because it sounds a little too much like a boondoggle."

"No seriously."

Matt smiled, "I'm glad to hear you're going, Nick. I'm just jealous. Why now, though? That must have all happened a while ago."

"It did. Most of the investigation was conducted a couple of years ago, but the Micronesian government just got the money back this past year. About all of it was moved offshore, and you know how long it takes when everything has to go through Letters Rogatory."

"Yeah, tell me about it," Matt agreed. "Is Honolulu your first stopover?"

"You've got it. I'll meet Laynie there, and then we'll go on to Pohnpei. She told me that we'd be flying the island hopper across the Pacific. Whatever that is."

"The island hopper, huh. Now, that's original," chuckled Matt. "Well, gotta go. See you in Agana, Nick."

Before leaving, Matt still had to call over to Cole Dawson at HRT, make airline reservations, and then let Jack Stacy know when he'd be getting into LA.

"Enjoy yourself in la-la land," Nick added, as Matt neared the doorway.

"You know me, I always do," laughed Matt.

"That's for sure," Nick agreed.

Stopping momentarily outside the door, Matt yelled back, "Don't get yourself hooked up with some honey in paradise, and forget to show up for the PTI."

"I'll try not to, but, if for some reason I'm a no show, just go ahead and start without me," Nick answered, laughing. "And, oh, before I forget, some of the officers attending the PTI will be coming from Laynie's territory, so she's planning to stay over with us for the opening ceremonies."

"Okay, I guess," Matt, muttered under his breath, as he walked to his office.

Nick's bringing up Laynie West's name caught him by surprise. Matt had never mentioned her name to Nick, nor anything about the stormy on and off relationship the two of them had going while both were assigned to the Chicago Division.

It was after the emotional break-up of their engagement that each sought transfers. Laynie went to Honolulu, where she became the FBI's Pacific Liaison Agent to a chain of island paradises linked half way around the world and Matt, later, went to the FBI Academy at Quantico. Neither had spoken to the other since leaving Chicago, and in fact, Matt did not even know that Laynie's last name was now Steele, although he had heard through the grapevine that she had married some guy who was a former Navy officer.

Whoever told him this knew that Matt had gone to the Air Force Academy and rubbed it in that this guy was an Annapolis grad.

Since Nick had been responsible for coordinating all of the arrangements for the PTI, Matt hadn't given a second thought that Laynie might also be participating, but now that she was, he was already feeling a bit uneasy about their being reunited in Guam.

CHAPTER EIGHTEEN

As far as Nina was concerned, her life as a trafficked sex slave could not get any worse, and this time she was determined to make good her get-away, no matter what the consequence. She had contemplated making an escape once before, but reconsidered after seeing what acid did to the face and breasts of another young woman following a foiled attempt.

With this john passed out on the floor from too much booze, she quietly slipped out the door of the first floor apartment. Remaining in the dim lighting and shadows along the hallway, she sneaked past the security control checkpoint where a guard sat fixated on the television set, cheering on his favorite team. Fortunately for Nina, another john was in the midst of leaving, and before the door could fully close and engage the automatic lock, she darted out through the slim opening and into the darkness where she hid behind some nearby bushes.

Since being trafficked from her native Indonesia to the U.S. only months earlier, this petite, seventeen year-old Asian beauty with shiny, long, black hair and a porcelain-like complexion lived a life of sheer terror.

Her blemish-free skin now revealed deep purple bruises along her legs and back, and needle marks and sores tracked down her forearms and along the bottoms of her feet. Around her mystical eyes hung dark rings, and those

Swashbuckler

luscious lips that had been so inviting remained swollen from a beating handed out only two days earlier by one of the guards. A john had complained that she was unwilling to fulfill his disturbed and bizarre sexual fantasy and this was the consequence.

In addition, Nina also suffered from at least one infectious disease that she knew of, and had become drug dependant due to the regular forced shoot-ups injected by her captors.

Now, looking around from the bushes where she was hiding near the entrance to the apartment building and noticing no one, Nina raced down the sidewalk and into the night. She knew that once it was discovered she had escaped, the search for her would be on. Her captors would put her picture out to their associates and a bounty would be placed on her head. If caught, she would likely be killed, since their punishment of acid disfigurement to faces and breasts seemed to be confined to those who had attempted an escape, but were found while still on or near the grounds.

Nina had no passport or other identification, as that had all been taken from her before she ever arrived in the U.S. Tucked inside her blouse, however, was a slip of paper she had saved for a moment like this, plus the cash she had lifted from the wallet of the drunk, abusive john she had been with prior to her escape. On the piece of paper was printed the name "Sam" and a telephone number.

Nina received the name and number from the Indonesian girl who suffered the brutal acid attack at the hands of their captors. A guy she had met at the club from which she was recruited in Indonesia gave her this information and told her she could call on this person for help in getting settled and additional work in the U.S. She did not get the opportunity to make the call, but saved the name and number just in case.

Fearful that her escape had been discovered and that her captors were already out looking for her, Nina wandered the area side streets throughout the remainder of the night, ducking into the shadows and behind trees and bushes whenever headlights shown her direction. Fortunately, there had been no sign of any of her captors.

As the hazy early morning sun was rising above an unusually heavy dose of LA smog, Nina recognized a familiar logo identifying an international fast food restaurant chain in the distance. There, she would be able to use the restroom to clean up a little, get something to eat, and change for the telephone.

Although Nina found it difficult to carry on a normal conversation in English, she could read some and spoke enough to be able to order something to eat and drink. Her native language was *Bahasa Indonesian* and she hoped that Sam, whose number she was now dialing, also spoke it and not another of the nearly two hundred other languages used throughout the archipelago.

During the next hour and a half, she tried dialing the number given her for Sam a half-dozen times, but all she kept getting was a message saying that the person was unavailable. She would try again, later.

Looking around for a phonebook, she noticed one hanging from a chain by a nearby phone. Locating a number for the Indonesian Consulate Office in Los Angeles, she picked up the receiver and dropped in her coins. The phone

CHAPTER NINETEEN

Exiting the gateway at LAX's Gate 54, Matt Kelly glanced first to the left and then to his right before stopping in front of the airline boarding agent's desk.

Standing over to the side was a guy who looked to be in his early fifties, about six-foot tall, a little overweight, with a red, ruddy complexion, and graying hair. He was wearing tinted glasses, the kind that change with the light, a blue cotton, starched shirt with a button-down collar, conservative striped tie, lightweight wool gray slacks, black wing tips, and a dark blue blazer.

He gave Matt a nod and started walking in his direction. Kelly knew that must be Jack Stacy. In all of his travels, there was rarely, if ever, another FBI agent holding up one of those cardboard signs with his name on it. Whether it was a bulge under his jacket; or the black fanny pack often worn strapped to the agent's waist to conceal a pistol when he was not wearing a jacket; or just something innate, Kelly wasn't sure. But, he and any other agents meeting him always seemed successful in linking up with one another.

"Matt Kelly?" the man asked.

Matt smiled and nodded, extending his hand.

"Jack Stacy," greeted the LA agent. "Welcome to California."

"Thanks. It's good to finally get off that plane," replied Matt, giving a sly smile and shaking his head.

Swashbuckler

was dead and her coins were gone. The coin return wasn't working either. Agitated, Nina slammed dow[n] receiver and tore that page out of the book, circlin[g] number for the Consulate Office with the piece of b[r] pencil that had been discarded on the shelf below the ph[one].

Since she knew the other phone was working, returned to it and started dialing.

"You have reached the Indonesian Consulate Offi[ce] Los Angeles. We are unable to take your call at this Please leave a message at the tone."

Speaking in her native *Bahasa Indonesian*, Nina i[denti]fied herself and rattled off details of the terror and s[exual] brutality carried out against her and other girls being captive in the apartment building. Suddenly there [was a] second tone sound and then nothing. The message rec[order] had clicked off.

Waiting another hour before again trying the numb[er for] Sam, Nina finally heard his phone ring.

"Hello," answered the person on the other end.

"Speak to Sam?" Nina asked.

"This is Sam. Who is this?" he replied.

"Nina," and she immediately started speaking in B[ahasa] *Indonesian.*

Sam responded in their native language and Ni[na was] relieved. As they continued to talk, she revealed mor[e of] her circumstances and sought his help. Sam res[ponded] sympathetically and their conversation ended wi[th Sam] suggesting they meet about eight that evening at [a] shelter located in the corner of a small park not f[ar from] where she now was.

"Not a great flight, huh?"

"I've had better," answered Kelly. "A middle seat in the back, with a wide body on one side, a hacking cougher on the other, and the seat back of the person sitting in front of me reclined as far as it would go."

"Sounds great," chuckled Stacy.

"It was," Matt sarcastically responded. "Five long hour's worth."

"When people put their seats back and I have no room for my legs, I try to make sure that their back gets a generous massage with my knees," Stacy said. "Sometimes they get the hint, and straighten the seatback up."

"That's occasionally worked for me, too, but it didn't seem to make any difference today," replied Matt.

"Some people just don't get it," noted Stacy.

"Or care about anybody else," added Kelly.

Stacy nodded, "Especially those with attitudes."

"Yeah," Matt agreed.

"Well, let's pick up your bags get out of here," Stacy said, as he pointed the two of them in the direction of baggage claim.

From the airport, Jack took Matt to his hotel so he could get checked in and drop off his bags. When that was completed, the two of them got back onto the 405 Freeway, north, to the Wilshire Boulevard exit. The FBI occupied several floors in the nearby Federal Building and there Jack would bring Matt up to date on where they were regarding the case.

As Jack was sliding his card into the reader to open the door leading into the FBI garage, a call came over the air for him to meet one of the other agents from the squad at a Beverly Hills parking lot.

"Looks like a change of plans," Stacy told Kelly as he reversed direction and the two agents headed for the meet.

The parking lot was only about ten minutes away. Jack spotted a Bucar in a side slot in the lot. He pulled into an empty spot a couple of spaces away. A tall guy, about Matt's age, wearing sunglasses and dressed in business casual walked over to the driver's side.

"What's up, Tom?" Stacy asked.

Not immediately responding, he slid the sunglasses down on his nose and glanced over at Matt, as if to say, "Who is this guy?"

Stacy reacted, "Sorry, Tom. I forgot you two didn't know each other. Tom Sanders, this is Matt Kelly."

Matt smiled and nodded, "Nice to meet you, Tom."

"Matt's out of Quantico. He's an OC money laundering guy who's going to be working with us for the next few days."

Sanders glanced back in Matt's direction, "Back to the street, huh, Matt?"

"Yeah, for a few days, anyway"

Sanders smiled, "Well, this old fart can use all the help he can get." Then, kneeling down beside the door so as not to appear too conspicuous, he said, "Jack, you wanted me to let you know about any more banks our guy went to, today."

Stacy nodded.

"There were those I talked to you about earlier."

"The ones you called me about while I was out at LAX," Stacy confirmed.

"Yeah, those, and then this one," Sanders responded, looking over toward the bank. "He got here about fifteen minutes ago."

"Anybody with him?"

"Nobody I saw. Just him and an aluminum briefcase."

"Before we go any further, Tom. Why don't you start with the grocery and bring Matt up to date on what you saw our guy doing at those other stops he made earlier, today?"

"No problem," responded Sanders, as he glanced over toward the car they had been tailing. "We were sitting on this little corner grocery store when our man pulled up in that black Mercedes. Where he'd been earlier in the morning or spent the night, we have no idea. Anyway, he went into the store with his hands empty and came out a few minutes later carrying an aluminum briefcase. From the grocery, his first stop was at one of those safe deposit box places. You know, the ones that have safe deposit box rentals, but they're not banks."

Matt acknowledged that he was familiar with them.

Sanders continued, "There, he took two aluminum briefcases in with him and came out about ten minutes later, but this time the two cases appeared to be considerably heavier."

Matt smiled and nodded.

"We then followed him to three banks. He stopped at each just long enough to go to a teller window, hand over some of the cash from one of the briefcases, and get what looked like a check in return."

"Probably a bank or cashiers check, responded Matt. "Sounds like he's acting as a 'smurf.' "

"A 'smurf,' huh," chuckled Sanders, envisioning one of those classic cartoon characters.

"Yeah, you know, one of those guys that goes from bank to bank exchanging cash for cashiers checks."

"I've heard about 'em, but this was my first time to see one in action."

Looking over at Matt, Jack Stacy smiled, "Let's take a walk inside and see what our 'smurf' is up to, here."

Going through the first set of double doors, Jack and Matt waited a few seconds in the bandit barrier for their eyes to adjust from the bright mid-day sun before proceeding to the second set. This barrier space, enclosed by pairs of tinted, heavy, bulletproof double doors at both ends could be locked electronically, creating a box from which more than one bandit wished he could have escaped.

Inside the bank, Matt looked to his right where several rows of bank employees were sitting in high back, black, leather chairs, behind rich-looking executive wooden desks. On each of the desks was an engraved, shiny brass plate identifying the person as a personal banker, loan officer, new account representative, and the like.

To his and Jack's left stood a long, dark, walnut counter fronting a line of teller stations, each with its own bulletproof glass window. Centered in front of the counter was a customer line winding through a maze of burgundy velvet ropes and chrome posts. Standing at the farthest window down the line was the guy from the little grocery store.

Dressed in a black shirt and khaki trousers, their man had a pair of two hundred dollar sunglasses flipped atop his slick, black hair. He had one of the aluminum briefcases propped up on the counter directly in front of him. The two agents arrived too late to see any exchange of cash, if in fact there had been any. All they saw their man do was take, what looked like a check from the teller, drop it into the case, and then struggle momentarily with one of the latches while attempting to get it closed.

Sensing he would be leaving shortly, Jack went back outside the bank to wait, while Matt continued to monitor what was going on inside. The surveillance agent that had followed their man into the bank also left when Stacy departed.

After the second lock on the case was closed, the subject turned and walked toward the first set of double doors.

As he approached, Matt looked down at his watch, still keeping him in sight out of the corner of his eye.

After the subject passed through the inner and outer doors, Jack signaled Tom Sanders. The agents watched closely as their guy made his way to the black Mercedes. From there, it was up to Tom and the others on the surveillance team to pick up the tail, while Jack and Matt followed up on what had transpired inside the bank.

CHAPTER TWENTY

Jack Stacy rejoined Matt Kelly in the bank lobby and the two of them immediately took an elevator to the fifth floor.

"The compliance and security director here at the bank is a guy named Harold Moore," Stacy told Kelly. "He's retired Bu. I first knew him years ago when he was on one of the BR squads. That was back in the days when the LA division had two bank robbery squads."

"I remember hearing about those days," nodded Matt, "A city and a county."

"Right," Stacy responded with surprise. "How did you know that?"

"My dad was on one of those BR squads for years. His name is Pat Kelly."

"Sure, I remember hearing stories about your dad," replied Stacy. "Harold probably knows him. Your dad was a 'heavy.'"

"Cigars and all," chuckled Matt.

Stacy smiled and nodded, "Cigars and all. Those were the days."

When they arrived at Room 502, no one was in the reception area.

"Sorry Monica isn't here for you to see and meet," Jack whispered.

Matt smiled and nodded. Noting the way Stacy said it, Matt thought, "I have a feeling that I'm sorry, too."

Swashbuckler

Jack led Matt to Harold's office. Tapping on the open door, he called out, "FBI, keep your hands where I can see them."

Moore laughed, as he looked up and smiled, "Come on in, Jack."

Motioning toward Matt, Stacy said, "Harold Moore, this is Matt Kelly. He's out of Quantico."

Extending his hand, Moore greeted, "Good to meet you, Matt."

"Likewise," Matt said, shaking Harold's hand.

Jack added, "Matt is Pat Kelly's son."

Harold gave a big smile. "Indeed it is a pleasure to meet you, Matt. I see your father regularly at the Former Agents' Society monthly luncheons. You graduated from the Air Force Academy, right?"

"Right," Matt nodded.

"Well we've certainly heard stories from him about you for years."

"Thanks, but please don't hold what he's said against me," replied Matt with a smile.

Harold chuckled, "It's all been very favorable, Matt. He's very proud of you. Besides, how often do you ever hear retired fathers say anything bad about their sons and daughters?"

"Or for that matter, even not-so-retired fathers," Matt responded, and the three of them enjoyed a good laugh.

"What brings you guys by today?" Harold asked.

Jack answered, "We were just downstairs keeping an eye on our man from the grocery store. You remember the one, Harold?"

"Sure," answered Moore, "Was he making another large deposit?"

"We're not exactly sure what he did. We got here just in time to see him put what looked like a check into his briefcase and close it up."

"Well, we can certainly talk with the teller. In fact, if you guys have time now, let's go downstairs and see what we can find out."

"Sounds good," replied Stacy.

While the three stood waiting for an elevator, Matt confirmed, "The bank does continuous digital recordings of the teller lines, right Harold?"

"All day, everyday," the retired agent assured them.

Jack requested, "Would you mind setting aside those taken of the teller line and lobby area when our man was in here today, so that we can have a look to see what he was up to?"

"No problem," Harold assured the two agents. "In fact, I'll also see what I can do about getting the recordings showing his other transactions, too, so that you'll have them all. I'll give you a call when I get everything together."

"That would be great," Stacy told him.

The elevator finally arrived and took the three of them downstairs. As they approached the teller window, Amanda Jamison was getting ready to take her break. Harold asked her if she minded the three of them joining her in the cafeteria and she agreed that would be fine.

Once everyone had their refreshments and were seated at an empty table, Harold opened the conversation. "Ms. Jamison, as I mentioned before, my name is Harold Moore.

I'm the director of compliance and security for the bank. These other two gentlemen are from the FBI."

"Okay," Amanda responded, somewhat hesitantly.

Noting the nervousness in her voice, Harold quickly reassured her that she was in no trouble, and that they were only seeking her assistance.

He then proceeded to explain, "We have a couple of questions regarding a transaction that took place at your window earlier this afternoon."

"All right," Amanda replied.

Harold continued, "The man involved in the transaction was wearing a black shirt and khaki trousers, and was carrying an aluminum briefcase."

"When you mentioned one of this afternoons transactions, I thought that was probably the one."

"Why do you say that?" Moore asked.

"Because everything else seemed pretty normal. That was the only unusual transaction I had."

"Unusual in what way?"

"This customer set one of those aluminum briefcases up on the counter, opened it, and started taking out stacks of bills. He told me he wanted to purchase a cashiers check. I asked him in what amount and he said $9,500. He then counted out the $9,500., and put the few remaining bills back into his briefcase."

"Did he have more stacks of bills in the briefcase?"

"I couldn't tell for sure, but I think so. He kept the briefcase closed most of the time."

"Then what happened?"

"I re-counted the cash and issued the cashiers check. The man took the check, put it into his briefcase, said 'thank you,' and left. That was all there was to it."

"Do you remember who he had you make the check out to?"

"Not exactly, but I can get it from our duplicate copy. As I remember, though, it was to a foreign company with an 'SA' behind the name."

"Would you please make a copy of the check for me, and I'll be by to pick it up, later?" Harold asked.

"No problem," Amanda said.

"Thanks for your help, Amanda, and sorry we had to interrupt your break."

As the three of them walked through the lobby and toward the first set of double, bulletproof, glass doors leading to the outside, Jack stopped and asked Harold, "I've got one for you. Why do you think he bought a check with the money instead of just depositing it?"

"I don't know for sure, but Bridgette Tomas mentioned something during that first interview that might fit. She said that was the third day in a row he had come to her window to make a large cash deposit. He had been paying attention to something else going on in the bank when he came up to her window. Then, when he opened his briefcase and handed her the cash, he suddenly saw who she was, and one of those, 'oh shit, it's not you again,' looks came over his face. She said that she reacted the same, and the two of them then completed the transaction as quickly as possible, and he was on his way out the door."

"I can just picture that," nodded Stacy.

Moore continued, "Come to think of it though, it might have been that after that little episode that he became cautious about making any more large cash deposits, and instead opted to exchange the cash for cashiers checks."

"Sounds like an explanation to me," agreed Stacy.

"I don't know for sure," shrugged Harold, "It's just a thought."

"And with those check purchases, the cash never shows up in his account," Matt noted, adding, "the checks can then be sent or smuggled out of the U.S., and subsequently deposited into accounts at banks around the world."

"Yeah, you're right," Stacy smiled, shaking his head. "It seems like whatever the mind can dream up, these money launderers will try."

Harold Moore nodded in agreement.

"By the way, Harold, Matt doesn't know all that's been going on. Why don't you bring him up to date on what's happened from your end and what you've come up with so far?"

"Okay," Harold replied, and he quickly ticked off the series of events that led to his filing of the Suspicious Activity Report (SAR) with the Treasury that had gotten them to where they were, today.

First, there was his meeting with Bridgette Tomas. Then, his review of the grocery store account's monthly statements in which he had identified numerous large cash deposits made not only at the headquarters location in which the three of them were presently standing, but also at various branches throughout the bank's system.

Also noted in his analysis, were six figure wire transfers sent out of the grocery store account whenever it appeared to have reached a predetermined balance. And, then there were those other related accounts he discovered for the restaurant and movie theaters and the large cash deposits made to them. Lastly, he mentioned this latest transaction involving the exchange of $9,500., in cash, for a cashiers check.

"Interesting. It looks like they're into a lot of different types of laundering," remarked Matt. "Everything except the wire transfers were probably kept under the ten thousand dollar threshold, so they wouldn't trigger any Currency Transaction Reporting (CTR) requirements."

Harold nodded in agreement.

"Oh, one other thing before we get out of here, Harold." Stacy asked, "How's the bank coming along on those subpoenas?"

"I think they're about finished getting everything together for the three business accounts."

"What about that personal account you found for Luis Ayala?"

"They should be getting that one processed before long, too. I'll let you know when everything is ready for pick up."

"Thanks, and please remind the legal department that all of those Grand Jury subpoenas have non-disclosure orders attached. The last thing we need is for Ayala or any of the other account holders to be notified that these bank records have been subpoenaed."

"I understand. I'll remind them," Moore assured Stacy.

CHAPTER TWENTY-ONE

Upon their return to the LA field office, Jack Stacy took Matt Kelly through some of the mounds of paper that had already begun to accumulate in the case. At the same time, Tom Sanders and the surveillance team remained locked onto this man identified in both the rental car agreement and the bank accounts paperwork as Luis Ayala.

Whether a relatively common name like Luis Ayala was their subject's true name, or an alias he had masterfully created with phony back-up documentation and a California driver's license, the agents could not be sure. An uncertainty as to positive identification on this guy though, was not going to affect their pursuit of the investigation.

From Harold Moore's bank, the tail had taken the team directly back to the little grocery where the agents now sat waiting.

Sanders finally called Stacy, "My butt's getting tired. How much longer do you want us to sit here?"

"Another hour or so, Tom, and if he doesn't go anywhere else, then call it a day."

"Okay," Sanders responded.

"Let me know if anything changes."

"Will do," replied Sanders, and he clicked off his cell phone.

Within minutes of completing that call, their man wearing the black shirt and khaki trousers emerged from the little corner grocery store. This time, though, he was carrying not only two aluminum briefcases, but also had a travel bag hanging from his shoulder.

Sanders hit the redial button on his cell phone, "Jack, it's me again."

"That didn't take long," Stacy responded.

"No, it didn't. It looks like our guy might be taking a trip. He just loaded two briefcases and a travel bag into the trunk of the Mercedes."

"Stay on him and keep me advised."

"Will do," Sanders told him.

When he hung up, Jack commented to Matt, "Looks like our man might be taking a trip."

Seeing him carrying the travel bag and two aluminum briefcases out of the grocery and putting them into the trunk of the black Mercedes, Sanders first thought was that he was probably going to go to LAX to catch a flight. If so, they would follow him to the airport, gather the flight information, and notify the field office or LEGAT at the other end to pick up the tail.

The phone rang at Stacy's desk. "Jack, it's me, Tom. I thought our guy would head for the airport, but instead of going north on the 405 and then west to the airport, he's heading east, and well, you know the way traffic is."

"Yeah," Stacy replied, "but stay on him."

"We will," Sanders responded, and clicked off the line.

Stacy rubbed his temples as he temporarily mulled over in his mind what he had been told by Sanders. Unable to come up with any answers, he returned his attention to his review of the case and evidence with Kelly.

A couple of more hours passed, and Stacy's phone rang again.

"Jack, it looks like we're on our way into the desert."

"The desert!" Stacy exclaimed.

"Yep. Right now we're on 15 headed toward Barstow."

"I'm losing you, Tom. Stay on him and give me a call when your signal's stronger."

Hoping Sanders had heard his reply, Stacy slammed down the receiver, "Damn cell phones and their dead spaces."

"I assume that was Tom," concluded Matt.

"It was," nodded Stacy.

"What did he have to say?"

"About all I could hear is that they're on I-15, headed toward Barstow."

"How about Las Vegas?" Matt replied. "I seem to remember 15 being the interstate we used to take to Vegas."

"Still is," remarked Stacy.

"Sounds to me like our man is up to one of two things," speculated Matt.

"What's that?"

"Either, he's planning to take the money out into the desert, and burying it, or else he's on his way to Vegas to do whatever with it."

"I'll put my money on the latter," responded Jack.

"Me, too," agreed Kelly.

"Then I think its time for us to hit the road and join 'em."

"Right on," Matt replied.

"I'll give Sullivan a call and tell him where we are. Assuming that neither he nor the Las Vegas division has any heartburn with our going over there, we'll plan to head out shortly. We can swing by the hotel and pick up your stuff on our way."

"Sounds good. What about you?"

"Oh, I'm okay. I've got a bag in the trunk. I started keeping a shaving kit and change of clothes with me a couple of years ago."

"Good idea."

"Its saved me more than once," Stacy replied, pausing. "Say, while I'm getting everything squared away with Sullivan and the Las Vegas division, you can give your folks a call."

"Yeah. I guess I'd better let them know I won't be making it for dinner," Matt replied.

"I just hope it doesn't take us too long to get everything approved and be on the road," Jack answered. Then, giving Matt a friendly dig, said, "But, you know the way those FBI supervisors are."

Matt smiled, and nodded at Stacy's jab.

CHAPTER TWENTY-TWO

Several years had passed since either Matt Kelly or Jack Stacy had spent any time on the Las Vegas Strip, but from what they could tell, the ambiance had not changed. Bright lights emanating from the LED multi-color signs and phosphorus glass tubes containing neon and argon gasses made it seem almost like midday. And, although it was already early morning, seas of people were still packing the wide walkways and crowding the overpasses and crosswalks. Las Vegas was certainly living up to its reputation as a city that never sleeps.

Sleep, however, was exactly what Matt was looking for. Having risen very early to finish packing and catch his morning flight from DC to LA, and then allowing for the three-hour time change between the East and West Coasts, plus their drive across the Mojave Desert; well, he was rapidly approaching twenty-four hours without sleep and fading fast.

Using the Bucar GPS, Stacy and Kelly had no trouble finding the imposing hotel-casino where they would be staying. Bold signs announced the name, and fiery torches lit the grand entrance.

After finding a space in the lower level of the parking garage and setting the car's alarm, the agents gathered their bags from the trunk and took the elevator to the lobby. The reception area décor was striking, and as was the case with most other lavish hotel-casinos located on or near the Strip, it was obvious that this awesome edifice had not been built on winning gamblers. Highly polished marble floors, ornate crystal chandeliers, chiseled columns towering upward to an inlaid gold sculptured ceiling, and magnificent artwork graced its interior.

As they approached the registration desk, the two agents overheard the clerk tell a bellman walking by that there were no more rooms available for that night. Stacy looked to Kelly and shrugged. Fortunately, for them, however, Sanders had already reserved rooms in their names at this luxuriously appointed hotel-casino located near the heart of the Las Vegas Strip.

After arriving and before registering, Sanders met with one of the security supervisors for the hotel-casino to see if he could take a look at the registration card completed by their man driving the black Mercedes. His review of the card showed the guy staying in Room 1301. Sanders requested a room on the same floor, and got it.

While he was doing that, the other agents on the surveillance team got checked in and continued to keep an eye on their man.

Sanders was now in a downstairs bar with one of the other agents watching, as their subject and two young women sat drinking together in a dimly lit, corner booth.

Sanders cell phone vibrated. He flipped open the receiver and noted the number appearing on the screen. Nudging his fellow agent and pointing to the cell phone, Sanders whispered, "Its Stacy. You stay here. I'll call him from the lobby."

Jack Stacy's cell phone rang as he was hanging his clothes in the closet.

"Where are you, Jack?" asked Sanders.

"We just checked in. I'm in my room, 1021. Why don't you come up."

"What about Kelly?"

"He's next door in 1023. I'll get him, too."

"Okay, I'll be there shortly."

In the meantime, Matt took a quick shower. That, a shave, and a fresh change of clothes gave him a second wind.

As the three sat in the Stacy's room, Sanders went over what the surveillance team had observed since their arrival.

"I met with one of the hotel's security guys and he pulled our man's registration card. As far as I could tell, there wasn't anything different from what you had already gotten from that rental car agency, Jack. The name on the card was the same, Luis Ayala, and the address given was the same as the little LA corner grocery we've been sitting on."

"Okay," nodded Stacy.

Sanders asked, "Did you get anything back on the other checks?"

"Nothing," responded Stacy. "Indices, NCIC, Criminal History, they were all negative."

"So we know nothing about this guy or who he really is," commented Sanders.

"Big surprise, huh," nodded Stacy, "But, we're still checking. I'm going to get with the Health Department Inspectors when we return to LA, though, to see if they have anything on him or that little grocery."

"Good idea," Sanders agreed. "I'll be surprised if they don't have anything on that place. I don't think I mentioned it to you, Jack, but I did walk in there, yesterday, to take a look around. What a pit. I can't believe anyone would shop there."

"Yeah, me either," Stacy replied. "Were there any customers?"

"None. I was the only one in there, and I sure wasn't going to buy anything."

Stacy nodded in agreement, and then asked Sanders to continue with what the surveillance agents had observed since their arrival in Las Vegas.

"I think he's stayed here before and must have dropped some big bucks."

"Why do you say that?" Jack asked.

"It looks like he's being well comp'd. Luxury suite, food, booze, and who knows what else. When I got a look at the room registration card, I noticed the rate showed 'no charge,' and at dinner tonight there was a crowd waiting for tables, but not our man. The maitre d' escorted him directly into the dining room, and from what we could tell everything he had looked like it was compliments of the house."

"Must be nice," responded Stacy.

"My thoughts, exactly," agreed Sanders. "After dinner, we followed him back to the registration desk where one of the clerks then escorted him through a locked door beside the counter leading to an area where the hotel's safe deposit boxes are located. He returned carrying one of the aluminum cases.

"I assume the second case was left in there," Stacy interjected.

"That would be my best guess," responded Sanders. "We never saw him take any cases into that safe deposit area. He must have done that as soon as he arrived."

"He probably didn't want to risk anything happening to all of that money while he was busy getting situated in his room," summed Stacy.

Sanders nodded in agreement, and continued, "He then went directly to one of the cashier's cages located in the far side of the casino. There, he took some cash out of the case, bought chips, and put those chips he purchased back into the case. It looked to me like he bought a few thousand dollars worth."

"Did you catch the time and which cage?" asked Kelly.

"Yeah, I've got it jotted down somewhere." Sanders quickly thumbed through his notes, "Got it," and after copying down the time and cage, handed the paper to Kelly.

"What did he do then," asked Matt.

"We followed him around the casino for a while and finally into the bar."

"Did he do any gambling while he was in the casino?"

"A little, but most of the time he just walked around eyeing the ladies. When he pulled a wad of bills out of the case and peeled off a couple of big ones and threw them onto the table, two of the local honeys wandered over and latched onto him pretty quickly."

"What was he playing?"

"Craps."

"Was he winning?"

"A little, maybe. My guess is he was about breaking even. He was playing pretty conservatively. Strange thing was, though, he never played any chips. It was always cash on the table."

"What about the chips he won?"

"They went into the case with the others."

"So, let me get this straight. Each time he played, it was with cash only on the table, and any winning chip payouts all went back into the briefcase and were never played."

"That's about the size of it," Sanders nodded. "Strange, huh."

Matt added, "I assume he was flashing around some of that cash to get the attention of the honeys."

Sanders nodded and smiled, "That's my guess. And, it must have worked, because he's in the bar with the two I mentioned, right now."

"Where's the rest of the team?" asked Stacy.

"One's sitting in the bar keeping an eye on our man and his ladies, and the other two are getting some rest so they can pick up the next shift."

"Let's all go down to the bar and see what's going on," suggested Jack.

Matt nodded in agreement. If he was going to stay awake, he needed to keep moving.

CHAPTER TWENTY-THREE

In a corner booth at the downstairs bar, Tom Sanders, Jack Stacy, and Matt Kelly joined their fellow agent and quietly talked and laughed as they watched Luis Ayala and his two playful companions become increasingly risqué.

Sensing that things might be getting out of hand, the manager went over to where they were lounging and handed Ayala a bottle of champagne and suggested that he might want to take the women somewhere a bit more private to pursue further fun and games.

Ayala gave an inebriated smile and nodded in agreement. He whispered something into the ears of his newfound playmates and they both giggled. It was obvious that before long, the real action would begin.

As Luis pulled the two women from the booth and they stood up, both teetered on their thin-strapped, three-inch stiletto heels.

With one hand gripping the aluminum briefcase, Ayala quickly got an arm around each of his newfound friends so that they would not fall, and the three of them clung to each another as they made their way out of the bar and onto the elevator.

Fortunately, for the agents and their surveillance, the trio seemed oblivious to anything else going on around them.

While Sanders joined a half dozen other hotel guests in taking the same elevator as Ayala and his two bimbos, the other agents followed in the next car up.

Pointing to an array of photos that hung on the elevator walls showing off the pair of luxury suites set aside on each floor for those guests who had attained a prescribed elite play level, the surveillance agent remarked, "So this is what our man is staying in."

Stacy nodded, "It must be nice, huh."

Beyond the double doors leading into each luxury suite was a sitting room with a huge plush sofa and big screen television, dining area, fully stocked wet bar, bubbling spa, marble bath with gold trim, and of course a giant oval bed to romp in. Through a second set of double doors opening onto the balcony was another spa, another bar, and a breathtaking view of the Las Vegas Strip at night. It was obvious that Ayala's little playground was a bit more luxurious than the queen size bed, basic bath, standard rooms occupied by the agents.

Once the trio arrived at the entrance to his suite, the women continued to hang onto Ayala as he fumbled around with the keycard trying to get the door unlocked. He slid the card in upside down and backward before getting it right. Finally, there was a click and a green light signaling him that the door on the right was now unlocked. He turned the knob and the three of them stumbled in. A few minutes later, a waiter knocked on the door to the suite to give Ayala the bottle of champagne that he had left on the table when the three departed the bar.

Since Sanders room was located just down the hallway from Ayala's, the surveillance would be continued from there. Sanders cracked the door open as far as the extended safety chain would allow and sat down. Although the view wasn't perfect, he could at least see part of the hallway and the double doors leading into the luxury suite.

Soon, Stacy and Kelly returned to their rooms to try to get a little sleep. One of the surveillance agents would call them whenever Ayala decided to leave his suite.

Curious as to whether the frolicking, or anything else for that matter, was still going on in Ayala's little playground down the hall, Sanders grabbed an ice bucket and decided to take a walk. As he slowly passed by the double doors leading into the suite, he paused to listen. Squeals, laughter, and lots of heavy breathing could be heard coming from inside.

"How much longer can they keep this up?" Sanders asked himself. "I'm dead on my feet."

While stretching his shoulders and rolling his head back and forth in an attempt get a grip on the mounting fatigue that had set in, Sanders spotted a welcome sight on the way. The agent up for the next shift was walking from the elevator toward his room. As soon as his relief was in position at his post behind the cracked doorway, Tom would finally have his chance to crash.

Things remained quiet on the thirteenth floor throughout the remainder of the night, and it was only after a spectacular early morning sunrise over the desert that the two inebriated bimbos finally emerged from Ayala's suite. Standing against the hallway wall, they rocked back and forth, as both tried to put on spike heels and get the rest of their acts somewhat together. One wiggled her hips and tugged at the hem of a black leather micro mini-skirt as she tried to get it down around her thighs, while the other pulled at the exposed cleavage portion of a low cut, skintight, V-neck knit top in an effort to better flaunt her pair of recently enlarged 40 D's.

Now ready, they each reached out, putting an arm around the shoulder of the other, and staggered down the hallway. At the elevator one opened the stuffed shoulder bag she was carrying, and out onto the floor fell a G-string, black and white feather boa, garter belt, and pair of black fishnet stockings. The two giggled as they quickly knelt down to pick up the items and put them back into the bag.

As the surveillance agent watched all of this, he could only imagine what else might be in those shoulder bags the two carried. To his surprise, though, the next item pulled out of one of the bags was not something kinky, but rather a fistful of dollars.

The one holding the bills waved them in front of the nose of the other and announced loudly enough for anyone within earshot to hear, "Not bad for a sandwich, huh?"

The other nodded in agreement, and the two bimbos exchanged high-fives.

CHAPTER TWENTY-FOUR

Noonday had come and gone before there was any sign of life coming from Luis Ayala. Donned in a white robe and slippers, he opened the door of his suite for the room service waiter who was standing there holding a covered tray. The waiter went into his room and soon came back out, closing the door behind him and stuffing the tip into his jacket pocket.

Within the hour, Stacy and Kelly received word from Sanders that their man had left his suite and was on his way downstairs. The two of them had been up since well before noon, grazing at one of those casino mega breakfast buffets, which over the years had been a big hit with agents from all agencies, especially back in the good ole' days when they were $1.99 specials.

Later, the two FBI agents wandered over to the baccarat tables and watched several high rollers drop thousands on a single hand.

"This is where you want to go with 'Banker,' and never 'Tie,' " Kelly whispered to Stacy.

Immediately following the phone call from Sanders, the two agents hurried out of the casino and into the hotel lobby. They spotted Ayala carrying a case as he walked over to the registration desk. There, he stood until a clerk escorted him through the locked door leading into the safe deposit box area. In the meantime, Stacy and Kelly stood by watching and waiting for Sanders to join them.

When Ayala came out of the room, the agents followed him into the casino. As opposed to his run of the previous evening, however, this time their man did not make a stop at the casino cage to purchase more chips. Instead, he went directly to the gaming area.

His first play was at one of the roulette tables. He took a long look at the tote board's list of the most recent winning numbers and colors before he placed a couple of hundred in bills onto the table and played red. Replacing the currency with chips, the dealer counted the currency and stuffed it into a narrow slot located in the top of the table that fed into the locked drop box.

Ayala smiled when the wheel stopped on red. He won, and the dealer slid the stack of chips his direction.

Instead of leaving the chips on the table, however, he followed his pattern of the previous evening, again dropping all of the chips into the case, and taking out several hundred more in currency and placing it onto the table for his next bet. As before, the dealer exchanged the currency for chips and stuffed the greenbacks down the slot in the table. This time, however, instead of selecting red or black, as he had done before, Ayala's wager was on any even number. The wheel spun and the white ball dropped into the slot numbered twenty-three. There were no winners, so that time the house collected on all of the bets placed.

Ayala continued to play these safer outside bets on black or red, and odd or even. He won nearly 50 percent of the time. That was until the little white ball dropped into green double zero and green zero on consecutive spins of the wheel and the 5 percent advantage the house got on these tables became dreadfully apparent.

Shaking his head in disgust, Ayala picked up his case containing the chips and greenbacks and headed toward a noisy craps table across the way that was attracting quite a crowd. He quickly moved up to see what was going on.

As the three tailing agents also approached, Kelly's suspicions were confirmed. There was a shooter on a hot roll.

Ayala watched for a while and then, after things had calmed down a bit, finally joined in. Once again, he continued his practice of taking currency from the case and playing it on the table instead of using any of the chips he had won. And, just as he had done at the roulette table, Ayala concentrated on the safest bets, putting his cash down on either the "Pass Line" or "Don't Pass," and then adding the "Odds Bet."

Stacy looked down at his watch and nudged Kelly. They needed to go to the director of security's office before he left for the day. With no clocks or windows in the immediate gaming areas of most of these twenty-four hour casinos, it was easy to lose track of time, and that was of course exactly what management wanted.

While they were gone, Sanders would continue to monitor Ayala's play at the craps tables.

CHAPTER TWENTY-FIVE

"Is the security director in?" asked Jack Stacy.

"May I have your names, please?" the receptionist replied.

"Sure. Jack Stacy and Matt Kelly. We're with the FBI."

"Just a minute, please." She dialed the intercom and relayed the information.

The door opened and out came a big man who appeared to Matt to be in his early sixties. He extended his hand, "Rex Thompson. I'm the security director for both the casino and the hotel."

Jack and Matt shook his hand and showed him their FBI credentials.

"What can I do for the bureau, today," he asked.

"We hope you can come up with a digital for us to take a look at," Jack answered.

Matt showed him the piece of paper with the cage location, and date and time on it that Tom Sanders had copied from his notes.

"This was just last evening?" Rex noted.

The two agents responded affirmatively.

"We should have it. With a thousand cameras recording everything that's going on around this place, though, it might take a few minutes.

"No problem." responded Stacy. "Did you say a thousand cameras, Rex?"

"Well, there are actually a few more than that. So be warned," he added, smiling.

"I'll be sure to keep that in mind," laughed Kelly.

"Let me have someone bring this up. When it's ready, we can take a look at it in the conference room next door."

While they were waiting, Stacy asked, "Do you know anything about the guy staying Room 1301?"

Rex went to his computer. "He's been here before and while not a whale, he's big enough to be well comp'd."

Stacy gave him a questioning look, "A whale?"

"Yeah, those are the really high rollers. All of the casinos are after them. These are the guys that bet anywhere from $25,000 to $250,000."

"You're not talking about a stay?" Stacy questioned.

"Oh no," Thompson replied. "That could be on a hand or a roll. Most of them will easily play a million or more during a stay. Some we'll even fly in on one of our private jets, and have a stretch limo waiting to take them to any one of a half dozen penthouses. They might even have a butler assigned."

"Those penthouses are just reserved for whales, huh?" asked Stacy.

"Yeah, most of them, anyway, and these guys get anything and everything they want."

Kelly's eyes rolled back, "Sounds like my kind of treatment."

"Mine, too," Thompson nodded in agreement. "As I said, this guy's not a whale, but he is big enough to be comp'd with one of our luxury suites. It's not a penthouse, mind you, but our luxury suites are pretty nice, too. And, he gets all the food, drinks, and tickets to any shows that he wants. All compliments of the house. So you can see, he is treated well."

"I'm sure he is," Stacy chuckled to himself. "You mentioned some will play as much as a million dollars on the tables during a stay. How do you know?"

"Our high rollers use players' cards which tracks their gambling electronically. Ninety-nine percent of those whales I mentioned are playing on credit."

"Credit, huh?"

"Yeah," nodded Rex, as he flippantly added, "First, you play, and then, you pay."

Kelly smiled, acknowledging the quip.

"Also, you guys have seen all the computers we have spread throughout the gaming areas."

The agents nodded that they had.

"Those computers and the cameras that I mentioned we have running twenty-four hours a day help us keep track of the high rollers and the other rated players throughout their play."

"So the casino knows how much this guy staying in 1301 bets, and wins or loses during his stays?"

Thompson gave a sly smile with his nod, "You could assume that. This casino wants to know who to give the comp's to in the future."

"And how much," Kelly added.

"You've got that right," nodded Thompson. "To put that in perspective, I've heard the number three million tossed around as the amount of dollars doled out each day in the way of comp's by the Vegas casinos."

"That works out to close to a billion a year, huh?" summed Kelly.

Thompson once again nodded in agreement.

Noticing an FBI National Academy seal hanging on the wall behind Rex, Matt remarked, "I see you're an NA grad."

"Yeah, that was a few years back. I was still with the sheriff's department then."

As the three of them continued to wait for the cage recording, each rehashed stories about what went on during his New Agent or National Academy training at Quantico. Their instructors, the range, jogs on Hoover Road, the NA Challenge, exams, papers, the PT sessions, the yellow brick road, the dorms, the beds, the cafeteria food, and of course the noisy evenings spent in the Boardroom, with pitchers of beer and peanut shells littering the tabletops.

There was a tap on the door. "We're ready in the conference room, Mr. Thompson."

Rex gestured, and the two agents followed him.

As the three concentrated on the digital playback, they could see Ayala hand the cashier a bundle of cash. She quickly, but carefully, counted out the $9,800., and exchanged it for a like amount of chips.

"That's what we needed to see," Stacy told Rex. "Thanks."

"Anytime. If I can be of anymore help to you guys, just let me know. Here's my card. Call that number. They pay for me to be at their beckoned call 24-7."

"Sounds like the Bureau," Stacy laughed.

"That's why we all make the big bucks," added Kelly.

As the three got up from their chairs and walked toward the door, Jack paused, "There is something. You can hang onto that recording for me and make sure it doesn't get lost."

"Consider it done," the security director assured him, and the three of them shook hands.

On their walk back to re-join Sanders, Matt commented to Jack, "He did it, again."

"What's that, Matt?"

"Your man, Ayala, stayed under that ten thousand dollar threshold, so his chip purchase at the cage didn't require a Casino Currency Transaction Report (CCTR). This guy sure seems to know about the reporting requirements and wants to make sure his name stays out of Treasury's Financial Database.

"But, we do know about the SAR filed by Harold Moore, for the series of deposits he made with that same teller, each time under ten thousand dollars," noted Stacy. "So he didn't escape it after all."

"Yeah, and what makes it even better," Matt added, "Is that he doesn't know anything about that SAR filing."

CHAPTER TWENTY-SIX

Rounding a corner leading into the lobby on their return to the casino, Stacy and Kelly spotted Sanders standing over near the registration desk.

"What's up, Tom?" Jack asked.

"I'm not sure," Sanders responded, and he went on to explain that he believed Ayala had apparently run out of cash and returned to the hotel's safe deposit box area for a refill.

"He still had all of his winning chips in the case when he returned here, though, right?" confirmed Matt.

"Yeah. As far as I could tell, once the chips went in, that was where they stayed."

Moments later, Ayala emerged from the door leading into the safe deposit box area, still carrying the case. Rather than returning to the hotel's casino, though, he strolled out the main entrance and down the strip, and into another casino located a little more than a block away.

As he made his way through the noisy casino and toward the cage, the agents followed him past rows and rows of slot machines with their ringing bells, flashing lights and metal trays specially designed to amplify the sound of winning coins as they dropped into them.

At the cage, Ayala purchased more chips. So far, following the same practice he had carried out the previous evening at their hotel's casino, the agents assumed the amount exchanged was once again for less than $10,000.

With both chips and cash now in the case, he walked over to the craps tables and started laying down more bets. As the red dice with their hand painted white dots continued to roll, his play remained very conservative. Other than an occasional "Come" and "Don't Come" bet being placed after a point had been established, he opted repeatedly for the "Pass Line" and "Don't Pass." In addition, just as before, every bet he made was cash on the table, and all of his winning chips went immediately into the case.

Once all of the cash was gone and only the chips he had purchased at the cage and won at the tables remained, Ayala took the aluminum case to the cashier's cage. There, the cashier counted the chips and handed him what appeared to be a casino check.

Following that, their man returned to the safe deposit area of the hotel for more cash, and repeated this same exercise of first converting the currency into chips, and then the chips into checks at two more casinos. He then retreated to their hotel where he ducked into one of the bars for a drink and something to eat.

As the agents watched their subject from a distance, and rehashed what had gone down so far, Jack Stacy was suddenly reminded of an earlier conversation he had with LA bank robbery supervisor Mike Mathis.

"I was talking with Mathis the other day," he said, "and as we were joking about some of the crazy bank robbery cases we've had over the years, I brought up the topic of literal money laundering. I mentioned to him a BR case of mine where the bait dye pack exploded and rather than trying to spend his bag of red dye-blotched currency and have questions raised, or throw it away, the bandit decided to toss the bills into a washing machine."

Smiling at the thought of money going through the cycles, Sanders asked, "What happened?"

Stacy chuckled, "Well, we've all had money go through the washing machine at one time or another and found that the bills, because they're made from cotton rags and the like, can survive the wash and rinse okay."

The agents nodded, acknowledging that they, too, had at times engaged in this kind of money laundering.

"But, in this case, the red dye bled, and the greenbacks turned into pinkbacks."

Everyone laughed.

"So what did he do with 'em, then?"

"Nothing," answered Stacy. "We got him while all the bills were hanging on lines spread throughout his apartment. Some of 'em still weren't even dry."

Sanders and the other agents just shook their heads and smiled.

Stacy continued, "So, as I've been watching our man throwing all those greenbacks onto the tables to be replaced by chips, I thought that might have been what my bank robber had in mind. Think about it. Pink money onto the table and down the slot into the drop box. Chips substituted by the dealer for that cash put down, and chips paid out for any winnings. All of those chips are then taken to the cage where they're cashed out for fresh greenbacks. Now, its time to go spend, and without any questions. What a deal."

"Yeah," Matt agreed. "It sounds like that might have been what he had in mind. My guess is, though, that those thousand cameras looking down from all over the place might have caused him some 'pinkback' problems. From what I hear, they can zoom in close enough to capture the serial numbers on the bills, so there should be no problem seeing colors or blotches."

"Probably not," Stacy agreed. "What about our man and his gambling? Any thoughts, Matt?"

"He's bet a lot of money," Kelly responded with a sly smile.

Stacy nudged Sanders, "Now, that's brilliant."

"Sounds just like a bureau supervisor," Sanders replied, laughing.

Matt smiled, and continued. "Seriously, guys, it looks to me like his objective is to avoid any Currency Transaction Reporting by converting all of that cash, first into chips, and then into casino checks, without sustaining substantial losses. You notice that most of his plays on the tables were in effect exchanging cash for chips and that he rarely played anything other than the safest, even money bets. That way he could come as close as possible to having the same advantage as the house and keep any losses to a minimum."

"Makes sense," agreed Stacy.

Matt added, "If he actually wins money in the end, fine, but I don't think his goal is necessarily to win. I think his goal is to convert as much of that cash to chips as he can, and that's just what he did. Any losses sustained at the tables are just a cost of laundering."

Stacy noted, "And, by keeping those initial cash purchases of chips at the cages below ten thousand dollars, and eventually having casino checks issued for all of the chips when they're cashed out, he's avoided having any Casino Currency Transaction Reports being sent to Treasury, because it's a check and not cash."

"Right," Matt agreed, "And later, if he's asked about where he got all his money, he says 'I'm a gambler, a big winner, and look at all of those casino checks I have to prove it.'"

"As I said before, it looks like he's got his act together," Sanders concluded.

"Hey look," Stacy said.

One of Ayala's playmates from the previous night was trolling through the bar. When she spotted him sipping a margarita and sitting alone, she wiggled over, tossed her shoulder bag on the other side of the horseshoe bench, and slid in next to him. It was not long before they were whispering into each other's ears, and while she was rubbing his leg, he slipped his hand under her micro mini-skirt and started edging his fingers up her thigh.

She giggled, and based on the smiles they exchanged it appeared that their negotiations were now complete. She had sufficiently aroused him to the point that the faster he could get her upstairs and into his suite, the happier he was going to be.

As he took hold of her hand, she grabbed her shoulder bag, and the two quickly moved out of the bar. When they did, the agents once again split up and followed at a safe distance. So far, they had been successful in Ayala not detecting them in either the hotel nor on any of the casino gaming floors, and they did not want to blow it now.

Entering the elevator, Ayala seemed totally oblivious to anything going on around him. It was obvious that he had only one thing on his mind at this point.

From Tom Sanders room, the agents once again took shifts monitoring both the traffic in the hallway and anything taking place outside Ayala's luxury suite.

With no one going in or coming out of the suite during the night, it was daybreak before an agent finally got a glimpse of life, as he watched Ayala's little playmate make her exit. Judging from her tangled hair, smeared make up, and wrinkled clothes, the two of them must have been engaged in some kind of a wild ride.

Several more hours passed before Ayala made an appearance. Opening the door and looking around, he gathered his copy of the local newspaper from the door handle. It appeared that the night had been every bit as rough on him as it was for the bimbo. His smile though, indicated that she satisfied him and that he had a good time.

Suspecting that their man might be getting ready to checkout, Sanders called security and asked them to check with reception to learn if Ayala was leaving. When told that he was, the agents quickly gathered their stuff and cleared their bills in preparation for a timely departure.

Shortly thereafter, Ayala left his room and proceeded directly to the reception area. From there, a receptionist escorted him through the locked door leading into the safe deposit box area. Several minutes later he emerged, carrying a pair of aluminum cases and went directly to the cage of a casino cashier. This time, however, there was no cash to be exchanged for chips. The cash he had brought with him to exchange was gone, and in its place were the casino checks received the previous afternoon and evening, and these remaining chips from the hotel-casino where he had been staying and playing. Now, all that was left for him to do was cash out these chips and receive a big casino check.

While waiting for his check to be prepared, a scantily dressed casino hostess walked by carrying a bloody mary. Ayala stopped her, took the drink, and tossed a twenty-dollar tip on her tray.

"Mr. Ayala," remarked the cashier, and Luis turned back. "Here is your check."

"Thank you," he responded.

After dropping this check into the aluminum case alongside those received from the other casinos, Ayala quickly grabbed his drink. A casino host standing nearby picked up the pair of briefcases, and followed as the two of them rushed off through the lobby and out onto the ornate covered drive up. Waiting there for Ayala was a valet and the bellman that had already gathered his belongings from the luxury suite, and loaded them into the black Mercedes for his return to LA.

CHAPTER TWENTY-SEVEN

Harold Moore left a message for Jack Stacy telling him that the subpoenaed bank account records were ready to be picked up, but by the time he and Matt Kelly arrived at Moore's office, Harold had already left for a meeting at one of the branches. He left instructions with Monica that if the agents came by she was to give them the envelopes with Jack's name on them.

After receiving the copies from Harold's assistant and walking down the hallway to the elevator, Matt commented to Jack, "Now, I know what you meant about it being too bad that I didn't get to see Monica the last time we were here."

Stacy nodded, replaying his brief comment to Moore when the subpoena was served. "I mentioned to Harold that, 'I think I'm in love,' " Jack told Matt.

"Me, too," Kelly smiled.

"Too bad you're not going to be out here longer, Matt," Stacy said.

"Yeah," Kelly agreed. "Getting a chance to spend some time with her might even be worth making a special trip out here on my own dime."

After returning the copies of the bank account records to the Federal Grand Jury, the two agents remained downtown at the Offices of the United States Attorney for the Central District of California to examine the documents they had received. These photocopied records mapped out a financial history and trail of transactions into and out of all three of the business accounts, as well as the individual account of Luis Ayala.

Stacy pointed out to Kelly that these deposits for the most part were made prior to the meeting Moore had with teller Bridgette Tomas, and his filing the Suspicious Activity Report.

"Her reaction must have caused him to reconsider what he was doing and how he was doing it, because immediately after that, the deposits tapered off dramatically," Stacy said.

"Yeah, that's probably when he started concentrating on 'smurfing' the cash for checks at all of those banks instead of depositing the money into the accounts," Kelly replied. "I wouldn't be surprised to see him or another guy take a trip out of the country before long."

"Why do you say that?" Stacy asked.

"Now that he's gotten all of those bank or cashiers checks made out to foreign corporations, he'll probably take them offshore for deposit."

"That makes sense," nodded Stacy. "Probably to some of the same banks where those six figure deposits were transferred into."

"You're probably right," Kelly agreed.

"And, speaking of checks," Stacy said. "Take a look at these from the Vegas casinos!"

Jack started tossing photocopies onto the desk. They were all casino checks deposited several months earlier into the personal account of Luis Ayala.

"I guess we now have a pretty good idea about what he's going to do with all of those casino checks we saw him collect on his most recent trip," Matt replied. "What do the monthly statements show?"

Stacy handed him the documents.

Matt thumbed through them until he found what he was looking for. "It looks like shortly after those casino checks were deposited, the money was wire transferred out."

"Where to?" asked Jack.

Matt found a copy of one of the wire transfers, "It looks like this wire went to a bank in Nauru."

"Nauru?" questioned Stacy.

"Yeah, it's an island in the South Pacific. Somebody told me it's the smallest republic in the world."

Kelly then showed him a photocopy of the transfer. "Here we have the bank and an account number, but the name of the receiver shows only 'Our Good Customer.'"

"And who's that supposed to be?" asked Stacy.

"Good question. My guess is the money didn't stay there long. It was probably wire transferred through banks in several more countries before arriving at its final destination."

"Wherever that is," Stacy replied, adding, "He just keeps wire transferring it from one haven to another throughout the world to hide the paper trail."

"Yeah. He's layering 'em one on top of another, and the longer he can keep us running into roadblocks at each of these confidentiality and secrecy havens, the happier he is."

Jack nodded.

Matt added, "And we also now have a pretty good idea of what his response will be when he's asked about the money."

Jack smiled, "Yeah. He'll say, 'I won the money gambling, and I have the checks to prove it.' "

"Right on," Matt said. "And it certainly won't be the first time we've ever heard that as an explanation."

"You mentioned that he or somebody else would probably be taking a trip shortly to deposit those 'smurfed' checks into an offshore bank account."

Matt nodded.

"I was just thinking," Stacy said. "Since it looks like he might be changing some of his strategy, whoever takes those bank cashiers checks might also add this latest round of casino checks to that offshore deposit?"

"That's certainly a possibility," Matt agreed.

After finishing their cursory review of the subpoenaed bank records at the offices of the United States Attorney, the two agents paid a visit to the offices of the Los Angeles County health inspectors. There, they hoped to determine if any sanitation actions had been filed against the small corner grocery.

The health agency's records identified numerous code violations and several fines issued. A blistering report from the most recent follow up inspection cited unsanitary conditions, mice droppings, expired goods, seeping cans, and the like. Also included in that write-up was an attachment from the inspector that read, "Upon leaving the grocery, I was told by one of the owners, 'You're going to regret filing this report.' "

When asked if they might speak with the inspector, the two agents were told by the clerk, "She was killed while crossing the street. It was a hit and run."

"Did they get the driver?" Stacy asked.

"Not as far as I know," replied the clerk.

"May I see the report?"

The clerk quickly searched through some files in the top drawer of a nearby cabinet, and after finding it, made a copy for Stacy. Jack scanned over it quickly. There was a handwritten note attached indicating that it was being referred to the LA District Attorney's Office for their investigators to follow up on. From the report, it appeared there were no witnesses and thus, no description of a car or any explanation about what had happened.

Stacy handed the clerk his card and thanked her for her help, adding, "If you hear anything more about this, please let me know."

She assured him that she would.

Stacy had his suspicions about what had happened, but suspicions were all he had for now.

Some years earlier, an Assistant United States Attorney (AUSA) who was the lead prosecutor on a major drug trafficking case Jack was investigating received a call that there was an accident involving one of her children. When she rushed out of the courthouse and started crossing the street, an SUV with tinted glass windows sped by and struck her down. No one got a license plate number, and the dark windows concealed the identity of the driver.

Later, a stolen SUV matching the description of the one spotted was found stripped. There were traces of her blood and hair found on the undercarriage, but agents were never able to make the case tying the drug kingpin to her death.

CHAPTER TWENTY-EIGHT

While Jack Stacy and Matt Kelly remained busy at the bank, the U.S. Courthouse, and the offices of the LA County health inspectors, Sanders and others from the surveillance team continued to maintain their tail on Ayala.

It was mid-morning before their man left the small grocery. His first stop was at one of the numerous bank branches for which Harold Moore was the compliance and security director. This time, however, there was neither a briefcase in his hand, nor stacks of cash to deposit into an account or exchange for a bank or cashiers check at the teller's window. Instead, he carried a large envelope, from which he took what the agents suspected were the checks he had received from the Las Vegas casinos and deposited them.

From the bank, the surveillance team followed Ayala to an apartment building located not too far from the FBI's office. This was a large, multi-story building that Sanders had probably driven by a hundred times before, but never paid much attention to until today. The exterior of the building was traditional LA stucco, and the landscaping and parking areas were well maintained.

Although noon was fast approaching, and one would have expected most of the residents and their cars to be gone by this time, there was a shortage of parking spaces beside and around the building. Ayala quickly slipped into a spot marked "Reserved," and as he walked toward the entrance, another man who had gotten out of a custom silver sports coupe moments earlier followed close behind him.

A pair of reflective glass windows near the dark, heavy wooden door at the entrance would not permit anyone to see in, but the surveillance agents suspected anyone on the inside would probably have no problem seeing what was going on outside.

Ayala pressed a button located near the entrance and as the door slowly opened, he was warmly greeted by an intimidating looking guy. It was obvious that the two of them were well acquainted. His greeter appeared to be near the same age as Luis and wore his slicked black hair in a ponytail. He was dressed in black slacks and a black shirt that he left unbuttoned half way down his chest, exposing dark hair and several thick gold chains.

Standing behind Luis was the man who had arrived in the custom sports coupe. He was well groomed and dressed in business professional, wearing an expensive tailored suit, fitted open collar dress shirt, jewelry, hi-quality custom made slip-on loafers, and the like. His greeting by the man at the door, however, was much more businesslike than that given to Ayala. After a brief exchange between the two, the man in black nodded and put up his finger indicating to the other man that he needed to wait while he and Luis went inside.

Less than a minute passed before the intimidating looking guy returned, motioning for the other man to come in. The assumption made by the surveillance agents was that some kind of a check must have been made before he was allowed to enter.

Staying less than an hour in the apartment building, the man returned to the custom silver sports coupe and drove away.

As the surveillance agents stayed put throughout the remainder of the afternoon and into the late night, they saw no fewer than fifty men ranging in age from their late-twenties to their mid-sixties go in and out of that apartment building. Most came alone, many were well dressed, and virtually all drove expensive luxury sedans or sports cars. Their stays ranged anywhere from a half-hour to all afternoon and well into the night.

All the while, Ayala had not reappeared, and his black Mercedes remained parked in the "Reserved" spot located next to the building.

CHAPTER TWENTY-NINE

It was mid-morning before Tom Sanders linked up with Jack Stacy and Matt Kelly in the squad bay.

"Good afternoon, Tom," jabbed Stacy.

"Afternoon? It should be evening," Sanders shot back.

"Long night, huh," Kelly chimed in.

"Yeah. I'll sure be glad when this guy is busted. We sat on an apartment building not too far from here for most of the night."

"Is that where our Mr. Ayala spent the night?"

"From what we could tell. We didn't see him leave and his car was still sitting in the same spot when I drove by this morning. My guess is he was there having a good time."

"Why do you say that?" asked Stacy.

"Something was going on inside," Sanders responded. "That place had no less than fifty guys going in and out between the time we got there in the afternoon and when we finally called off the surveillance around midnight. Most stayed there anywhere from a half-hour to all afternoon, and I assume some were even there all-night. Several of the cars from yesterday were still parked there when I drove by a little while ago."

"What about those guys, anything in particular?"

"Other than most of 'em must have big bucks, you should have seen some of those cars, Jack."

"Like my Bucar, huh?" Stacy smiled.

"Yeah, just like your Bureau steed, Jack," laughed Sanders.

Tom continued, "I'd say the guys going in and out ranged in age from their late-twenties to their mid-sixties with most of them being somewhere in the middle."

"Alone or in groups?"

"Most arrived and left alone."

"Any women?" asked Stacy.

"None that I saw," Sanders replied. Then checking his shirt pocket said, "By the way, Jack, here's the address," and handed him a slip of paper.

As Sanders and Kelly looked over his shoulder, Stacy typed the address into the FBI indices. He came up with no recent open or closed case file references, but did notice a query from Teri Lee, an agent with the Bureau of Immigration and Customs Enforcement (ICE).

Several days before, she had requested any information the FBI might have pertaining to criminal activity going on in some local area apartment buildings, and left half a dozen addresses to be run. One of those addresses turned out to be the apartment building Sanders and his team had been sitting on. She left a number.

"Teri Lee," she answered.

"Teri, this is Jack Stacy at the FBI. I saw where you had requested any information we have on some apartment buildings."

"Yeah, one of your guys already ran the addresses and called me back. He said you had nothing."

"Well, that was before. As of last night, it looks things might have changed," he responded. "What's going on?"

"I'd rather not do this over the phone. Let's get together," Lee responded. "Your office in an hour?"

"That'll be fine," Stacy agreed. "See you then."

ICE Agent Teri Lee followed the three FBI agents into one of the FBI interview rooms.

Jack Stacy took a minute to introduce her to everyone. "Matt Kelly's an instructor from our academy at Quantico. He specializes in organized crime and money laundering. Tom Sanders is a team leader on the surveillance squad here in LA, and I'm assigned to one of the OC squads."

"Nice to meet everyone," she responded.

Stacy directed his question to Lee, "What's this about?"

Lee proceeded to explain. "The day before I made that call to you guys, I received a call from the Indonesian Consulate Office, here in LA. A young Indonesian girl identifying herself as Nina left a long message on their recorder."

"Any last name?" asked Stacy.

"None was given, and that's pretty common. Quite a few Indonesians go by only one name." Teri continued, "Anyway, they asked me to come by, and I told them I would. By the way, it turned out that this message was in one of their native languages, so other than hearing the panic in her voice I couldn't tell much. Fortunately, they had one of the translators from the Consulate Office there to interpret the recording for me as I listened."

Stacy nodded.

"In her message, Nina talked about Asian girls being smuggled into the U.S. and held prisoner in an apartment building. From what I gathered, she had escaped the night before and was afraid they were now out to kill her. She mentioned that another girl had tried to escape a couple of months earlier, and didn't make it. I guess her captors wanted to make an example of her and threw acid onto her face and breasts."

Infuriated at the thought, Stacy and the other agents gritted their teeth and shook their heads.

"What else did she say?" asked Stacy.

"They're sex slaves," Teri answered.

"Sex slaves!" Stacy replied.

"Yeah, we're seeing more of this international sex trafficking going on all of the time. These scum bags start out by promising teens and young women great jobs as models, waitresses, hostesses, or whatever, here in the States. Once recruited, they smuggle them in by plane or boat, confiscate their passports and ID's, and put them to work on their backs. And, in Nina's case, it sounds as though it got even worse. In addition to being held as prisoners, those girls were also being forcibly shot up with drugs by their captors until they were addicted. Then, once they're totally dependent upon their captors for their next fix, they become these bastards sex slaves for life."

"For however long or short that might be," added Stacy. "Do you believe her?" he asked.

Teri nodded that she did.

"How did you come up with those addresses?" Stacy asked.

"In her message, Nina briefly described the apartment building and generally where it was located. With that, our agents then drove around the area and were able to narrow it down to about a half dozen possibles. Those were the ones I called your office about. Then, a couple of days later, I got a call from an LAPD homicide sergeant named Cassidy."

"Jim Cassidy?" Stacy interrupted.

Lee thumbed through her notes, "Yeah, that's his name, and here's his number. Anyway, he asked if we were doing anything on the call a young woman made to the Indonesian Consulate Office here in LA. When I asked him, why, and how he knew about that, he said there was a young woman in the morgue who had a page torn out of the LA phonebook in her pocket with the number of the Indonesian Consulate circled. When he called the Consulate, they told him about the recording left on their machine and that they had called me. He said a patrol unit found the body the day before, under a clump of bushes beside a shelter in one of the nearby parks. Her throat was slit."

"Any ID?"

"None when we talked, but I haven't talked with Cassidy since." Teri paused, shaking her head and pondering, "The panic in her voice, the circled telephone number, that call to the Consulate, the body being found in the park, and now your surveillance. This all could just be coincidence, but I don't think so."

Stacy nodded in agreement, "I think we should get on this now. I'll get in touch with Cassidy and see if he has anything more."

CHAPTER THIRTY

"Homicide. Sergeant Cassidy," answered the officer on the other end of the line.

"Jim, it's Jack Stacy over at the FBI."

"Jack Stacy. Now, that's a name out of the past," Cassidy responded with surprise. "How long's it been since that kidnapping case? I thought you'd be retired by now."

"Nearly ten years, and I thought the same about you, but instead I hear they've transferred you over to homicide."

"Yeah, about two years ago. It was time for a change, and I wasn't ready to pull the pin, so this opened up and I moved over. It's been good for me."

"Jim, I'm on the speaker phone in one of our interview rooms. With me is Teri Lee from ICE, Matt Kelly from Quantico, and Tom Sanders from our surveillance squad. We've been discussing the possibility of a link between an apartment building that's come up in a case of ours and one of your homicide cases."

"Let me guess. We're talking about the girl found in the park. The one I called the Indonesian Consulate about."

"You've got it."

"Before I forget, Jack, do I get in the press release this time?" Cassidy asked.

"I'll see what I can do, but keep in mind that your name will have to come after mine," Stacy jabbed, remembering that neither of their names were ever mentioned in the high profile kidnapping case the two of them had solved years before.

Names in the newspapers, TV and radio interviews, and photo ops seemed to fall on an elite few within the law enforcement community, and those chosen were usually part of the hierarchy. Rarely did it seem that the press recognized those doing the real investigative work, but that was the way it is, and it's probably due more to the agencies and their policies than the media itself.

Stacy continued, "Tom's surveillance team tailed a guy we're investigating to an apartment building in the area. During one afternoon and evening, at least fifty guys, driving expensive cars, went in and out of the place. Some stayed thirty minutes, while others were in there for several hours or more. When we checked our indices, it turned out that the address of that building matched one that ICE had requested information from us on, so I called Teri Lee. She came over and has just finished telling us about the recording left at the Indonesian Consulate, and your call to her. That's where we are, now. Did you get anything back from the coroner, yet?"

"Yeah, just today," Cassidy answered. "The report described her as an Asian female, approximately eighteen years of age. She died from strangulation. Her assailant then slit her throat, I guess to make sure she was dead. They said it looked like she had been the victim of numerous brutal sexual attacks carried out over an extended period of time. There were also bruises over much of her body and needle tracks along her forearms and on the bottoms of her feet."

"Has your investigation turned up anything else?"

"A slip of paper with a name and phone number on it, and some cash."

"I guess the cash probably rules out robbery as a motive," Stacy remarked. "What was the name on the piece of paper?"

"Sam"

"S-A-M?"

"Yeah, just Sam and a number. The number's a cell phone and it came back to some guy named Sam Smith."

"That's original," chuckled Stacy.

"Isn't it," Cassidy agreed. "We checked the billing address and it turned out to be one of those suites. You know the ones I'm talking about. Walls and walls of mail box suites, all in one room, and at the same address."

"The kind some people use to make it appear they have a prestigious office address, but really don't," Jack replied.

"Yeah, one of those," responded Cassidy.

Over the years, investigators had become all too familiar with these kinds of drops in their attempts to locate people.

"Did he by chance pay his monthly bill with a check?" asked Stacy.

"We should be so lucky," Cassidy answered. "No, he used money orders."

"And he bought 'em with cash."

"That's what I would assume."

"Anything on the numbers he called?"

"Not yet, but I got a call about thirty minutes ago that the printout is ready to be picked up. Do you want to meet?"

"Yeah, how about in an hour. The cafeteria downstairs, here, in our building," Stacy answered. "I'll even buy."

CHAPTER THIRTY-ONE

The three FBI agents and ICE Agent Teri Lee were sitting around a circular table in the corner of the Federal Building cafeteria when the slightly paunch and follicle-challenged detective in his mid-fifties came through the door.

"Jim Cassidy," Stacy yelled, and motioned for him to come over to the table.

After being introduced to everyone and receiving the promised cup of coffee from Stacy, Cassidy quickly briefed everyone on his initial analysis of the subscriber information, and put summaries of the calls placed to and from Sam's cell phone on the table. Already high lighted were those days surrounding their finding of the body. One call was made from that number the day the body was found, and another half dozen were made to and from it the day before. There were no calls the day after.

The agents noticed that the single call made on the date the body was found was to a number assigned to the same address as the apartment building Sanders had been staking out. On the day before, there were two calls made to that same number and one incoming call from an area pay phone.

Also included in this most recent monthly listing were a number of international calls. From the country codes, the agents and Cassidy were able to discern that they were made to or from, and received from, parties in Indonesia and the

Philippines, but no additional subscriber information was available.

Getting into that apartment building, and soon, was something all agreed had to be done, but first, they were going to have to firm up the probable cause before a magistrate or judge would be inclined to issue a search warrant.

"Let's continue to sit on the place and see if we can come up with anything more," suggested Stacy.

Everyone nodded in agreement, and since Tom Sanders was most familiar with the location, it was agreed that he would set up and handout the surveillance assignments.

Matt Kelly would take another Bucar and position himself on the other side of the street from Jack Stacy at one end of the block. Teri Lee and Jim Cassidy would station themselves accordingly at the other end, and Sanders would remain in the parking lot across the street. From these locations they should be able to run the plates on any vehicles the guys drove to and from the building and determine from the registrations if there are any wants and warrants outstanding on the owners.

"We'll get our portables for you two," Stacy told Lee and Cassidy. "That way we can make sure we're all on the same channel."

"I'll alert the patrol units working the area, just in case we need to call on them to make a stop," volunteered Cassidy.

It didn't take long for their multi-agency team to hit the streets, and shortly after his arrival outside the apartment building, Tom Sanders came over the air with a hit.

"Jim and Teri, a yellow Corvette moving your way comes back to a California parole violator."

"Teri, if you'll continue to cover this end of the block, I'll stay with him and have a black and white make the stop once he gets a couple of blocks from here," responded Jim Cassidy.

"Will do," answered Teri Lee.

The next call over the radio was from Cassidy, with his location.

"We've got him. Do you want to come here, Jack? I'm six blocks straight ahead from where you're sitting."

"I'm on my way," Stacy responded.

By the time Stacy linked up with Cassidy, their con man parole violator was already in the backseat of the homicide detective's car trying to work out some kind of deal for his cooperation.

"Okay," he concluded with a sigh, "What's in it for me?"

"You know you're already toast," Cassidy responded. "But I can tell your parole officer you cooperated, and that certainly can't hurt."

The forty-five year-old con man, dressed in a multi-colored, open-buttoned silk shirt, leather sport jacket, tailored slacks, Italian slip-ons, and expensive jewelry, gave a shrug.

"Okay, if that's the way you want it," responded Cassidy, as he opened the door to return this violator to the patrol unit.

"No. No. Wait a minute!" protested the con man.

"Then, let's hear what's going on inside that apartment building."

"You promise you'll put in a good word for me?"

"I told you, I'll let your parole officer know that you cooperated," Cassidy again told him.

"Okay, okay." The con man paused. "I go there for a good time. You know what I'm talking about," he added, giving one of those all assuming looks.

"Yeah," Cassidy replied sarcastically, "but why don't you humor me by telling us, anyway."

"Ya know. Fine women, gettin' laid, and all that."

Cassidy nodded, "How did you learn about the place?"

"Word on the street."

"What did you hear on the street?"

"That you could go there and get any kind of action you wanted. They had teens and young women brought in from overseas who would do anything."

"What do you think they meant by 'anything?'"

"Ya know, 'anything.' Two, three, even four at a time. Sandwiches, handcuffs, whips, leather, all that. I'm not into the real kinky stuff, myself," he stressed, shaking his head, "but with all the business that place gets, there sure must be plenty of guys around that are, and all with big bucks."

"Why do you say that?"

"Because the place is not cheap. As I said, the girls will do anything, and you're treated first class, but you pay for it. They don't shove you into some dingy, shabby, little room with used condoms on the floor, dirty sheets on the bed, and no A/C. Believe me, I've seen those, and never again after experiencing this. The apartments in this place are great.

They're loaded. Fully stocked bars, hot tubs, sound systems, and showers big enough for two or three to share. They even have flat screen TV's hanging from the ceiling over the beds and stag videos running all the time." He stopped and smiled, "Did I forget to mention that this place has it all?"

"No, you made that pretty clear. You did mention that it's not cheap, though."

"Yeah, depending on what you're after and for how long, my guess is a visit would run anywhere from a few of hundred, to several thousand. Since I'm not into all of the kinky stuff and usually just stay long enough to take my shot and leave, I'm at the lower end of that payment scale."

"Any idea how many girls we're talking about working there?"

"None, but with all of those apartments there must be a bunch, and the ones I've had are young and hot."

"Have the girls said anything to you?"

"Other than asking me what I want them to do?"

"Yeah," Cassidy told him.

"Well, they haven't said much, and since I'm in there for action rather than talk, I don't say much, either. But, I don't think most of them speak much English, anyway."

"What about the guys running the place. How's their English?"

"Broken. Most have accents."

"Any idea where these girls and the guys running the place are from?"

"My guess is somewhere in Asia, but I don't know."

"What about drugs?"

"None for me," replied the con man, defensively, "but, those tracks on the arms of some of the girls tell me they must be around there somewhere."

"How many guys do you see around there running the place?"

"There's usually one or two at a security checkpoint, near the front door, and I've seen others walking around. One time I looked behind a half opened door and a guy was sitting at a desk in what I figure must be the office."

"Any guns?"

"None that I saw, but I'd expect they'd have them around somewhere. Those guys have always been okay to me, but I sure wouldn't want to cross any of them. I think they could be real nasty."

"What else?" Cassidy asked.

"Not much," the guy responded. "Do you think this is one of those sex slave operations you hear them talking about on the news?" he asked the detective.

Cassidy shrugged, "Could be."

Before returning him to the patrol officers for his ride downtown, Jack Stacy handed the con man a clipboard and a couple of sheets of paper. He asked him to make a sketch of the inside of the building, as best he could remember. Of particular interest, Stacy told him, were how the floors were laid out, building and floor entrances and exits, stairways and elevators, and any guard positions.

The con man started drawing, and after asking for another sheet of paper, continued for a few more minutes. Responding nervously, he handed the paper back to Stacy,

"This isn't to scale and it's only as best I can remember. I've only been in there a few times."

Jack nodded, adding, "Oh, one other thing. Is there anything special about the front door?"

"Nothing, other than it's re-enforced and looks really heavy," the con man said.

Stacy looked at Cassidy, "I think that should do it for me, Jim."

"Me, too," Cassidy nodded, as he opened the door to return the con man to the patrol car.

"You'd better be telling the truth on everything, or else," the detective told the parole violator as they walked back.

"I am, I am, I swear," the con man assured Cassidy.

"We're finished here," Stacy called over the radio. "Everybody meet at the office in the FBI garage in twenty."

Kelly, Sanders, and Lee were already sitting in the garage office talking about what they had seen when Stacy and Cassidy walked in.

"Jack," Sanders called to Stacy, "After you left, you'll never guess who pulled his black Mercedes into the "Reserved" space next to the building?"

Stacy smiled, "How long did he stay?"

"He was still there when we left to come back here. Maybe he's there for the night, again."

"Good," replied Stacy. "Hopefully he's planning to spend a lot of time there in the next few days, because we need him inside the building when we hit the place."

"When's that going to be?"

"Can't say for sure, but we need to do it soon."

Stacy turned to Agent Lee and Sergeant Cassidy for their reactions.

Teri Lee responded, "I'll start working on getting people and transportation together to detain and process any girls who are here illegally."

"I'll get with vice and patrol to make sure we have enough officers available to get the place shut down and the johns and the guys running the place taken in," added Cassidy.

"Tom, I want you guys to maintain the surveillance on the apartment building. As I mentioned before, we need to know when Ayala's usually there, since he'll be ours."

Sanders acknowledged that they would.

"In addition to Sullivan and the agents from our squad, I'll also alert SWAT," Stacy told the others, finally adding, "I know its going to take time for everybody to get everything together, but. . . ."

They all acknowledged that they understood.

"Who's the AUSA on this?" asked Teri Lee.

"Cheryl Rathmann," answered Stacy. "I'll get with her so we can start drafting the search warrant affidavit. As soon as we get it done and signed by the Magistrate, I'll let everyone know so we can get back together and go over the final raid planning."

"I assume the guy driving the yellow 'Vette' came through with the additional probable cause," Kelly surmised.

"That he did," confirmed Stacy.

CHAPTER THIRTY-TWO

"I see you made it back from the Philippines," Special Agent-in-Charge (SAC) Winston Lange III, of the FBI's Honolulu Division, remarked as he greeted Supervisory Special Agent Laynie Steele in the FBI parking garage.

"It was a good trip," replied Laynie, adding, "You were gone when I returned so I didn't have a chance to brief you."

SAC Lange nodded, "It's been a while. I was on leave back home in Texas, and from there I went to the SAC Conference in Washington. I just returned this afternoon, and am on my way up to the office now."

"Anything new from the puzzle palace?" she asked.

"Not much, and it doesn't look like our division's going to be getting more agents in the near future."

"That's too bad, especially after what I heard at the Philippine conference."

"What was that? And, by the way, who all was there?"

"Most of our LEGATS from Asia and the Pacific Rim, plus a couple of unit chiefs from Terrorism and Asian OC Units at HQ. The reason I said 'that's too bad,' was that in addition to the terrorist threat appraisals, which were obviously high on the list, they also discussed significant increases in Asian syndicate involvement in human trafficking, drugs, and money laundering."

"All areas I think our division needs to get more involved in," the SAC responded. "Now, if we could only get headquarters to give us more agents."

"For sure," Laynie agreed.

"How was the weather in Manila?" he asked.

"Hot and humid."

"Sounds normal," the SAC replied. "Are the Jeepney's still packed full of people and running up and down the streets?"

Laynie laughed, "I'd say it was more like crawling, but yes, they're still out there in force."

"Traffic's still bad, huh?"

She nodded, "Terrible."

"From what you're saying, it appears things haven't changed much since I was there a year ago. By the way, is Bill Robinson still the LEGAT?"

"He is, and he asked me if I'd ever seen you get up in front of a group and sing karaoke." She smiled, "I told him 'no,' but that I had seen you on stage doing the hula with a group of Tahitian girls."

The SAC gave her one of those perfunctory chuckles regarding his brief stints at hula dancing and singing karaoke, but Laynie could tell he was not particularly amused with her quip. That was probably to be expected, however, since he had always been regarded as somewhat of a stuffed shirt.

Winston quickly changed the subject, "How's the baby?" he asked.

"Growing. She'll be a year old before we realize."

"And your husband?" he paused, obviously unable to recall the first name of Laynie's spouse.

Laynie hastily interjected, "Oh, Clay is doing fine."

"I assume he still stays busy writing?"

"That, along with taking care of Ashley, volunteering as a youth swim team coach, and being a deacon at our church," she answered.

"Well, it sounds like he has his hands full," Winston replied. "When's his next novel due out?"

"It's with editors now. So, it should be available through the website dot com's and for order from the bookstores in about nine months."

"I'll have to remember to get a signed copy. Be sure to let me know when it hits the shelves."

"I will," Laynie assured him.

"Well, where are you off to now?" the SAC asked.

"I'm on my way to the airport to pick up Nick Costigan and take him to his hotel."

"Nick Costigan," Winston smiled. "We were in the same new agent class. I guess this has to do with the award I remember seeing something about you two receiving, huh?"

"Yes, it's from the government of Micronesia," Laynie said. "We're leaving for Pohnpei tomorrow morning on the Island Hopper."

"I'm going to have take that flight sometime when I go to the Guam RA. I've heard and read so many stories about it," remarked the SAC.

"Like that it takes nearly fifteen hours?" Laynie replied.

"Yeah, I've heard that it's not only long, but it's also different."

"It's different all right. Short runways, up and down, up and down, on the various islands, and cabin sprays on all the landings," she laughed. "Plus, you get the added benefit of seeing a wide variety of carry-on's, many the likes of which you have probably never seen before."

"Sounds interesting."

"Oh, and I almost forgot to mention that they even bring a mechanic along in case the plane needs to be repaired on one of the islands."

A smile came over the SAC's face. "That's reassuring," he laughed. "After Pohnpei you're going somewhere else, right?"

Laynie nodded. "To Palau, and then back to Guam for the PTI."

"Well, it's good to see you, Laynie," the SAC told her. "I'd better get on my way and let you get to the airport. You have a good trip and be sure to tell Costigan that I said, 'hello.' "

"I will," Laynie replied, as she pushed the button on her key, unlocking the driver's door of her Bucar.

Traffic was heavy and by the time Laynie arrived at the Honolulu terminal, Nick's flight had landed, so she went directly to the baggage claim area.

The Wiki Wiki trams carrying Nick and the other passengers on his flight to the baggage claim area had not yet arrived, however, so Laynie stood to the side and waited.

When Nick walked in, the two made eye contact almost immediately. They had talked regularly during the Pohnpei investigation, and met on at least two occasions at FBIHQ.

"Nick," Laynie called and waved.

He smiled and walked over to where she was standing.

"Good to see you, Laynie," he said.

"Aloha," she responded, and placed a Hawaiian lei over his head and around his neck.

"Thanks," Nick replied. "That's very nice of you."

"Since you mentioned in our last telephone conversation that this would be your first time to paradise, I thought you deserved a real Hawaiian lei."

As Nick looked down at the fresh lei and smelled the flowers, a smart-ass response immediately came to mind.

Laynie noted the sly smile now spreading across his face, and quickly said, "I knew I shouldn't have said that when it came out. Those are sold on the streets and not in the flower shops," she joked.

With the sly smile still on his face, Nick shook his head, "Now, I might not have been thinking that at all."

"Sure," Laynie replied laughing. "Like I don't know what you guys are thinking after all of these years on the job."

From the airport, it took about thirty minutes to reach the Waikiki beach hotel area where Laynie had made reservations for Nick to stay. During the drive, she gave him a quick rundown on their upcoming travel itinerary and suggested several restaurants for them to go to. All of her suggestions sounded good to Nick, and since it was already after nine o'clock WDC time, he was long past being ready for dinner.

After getting him checked into the hotel, they immediately went to eat. The restaurant was only a short walk. It was nothing fancy, but well known by the locals as the place to go for traditional Chinese food, and Laynie had never been disappointed. At first, Nick had a little trouble getting the hang of using chopsticks again, as it had been a long time since he had tried them. He persevered, though, and with some help from Laynie, managed to get his fingers and the sticks together, and most of the food up to his mouth. It took him a little longer than most to finish, but this dinner proved to be well worth the extra effort.

After leaving the restaurant, Laynie took Nick for a tour along the torch lit pathway running between the Waikiki beach and the nearby string of luxury hotels. The two agents got a great view of a brilliant sunset, and as they looked back in the distance toward Diamond Head, everything appeared even more picturesque than any postcard could ever depict.

It was easy for Nick to now understand why Laynie had been so high on living there. She mentioned during dinner that some people had difficulty with a thing they referred to as "island fever," but that problem had not affected her and she hoped it would not. From his brief take on Hawaii so far, a walk along the beach, some great food, the relaxing lifestyle, and a welcome, but unexplained sense of relief from stress, he could certainly appreciate why so many honeymooners and vacationers had chosen these islands.

Spotting a commercial flight rising in the distance, Nick was reminded of the 7:00 A. M. flight departure time Laynie had mentioned earlier. Although the jet lag didn't seem as bad to him going west as it did east, the travel time gap remained, and as they neared his hotel, Nick was ready to call it a night. After all, he had already been up since 4:30 that morning, and that was Washington, DC time, not Oahu.

After agreeing to meet at the Honolulu Airport check-in at 5:00 A. M., Nick went up to his hotel room and Laynie returned home. She arrived just in time to join Clay in reading Ashley a story before saying prayers and putting her to bed with a goodnight kiss.

CHAPTER THIRTY-THREE

As the 737 lifted upward, Nick peered out his porthole window and watched as a myriad of colorful rays from the early morning sun danced off the clear blue waters and whitecaps that lie below. Fading in the distance was Diamond Head, Waikiki beach, and the string of towering hotels they had walked past the night before. Soon the entire vista of Oahu disappeared and all that remained was the vastness of a deep, blue, beautiful Pacific Ocean.

Laynie was already asleep in the aisle seat of the same row as Nick. Upon boarding, she had quickly grabbed a pillow and blanket and proceeded to take advantage of this time get some much-needed rest. Since the flight wasn't full, it appeared that her frequent flyer status had once again pulled a little weight, blocking the availability of the seat between the two of them so that it would remain unoccupied on this initial segment.

After reaching cruising altitude, the captain announced that their fourteen-plus hour flight would be taking them on a southwesterly course, where they would be passing over Johnston Island, and crossing the international dateline before making their first stop.

Following breakfast, Nick felt very relaxed and relieved, as he sipped a second cup of black coffee and thumbed through the airline magazine he found in the seat pocket. In it were several articles and photos about some of the island nations on which they would be landing. After finishing the articles, he went back to staring out of the window, spotting only an occasional ship, island, or atoll, before finally dozing off.

Nick woke up when the captain advised everyone onboard that their flight was approaching the Marshall Islands and that they would be landing on the island of Majuro, shortly. He glanced out the window and attempted to spot the island in the distance, but no such luck. The cloud cover wasn't cooperating.

Laynie also stirred from her sound sleep, and as the flight attendant walked through the cabin, she asked her to double check that the seatback was upright. Laynie groggily complied.

Soon, the attendant announced the local time and date. She made a special point to remind the passengers that they had crossed the international dateline en route, and so now not only had the time changed, but they were a day ahead from when they left Hawaii. Nick pressed the change buttons on his new GPS watch and hoped the adjustments he had made were correct. As he had gotten older, it was getting harder and harder to see those tiny morning or afternoon identifiers and to make sure everything was right so that he would not be twelve hours off, and consequently on the wrong day half of the time. He had also mistakenly pushed the wrong button on more than one occasion on his old watch, causing him to be wake in the middle of the night when his alarm sounded.

Just prior to landing, a flight attendant walked through the cabin once more. This time she had a can in her hand, and sprayed what Nick assumed was some kind of repellant.

One of the articles in the airline magazine Nick had been reading mentioned the Marshalls and identified Majuro as the capital of this North Pacific island group. The article went on to explain that the islands' name came from a British captain named John Marshall who first set foot on them in 1788. Later, the islands became a German protectorate in the 1880's, before being seized by Japan in 1914.

After World War II, the Marshalls were placed under the protection of the United States as a Trust Territory and remained in that status until 1986, when they became self-governing.

Today, the Marshall Islands are inhabited primarily by Micronesians and Polynesians and are probably best known for their nuclear weapons testing sites of Bikini and Enewetak.

At Majuro, their flight remained on the ground only long enough to allow departing passengers to get off, unload mail and cargo destined for the island, and then board the like.

CHAPTER THIRTY-FOUR

Once again airborne, Nick leaned over to Laynie and asked, "How was your nap?"

"Great, I really needed that. Did I miss anything?" she asked.

"Breakfast, but other than that probably nothing you haven't seen before."

"Probably not," Laynie replied. "I don't know how many times I've taken this flight, but it's been a lot and I haven't noticed the Pacific view changing much at 32,000 feet."

The flight attendant stopped her cart next to their row and asked, "May I get you something to drink?"

"I would love a cup of coffee, with cream and sweetener," Laynie answered, as she lowered her tray table.

After handing her a cup and napkin, the attendant glanced at Nick.

"Coffee for me, too," he said, "but make mine black."

When the attendant moved on, Laynie continued their conversation. "Oh, I almost forgot to mention that our SAC wanted me to tell you 'hello.' He said that you two were in the same new agent class."

"Yeah, we were," acknowledged Nick, as he raised his eyebrows and gave her a sly smile.

Laynie grinned. "Why the look?" she asked.

"He was our class spring-bud."

"Every class has one of those," Laynie chuckled, "always raising their hands, and popping up with one question or answer after another."

"Or even answering for you when you're asked a question," Nick added. "Anyway, Winston was ours."

"Did he have a blue flame back then, too?" she asked.

Nick nodded, "He had one a mile long. All we heard from day one in training school was about how he was going to be an SAC or AD someday."

"Well, it looks like he made finally it," she replied.

Nick smiled. "Yeah, and I'll bet there's an 'I Love Me' wall in his office that's loaded with signed photos of every recognizable person he has ever met."

Laynie laughed. "Well, it's really more like two walls."

"As I would have expected," chuckled Nick. "He's been the SAC in Honolulu now for quite a while, right?"

"Yeah," Laynie answered. "Winston came here shortly after I was assigned as the pacific liaison agent."

"I was trying to remember when you first contacted me about the case in Micronesia. It must have been about three years ago," Nick said.

"That sounds about right. It was before Clay and I were married, and that's been nearly two and a half years."

"Did you two know each other before Hawaii?"

"No, we first met on a packed redeye flight from Pago-Pago to Honolulu. Clay had the window, I drew the middle, and in the aisle seat was one of the biggest Samoan guys I've ever seen. He had to have been 6'7" and weighed at least 325 or more, and with Clay not being a particularly small guy either, you can imagine how scrunched I felt sitting between the two of them. Well anyway, the Samoan guy slept most of the way while Clay and I read and talked. As we chatted, Clay told me that he did some work as an advisor for the U.S. government, but was primarily a fiction writer."

"I noticed that you didn't say for which government agency or department he's an advisor," replied Nick.

Laynie just smiled, not answering.

Returning a sly smile, Nick cracked, "Ok-a-a-a-y."

This reminded him of a retired FBI agent and close friend from the Academy, at Quantico, who was now a fiction writer and periodically received one and two-week international assignments to travel to hot spots around the world. Having a suspicious nature, Nick had his own idea about who this friend was really working for, and believed that the company name or government entity noted on his business cards was likely not the same as that agency. Nick knew better than to ask, however, since he was sure that even if this were the case, his friend could never confirm those suspicions; and even if he did not work for them, well. . . . At least all of it made for some intriguing conversation among those who knew this retired agent.

Sensing Nick's note of skepticism, Laynie paused, adding, "Clay also does some training."

"Oh, training, too," Nick smirked, recalling that his friend had also mentioned doing training in his international travels.

"Yeah, from time to time they send him around the world doing teaching and consulting in the anti-money laundering and terrorist financing areas," Laynie added.

"Is he an accountant?"

"That's great. A neighbor lady like that helped me out with my kids."

"How many kids do you have, Nick?"

"Two. They're both grown. In fact one lives out here in Micronesia, on the island of Chuuk."

"Doing what?"

"Eric works on a dive boat as a scuba instructor and wreck diver. He leads visiting divers on dives into the Truk Lagoon."

"That sounds like fun."

"He seems to enjoy it. The money isn't great, but he's single and doesn't need a lot, and he definitely seems much happier than he did working in software development. He couldn't seem to get into the hang of having to stare at a computer screen and strings of code all day long."

"I can go along with that," Laynie responded. "You mentioned another child?"

"Teresa. She's a civil engineer and has moved back to Fredericksburg."

"So she's close to where you are."

"Yeah, she and her black Lab, 'Alli,' are over at my house most weekends and the two of them take care of things while I'm gone."

"Alli?"

"I gave her that nickname. It stands for alli-gator, because of the way her mouth curls when it looks like she is smiling."

Laynie laughed to herself, "I've seen Labs do that. It sounds like you have a nice family, Nick."

"The kids are great. At times, it was a little tough raising them after I lost my wife to cancer, but they seemed to come through it in spite of my shortcomings."

"It doesn't sound like there were many shortcomings to me. I know several other agents like yourself, who have also gone it alone, but I don't know how I could do it with Ashley if it weren't for Clay."

"You could have if you had to," Nick assured her, "but on occasion it can be a little tough on both the kids and the parent."

As their flight approached the island of Kwajalein, the passengers were once again directed to stow their tray tables, bring their seatbacks upright, and put away anything they had taken out during the flight. While one of the flight attendants picked up any remaining trash, another walked through the cabin with a spray can, and a third made a date and time announcement so all could adjust their watches as need be.

Once at the gate, a couple of guys with close-cropped hair and carrying bags with "U.S. Army" printed on the side got off, but no additional travelers boarded.

"No, but after the Navy, he did study finance and was a stockbroker for a while."

"You didn't mention the Navy before."

Laynie smiled and reacted, "Oh, yeah. I forgot about that. After graduating from Annapolis, he was assigned to naval intelligence."

Looking amused, Nick surmised, "So we have a Naval Academy grad that was a military intelligence officer and now works as an international advisor for an unnamed government agency or department, but is really a fiction writer. Sounds like a pretty good cover to me."

"I didn't say unnamed," laughed Laynie. "There is a name; it just may not be the same department or agency you see on his business card. Remember, though, he really is a fiction writer."

"I see," Nick smiled, "and my guess is that his employer goes by three letters, and those letters are not FBI."

Laynie just smiled, again, not saying anything.

Nick quickly added, "And, I doubt that most of these trips he now goes on are to your traditional vacation destinations, either."

"You might say that," Laynie chuckled. "Places like London and Paris, or Tokyo would more than likely be airport transfer or layover points than final destinations."

Nick nodded, and from his reaction, Laynie could tell that he clearly understood what she had really been saying.

"So it was then that he asked you for your number?"

"In a round about way," she coyly answered. "As we were leaving the flight he asked me for my card and I gave it to him. To my surprise, the next day he called me at the office and asked me out to dinner. One thing led to another and six months later we were married."

"That's great. And you mentioned last night at dinner that you two now have a daughter?"

"Ashley," Laynie said, beaming and pulling her wallet from her purse to show Nick a picture.

"She's very cute," Nick responded. "And that must be her daddy holding her."

"You've got it," Laynie proudly answered. "Ashley definitely loves her daddy. Being a stay at home dad when he's not away on assignment, Clay takes care of her during the day, and I might add does a great job of it. It's cramped his writing a little, but he still manages to get his necessary research done and a couple of pages out on most of those days."

"Does his research require him to do much traveling?"

"Do you mean in addition to that he does for the government?"

"Yeah," Nick nodded.

"Some, but he's able to draw a lot from his experiences, and he also spends hours at a time on the Internet."

"Do you have any other help with Ashley?"

"There's daycare available at a nearby center that we use, and we also have a wonderful neighbor lady we call 'Nana,' who is also a grandmother and she loves to take care of Ashley. She has even kept her overnight for us. One time when Clay was traveling out of the country on one of his assignments, I got called out on a shooting on the Big Island. 'Nana' came over and stayed at our place with Ashley until I got back two days later."

CHAPTER THIRTY-FIVE

After leaving Kwajalein and reaching cruising altitude, the captain announced that the next group of islands on which they would be landing make up the Federated States of Micronesia, and that the island of Kosrae would be their first stop in the FSM.

During that leg of the flight, the cloud cover had gradually lifted, and as they approached the Kosrae International Airport, Nick spotted an airstrip on a small peninsula. He also got a clear view of the lush green vegetation covering the steep mountainous terrain of the island, and the beautiful pattern of contrasting turquoise and deep blue waters that surrounded it.

As the 737 was preparing to land, the captain set the flaps to forty, and at touchdown, the engines were set into reverse thrust and the braking system set to medium.

Nick and his fellow passengers felt the jolt, and he hoped that they didn't run out of runway.

Fortunately, there was enough runway, and as the plane taxied over to the tarmac and came to an abrupt stop, Nick looked over to Laynie and silently mouthed, "Is this normal?"

Laynie laughed, "This is smooth. You should feel it sometimes."

"Short strips on some of these islands, huh?" he responded.

"You might say that," Laynie replied with a smile. "Be sure to hang around for the take-off."

"Can't wait," Nick chuckled.

"They told me one time that the landing strip on Pohnpei is a little over 6,000 feet and I don't how long the other ones here in the FSM are, but I think this one at Kosrae is the shortest. The closest I've come to one of these in the States is flying into and out of John Wayne in Orange County. After landing there one time, I talked to the pilot and he told me that they like to have 8,000 feet for these 737's. When there's less runway than that, I guess they have to compensate."

"And, I'm sure they do," Nick agreed. "My closest call to this was while I was in Vietnam. Air Force pilots took one of the platoons from our MP Company into a firebase near Phan Thiet. The temporary landing strip used there was made of individual sheets of metal hooked together. I think they called the stuff PSP. Needless to say, that strip was short and bumpy, and I suspect the pilots had to almost start reversing the engines before we hit the ground in order to get that big C-130 stopped in time."

"Sounds like those guys did some kind of flying," Laynie replied.

'Yeah. They did, and no matter how short these island strips are, they have to be better than those made with metal PSP strips. Also, the seats on these 737's are definitely more comfortable than the hard floor of a C-130, where combat loaded troops sit there holding onto straps stretched across the floor of the cargo area."

Laynie smiled as she looked down toward the seat and then toward the cockpit where one of the pilots was standing in the doorway, "These guys do a good job, too."

"That's really good to know," Nick said as he smiled and nodded.

Because there were more passengers boarding the plane than had gotten off, most of the seats that had remained open to this point in the flight were now occupied. At first, Laynie and Nick thought they had lucked out and were going to have the middle seat between them remain vacant, but that was not to be.

A large woman carrying a roomy bag made of woven leaves boarded late and came down the aisle. Arriving at their row, she looked down at her boarding pass and pointed at the middle seat between the two agents. Laynie got up and stood in the aisle while the woman lifted the armrest and slid into the seat.

Now, lowering the armrest and turning to look toward Nick, she gave him a big smile and a brief glimpse of her deep red stained teeth.

Nick returned her greeting with a nod and a smile.

In preparation for take-off, the captain alerted the passengers about what was to happen. Reminded of Laynie's earlier comment, Nick looked over to her with a smile.

Once the 737 had taxied to the end of the runway it came to a complete stop. There, the engines were set to maximum power, and as they came to a thunderous roar, the brakes were released, the plane shook, then shot forward, pinning the agents and other passengers against their seatbacks.

Success! They were once again airborne.

The newly boarded plus-size passenger sitting between the agents wore sandals and a loose fitting, brightly colored dress that hung down well below her knees. Her black hair was long, straight, and coarse, and atop her head, sitting like a crown, was a flowered wreath that emitted a strong scent.

During the flight, she looked over at Nick from time to time, and finally, as they were nearing Pohnpei, asked him where he was going.

Nick answered, "Pohnpei."

"That is our islands' capital," she responded. "Have you been there before?"

"No, but I have heard many nice things about it. In fact, this is my first time to visit any of these islands. Are you from Kosrae?" Nick asked.

"No, but I have family there. We had a nice visit. I am from the island of Chuuk."

The mention of Chuuk sparked an immediate response from Nick, as that was the island where he planned to take a few days of annual leave before returning home from Guam, after the conclusion of the PTI.

"That's where my son lives," Nick told her.

She responded with pride, "You know, our Truk Lagoon is a historical monument."

"That's what I understand. My son told me that more than sixty ships from the Japanese Imperial fleet were sunk there in a surprise bombing attack during World War II, and that it is one of the top wreck diving spots in the world."

She smiled in agreement. "It is," and Nick got an even better look at her deep-stained, red teeth. "We have a very beautiful island, you know. You will have to come see it."

"That's what I plan to do at the end of this trip."

"When will that be?" the woman asked.

"In a couple of weeks," answered Nick.

"When you do, bring your son and come visit my family," she told him.

Nick would have normally just smiled appreciatively and left it at that, but because she seemed so nice and genuine, he replied, "Thanks, we will try to do that," and pulled two business cards from his pocket. He wrote Eric's name on the back of one for her to keep, and asked her to write her name and telephone number on the back of the other one and give it back to him.

As she was finishing writing the information on the back of the card, an announcement came over the speaker that they were descending into the Pohnpei International Airport and the captain asked that the cabin be prepared for landing.

She quickly handed the card with her information on it back to Nick and put her tray table up.

"We will look forward to seeing you and meeting your son," she said.

Nick smiled, "Thank you. I also look forward to meeting your family."

Once again, as the 737 was setting down, the captain repeated the protocol he carried out while landing on the previous short strip.

Nick felt a jolt similar to the one he had experienced at Kosrae, but this time he was better prepared and as a result didn't seem to notice it as much.

Shortly, the 737 came to a stop on the tarmac near the lone boarding gate.

CHAPTER THIRTY-SIX

Welcoming Laynie and Nick as they stepped off the plane and walked down the steps at Pohnpei International Airport was not only the attorney general for the FSM and her chief investigator, but also the President and his bodyguard.

To say Nick was impressed with this high-level reception would have been an understatement. Never before, in all of his international travels had he ever been met by anyone approaching the position of the president of a country. This was a first for Laynie, also. On her previous trips to Pohnpei, the AG met her at the airport without fail, and on one occasion the head of the FSM Senate Judiciary also accompanied the AG, but never the President.

Two of the island's most popular entertainers, who after presenting them with leis and kisses, joined the agents in following the president and AG to an area that had been set aside for a newspaper photo op. The AG explained to Laynie and Nick that this award was a big thing in the FSM and the photo and accompanying story regarding the investigation would likely make front-page headlines in newspapers throughout the region. As the group gathered in front of the Pohnpei International Airport sign for pictures, the photographer requested that the president and attorney general move to the center, and that Laynie and the male entertainer stand on one side, and Nick and the female entertainer on the other.

Once the photo session was finished, the agents gathered their bags, and after clearing immigration and customs, were driven to the Kolonia town area where a celebration in their honor had been arranged at a feast house or *nah*.

As Laynie, Nick, and their hosts approached the thatched-roof, open-air *nah*, a man standing near a pile of coconuts, picked them up one by one, and after whacking off the tops with a machete, handed one to each of the attendees for their drink. With the temperature climbing into the high eighties and the humidity exceeding 90 percent, the fresh *uhpw*, also known as coconut milk, was a welcome refreshment.

Off to the side under a sheltered cooking area, a group of men finished wrapping a dressed out pig in banana leaves. They put the pig on a bed of hot coals and rocks, placed breadfruit around the border of the pit, and carefully added more long green banana leaves to the pile. As smoke seeped through the banana leaves and trailed upward, a tempting aroma filled the air.

When they entered the feast house, Nick's attention was immediately drawn to the rhythmic pounding noise and two groups of men sitting in recessed pit-like areas. Each group of these large, bare-chested, copper-skinned men sporting traditional tattoos encircling their biceps, sat around elevated giant flat stones that were at least five feet in diameter. As the men simultaneously raised smaller stones high in the air and hit them in cadence against the large flat stone in a rhythmic beat, a ringing tone was produced.

"They're making *sakau*," Laynie whispered to Nick.

"*Sakau*?" Nick gave her a puzzled look indicating, "What in the world are you talking about?"

"It's a drink they have at sakau bars and also offer at special ceremonies like this. One of the other ceremonies I attended was commemorating the completion of a canoe and another was for a birth. They also hold them for marriages, returning friends, and so forth. This one is being held to honor us," she told him appreciatively.

"That's very nice of them," Nick agreed. "And what is that they're beating with the rocks?" he asked.

Laynie answered, "That's the *sakau*. It's the root of a pepper shrub. They grow it here on the island. My first chance to experience something similar was in Samoa, but there they call it *kava*."

"Interesting," Nick nodded.

"These men will pound the roots with the stones until they have pulp. The pulp is then squeezed into juice, and after adding some water, it is ready to serve. They'll bring the *sakau* to us in a coconut shell. Just wait and see."

Nick gave her a smile and one of those subtle looks indicating, "I can hardly wait."

While they sat and waited, local people carried colorful fish hung from bamboo poles over their shoulders. They paraded up to the front of the *nah*, where those with high titles were positioned. After presenting the fish as gifts, those people re-joined the other attendees.

When the ceremony began, Laynie leaned over to Nick. "It is all very formal at these *sakau* ceremonies and they follow a set procedure. Everything is carried out in accordance with position or title. The *Nahnmwarki* or *Nahnken* is always served first."

"The *Nahnmwarki* or *Nahnken*?" questioned Nick.

"They're the two paramount chiefs or traditional leaders of each community," whispered Laynie.

As the cups were presented, Nick noticed that they did not pass the cup of *sakau* on from one person to another, but instead, each participant appeared to drink all of it before handing the cup back to the server to be refilled and given to the next attendee.

Being honored guests, Laynie and Nick were included in the first group of those receiving the *sakau*. Along with the two FBI agents were all of the chiefs and their wives. Nick watched closely as Laynie received her cup and drank it all in one gulp. That looked easy enough he thought.

When it was his turn, he took the cup and looked down into it. Brown colored water, Nick thought, and followed Laynie's lead, downing it all just as she had.

Nick's tongue and lips soon went numb. Putting his finger to his lips, he looked to Laynie and whispered, "You didn't tell me about that."

Laynie smiled and laughed to herself as she quietly replied, "I didn't want to give everything away."

"Thanks," Nick told her under his breath.

"And after another cup or two we might even have a little trouble understanding you," she added.

"I've got it. So along with my mouth going dead, I won't be able to talk."

"Well, I think you'd still be able to talk, but it would probably be a bit slower."

"How long will my mouth feel like this?" he asked.

Still smiling, Laynie assured him, "Oh, you'll be fine by tomorrow. If you would like, though, we could ask them to take us to a *sakau* bar tonight where we can get some more. There are a number of those little bars around the island."

"No, I think this will be fine," he assured her. "One is enough."

After everyone finished partaking in the *sakau* ceremony, they gathered to share taro, fresh fruit, and other food that women from the island had brought to the gathering. This was all in addition to some of the colorful fish presented as gifts, and the roasted pig and breadfruit that had been simmering in a pit under the nearby shelter. The fresh fish that was not eaten was available for anyone who needed the food for their family, or to be taken and shared with others on the island.

When the ceremony concluded, Johnie, the chief investigator from the AG's office with whom Laynie had worked during the investigation, invited the two agents to come to his house that evening to meet his wife and have dinner.

Before they left, however, Johnie gave the agents brightly colored *lavalava's*, sometimes referred to as *sarongs*, as gifts to wear. Laynie had started wearing them during her earlier visits to these Pacific island nations and loved them, but since this was something new for Nick, Johnie gave him a quick lesson on how to wrap the *lavalava* around his waist and tuck it in so it did not fall off. Seeing the apprehension this demonstration left on her fellow agent's face brought a smile to Laynie. Whether Nick's uneasiness had to do with feelings about his masculinity being tested, since this was the first time he had ever worn a wrap, or did he have some serious concern about whether it was going to stay up, she didn't know, but his anxiety crisis was fun to watch.

"You remember how to get to my house, don't you?" Johnie asked Laynie.

"I'm sure I can find it," she answered. "We'll see you in a couple of hours."

Slowed by holes, ruts, and narrow stretches on dirt roads leading both away from their hotel and into the water's edge where Johnie lived, the agents arrived a few minutes late. It was in time, however, to see one of the most inspiring sunsets Nick had ever witnessed in his life, as the bright orange ball slowly disappeared into the Pacific amidst a colorful array of clouds.

Walking through the gate, Johnie explained that some of the houses on the island now used concrete and corrugated metal for walls and roofing, but that his house was built in the traditional style. The sleeping room had woven pandanus sleeping mats on the floor and the walls were made from reeds. The wood used for the floor came from breadfruit trees. A large outdoor kitchen area was attached, and the wood used for the supports and rafters in this open-air great room came from a grove of nearby mangrove trees. The roofs covering the family house, the outdoor kitchen, and the nearby canoe house were all constructed from thatched palms.

"Laynie, I know you would probably like some mango juice," offered Johnie.

"Definitely," she nodded.

"Can I get you some mango juice, papaya juice, coconut milk, a soft drink, beer?" Johnie asked Nick.

"I'll go for the mango juice, too," Nick replied.

When he returned with their drinks, Johnie pointed to a nearby tree and said, "That's where it came from. We also have papaya trees over on the other side."

"It looks like you get most of what you need from right around here," Nick remarked.

"We do," Johnie agreed. "In addition to gathering fruits and raising vegetables, I also go spear fishing every week or two and get enough fish to usually take care of us and our parents until I can go out again."

"Isn't that a little dangerous?" Nick asked.

"It can be," Johnie answered. "Our greatest risks usually come after we have been out for a while and have a string of fish attached to our belt lines. Those strings of fish sometime attract sharks."

Nick gave a serious nod.

Johnie then quipped, "But we usually get the fish rather than letting them get us."

Nick smiled, "That's good to hear."

"Who climbs the trees to gather the coconuts?"

"Most of us here know how to, and I still get some, but it seems like the older you get the harder it is to get up there."

"I can go along with that. Just don't ask me to try," Nick noted.

"I won't," Johnie assured him. "If I'm going to get to go to your upcoming training program in Guam, I can't have you falling out of trees."

Nick laughed, "So you're coming to the PTI?"

"I am," Johnie answered. "The FSM got four slots. There will be one of our people coming from Chuuk, one from Kosrae, one from Yap, and me from Pohnpei."

"I will look forward to having you in our class."

Johnie's wife, Lena, signaled him that dinner was ready.

After sitting down at the table, Johnie said grace and Lena passed the food. Simmering on the platters were tender, but firm, mouthwatering tuna steaks, the likes of which Nick had never before experienced; and succulent giant crab claws that had been cooked over an open fire, and melted in your mouth when dipped into the warm butter. Once those scrumptious seafood platters had made their way around the table, Lena passed several hand-carved wooden bowls filled with boiled taro, baked breadfruit, and yams.

"Did you catch that great tasting tuna?" Nick asked Johnie.

"No, a friend of mine caught this yellow fin when we were out on his boat last weekend. It weighed thirty-two pounds. The crabs did come from my traps, though."

Nick gave an appreciative smile. "And this pepper," he added, as he sprinkled some more on his food, "I've tried both the black and the white and this is the best ever. Is it from here, too?"

"Yes," answered Johnie, as a broad smile spread across his face, "I ground it from our local Pohnpei peppercorns."

"Well, everything is wonderful," Nick gratefully told his hosts, and Laynie concurred.

Johnie and Lena nodded appreciatively.

After stepping away for a short time, Lena returned carrying a tray loaded with fresh fruit and banana pudding. This was Nick's first opportunity to try the local finger length bananas that Laynie had told him were so good, and she was right. These were the best bananas he had ever eaten.

As they sat around talking after dinner, Johnie took out some green nuts and asked Laynie and Nick if they would like to join him and Lena for a chew.

Laynie smiled and nodded, "Okay."

Following Laynie's lead Nick responded that he would also, but then asked, "What is it?"

"*Pwuh*," Johnie answered.

"*Betelnut?*" questioned Nick.

"You're learning Pohnpeian very quickly, Nick," Johnie said.

Nick watched intently as Johnie cracked the green nuts in half with his teeth and took the seeds out of the center, before sprinkling them with some kind of powder."

"What's that powder?" he asked.

"Lime and crushed coral," Johnie answered. "It makes your mouth water."

Next, he wrapped the nut in a pepper leaf and asked if either of the agents wanted him to add part of a cigarette to theirs, as he was doing with his and Lena's. Nick and Laynie graciously shook their heads.

They each popped a small green lump into their mouths and began chewing, while at the same time spitting the deep red juice into cans they were handed.

"Glad I tried the *betelnut*," Nick thought to himself. "But, like the *sakau*, where one drink was enough, I'm fairly certain that this single chew will be sufficient."

These opportunities to experience different cultures and traditions were something Nick had thrived on, and this memorable evening in Micronesia, with respect to their customs, was ranking right up there with another trip he had recently completed to Kazakhstan. There, he and others sat on a carpet around a low table in a nomad *yurt*. After enjoying interpreted conversation and exchanging vodka toasts, Nick, serving as the training team leader and honored guest, was presented with a cooked sheep's head, which he immediately and "generously" shared with all of the others. His hosts anxiously awaited his reaction and enjoyed watching the expressions on his face as he ate a bite of the tongue, plucked a bulging eyeball, and spooned some brains onto his plate. Both this enchanting evening enjoyed on the shores of a Pacific island paradise and that most interesting experience he had in Genghis Khan's Central Asia were dining happenings Nick was likely never to forget.

While Nick and Lena listened and laughed, most of the evening's after-dinner conversation centered on Johnie and Laynie's local war stories, and the cast of characters in the fraud investigation for which the FBI agents were there to receive the award.

Just before they were ready to leave, Laynie asked, "Any progress on the restoration of Nan Madol?"

"Glad you brought Nan Madol up," Johnie said.

"Why's that?" she asked.

"Well, this has nothing to do with restoration, but just yesterday, I was talking with a guy I've known for years who lives down near there. He was telling me about spotting a ship sitting not far off the coastline. A couple of outboards had been running between it and the shoreline, and it looked to him like they were moving something from the shore and back to the ship. He couldn't tell for sure what it was they were moving, but told me he was going to snoop around a little and give me a call back if he came up with anything."

"Have you heard anything more from him?"

Johnie shook his head, no, and replied, "So it was probably nothing. However, just in case, I thought you two might like to take a run with me down to Nan Madol after tomorrow's ceremony? We'll take the AG's boat, and it will give Nick a chance to see some more of our island and give you some time to catch some rays, Laynie." He paused, "That is unless you two have something else going on."

Nick looked at Laynie. "I'm all for it," he responded.

"Sounds good to me," Laynie agreed.

"Fine, I'll make the arrangements," Johnie smiled.

As they said their good-byes for the evening, Nick asked, "By the way, Johnie, who or what's a Nan Madol?"

"Oh, that's a reef area down off the southeast coast of our island. We have some ancient ruins there."

"Ruins, huh? How old are we talking about?"

"I've heard anywhere from 200 B.C. to 1500 A.D. mentioned, depending on whether they're talking about occupation, or construction of the man-made islets, but I don't think anyone really knows for sure. It's safe to say that they are really old, though."

"I look forward to the trip and seeing them," Nick remarked, as he squeezed into the compact car the agents had rented.

Driving back to where they were staying, Laynie pointed out a *sakau* bar to Nick. Around the corner, they came upon an old car that was barely creeping along the narrow dirt roadway.

"He must have just come out of that *sakau* bar we just passed and is now on his way home to get something to eat," she surmised.

"Why do you say that?" Nick asked.

"After a night of drinking at one of these bars, drivers tend to go extremely slow. I don't know exactly why, but it has something to do with the way their system reacts to the *sakau*."

"And what about all of those we see walking?"

Laynie laughed. "Well, sometimes there's a little problem getting both feet going the same direction, but they do seem to eventually make it back to their houses. Surprisingly, their heads usually remain pretty clear, and any problems seem to lie with speech and motor skills."

Upon reaching their quarters, Laynie decided to call it a night and followed the torch lit trail to her thatched roof hut, where she went directly to bed.

Nick, however, could not resist the urge to take a walk into this starlit darkness and took a path that led him onto the peaceful and deserted nearby sandy beach.

Unfolding overhead on this incredibly clear night was a celestial gathering of greater proportion than anything he could have ever imagined possible.

As the tide rushed to shore, Nick sat for nearly an hour pondering the wonderful times he and his deceased wife had together and how much he missed her and wished that she could be there with him as he experienced this spectacle of the universe.

CHAPTER THIRTY-SEVEN

Before going to the morning ceremony, Laynie took Nick to a local restaurant known for its legendary Pohnpei banana pancake breakfasts. Since her first visit to the island, she had made it a habit to stop there at least one morning each trip and Nick quickly understood why. After finishing a short stack topped with melted butter and syrup, he seriously considered ordering a second but knew he had better stop; especially after all he had eaten the previous afternoon and evening. It was certainly tempting, however.

The drive from the Kolonia restaurant to the FSM capital at Palikir was about five miles. By the time the agents arrived at the Congress Chamber both the attorney general and Chief Investigator Johnie were already there and waiting outside for them. Soon, three judges from the Supreme Court, and the representatives from Chuuk, Yap, Kosrae, and Pohnpei also arrived and everyone entered the chamber together. The only ones missing were the President of the FSM and the head of the Senate Judiciary. The AG advised that they were together, and had telephoned saying they would be arriving momentarily.

The festivities opened with a flag ceremony and introductory remarks from the attorney general. The head of the Senate Judiciary followed with comments describing how the FSM Attorney General's Office and the FBI worked closely in the past and that this investigation demonstrated what can happen when everyone pulls together.

He concluded by saying, "Over ten million dollars was located and returned to the coffers of the FSM and I think we would all agree that those dollars would not be available today if it were not for the efforts of FBI Supervisory Special Agents Laynie Steele and Nick Costigan." That brought a rousing applause.

Next, the President came to the podium, and after joining the others in expressing his sincere gratitude, he asked the AG, Johnie, Laynie and Nick to join him at the podium. After shaking their hands, he presented each with a certificate of appreciation from the FSM, and also gave the two agents hand-carved Polynesian handicrafts, a beautiful mangrove wood dolphin for Laynie and a shark, with teeth, for Nick.

Following a brief reception, most of those in attendance returned to their offices. Johnie told Laynie and Nick that he would go to his office to change clothes and pick them up at their hotel in about an hour. From there they would all go to the dock and depart for Nan Madol.

Dressed in shorts and tank tops over their swimsuits and wearing surf shoes and baseball caps with sunglasses resting on the bills, the two agents stood outside their hotel awaiting Johnie's arrival. When his yellow Jeep pulled up, they tossed the bags containing their towels, snorkels, masks, suntan lotion, and binoculars in behind the driver's seat and Laynie stepped into the front seat while Nick jumped over the side and into the back.

Catching Nick's attention as they neared a thatched roof open-air bar and small dock where the AG's boat was moored alongside several others, were two ladies wearing brightly colored *sarongs* wrapped around their lower halves, but little else.

Noting his interest, Laynie smiled, "As you can see, Nick, customs in the region have some of the women more concerned about covering their hips and thighs than their breasts."

"I noticed," he replied with a smile.

The boat used by the Attorney General's Office had no cabin, no bridge, no place to sleep, and no toilet. In fact, there was not even a windshield or steering wheel like Nick had envisioned they would be using when going out into the Pacific. Instead, he found himself sitting beside Laynie on a flat, no-back seat located in the mid-section of a sixteen-foot open-bow runabout. Seated behind them with one hand gripping the seat and the other on the tiller handle of a forty horsepower outboard motor was their chief investigator host.

As Johnie accelerated, the salty spray peppered their faces and the brisk ocean breeze tangled Laynie's hair. Spotting a body floating on the surface with his head bobbing face down in the water directly ahead, Johnie slowed, and as he got closer, the man looked up and waved. Johnie yelled, and motioned for him to go over to a nearby rock, commenting to the agents that this was a friend.

The man swam toward the rock and the trio followed slowly in the boat. There, Johnie's friend raised the mask and snorkel to his forehead, and gave a big grin, revealing a mouth of deep red beechnut stained teeth and gums. Pulling himself up and onto the rock, he stood, holding a spear gun pointed upward in one hand and lifting a stringer of colorful fish high above his head with the other. This was his catch for the day.

"That should take care of the family for another week," Johnie yelled. "Thanks for letting us see what you caught."

The friend nodded and again gave a broad smile.

Waving good-bye, Johnie reversed the outboard motor and their boat drew back into the deeper water. Nick leaned over the side of the boat and looked down. Resting unspoiled just below the surface of the crystal clear waters was the most vivid array of pastel colored coral he had ever witnessed in his life. It was truly a breathtaking collage.

Heading back out along the coastline, Johnie once again brought the runabout to full throttle. As the small craft cut through the water, and the waves pounded against the hull, Nick took out his binoculars for a better look. Johnie pointed out several nearby coves and atolls, and Nick brought a couple of plunging waterfalls to everyone's attention.

Suddenly, Johnie shouted, "That's Nan Madol," pointing ahead at a collection of huge basalt slabs and inland waterways looming in the distance.

Nick got his first good glimpse of what he was soon to come to believe might truly be one of the wonders of the ancient world.

He yelled back to Johnie, "Unbelievable!"

Johnie slowed the boat and entered the channel in front of the Nan Douwas islet. He cut the engine and guided them to a point nearby where they dropped anchor and tied up.

What caught Nick's initial attention was the massiveness of some of the walls. Seeing the dark, log-like basalt stones alternately stacked atop bases of huge basalt boulders, he wondered how these immense and impressive structures, like those he had also previously visited in Egypt, Mexico, and Peru, could have been constructed without the aid of modern-day equipment and technology.

"How many of these are there?" Nick asked.

"Islets?" Johnie clarified.

"Yeah."

"I've been told ninety-two, but never counted 'em all. This area they are on covers about two hundred acres."

"Amazing!" Nick replied.

After getting out of the boat, the trio entered Nan Douwas. The coral rubble crackled under their feet as they followed walkways outlined by the heavy black logs laid end to end, and climbed a series of basalt steps. Palm trees swayed majestically in the wind and green foliage sprouted through crevices and into openings in the walls and along the pathways.

Stopping to look up and around, Nick commented, "Some of the walls on these must be twenty-five feet high."

Johnie and Laynie nodded in agreement.

Pointing in another direction, Johnie said, "Let's head this way and see a couple of the other ruins."

Johnie told them a little about the oral history of the ancient city. He explained that legend had it that two brothers, *Ohlosohpa* and *Ohlosihpa* had set out to build a religious center to worship *Nahnisohnsapw*, which translated meant the "honored spirit of the land." After considering several other possible sites they finally settled on Nan Madol, and as a result constructed the islets.

Nick lifted his binoculars. "This place is incredible," he remarked, as he gazed out over the area. "With all of the inner-waterways, it must have been something akin to an ancient Venice of the Pacific."

"And, with all of these islets and ruins, there must have been thousands of people living here at one time," Laynie noted.

"Yeah, it makes you wonder what happened to their civilization?" questioned Nick.

"Mysterious, huh?" added Laynie.

Nick and Johnie nodded in agreement.

Suddenly, Nick spotted something in the distance and pointed, handing Johnie the binoculars.

"Is that what it looks like?" Nick asked.

After taking a look, Johnie answered, "I sure hope not. Let's head in that direction and see."

"What's up, Johnie?" Laynie asked, as the three of them rushed back through the ruins and toward the boat.

"Maybe nothing, but it looks like it could possibly be a body," he answered.

CHAPTER THIRTY-EIGHT

Nick, Laynie, and Johnie ran up to the body lying in the coral rubble on the islet.

Johnie cried out, "Richard!"

"You know him?" Laynie asked.

"He's the guy I told you about who lives down here and called me."

"The one who saw the boats running between the ship and shoreline?"

Johnie nodded, as he slumped and lowered his forehead into his open hand. "I told him to be careful. I think we both suspected what might be going on, but since he didn't call me back, I just figured it was nothing."

Laynie put her hand on his shoulder. "Johnie, it's not your fault."

"I should have come when he called, though."

Still trying to console him, Laynie added, "You had no way of knowing, Johnie. As you said, he didn't call you back."

Focusing on the deep slit across his throat, and the dried blood where Richard's lopped off ear once was, Johnie repeatedly pounded his fist into the coral rubble and exclaimed, "Damn pirates! Those damn pirates!"

From the bloated appearance and strong odor emanating from the body, the two agents suspected that Richard was probably killed not too long after he placed the call to

Johnie, but they had no way of knowing for sure. That determination would have to be left up to others.

Johnie scrolled through numbers on his cell phone. His first call was to his AG boss and then to the police chief in Kolonia to tell them what he had found.

After he completed those calls, Johnie briefly explained to Nick that for nearly a year investigators from throughout the region had been passing along informant information that traffickers growing *maru* on Peleliu had started expanding their operations.

"I guess we must be one of the places they've added," he concluded.

"*Maru* and Peleliu?" Nick replied, displaying a puzzled look on his face.

"*Maru*? Oh, that's our name for marijuana," Johnie explained. "And Peleliu? Well, that is one of the islands in the Palauan group. You might have heard of it in connection with World War II."

"Now that you mention it, I do remember reading about some of the fiercest fighting and biggest battles in the Pacific taking place around there," Nick recalled.

"And, marijuana has been grown on that island for a long time," Laynie added. "But, from what I heard at a recent OC conference, it's only been of late that the Asian wiseguys have started muscling in on the action there."

While they continued waiting for the AG, police, and the coroner to arrive, the three investigators secured the crime scene and began an intense search for evidence.

CHAPTER THIRTY-NINE

Because they spent the rest of the afternoon and most of the night assisting at Nan Madol, Nick and Laynie had to hurry back to Kolonia to gather their bags from the hotel, and arrive at the Pohnpei International Airport in time to catch their flight. With very few flights scheduled in and out of PNI, and those not necessarily on an every day basis, their missing the flight was not an option.

"If you come up with anything else, or if we can help in any way, just give me a call on my cell phone," Laynie told Johnie and the AG.

"Thanks. We will," the AG replied.

"See you next trip and thanks for everything," Laynie yelled back, as she and Nick waved good-bye to their hosts.

They adjusted the scented, flowered wreaths placed on their heads as parting gifts by Johnie and the AG, and walked through the customs and immigration area before boarding the plane.

Now settled into their seats and buckled up, the captain of this 737 came over the speaker and just as they had previously experienced in preparation for their take-off from Kosrae, alerted the passengers about what to expect.

After taxiing to the end of the runway, the aircraft came to a complete stop. There, the engines were set to maximum power, and after coming to a thunderous roar, the brakes were released, and the passengers were pinned against their seatbacks.

As the plane lifted off and climbed toward the clouds, Nick caught his last glimpse of the Island of Pohnpei, and the Sokehs Rock landmark as it rose above Kolonia Harbor.

"That was probably as close to paradise as I can ever expect to get," he told Laynie.

"But there are no high-rise buildings or big name hotels," she teased with a sly smile.

"And no chain or fast food restaurants, either," Nick added. "Just thatched roof bungalows, melt in your mouth fresh seafood and the best finger length bananas I've ever tasted."

Still smiling, Laynie added, "And don't forget about those banana pancakes. They aren't bad either."

"Those, too," he agreed.

"I guess you're just another one of those hopeless island romantics," Laynie laughed, "Albeit a hungry one."

Nick nodded, as he smiled in total agreement.

"If you're referring to a man impressed by breathtaking sunsets, clear nights where you can see the stars forever, palm trees swaying in the Pacific breezes, and last but not least, great food, then I guess that's me," he said.

Laynie added, "And these are some of the least materialistic people you'll ever meet in the entire world."

"Yeah, I didn't see much in the way of luxury cars and big, expensive houses."

"And there probably aren't many high mortgages, either."

Nick smiled. "Yeah, I think even I could afford the mortgage on one of those thatched roof beach bungalows."

"Only one problem," Laynie responded. "You're not Pohnpeian."

"So, I guess you're telling me that I don't need to plan on retiring there if I'm not a member of one of the clans and able to own land, huh?"

Laynie nodded, "I think you're probably right."

"Well, I can always dream, though, can't I?" sighed Nick.

"You can certainly do that," agreed Laynie.

CHAPTER FORTY

Everything in LA had gone like clockwork to this point. The preparation of the affidavit, getting the search warrant signed by the magistrate, and the planning meetings for the raid on the apartment building all went off without a hitch.

In anticipation of the afternoon execution of the search warrant, agents from the FBI surveillance team had taken up positions near the apartment building earlier that morning.

Luis Ayala's black Mercedes had been parked in the "Reserved" space when they drove by the previous evening, but it was now gone. Since they wanted him there, all they could hope for was that he'd make a re-appearance before long.

By noon, all of the raid teams were assembled in the FBI parking garage and awaiting the final word to go in on the search. This garage was selected because of its secure location and its reasonably close proximity to the apartment building.

While everyone anxiously awaited word to get things rolling, Jack Stacy methodically went over the raid plan with them one more time.

"Any questions?" he asked.

There were none, and the patience of some of the officers and agents was beginning to wear thin. Periodic calls were coming from those just standing around for Stacy to get things moving, and each time they did, Jack would reemphasize the need for Ayala to be present in the apartment building. Everyone understood the reason why, and having to sit and wait was nothing new for those who had been in law enforcement for any length of time, but these kinds of delays remained frustrating no matter how long you had been on the job.

Shortly before five, the call everyone had been waiting for finally came in.

"He's here, he's here," an excited Tom Sanders called over the air.

A cheer went up throughout the garage, and Stacy yelled out, "Let's hit it."

Fortunately, Jack had insured their search warrant would also be good for a nighttime execution, so they would be okay even if everyone didn't get out of there until well after dark.

Not wanting to attract any undue attention, the raid teams took several different routes from the FBI garage to their assigned locations surrounding the apartment building. Each team leader would notify Stacy when their team was in position and ready. Once Stacy heard back from everyone, and the patrol units had roadblocks set up at the both ends of the street it would be time for the raid to get underway.

"We're going in!" Stacy told everyone.

Anticipating that there was at least one security camera focused on the front door, and most likely, someone standing nearby observing through the one-way glass anyone coming and going, the FBI entrance team was on the run when they approached the front door.

Pounding on the door, Stacy bellowed, "FBI! Open up! We have a search warrant!"

There was no immediate response.

A pair of agents carrying a two-man blunt end metal ram started toward the heavy, re-enforced, solid wooden door. One jarring hit was followed by another until they were able to break it open.

Guards standing behind the door quickly scattered, setting off alarms as they ran out other doors and into the hands and arms of waiting police officers. All of the exits were well covered by the police. No one would escape.

With their weapons drawn, Stacy, Kelly, and Sanders cautiously led the charge through the front door, and systematically covered one another as they moved down the entry hallway. Remaining behind and protecting the backs of their fellow agents were the two agents that broke open the door using the metal ram. They would also be screening anyone trying to get in or out the front.

Kelly tried to open a door leading into a room that the sketch the con man gave had led them to believe was likely an office. The door was locked. He turned and gave it several swift kicks. The door popped open. A startled Luis Ayala looked up and bolted out a side door leading down another long hallway. In his hand was a canvas bag that he had been hurriedly filling.

"Halt! FBI!" yelled Kelly.

Ayala turned, looked briefly, and resumed running.

Kelly pursued, and as both neared a fork in the hallway, Matt lunged and caught Ayala's foot. Both went down to the floor. When they did, greenbacks stuffed into the partially open canvas bag scattered all over the floor in front of them. As Ayala tried to get back to his feet, Kelly quickly put a knee into his back and grabbed his wrists, closing a pair of handcuffs tightly around them.

In the meantime, Stacy had arrived and was gathering up the strewn money. Once all the greenbacks were packed back into the bag, Kelly and Stacy took Ayala and the money back to the same office they had all ran out of only moments earlier.

"Luis Ayala, or whatever your name is, you're under arrest," Matt Kelly told him.

Jack Stacy then read their subject his rights.

He responded with a look of disdain and then spat in their direction. Fortunately his discharge landed on the floor and not on the agents, but his message was clear. They would get nothing out of him at this time.

Tom Sanders opened the remaining locked exit doors and assisted the search and arrest teams in clearing the stairwell and securing each floor so the apartment searches could begin.

"ICE! Open up! We have a search warrant!" announced Agent Teri Lee as she pounded on the door of one of the apartments located on the top floor.

When she did not hear a response, but heard voices and a rustling sound coming from inside, she issued a louder and even terser command.

"Just a minute," replied a male voice from behind the door.

Noise could be heard from inside that sounded like someone fumbling with the lock, and the door slowly opened. The police officer standing beside Agent Lee gave the door a sudden jolt with his shoulder and with that, he, Teri Lee, and a female ICE officer were able to force their way into the apartment.

To Teri Lee's surprise, a john was standing there zipping his fly. He was someone she vaguely recognized, but from where, Teri couldn't immediately recall. Behind him, huddled in a nearby corner, were three girls who appeared to be in their late teens. Disrobed and frightened, only the girls' long, black, silky hair covered their bare breasts.

Suddenly it came to her. This john was one of those "talking heads" Teri had seen on nighttime television talk shows where politics was discussed. He always staked out the high moral ground and being somewhat conservative herself, she usually tended to side with him.

"What a hypocrite," Teri thought. "Too bad the viewers can't see him now and know what he's really like."

Joining an assortment of kinky sex toys scattered about the living room were a collection of skimpy bikini tops and bottoms dropped along a path leading into the glass room that housed a bubbling hot tub.

In the bedroom, huge mirrors covered much of the ceiling, and an erotic film played on a giant, flat screen TV that hung on the wall directly in front of the king-sized bed. Bottles and half-empty glasses of booze were on the floor beside the bed, and the extra large plush pillows and satin sheets covering the bed were in total disarray.

It was obvious that this foursome had been doing more than just sitting around having a couple of drinks and discussing politics.

CHAPTER FORTY-ONE

After being advised of his rights by the police officer, the "talking head" john was taken to one of the waiting paddy wagons where Luis Ayala, the guards, and a number of other johns were already sitting.

Teri Lee and the female immigration officer remained behind while the three frightened girls got dressed. Once that was completed, these girls would join others in an empty apartment on another floor that the ICE had set up for use as a temporary holding facility.

"Where do you girls stay?" Lee asked.

One of them glanced upward toward the ceiling.

Teri Lee pointed, "Up there?"

All three girls nodded.

"How do you get up there?" asked Lee.

One of the girls gestured that she would show her.

While the immigration officer remained behind with the other two, Teri Lee followed the third girl down the hallway.

Reaching a point near a doorway with stairs leading downward, the girl stopped and pointed up.

Lee could see slight gaps around a set of decorative rectangular moldings overhead.

"You go up there?" asked Lee.

The girl nodded.

"How?"

She flicked a wall picture to the side, and behind it was a recessed button.

"You push the button and stairs drop down?" Lee asked.

"Yes," the teenager responded.

"Are girls up there now?"

She nodded there were.

"How many?"

The girl shook her head indicating she did not know, but quickly added, "Careful. Men have guns."

Unknown to either of them, a video monitor being fed by a pinhole camera provided armed guards located overhead with a clear view of everything going on in the hallway in which Teri and the girl were now standing. It had been the guards' intention to remain there undetected, and escape when everyone was gone, but this disclosure by the girl had changed everything. They were going to have to make a run for it.

As Lee and the teenage girl started back down the hallway, they heard a noise. The ceiling area leading to the attic hideaway opened behind them and a mechanical stairway unfolded.

Lee quickly grabbed the girl by the arm, and as the two of them raced toward the apartment, a single gunshot rang out. The bullet hit its mark and the wounded girl screamed as she stumbled to the floor in front of the door leading into the apartment.

Hearing the shot, the female immigration officer who had remained behind in the apartment rushed to the door and opened it. Seeing the girl lying on the hallway floor, she grabbed her around the shoulders and dragged her through the doorway. Agent Lee looked to return fire, but after spotting no one, quickly slammed and bolted the door shut.

Her pulse racing, Teri Lee shouted frantically over the radio, "Jack, Jim. One of the girls has been shot in the back! We need an ambulance!"

"Where are you, Teri?" Stacy yelled into the radio.

"Apartment three, top floor. Hurry! I'm trying, but can't stop the bleeding!"

"I'm calling for an ambulance team, now," Cassidy told her.

"Any idea where the shooter is?" asked Stacy.

"None," answered Lee, nervously. "There's a hidden attic above this floor and I'm pretty sure when the stairs came down that he came down with them."

"Alone?"

"Don't know. I didn't see anybody."

"We're on our way," Stacy told her. "Keep the door locked and protect the girls."

"Be careful, Jack!"

With no time to get a SWAT team, the FBI agents started up the stairwell while Cassidy and two patrol officers waited near the elevator for the medical team to arrive from the ambulance.

Their forty caliber pistols in their hands, and wearing bullet-proof vests under their blue raid jackets with the letters "FBI" emblazoned in gold on the front and back, the three agents covered one another, as they carefully leap-frogged their way up the concrete stairs and onto the landings. When they neared a steel fire door leading into the top floor, they could hear muffled sounds of rounds being fired in the distance.

"They're shooting through the door," Teri Lee screamed into the radio.

"Keep the girls behind cover," Stacy responded. "We're almost there."

Matt Kelly opened the door leading into the dimly lit hallway and motioned for Stacy and Sanders to cover him while he ran to the recessed entryway leading into a nearby apartment.

Sanders and Stacy nodded they would.

Breaking from the doorway in a sprint Kelly caught a brief glimpse of two silhouettes standing in the distance. Fortunately, he wasn't noticed.

It was now Tom Sanders turn. As he darted toward Matt, one of the figures spotted his dark form. The agents saw flashes and heard pops from two rounds.

Stacy and Kelly returned fire, but the poor lighting coupled with shortness of breath and racing heart rates resulting from having just sprinted up flights of stairwells did not help their accuracy.

As Matt ran toward the next apartment, shots once again rang out. This time, one of the rounds temporarily stunned him as it lodged in his vest.

Stacy and Sanders fired back.

Dropping to the carpet, Matt rolled into a prone position in the nearby recessed entryway. Closer now, he was able to see the two images more clearly. Kelly fired bursts of two rounds each.

One of the gunmen dropped to his knees, and after firing more rounds in Kelly's direction, fell to the floor.

As Matt was ejecting one magazine and reloading with another, the other subject fired several rounds his direction and charged him in a crazed rage.

Stacy and Sanders unloaded a barrage of fire, and after multiple jarring hits to his torso, the gunman stumbled and fell face down next to Kelly.

Reaching out to check for a pulse, Kelly yelled out to Stacy and Sanders, "I think this one's dead."

Stacy and Sanders now rushed to the other body. "No pulse here either, Matt."

Kelly remained in a prone position covering Stacy and Sanders while they prepared to finish clearing the remainder of the hallway.

At the same time, another team of FBI agents came through the stairwell doorway.

Trying to keep an eye on both directions at the same time, Kelly yelled to the team just arriving, "Check the attic!"

"Will do!" one of the agents yelled back.

While the newly arrived team of agents started up the dropdown stairway leading into the attic, Kelly continued to cover Stacy and Sanders as they moved past the elevator and on to additional apartments.

When they got to the end of the hallway, Stacy shouted back, "All's clear at this end."

The three assembled outside the bullet-ridden door leading into apartment three.

Stacy knocked. "Teri, it's Jack. You can open up."

Teri Lee rushed to the door, looked through the peephole, and then opened it.

"Where are the paramedics?" she asked frantically. "I can't get the bleeding stopped."

The elevator doors opened and Cassidy, two other police officers, and three paramedics carrying medical kits rushed down the hallway.

"A stretcher will be coming up on the next trip," Cassidy yelled.

One paramedic went into the apartment to attend the wounded girl, while the others made their way to the two gunmen lying on the hallway floor.

CHAPTER FORTY-TWO

While Jack Stacy and Tom Sanders remained in the apartment with Teri Lee, Matt Kelly climbed to the top of the foldaway stairway leading into the hideaway. There, he joined the other team of FBI agents as they prepared to make a sweep.

The attic was poorly lit, but there was a sliver of light emanating through a partially open doorway leading into a room located in one of the corners. Several large mirrored windows surrounded the doorway. These windows allowed anyone inside to view everything taking place in the rest of the attic while those observing remained concealed.

"That must be the control center for the guards," the agent taking the lead turned and whispered to the others.

Believing that they would have already more than likely been met by a barrage of gunfire had any guards still been in there, the agents opted to make their move.

"Cover me," one of them said as he rushed and kicked the door open the rest of the way.

Matt and two other agents quickly followed, stepping in and clearing the room, while another remained outside the doorway watching their backs.

Although no guards were found inside, there were plenty of weapons and ammo, and a bank of video monitors covering not only what was going on in the attic, but also the hallways below. In this temperature controlled center they also found a couch, a big screen TV, a table and chairs for playing cards, and a refrigerator well stocked with cold ones.

Stepping out of the air-conditioning and bright lights of the control center, and back into the stale, hot air hanging over the rest of the dimly lit attic, the agents stopped to turn on flashlights and let their eyes adjust.

To one side were hooks holding kinky sex objects, chains, whips, and leather for the girls to use on and with the johns. Near the other wall were racks of brightly colored feather boas; alluring dresses; micro-mini skirts and split tops; bins of seductive sleepwear; see though tops and bottoms; scanty undergarments; every imaginable type of garter belt: sexy stockings; and rows of spike heels.

A huge, twelve-foot high, steel-framed cage was straight ahead. The top and all four sides were covered with heavy gage chain link fencing. The only access point was a barred gate. The agents tugged on the gate, but found it locked.

Matt Kelly hurried back to the guard control center to retrieve a large, heavy key he had earlier seen hanging on the wall. When he slipped the key into the lock and turned it, the gate opened.

The agents entered the cage and stopped only long enough to get a quick look around. There were about thirty bunked beds, a few small beat-up dressers with cracked mirrors, a bathroom and shower area, and a washer and dryer. There was also a small open kitchen area where it appeared the girls prepared and ate their meals. Hanging in clear view on all of the walls outside the heavy chain link were posters showing a young woman's acid scarred face and breasts, with the words "NO ESCAPE" written in a bold, crossed out red circle.

As the agents gripped their pistols tightly and moved forward, the stench permeating this caged area was so overwhelming that it nearly caused a couple of them to vomit. Suddenly, one of the agents spotted movement near the rear of the cage, and motioned to the others.

"FBI. Come out with your hands up!" he shouted.

With their heads down and hands raised, a half dozen petite teenage girls and young women came shuffling slowly forward.

Quivering and sobbing, the girls cried out, "No Shoot! Please!"

"Don't worry. We won't," one of the agents assured them.

As the girls squatted on the floor in front of the agents and lowered their heads, a young agent commented to the others, "I've never seen anything like this. Teenage girls and young women locked up in a cage like animals and used for sex slaves. What's this world coming to?"

"Yeah. This place is twisted," remarked another.

"And escape doesn't look like an option from this hell hole, either," added Matt Kelly, as he glanced over at one of the posters. "It looks like if they don't go along with the program, acid scars them for life."

"Or they're killed," said the senior agent on this team.

While one of the agents remained behind with the girls, the others continued their search. When no more girls or guards were found, the sweat drenched agents assembled near the front of the cage. They stayed there until the ICE officers arrived to remove the girls from the attic.

Meanwhile, Teri Lee assisted one of the paramedics as he treated the young wounded girl. He had stopped the bleeding and started an IV. Now, he prepared her for the ambulance trip to the ER.

Stacy, Sanders, and Cassidy had initially assisted the other two paramedics as they were online with ER doctors going through the prescribed protocol on the gunmen who were lying in the hallway. Once the two had been pronounced dead, Stacy told Cassidy he would notify the FBI shooting team so they could carry out their required post shooting investigation, and asked Cassidy to do likewise with the police detectives who would be investigating. Cassidy would also put in a call to the medical examiner.

While Cassidy and the two uniform officers remained in the hallway waiting for the ME and the shooting team investigators, Stacy and Sanders returned to the first floor office to finish the inventory they had started earlier.

By the time Kelly got back downstairs, Stacy was finishing going through the desk and Sanders the safe. So far these searches had yielded more stacks of cash, and more importantly, passports. Waving a handful of the passports, Sanders remarked to the others, "I wonder if one of these belongs to the murdered girl in Cassidy's case?"

Stacy shrugged. "Set 'em aside for Jim and the ICE agents to take a look at. My guess is that all or at least most of them were taken from these girls when they arrived here in LA."

"I think you're probably right, Jack," Sanders added. "And, if that's the case, the job for ICE in making positive ID's on those girls has just become a lot easier."

Stacy nodded in agreement. Then, looking over to Kelly, he suggested, "While we're finishing the desk and safe, Matt, can you go through the trash? Later, the three of us can tackle the file cabinet."

Kelly nodded. There was little in this world that he despised doing more than rummaging through someone else's trash, but that was where some of the best evidence often came from. Anyway, he smiled to himself, somebody was going to have to do it, so who better than an FBI agent supervisor from Quantico.

After putting on latex gloves and picking through a collection of marijuana roaches, filtered cigarette butts, greasy fast food wrappers, dirty tissues, orange peels, coffee cups, beer cans, and the like, Kelly finally neared the bottom. There, he found several torn up bank deposit slips and a crumpled sheet of coffee stained paper that, when opened and flattened out, appeared to be a note left for Luis Ayala.

"Luis,
I have been called to Manila.
Will be leaving tomorrow morning.
Sam."

Since the note was undated, they would have to rely on Luis Ayala to tell them when it was written, and so far, he wasn't talking, but. . . .

Next for them to tackle was the four-drawer black metal filing cabinet. In the top drawer were two separate groups of files. Printed labels identifying banks and account numbers appeared on those folders located in the front. The banks were both domestic and foreign, and the files appeared to be reasonably well organized. A cursory check showed them to essentially contain a collection of monthly statements, cancelled checks, and wire transfer memos.

Pausing a moment to take a closer look at the second group of files in that top drawer, Matt noticed that all of these folders appeared to have country names posted on the outside tabs, and the names of people or businesses, with code numbers stuffed inside.

"Hey, it looks like we might have some 'hawala' transactions, here," Kelly told the others.

"Hawala?" Jack asked, as he and Tom looked to Matt.

"Yeah, no banks involved, just informal payment transfers and people trusting one another," responded Matt.

"So we're talking some of that 'underground banking' stuff, huh?" clarified Jack.

"Something like that," Matt agreed. "Let's say a guy here takes cash into a local money mover – merchant, who is called a 'hawaladar,' and tells him that he wants the money transferred to another country. Our 'hawaladar' here notifies the 'hawaladar' in that other country of the payment and gives over verification information that will be used by the person picking up the money there. The 'hawaladar' then pays out the money in the local currency to the person there."

"H-m-m-m-m," Jack replied. "Doesn't leave much in the way of a paper trail for us to follow, huh?"

Matt nodded, "Certainly not like the traditional banking paper trail we're used to."

The agents secured the top drawer's contents as evidence and recorded the files onto the sheets identifying these items and others taken during the execution of the search warrant. The records from this file drawer and other items located during the search would be gone over in detail later by agents and financial analysts assigned to the FBI's Los Angeles Division.

Drawer number two was a bit more diverse. In it were folders marked "Grocery," "Restaurant," "Movie Theaters," "Strip Clubs," "Video Arcades," "Video Rentals," "Gold," "Jewelry," "Concerts," and "Fights." With the exception of the last two, all of the files were thick. The last two folders appeared to contain only a few newspaper clippings and magazine articles telling about how others had acted as promoters and used them to launder cash. Kelly guessed that promoting concerts and fights might be a couple of new high cash businesses Ayala and his associates were looking to get involved with in the future.

Drawer number three was filled with file folders relating to real estate. Included, were not only this apartment building and what appeared to be several others like it located in the greater Los Angeles area, but also a number of strip malls. For this building there was an individual folder for each apartment, and strangely enough, those records showed most, if not all of these apartments were leased to individuals. All Kelly could figure was that Ayala issued phony rental agreements in the names of ghost renters for the individual apartments in these places and used that as another way to launder. He had seen something similar in an East Coast organized crime case a couple of years earlier. There, the wiseguy created ghost renters and paid their "rents" with dirty cash. By doing this, he was in effect, taking the dirty money out of one pocket to pay the rents and laundering it back into the other pocket as legitimate income. This helped him justify his lifestyle and spending.

In addition to commingling and depositing any legitimate income received from the grocery store, restaurant, movie theaters, and other like businesses with dirty cash generated from the sex slave trafficking, Kelly suspected that Ayala also took additional dirty money and deposited it in the form of phony "rents." These "rents" would likely be received from not only the apartments in this building, and others like it, too, but also some of the businesses located in the numerous strip malls that they appeared to own.

Near the back of that same drawer were several additional file folders that did not appear to be tied to the bank accounts, the apartment buildings, the strip malls, or those numerous businesses already discovered.

Matt chuckled to himself as he opened one that was oddly enough marked, "*Fantom.*" There was nothing inside and he wondered if this was just a misspelling, and actually stood for "phantom," rather than "ghost" employees. He had certainly seen his share of OC and corruption cases where regular payments made to "no-show" or "ghost" employees had been integral parts of the laundering schemes carried out.

The bottom drawer of the file cabinet was stuck. Sanders gave it several kicks, but to no avail. Finally, Stacy grabbed a sledgehammer used by one of the teams to open a side door and gave it a whack. Whatever was holding it closed was jarred loose and they were able to slowly slide the heavy drawer open. Inside there were no files or records, but in their place was an adequate stash of revolvers, pistols, magazines, and plenty of ammunition.

Fortunately, for everyone, Luis Ayala must have also had trouble opening the drawer when they made their assault on the office, or things might have gone quite differently.

CHAPTER FORTY-THREE

Like many Indonesians, Sam went by the single name, adding "Smith" only after he arrived in Los Angeles. His menacing stare, pockmarked face, and jet-black hair, slicked back into a ponytail at his neck made him appear more intimidating than a person of his stature might normally warrant. Growing up in squalor on the streets of an infamous section of Jakarta, Sam was attracted to the underworld by an aura he saw surrounding several local hoods. They had it all – beautiful girls, expensive cars, plenty of money to flash around, and the knowledge that their mere presence could strike fear in faces of others. "What more could anybody want out of life," he thought.

Shortly after turning fourteen, Sam made it clear he was willing to do whatever it took to join them, and it didn't take long for him to get his chance. A ride by hit had been ordered on a local money laundering banker turned informant, and Sam, with the loan of a motorcycle and a gun, was given the opportunity to prove he had what it took to get the job done.

Wearing a bandana mask across his nose and mouth, dark sunglasses covering his steely eyes, and a multi-colored headband tied in the back, Sam watched and waited for the right moment as his vulnerable prey emerged from the bank and walked toward his car. Sam revved-up his motorcycle and raced in the direction of the his target, pausing only long enough to empty a full magazine of 9mm rounds into the banker before lifting the front wheel of the cycle high into the air and squealing away. Passersby screamed as blood splattered around and on them, and the victim dropped lifeless onto the pavement.

For his handiwork, the loan shark rewarded Sam with the motorcycle he rode, the pistol he used, and a 200,000 *rupiah* payday.

Sam later learned that he was selected because if he happened to get caught or killed in the act, there would be no ties leading authorities back to any of those for whom the banker had been laundering money. In addition, Sam knew none of the higher ups, and he was certainly not about to turn on the goons who hired him, that is, if he wanted a future in their organization.

That proved to be only the beginning of his life as a contract killer. Now in his late twenties, Sam could lay claim to more than thirty execution style murders and as a feared hit man was a respected member of an international crime syndicate.

CHAPTER FORTY-FOUR

The hour of three in the morning had come and gone before Sam returned to his luxury hotel suite in Makati. Known as the Wall Street of Manila, Makati's clogged roadways border an assortment of towering skyscrapers, high-rise apartments, hotels, restaurants, mega malls, and numerous gala nightclubs.

It was at a couple of those clubs that Sam and associates from his crime family and several other Asian organized crime syndicates had drank and played grab ass with hostesses and strippers throughout the evening. Two of the girls engaged in lap dancing at the last club made plays to go with Sam and one of the other guys as they prepared to leave.

This was the first time Sam had met the other guy, but one look at his left hand gave him a pretty good idea as to what had happened. The missing end joint of the pinkie had probably been severed with a silver knife and put into a small bottle of alcohol with the guy's name on it and sent to another member of that syndicate as means of repentance. Sam also suspected that the guy had likely withstood a hundred or more hours under the tattoo needle, getting a full body design. Both were characteristic of his membership in a nearby country's OC syndicate. He was sure the guy was tough. These guys were all tough.

Still trying, however, to recover from the wild ride a local honey had taken him on the previous night, Sam passed on the offer made by one of the lap dancers' to go back to his room for some added entertainment. The other guy was not about to miss out on such an opportunity though, and stepped up, leaving with one girl hanging onto each arm.

Sam immediately returned to his hotel suite where he didn't even take time to strip off his clothes before crashing into bed.

Two hours later the phone rang.

"Hello," Sam groggily grumbled.

"Sam, its Mitchell Kip."

Sam's head pounded as he squinted to focus his eyes on the illuminated clock sitting on the stand beside his bed. He finally made out that it was 5:30 A.M.

"Do you know what in the hell time it is, Mitchell?"

"In LA or Manila?" Kip responded.

"Here," Sam groused. "It's 5:30 in the morning!"

"Sorry about the wake-up call, but I thought I'd better get word to you, so you can let the others know. The FBI arrested Luis Ayala on Money Laundering and RICO."

"Who in the hell is RICO?"

"No, you mean what in the hell is RICO," responded Kip. "It's the Racketeer Influence Corrupt Organizations statute. The Fed's use it when they're trying to get heavy sentences and forfeiture for people and organizations like yours."

"Those ass holes," grunted Sam. "Where is Luis now?"

"With the marshals. I just left his arraignment. No bail for him yet, but I'm working on it."

"You do that, and let us know when he is out."

"I will," Kip assured him.

"Okay, now tell me what happened?" Sam asked.

"An LA apartment building was raided. Two guys were killed, and there was something about finding teenage girls and young women being held in there as sex slaves. It is getting a major play here, front-page headlines, and was the lead story on the news. It's everywhere. Why don't you turn on your TV and see if it made it onto the international news, there?"

Sam mumbled something that sounded to Mitchell like, "Okay, I will," and clicked on the remote.

"I'll see what else I can learn, and get back to you," Kip told him.

As Sam hung up the phone, the worldwide weather map came into full view on the screen. Shown were two whirling disks. One was located in the Philippine Sea off the northern coast of Taiwan and was currently categorized as a tropical storm with sustained winds of between forty and seventy-five miles per hour, while the other was a full blown Pacific typhoon spinning toward Guam.

The mention of typhoon in the same sentence with Guam brought back horrifying memories. On a previous trip to the Philippines, Sam was stranded for nearly a week at a luxury hotel in Guam's Tumon Bay after a super typhoon with winds registering nearly 240 miles an hour crashed onto the island.

Seemingly a magnet for natural disasters, Guam and its people were better prepared than most to deal with such a catastrophe, though. Sturdy cinderblock houses and solid concrete power poles stood across much of the island, but even those structures could be impacted by pounding surf and whirling winds exceeding two hundred miles per hour. Hospital and emergency centers were packed, and food and water were in short supply. The only power to most locations came from independent generators scattered throughout the island, and flights in and out of Guam's Won Pat International Airport were cancelled or delayed for several days.

Following the weather summary, Sam's attention was immediately focused on the headline for an upcoming story.

"Next – SEX SLAVES in LA," scrolled across the bottom of the screen.

While he waited for another series of commercials to finish, he sat up in bed and lit a cigarette.

When the newscast returned, the anchor led with, "Two men were killed, and numerous others were arrested as an international sex slave trafficking ring was uncovered in Los Angeles."

An on-the-scene female correspondent continued, "Agents of the FBI and the Bureau of Immigration and Customs Enforcement, and officers from the LAPD raided this Los Angeles apartment building."

With the apartment building as a backdrop, she interviewed media representatives from the various enforcement agencies. Footage showed agents and officers with raid jackets with the bold letters FBI, ICE, and LAPD emblazoned across the back.

Evidence team members carried out boxes and loaded them into waiting vans. There were glimpses of several of those arrested as they lowered their heads in attempts to hide their faces from the onslaught of reporters, with their bright lights and cameras.

Suddenly, Sam caught a glimpse of Luis as he was being herded out.

"You bastards!" Sam yelled.

This story had it all. Sex, international intrigue, a shootout with FBI agents, and all of it taking place in a West LA neighborhood.

When the story was finished, Sam contemplated his next move.

Although the newscast made no mention of the girl murdered in the park, he was now hesitant to return to LA, since the report did say that they found passports of young Asian girls during the raid. Sam could only assume that the murdered girl's passport was one of those. If so, it would be only a matter of time before the investigators identified her as having been one of those in the apartment building. Also, if one of the guys arrested gave up Sam as part of a deal to save his own skin, Sam wouldn't know until he arrived at the LAX terminal and his name came up as a hit on the computer when he tried to clear immigration. If that happened, he would be arrested on the spot.

His mind continued to race.

Even if the FBI or the LAPD found out about him and got an arrest warrant issued, Sam felt confident that as long as he remained in the Philippines or Indonesia he'd never get caught. After all, there had been warrants out for fugitives who had been eluding authorities and hiding on those islands for years. So long, in fact, that some of them were probably dead from old age by now and those looking for them did not even know it.

"Guess I should stay put for now, and wait until Mitchell Kip gets back with more details before contacting the others," Sam sighed to himself.

As he lay back down and tried to go back to sleep, the events of the early morning began weighing more heavily on his mind. Finally, after tossing and turning for more than an hour, Sam gave up on sleep and called for room service to bring him some breakfast and a pot of hot coffee.

While he sipped a second cup of coffee, the phone once again rang. He tossed the TV remote he had been using to channel surf during this ungodly hour back onto the nightstand and picked up the receiver.

"Hello," Sam answered.

"It's me again, Mitchell," came the response.

"The story was on the International news. I saw Luis trying to hide his face from the cameras, but I didn't see you," Sam replied.

"That's because I stayed away from the cameras," responded Kip, adding, "I didn't want to talk with them, yet. Timing isn't right."

What a switch, Sam thought to himself. Mitchell Kip sought high profile cases and all of the media attention and hype that went along with them. He was certainly never one to shy away from a camera or an interview.

"I've got more bad news, Sam. The FBI has already started freezing bank accounts and getting seizure orders issued on them and other property."

"What other property?"

"The apartment building they raided, three movie theaters and one restaurant, so far. And, I heard that shortly after Luis was arrested, the health department went in and padlocked the little grocery store down south."

"Wonder how many of the bank accounts they know about?" Sam asked.

"Don't know," replied Kip. "We also don't know what other businesses they might know about, either."

"You be sure to let Luis know what's been frozen or taken."

"Oh, I will," Kip assured him.

"Luis will have to get out and work on all of that. Any more word on when that will be?"

"None. The prosecutors were pushing for no bail and the Judge has already ordered his passport be turned in. I was optimistic about getting him out on bond when we talked earlier, but now that the Fed's have begun issuing seizure orders and tying Luis to those bank accounts and the properties, it could be tough, real tough. They're going to be making him out as a major launderer."

"Yeah," responded Sam somewhat pensively.

It would now be his job to let the others know what Mitchell Kip had said and get further direction.

CHAPTER FORTY-FIVE

"Angaur and Peleliu on the horizon," First Mate Tomy yelled, as these two southern islands located in the Palauan chain came into view.

"Get those whores locked-up and all hands to their posts," bellowed Captain Buruk.

"Aye, aye, Captain," Tomy responded, as he quickly headed down to the lower deck.

Looking and listening, Tomy heard cries coming from the sleeping quarters of several mates and headed in that direction. Inside the cabin were two girls lying on bunks and whimpering as one crewmember after another took turns forcing themselves onto each of them.

"Time to stop screwin'," the cruel first mate snickered. "Get 'em out of here. The captain wants all of you to your posts."

Tomy threw the girls their clothes and motioned for them to get back with the others.

With their heads lowered and bent over in pain, the girls complied and ran back to their steamy metal container box.

Buruk took the *Fantom* to an area just beyond a protected cove on the seven-mile long island of Peleliu. This was a point near where he had dropped anchor before, and because of the depth, the currents were not as strong as in many other locations around the island.

Since he anticipated bringing marijuana, or *udel* as the locals referred to it, from the island and loading it onto the *Fantom*, Buruk wanted the best possible water conditions available for running small craft to and from the island.

After taking one of their small boats to shore, the captain and his first mate walked inland to an area covered by dense, heavy vegetation. This was where the high-grade marijuana they were there to pick up was cultivated.

The man they were there to meet emerged from his compound. Buruk and Tomy knew him only as "*Smuuch*" or "Stonefish." Buruk assumed that the locally acquired name came not only from his genuine meanness, but also from his large mouth, and the ugly, warty look he shared with the deadly scorpion fish. Fortunately, however, his spine did not possess the stonefish's paralyzing venom.

Smuuch's imposing size and his nasty demeanor insured that most of the locals kept their distance from both him and his crop. He was, however, just the type of guy that Buruk got along with, and although the two of them never said much, their inherent abusive tactics and heartless attitudes toward others had helped establish a mutual respect from the beginning.

"Got message, you coming to pick up load," grunted Smuuch to Buruk, as he stopped to spit a stream of red *betelnut* juice through a wide gap in his front teeth.

"Yeah," Buruk nodded.

"*Udel* not ready," Smuuch replied, as he looked in the direction of his crop.

"When?" asked Buruk.

"One week," Smuuch answered.

"I will be back then," Buruk told him.

Smuuch nodded approvingly, and Buruk and Tomy turned away and left the site.

"Doesn't say much, huh?" Tomy snickered to Buruk.

"He's no bullshit, and that's the way I like it," Buruk answered.

"Right," Tomy responded in a condescending, more serious tone. "Since the pick up here will not be for another week, what will we do now, Captain?"

"We'll dock at Palau and wait 'til we can set up a meet to swap the whores for that marijuana coming in on the ship from Pohnpei," Buruk told him.

"The girls will stay with us until then?" said Tomy with sinister anticipation.

"Yes, you can still have your fun until we make the swap," Buruk assured him.

"Good," responded Tomy, as a menacing look and evil, scary smile spread across his face.

Walking along dirt roads and trails on an indirect route back to their small craft and onto the *Fantom*, Buruk and Tomy passed by an old airstrip and a cemetery with two crosses made of metal strips and rusted helmets hanging on them. They spotted a rusted out American tank with the white U.S. star still barely visible, and a corroded Japanese canon, all leftover from World War II.

Resting at the bottom of the waters surrounding the two hundred limestone Rock Islands and Palau are graveyards for over forty-eight Japanese ships sunk during air raids in 1944, as well as an occasional aircraft here and there. It all served as a reminder of the Battle of Peleliu, which was one of the bloodiest of the Pacific and accounted for some 9,800 American and 13,000 Japanese casualties.

Awaiting Captain Buruk upon his return to the *Fantom* was an urgent message and number scribbled on a pad for him to call Sam in Manila.

Tomy stood at the ship's controls and waited while the captain placed his call.

"Sam, this is Captain Buruk. I got your message."

"Yeah, Captain. Don't swap the whores for that marijuana coming in on the ship from Pohnpei until you hear from us," Sam replied.

"No problem," Buruk answered, adding, "That weed I was to pick up here from Smuuch isn't ready yet, either."

"Okay," Sam responded.

"What have you heard from the captain I was to meet for the bitch swap?" asked Buruk.

"Not much other than they were buttoning down for a typhoon," Sam answered.

"Any word from them, since?"

"No, nothing."

"Once contact is made with that ship, how long before the swap?" Buruk asked.

"It should not be long, Captain. We need that marijuana from both Smuuch and Pohnpei as soon as we can get it."

Buruk gave an approving grunt.

Sam then added, "What happens to those girls once they are swapped off your ship and onto the other one for the rest of their trip to the U.S. though, depends."

"Depends on what?" asked Buruk.

"When we can get things back up in Los Angeles."

"What things, Sam?"

"The girls back into business and Luis out of jail."

Before Sam could finish, Buruk interrupted, "Luis out of jail! What in hell are you talking about? What is going on?"

"The FBI arrested Luis and some others when they took down one of our operations there."

"Luis is my brother!" roared Buruk.

"Yeah, I know," Sam responded.

"What is he charged with?"

"Something called RICO, and also money laundering."

"When is Luis getting released?"

"Don't know, Captain. Our attorney is working on it. The Judge took Luis's passport and the prosecutors are going for no bail. They're also taking our money and property."

"Those bastards!" Buruk yelled into the phone, "What is this attorney doing?"

"Whatever he can," Sam assured him.

"Attorneys, they're all pussies," grumbled Buruk under his breath. Then, throwing the phone onto his captain's chair, he yelled loud enough for anyone within earshot of the bridge to hear, "They're all pussies!"

Even though Tomy had only heard one side of the conversation, he shook his head forcefully in agreement. Besides, the first mate rarely disagreed with his captain on anything, especially when his mood was like this.

Turning to Tomy, Captain Buruk bellowed, "Make way to the port!"

"Aye, aye Sir," the first mate boldly answered.

CHAPTER FORTY-SIX

On the morning following the successful raid on the West Los Angeles apartment building, Matt Kelly returned to LAX to begin his long trip across the Pacific.

With the exception of nearly being bumped off his flight on the Los Angeles to Honolulu leg, due to an overbooking, Kelly's arrival at Guam's Won Pat International Airport went about as smooth as could be expected. And, since he took a direct flight from Hawaii to Guam, his travel time was nearly half that experienced by Nick and Laynie on the Island Hopper.

He would check into his Tumon Bay hotel room and try to get a little sleep before placing a call to Nick, in Palau, and continuing their preparations for the FBI's upcoming Pacific Training Initiative.

CHAPTER FORTY-SEVEN

Known as a premier diving destination, Palau has some of the most beautiful and pristine waters to be found anywhere in the world, and Nick Costigan was not about to let his once in a lifetime opportunity there pass without soaking in every breathtaking minute. Sitting on a small deck outside his bungalow, he sipped a glass of fresh guava juice and watched the majestic sun as it gradually rose over the Pacific and these amazing Rock Islands of Palau. This unforgettable scene and the rhythmic sound of gentle waves washing up on the sandy beach and against the pilings of his thatched roof hut, could have easily made its way in or onto any popular travel log.

Returning to his desk inside the bungalow, Nick paused a few moments to take in the artisanship of a long, dark, hand-carved Palauan storyboard, entitled, "The Stone Money of Yap."

On the flight from Guam to Palau, the plane made a stop on the island of Yap, and while he was there, Nick noticed on display a giant, flat circular stone with a large hole cut in the center. Laynie told him that it was a piece of Yapese Stone Money, and went on to explain about the Yapese myth, and the many pre-1900, 250 mile journeys made from Palau to Yap by brave men in small canoes, carrying these quarried, hard, sparkling stones. The colorful, glistening limestone making up these rocks was unlike anything seen by them on Yap.

In this discussion of unusual types of money, Laynie had also mentioned that when they arrived on Palau, Nick would likely hear of Palauan money. She explained that these were valuable and highly regarded colorful, clay-like bead pieces known locally as *Udoud*, and were not given as gifts nor sold to foreigners. Strung onto necklaces, this money was tightly controlled by the clans and worn by clan women on special occasions.

The telephone rang. It was Matt.

"Nick, I made it, and am having coffee here in the RA with Ty."

SSRA Ty Wong had been the senior supervisory special agent for the FBI in the Guam Resident Agency (RA) for a little over a year now. Prior to that, he was assigned to the Law Enforcement Communication Arts Unit at the FBI Academy where he taught interviewing to the new agents and police media relations to the FBI National Academy officers. Both Matt and Nick had gotten to know him at Quantico.

"It looks like Ty's about gotten everything arranged here, and our attendees will start arriving day after tomorrow," Matt said.

"Did Ty tell you how close we came to having to delay or even cancel the training due to a typhoon that was passing through the region?" asked Nick.

"Yeah, he mentioned that. Fortunately, Guam escaped this one. I guess it gained a lot of strength over waters south of here, though, and he told me that it reportedly sank two ships."

Swashbuckler

"Any survivors?"

"Haven't heard."

"Laynie and I will finish here today, and we're scheduled out on the Air Mike flight tomorrow. You have a copy of our itinerary, right?"

"We have it," Matt assured Nick. "Ty and I will meet you and Laynie at Won Pat and from there the four of us can go to the Navy Club for their famous Mongolian stir fry."

"Sounds good. Laynie has already gotten me primed for that," Nick said.

"See you two then," Matt told him.

As Matt was about to hang up, Nick heard Ty flippantly remark, "Don't ruin our relations with the police there."

"Tell Ty that I promise not to set things back more than ten years," quipped Nick.

"I will," laughed Matt as the call between the two Quantico agents was concluded.

Now, turning his attention to the matters at hand, Nick opened his laptop and added the final touches to the remarks he would be making later that morning before the Palau Legislature. The topic:

"**Money Laundering and its Negative Impact on Today's Society**."

Most of the additions to be included had come by way of a telephone conversation Laynie had with Bill Robinson the previous evening. The Manila LEGAT had mentioned several additional terrorist organization money laundering examples from the Philippines that he thought might be good to pass along to the Palauans.

CHAPTER FORTY-EIGHT

Nick and Laynie completed their presentation before the Palau Legislature and from questions received and remarks made by the attendees at the conclusion, what they had said appeared to have been well received. Shortly thereafter, they returned to the ocean-side bungalows where, after changing, the two agents rushed to the beach to meet up with Assistant Police Commissioner Adze. He had promised them a tour of the Rock Islands.

Nick found Adze, named for an English word and traditional Palauan sharp bladed tool used in building canoes and houses, to be outgoing, intelligent, and likable. Standing nearly five feet ten, he had a medium build, dark copper skin, black hair, a bushy mustache, and red *betelnut* stained teeth. His career had taken him through all of the police ranks before finally reaching the position of assistant commissioner. And now, following the recent unexpected and tragic death of the former commissioner in an offshore accident, Adze was in the process of being confirmed as the commissioner of police for Palau.

"I think you got through to them in your presentation," remarked the assistant commissioner to Nick and Laynie as they boarded the white fiberglass police runabout. "Maybe now, those who have been questioning some of what we have been doing will begin to take the thought of dirty money coming into here a bit more seriously."

"I hope they do," Nick agreed.

Adze added, "If they don't, and the bad guys get a small island nation like ours dependant on their deposits, who knows what the end result might be."

Laynie nodded, "That's right."

"Well, at least you told it to 'em like it is," Adze said.

"We tried," Nick replied. "Maybe by the time your confirmation is completed, everyone will be onboard and convinced that the get tough approach is the only way to go."

"I hope so, and I know, I'm preaching to the choir, but somehow people have to get over this thinking that any money is good money. What do they think all of these terrorists, mafias, syndicates, cartels, and whatever else there is out there do with all that money they get."

"Bury it in their backyard?" cracked Laynie, in jest.

Adze laughed. "I see it is time for me to step off my soapbox and get us going. Are you two ready for the tour?" he asked.

The agents nodded and gave him a strong thumbs-up.

Powered by a 225 horsepower outboard motor, the closed bow runabout started out from the small dock. They took little time getting up to top speed, and as the trio skimmed across the surface of these arresting Pacific waters, Nick looked over to Laynie and smiled broadly.

She hadn't said much to him about what he was in for, but having been diving in Palau several times before, she knew he was in for a treat and would be seeing some sights of a lifetime. Nick would soon understand why these waters and this island chain is regarded by many as the diving capital of the world.

Racing through a narrow passageway running between two dark green, exotic flora-covered Rock Islands, Nick could not help wondering what would happen if another boat came speeding around the corner in the opposite direction. There would be very little time to adjust and not much room to pass. Fortunately, however, there were no other boats in the immediate area.

In addition to noticing the giant umbrella-like foliage covering the isles, he saw that the ocean had worn away the bases and carved many caves into the limestone and coral at the shoreline of these Rock Islands. Noting his interest in one of the nearby caves, Adze slowed the runabout and headed toward the broad opening. As they entered the semi-dark cavity, Adze flipped a switch on the control panel to turn on a bright spotlight located near the front of the bow. As they floated around the interior of the cave, Adze slowly directed the spotlight and their attention to different parts.

"Look," he said, pointing at the illuminated wall, "historic pictographs from one of our ancient civilizations."

"And, are those bats I see?" Nick asked, as he stared upward into the darkness.

"They are," Adze replied, "and you can see the stalactites, too."

"Yeah. This place is amazing," Nick responded.

"Well, time to move on," Adze said, as he turned up the power and headed out of the cave toward Ngeremdiu reef. There they all had a chance to snorkel and see how each could fit into a sunken Japanese Zero.

After snorkeling at the site of the Zero and trying out the cockpit's close quarters, they re-boarded the runabout, and

Adze took the two agents along a stretch of reef where there was a deep drop-off. Not being a certified diver, Nick snorkeled near the surface, spotting countless bright yellow butterflyfish; blue, green, and gold triggerfish; parrotfish; several manta rays, and a pair of sharks swimming in the crystal deep. He also caught glimpses of Laynie and Adze as they remained below, diving the wall.

Back to the surface and out of their dive and snorkel gear, the three once again boarded the runabout.

"The water was so clear and you could see so far down the wall," Nick remarked.

"The Blue Corner and Blue Holes are a couple of other great ones, too," Laynie added.

"Yeah, it just doesn't seem like there are ever enough hours in the day," Adze said, adding, "I would have also liked for Nick to have snorkeled in Jellyfish Lake and visited our only remaining *Bai*."

"Swim with jellyfish, huh?" Nick noted.

Detecting the uneasiness in his response, Laynie added, "Yeah, millions of them." She then paused to get a reaction, before laughing, "But, these won't sting you."

"That sounds better," Nick agreed. "And, what is a *Bai*?"

"It's a traditional village meeting house that looks like a huge A-frame with a thatched roof," Adze answered.

"Yeah, I'd like to see and do everything," Nick agreed. "I can't wait to get back here. This place is great!"

"The next time you come for a visit, we will take them all in," Adze assured him.

"Sounds good to me," Laynie said.

Although she had visited Palau numerous times in her work, the word "spectacular" still summed up her thoughts best, when she described this underwater paradise and its majestic Rock Islands.

With a vibrant and fiery sun starting its rapid descent amidst a cloud-filled sky, Adze looked to the agents and said, "I hate to have to do this, but it looks like its time we have to head back to Koror."

Nick and Laynie sighed appreciatively, acknowledging that time was fleeting and they understood the necessity to return, but wished this afternoon on these incredible waters didn't have to come to an end.

"I wonder if we'll catch sight of that 'green flash,' I've heard tales about when the sun sets?" Nick remarked with anxious anticipation.

Adze and Laynie looked at one another, raised their eyebrows, and shrugged.

"You never know...," Laynie teasingly smiled.

CHAPTER FORTY-NINE

"Bring on the girls and let's party!" Tomy yelled to a mate standing near one of the sweatbox containers.

Having dropped anchor near the port at Koror, Palau, or Belau as the locals referred to it, Captain Buruk and his pirate crew waited here for word to arrive from Sam that the syndicate was ready for them to meet with the other ship and complete the swap of the girls for the weed. In the meantime, there was an ample supply of booze and all of these girls aboard the *Fantom* to satisfy any urges or fantasies Tomy and the others might want fulfilled.

Shortly before the partying was to begin, Buruk boarded a small craft and headed for shore to link up with a syndicate guy known to him as Es. "*Es*", a *Bahasa Indonesian* word, which when translated means "ice" in English, got his nickname for the cold and calculating manner in which he carried out his sadistic specialties of booby-trapping, arson, and extortion bombings.

After leaving Indonesia for the Philippines, he had rapidly become one of the most notorious fugitives in all of the islands. When agents from the Philippine National Bureau of Investigation (NBI) began closing in, the syndicate secured a new passport for Es under a different name and linked him up with Captain Buruk. The pirate Captain moved quickly, and quietly slipped him aboard his ship and out of Manila late one night.

Buruk eventually dropped Es off on Peleliu and put him in touch with Smuuch, with whom he stayed for a few months before moving on to Koror and opening a small bar there.

While waiting in the port store for Es to show, Buruk picked up a newspaper and noticed a headline near the bottom of the first page.

"Dirty Money Flowing Into Belau?"

The story led with an interview of FBI Manila LEGAT Bill Robinson regarding terrorist financing in the Philippines and his concern that if anti-money laundering legislation and enforcement actions were not implemented immediately, the entire region might be in for a series of perilous consequences that could last for decades to come. The article concluded with a short paragraph telling about the arrival on Koror of FBI Agent Nick Costigan of the FBI Academy and FBI Pacific Liaison Agent Laynie Steele, and that the agents would be making a presentation before the Palau Legislature that same day.

While Buruk's attention remained focused on the story, Es came up from behind and surprised him with an Indonesian welcome.

"Captain, *Selamat datang!*" he said.

Buruk quickly acknowledged Es's presence, and then grunted as he pointed to the names of the two FBI agents.

"Do you know where they are staying?" the captain asked.

Es shook his head. "But, I find," he said.

"How long will it take?" shot back Buruk.

"Not long," Es nodded assuredly. "Let us go. We find."

Buruk quickly threw down some coins on the counter for the newspaper, and the two men rushed out of the store and got into Es's pickup truck. While driving to Es's bar, Buruk told him about his half brother's arrest in LA, and that the article in the newspaper had given him an idea.

"That is why I need to know where those two FBI bastards are staying," Buruk told Es.

When they arrived at the bar, Es called out for three young toughs who hung out there to come over to a corner table. There, he and Buruk showed the trio the newspaper article.

"Three hundred big ones for where these two are staying," Es told them, pointing at the paragraph with the agents' names identified, "Plus three hundred more if you can get me their room numbers, too," Buruk promised.

"No problem," responded their leader.

"These guys can find out anything about anybody around here," Es assured Buruk.

While Es and the captain remained at the bar in the company of Es's girlfriend, Rena, the trio fanned out around the island making their contacts.

It did not take long before they returned.

Standing inside the bar with the name of the resort and the bungalow numbers for each agent, the three anxiously awaited their payoff.

Buruk laid the money on the table and started counting, "One, two, three, four, five, and six."

The eyes of all three young toughs locked onto the six crisp, new one-hundred dollar bills.

Concerned that the captain might change his mind, each man quickly snatched up his share and ran out of the bar.

Captain Buruk and Es got up and left in the pickup truck, heading toward the resort so that Buruk could view the layout. In order to avoid having to pass through a secured gate entrance where cameras recorded all of those coming and going 24-7 and guards would ID them, they opted to park outside and away. From that point, they followed a high fence around the perimeter and into the water, where a low tide made it relatively easy to walk into the resort area. Inside, they studied the grounds and Es pointed out the two bungalows where the agents were staying.

"She in that one, and he over there," Es told Buruk.

When they finished casing the resort, Buruk and Es returned to the dock, where they took Buruk's boat back to the *Fantom*. There, the two of them would put the final touches on preparations they were completing for a very early morning surprise.

CHAPTER FIFTY

A cloud-darkened sky was shielding any light from the moon and stars, as an alarm sounded aboard the *Fantom*, and hoists began lifting the outer shells off the black, high-speed, open-hulled fastboats.

"Mates, board your craft," ordered Captain Buruk.

Dressed in camouflage fatigues and jungle boots, and carrying a collection of guns, knives, and grenades, these shock troops scrambled to the special craft.

When everyone was aboard, the captain motioned for Es to join him, and all of the sleek, high-speed boats were lowered into the calm Pacific. Buruk flashed a signal for the pirate crews to start the powerful engines. Soon, a second signal was given and the buccaneers and their crafts charged into the darkness.

Travel time to the resort took less than thirty minutes.

As the fastboats neared the shore, they slowed and the pirate crews cut the engines and dropped anchor. Jumping out of the open-hulled craft and into the waist-high water, Buruk and Tomy led their crews of swashbucklers onto the sandy beach.

Walking silently up a slight hill that led to a row of secluded bungalows, the captain raised his arm and the two crews stopped. Buruk directed Tomy and his crew to advance toward the bungalow occupied by Laynie, and signaled for the others to follow him to Nick Costigan's.

After waking up from a bad dream and having difficulty getting back to sleep, Laynie was sitting-up in bed finishing a re-assuring telephone call home. Since her cell phone was now turned off and charging, Laynie was calling from the phone sitting on the nightstand. She had been having trouble with her phone the previous afternoon and was in hopes that this temporary shutoff and re-charging would correct any problems.

"I can tell Ashley is sure missing her mommy," Clay told her.

"Give her a big hug and kiss for me, honey," she replied. "Just a few more days and I'll be home."

"Can't wait," Clay responded, with a note of anticipation, adding, "You know I love you and miss you very much."

"I love you, too," Laynie assured him. "Oh, before we hang up, let me give you the name of the place where I'm staying and the number."

"Just a minute," Clay replied. "I need to get a piece of paper and something to write with."

Suddenly, there was a noise. "Clay, I hear something outside my door," she whispered.

Before Clay could answer, she put down the receiver and started to get up.

Clay heard a loud noise that sounded like a door being kicked in, followed by a scream and what he assumed to be the receiver dropping onto the floor.

"Laynie! Laynie!" Clay repeatedly shouted into the receiver.

There was no response.

All he could hear in the background were men's voices yelling, and something mumbled that sounded like, "Shut up, you FBI bitch, or I kill you!"

"No! No!" she cried. There were more screams, and then nothing. The phone went dead.

In a nearby bungalow, Nick experienced a similar attack. He was asleep when his door was busted open and before he could do anything, Buruk and his armed men were on him, waving their guns and knives in his face.

With the razor sharp edge of a twelve-inch knife blade now resting firmly against Nick's throat, Buruk ordered, "Don't say a word or you're a dead man!"

Nick glared up into Buruk's threatening eyes.

Buruk lifted the knife away from Nick's throat long enough to cut the telephone line and then growled, "Get up."

As Nick slid out from under the sheet and put his feet onto the floor, he subtly reached for his GPS wristwatch as it lay on the nightstand. Buruk reacted immediately with a hard hit on the back of the agent's hand before Nick could push the "emergency" button, and brushed the watch onto the floor. Then, with the full force of the heel of his boot, the captain ground the watch into the thatched mat on which he was standing.

"Now stand!" ordered Buruk. "Put your pants and shirt on."

Nick complied.

"Give me your cell phone," snarled the captain.

Nick pulled the phone from his pocket and handed it to Buruk. After checking to insure that the phone was turned off, the captain hurled it against the wall.

"Tie his hands," he told one of his men.

The crewman yanked Nick's arms behind him and tied them tightly.

"Now, hold him up," the captain sadistically ordered.

Two of his men grabbed Nick by the arms.

As Nick stood with his hands tied behind him, Buruk pulled a pair of brass knuckles from his pocket and snarled, "You FBI bastards, this is for Luis!"

His first shots were to Nick's face. Blood spewed from his mouth and nose as the pirate captain's strikes jerked his head back and forth like a punching bag.

While the pummeling continued, Buruk cried out, "I'll show that pussy attorney. If he won't do anything, I will!"

Inflicting additional blows to Nick's rib cage and stomach, Buruk made a final thrust to the groin with his knee. Those holding Nick let go and he dropped with a thud onto a thatched floor mat next to the bed.

Each pirate then followed the captain's lead and gave the agent a final savage kick to the ribs and abdomen.

As Nick lay motionless on the floor, Buruk spit onto his face and snarled, "Mates, away with this FBI piece of shit."

Obeying the captain's orders, the swashbucklers grabbed the unconscious, bloodied agent and dragged him out of the bungalow and down onto the beach where a fastboat was sitting ready to take him to the *Fantom*.

Buruk and Es remained behind to finish the job they had started. They would follow along later.

CHAPTER FIFTY-ONE

"FBI," answered the night clerk on duty at the FBI's Honolulu Division headquarters.

"This is Clay Steele, Laynie's husband. I have to talk to Mr. Lange. This is an emergency!"

"Just a moment, Mr. Steele," the clerk responded, "He's at home. I'll patch you through to his house."

"This is Winston Lange," answered the SAC.

"Winston, this is Clay Steele. Something has happened to Laynie. I was just talking with her on the phone. She heard some kind of noise outside her room, and the next thing I heard was what sounded like some guys busting into her room and her screaming, 'No! No!' They said something that sounded to me like, 'Shut up you FBI bitch, or I'll kill you!' and then the line went dead."

"Where is she?" asked the SAC.

"Palau. I don't know which hotel."

"Let me call Ty Wong at the Guam RA, and I'll get back to you shortly. If she calls again, or you hear anything more, be sure to call me immediately."

"I will," he assured the SAC.

While he waited, Clay placed a call to Langley to let them know what had happened and ask them to start checking sources and contacts for any information.

"Hello, Ty. This is Winston. We've got an emergency."

Still half asleep, the Guam FBI Resident Agency supervisor sat up in bed and responded, "What is it boss?"

"I need you to get in touch with the Palau police. The details are sketchy, but we think something has happened to Laynie Steele. She was talking with her husband, Clay, a few minutes ago when he heard a scream and what sounded like men breaking into her room, then, the phone went dead. That's all we know."

"As soon as we hang up, I'll call Assistant Police Commissioner Adze and ask him to check it out," Ty assured his boss. "Laynie told me that they would be staying at a place the police had made reservations for them at."

Ty immediately jumped to his feet, and after grabbing the cell phone from his dresser began scrolling down the directory for Adze's number.

CHAPTER FIFTY-TWO

The sun was already beginning to rise over the majestic resort hotel by the time Assistant Police Commissioner Adze and a small group of his officers arrived at the front desk. They tried stiffing calls into both Laynie's and Nick's rooms, but the phones did not ring into either. They assumed the lines had been cut since the night clerk assisting them reported no other outage problems. The clerk told them he had been making calls into and receiving calls from rooms around the complex throughout the night.

Adze directed the night clerk to call all of the residents in the other bungalows. They were told to lock their doors, close the drapes, and remain in their rooms until they received a call telling them it was safe for them to come out. Due to a one-day delay in a tour group's arrival, occupancy at the resort on this night was much lower than normal, and as a result, the bungalows on either side of both Nick and Laynie had remained vacant.

While the Palau Police SWAT Team sat nervously awaiting the arrival of the additional officers needed to finish securing the perimeter, other officers were crawling up into areas where, with the use of binoculars, they could get a good view of the entrances leading into the two bungalows. Unfortunately, the drapes were pulled covering the windows, and the doors leading into both were closed. They could also not hear anything, but that was to be expected, considering the distance they were away.

Adze had also ordered the pre-positioning of two high-powered police runabouts equipped with scuba equipment and experienced dive officers onboard to be available for any intercepts that might be required on or below the surface.

When everyone was in position, Adze announced over a bullhorn, "This is Assistant Police Commissioner Adze of the Palau Police. Release the FBI agents and come out with your hands raised high over your head."

There was no response.

AC Adze repeated his order.

Again, there was no response.

One of the SWAT team members approached Laynie's bungalow, getting close enough to listen for any noise coming from inside. There was nothing. He moved back a safe distance and reported his findings to Adze. Another officer approached Nick's bungalow in the same manner and reported similar results.

"Take Laynie Steele's room first and then Nick Costigan's," Adze told the SWAT officers.

With protective vests on and weapons locked and loaded, the team hit Laynie's door with a heavy ram. It went down without a problem.

"No one here," the team leader radioed to the assistant commissioner.

"Hit the other one," Adze radioed back.

The team reassembled in preparation for the assault on Nick's bungalow just as they had for Laynie's. As the ram hit this door and it separated from the lock and hinges, nylon lines pulled pins from grenades left attached to each side of the frame.

The grenades exploded and shrapnel flew in all directions. Shrieks and cries of pain could be heard coming from the SWAT officers who had been standing in and around the doorway. As they fell slowly to the ground and floor, other officers moved forward providing additional cover. The remaining team members rushed to the aid of their fallen comrades.

From what they could see looking through gaping holes left by the grenade explosions, there was no sign of Nick or anyone else inside the bungalow.

"Call the hospital and tell them to get prepared. We are taking these men in!" Adze shouted.

Fellow officers and EMT's standing nearby did what they could to slow or stop the bleeding and quickly loaded the wounded into vehicles that had been brought forward for transport. There was no time to wait for additional medical help to arrive.

As soon as they removed these wounded officers and secured the area, the remaining officers cleared Laynie's room and what was left of Nick's for any additional booby traps, and continued their search for the two agents.

As his second in command was preparing to leave for the hospital with the remaining wounded officer, Adze instructed him, "Let me know what the doctors have to say as soon as they examine our men. And, on your way, call my wife and have her call these officers' wives and families so they can all meet you there."

"Will do," his number two yelled back.

Adze and his men carefully entered Nick's bungalow through the gaping hole left where a door and wall once stood, and gingerly searched for signs of additional booby traps. No more were found. Adze did, however, pick up a crushed GPS wristwatch that he assumed belonged to Nick and was probably taken off before he went to bed. It was lying on a small blood-soaked, thatched mat near the bed. The blood must have also been from Nick, since it was not near where any of his officers had been when the grenades exploded.

Their subsequent check of Laynie's room revealed no booby traps, but the room was in disarray, and a ripped sheet and blood splattered on the floor indicated there had likely been some kind of violent struggle carried out on or near the bed.

Adze's cell phone rang. "One has died, another is not expected to make it, and two are in very serious condition," his second in command reported. "We are working on getting the wounded out on flights to Guam."

The assistant commissioner's head dropped in disbelief and tears came to his eyes.

Adze dialed Ty Wong's number, and the secretary for the RA answered, "Hafa Adai, Guam FBI. May I help you?"

"This is Assistant Commissioner Adze," he replied in a solemn voice. "Is Ty there?"

"Just a moment please."

"It's Commissioner Adze and he sounds upset," the secretary told Ty as he stood drinking a cup of coffee with Matt and two other agents while they anxiously awaited news from Palau.

Rushing to his phone, Ty answered, "Commissioner, any news?"

"Too much bad news," a choked up Adze responded. "Your FBI agents are missing. We don't know if they are alive and missing, kidnapped, or dead, and I have one officer dead, another near death, and two more in very serious condition."

Ty slumped to his chair and shook his head in disbelief.

Rushing over to where he was sitting, Matt asked, "What's up, Ty? How are Nick and Laynie?"

"We don't know," Ty somberly responded. "It's unbelievable over there right now."

"Commissioner, I'm going to put Matt Kelly who works with Nick at the FBI Academy, and two agents from the RA who are also here with me on the line, if that's ok?"

"That will be ok," Adze answered.

"We're all on the line now," Ty replied. "Please tell them what you just told me, along with any additional details you can give us at this time."

"As I told Ty, we don't know much. There is no sign of your FBI agents. They are gone from their rooms and we have no idea if they are alive and missing, kidnapped, or dead, we just do not know. I have one officer dead, another near death, and two in very serious condition."

The four FBI agents just stared at one another not knowing what to say.

From there, Assistant Commissioner Adze presented a graphic picture of their early morning raid.

As Adze was about to conclude, Ty looked over to the two Guam agents listening in. "We'll have two agents...,"

Matt caught his eye. "No, make that three agents on the next flight out of here to Koror, and I'll be back in touch after I talk with the SAC in Honolulu. Is there anything you need?"

"Prayers," Adze replied, "Prayers. When I get a better handle on everything, I'll let you know what we'll need in the way of additional assistance."

As soon as they hung up, Ty called the SAC in Honolulu while Matt used another line to call Will Crane, his Quantico ITU chief.

When the call came into Honolulu, the SAC was waiting in his office with Clay Steele. After Ty finished relaying to SAC Lange what Adze told him, the SAC immediately passed that along to Clay, and placed a call to FBIHQ to report the solemn news.

Clay stood emotionally spent, exhausted, and angry. He had been through his share of stressful times in his life, but this was probably the greatest he had ever experienced. The thought of a violent attack having been carried out on the one he loved so very much, her horrifying screams, and her cries of "No! No!" What were they doing to her? Is she alive or is she dead? These thoughts and others kept reverberating through his head.

When word that two special agents were possibly kidnapped or killed arrived in the corridors of FBIHQ, the assistant director of the Criminal Division placed emergency calls to both the FBI director and his deputy director.

Next, the AD rushed to the Strategic Information Operations Center (SIOC). There, he ordered the immediate notification to all Field Offices and LEGATs around the world that two agents were missing in the Pacific and believed to be kidnapped or killed. At the same time, another call went out from the SIOC to the SAC of the Critical Incident Response Group (CIRG) for him to alert the hostage negotiators and the commander of the Hostage Rescue Team (HRT) to prepare for possible deployment.

With an open line now established between the FBI SIOC and both the Honolulu Division and the Palau Police Department, the FBI from Guam to Washington sat anxiously awaiting any word. In the meantime, the Honolulu SAC ordered his SWAT team to prepare to leave for Guam, and an Evidence Response Team (ERT) from Quantico received an alert from FBIHQ to pack-up and be ready to head for Palau on a two-hour notice.

When he returned home, Clay found his neighbor, Nana, still up and holding Ashley in her arms as the two of them rocked back and forth in Laynie's grandmother's antique wooden rocker.

Nana whispered, "She was crying for her mommy, so I picked her up out of bed and started rocking her about an hour ago. She finally fell back asleep."

Clay carefully lifted Ashley from Nana's arms and carried her into her bedroom.

When he walked back in, Nana was getting ready to return home.

"Thanks for your help," Clay told his neighbor, "I don't know what we'd do without you."

Nana's response was most comforting. "You just call me anytime, day or night and I'll come right over."

"Thanks. That's a relief," Clay responded. "If you can come back and stay with Ashley until we get back, I'll plan to leave for Palau on the next flight out."

"Sure," Nana nodded, "I'll be waiting for your call. I can stay with her for days or even weeks if you need me to."

With Nana gone and Ashley asleep, Clay called his CIA chief at Langley to bring her up to date on what he had been told and learn if she had heard anything.

"We just received a notice from the FBI SIOC, but that's all we have, Clay. We're continuing to check with NSA to see if they're picking up anything and I have already put out a notice to our people throughout the region. You know we'll get back to you as soon as we hear anything," she assured him.

"I plan to be on the next flight to Guam and on to Palau," he told her.

"Be careful," she said, "and let us know if you need anything."

CHAPTER FIFTY-THREE

The fastboats were all safely cradled aboard the *Fantom*, and the last of the specially constructed container outer shells was now being fastened down.

With tears streaming down her bruised cheeks and crusted blood collected around the numerous cuts and scratches sustained during the violent attack that had taken place at the hands of Tomy and his band of renegades, Laynie sat propped up against a rusting wall in one of the ship's old empty metal containers. She was mentally exhausted and physically beaten, battered, and bruised, but at least she was alive.

Lying unconscious on the floor next to her was Nick. The blood had stopped spewing from his nose and mouth, but the broken ribs and internal hemorrhaging resulting from the brutalizing punches and kicks he took from Buruk, Es, and the others remained. Laynie could see he was still breathing, but that was about all she could tell of his condition.

On the bridge, Captain Buruk finished scrolling down the directory on his cell phone and pressed the call button.

"Captain," Sam answered.

"I see your Caller ID is working," Buruk responded.

"It is," Sam assured him, adding, "Before I forget, they wanted me to check and make sure that armor plated SUV you picked up on Flores was turned over to the man in the southern Philippines?"

"Yeah, I made the drop," confirmed Buruk.

"I will pass that along," Sam told the captain. "And, I still haven't heard anything more about your linking up with that other boat to swap the whores and the pot."

"No, no, that is not what this call is about."

"Then, what is it, Captain?" questioned Sam.

"I needed to let you to know that I DID IT!"

Not understanding what Buruk was talking about, Sam asked, "What did you do, Captain?"

"Remember, you said that pussy lawyer in Los Angeles couldn't do anything to get Luis released."

"Yeah, I remember," Sam answered.

"Well, I did something," bragged Buruk.

"What?"

"I got myself two FBI agents."

"You got what!" exclaimed Sam.

"Two FBI agents," boasted Buruk. "Two for one."

"Two for one?"

"Yeah, you call those FBI bastards and tell them if they want to see their two agents alive, they have to release Luis."

"Did the bosses approve this?" Sam asked.

"No. They don't know anything about it, so don't you say anything to them."

Pausing a moment before responding, Sam swallowed and hesitatingly responded, "Ok-a-a-ay?"

"Good," Buruk answered.

"But who are they, Captain?"

Pulling the newspaper article he had saved from his pocket, Buruk read the names to Sam, "Nick Costigan and Laynie Steele. You tell the FBI we have both of them."

"Uh-huh," Sam responded, as he held the phone between his ear and shoulder, and wrote the names on a pad.

"Let me know what they say."

"Just a minute, Captain. I am still writing." Sam paused, "Now, what is that again you want me to tell them?"

"You tell the FBI that if they ever want to see these two agents alive, they will fly Luis to Manila and release him."

"Anything else?" Sam asked.

"This is no bullshit, Sam," grumbled Buruk. "If Luis is not released, these FBI agents can kiss their asses good-bye. I will personally insure that both of them are killed. The guy is almost dead already, anyway."

Noting Buruk's furious tone, Sam vowed, "Don't worry, Captain. I will make the call and tell 'em as soon as we hang up."

Sam opened the telephone book and jotted down the number for the American Embassy. They should be able to connect him to the FBI, he thought.

Since making such an ominous call from his own cell phone was out of the question, and he was unsure about the tracing and tracking capabilities of law enforcement when "throwaway" cell phones were used, Sam left his Makati hotel room in search of a phone booth. There were pay telephones in the hotel lobby, but a call from there could be easily traced to where he was staying, so he walked to a nearby busy shopping mall where he knew several pay phones were located and he could blend in with the crowd.

Sam dialed the number.

"American Embassy," answered the operator.

"I want to talk to the FBI," Sam replied.

The phone rang several times before Bill Robinson could get back to his desk and pick up the receiver.

"Legal Attaché," answered Robinson.

His voice quivering, Sam nervously responded, "Are you FBI?"

Robinson replied, "Yes, I am the FBI LEGAT here in Manila."

"Listen to me closely," Sam said. "We have two of your FBI agents and they will die if you do not free Luis Ayala."

Quickly recalling several tips from a presentation made at a recent training seminar, Robinson knew that he should attempt to calm the caller and keep him on the line as long as possible. He would also attempt to determine the condition of the agents and listen to the demands made by their captors, but not give in.

LEGAT Robinson clicked on the phone recorder, as he took yet another look at the top priority message sitting on his blotter, and coolly responded, "Say that again. I don't understand what you are talking about?"

Sounding frustrated, but expressing himself a bit more forcefully this time, the voice on the other end of the line repeated, "I told you, we have two of your FBI agents and they will die if you do not free Luis Ayala and fly him to Manila."

"Which agents?" asked the LEGAT.

Sam looked at the piece of paper. "Their names are Nick Costigan and Laynie Steele. That is all for now. I am hanging up."

"Wait, wait," Bill Robinson said. "Where is Luis, now?"

"Los Angeles. The FBI has him there."

"How do you know?" Robinson asked.

"I saw him on television. I am hanging up."

"Wait, wait," LEGAT Robinson again responded. "Let me talk to the agents."

"No!"

"How do I know you have them and that they are alive?"

Sam paused, his voice still quivering as he curtly said, "You have to trust me. I told you they are both alive. That is all for now."

"Where are the agents?"

"Later," Sam replied.

"How is the exchange to be made?"

There was no response.

Robinson followed with, "How do I contact you?"

"We will call you," Sam responded. "You just make sure Luis is freed and brought to Manila."

Then "Click." The phone went dead.

Robinson hit the replay button. Fortunately, everything worked as it was supposed to, and he was able to get a good quality audible recording. Now, he had to make the grim call to FBI Headquarters reporting that two special agents were being held hostage or, even worse, possibly already dead.

A hushed uneasiness hung over the SIOC as word of the fate of the two missing agents spread. Solving kidnappings and returning victims safely to their families was something the FBI had built its reputation on, and who should be better to handle it, but. . . these were two of their own and would they be successful in getting them returned unharmed? Who would be so brazen?

Calls went out for any available CIRG hostage negotiators to pack their bags and equipment, and standby. A subsequent contact made with FBI air force operations revealed that all of the Bureau aircraft designed to fly nearly half-way around the world were either already committed on other missions or in required maintenance. As a result, it was decided that the most expedient option to get the special agent negotiators, to Manila, would be for them to fly commercial. As soon as reservations could be confirmed, they would depart Quantico for Dulles Airport.

The FBI's number two man was already on the phone with the assistant director of the Los Angeles Field Division. Although thousands of cases are ongoing in the LA Division at any one time, the sex slave trafficking case had sparked both national and international media attention and as such, both the AD and Criminal Division SAC there had been receiving regular status updates.

The LA assistant director quickly brought the FBI deputy director up to date on the arrest of Luis Ayala, his ties to suspected money laundering, and the raid on the apartment building where the sex slave trafficking took place.

Swashbuckler

In the meantime, Jack Stacy received an urgent page to report to the assistant director's office. When the AD saw him waiting outside the open double doors, he motioned for Jack to come in.

"That was the deputy director I was just on the phone with," he told Stacy. "Two of our agents have been kidnapped and are being held hostage. They're demanding that Luis Ayala be released and flown to Manila for the exchange."

"So that's what this is about?" Stacy asked.

The Los Angeles assistant director nodded.

"You're sure this Luis Ayala they're talking about is the guy we arrested?" a surprised Jack Stacy replied.

"The very same," confirmed the AD.

"Who are the agents?" asked Stacy.

"Laynie Steele, our Pacific Liaison Agent, and Nick Costigan out of the Academy."

"I don't know Laynie, but Nick Costigan works with an agent named Matt Kelly who was just out here helping us on this case. Kelly told me he was on his way to meet up with Costigan in Guam. Some training gig they were doing out there. Any idea who has them?"

"None. The call for the swap went to LEGAT Manila."

"Were they snatched out of the Philippines?" Stacy asked.

"No, they were working in Palau," the AD responded. "Whoever did this, took them from their rooms. When the Palauan police went in, the agents were gone but there was blood in their rooms and one of the rooms was booby-trapped."

"Booby-trapped?" questioned Stacy.

"Yeah, grenades exploded when the police went in," the AD solemnly replied. "One officer is dead, another is fighting for his life, and two others are in serious condition."

Visibly upset and shaking his head as he left the office, Stacy told the AD, "I'm on my way to the AUSA's. I'll let you know as soon as we catch up with Mitchell Kip and learn what he's willing to give us on his scumbag client."

Cheryl Rathmann had been assigned as the Assistant United States Attorney on this case. In addition to being a tough, type-A, tenacious attorney, she was also a gifted and talented black belt in karate, and her first successful prosecution in the Central District of California was a BR note job on which Jack Stacy was the case agent. That was nearly ten years ago, and since that time, the two of them had teamed up on many more cases. Most ended in convictions, but there were a couple of acquittals mixed in, along with a hung jury. That hung jury was in a public corruption case on a "special" Jack had been assigned to, and it remained stuck in Stacy's craw to this day. There was no question in his mind that the corrupt politician was guilty of everything charged, and probably much more, but. . . .

The call from Cheryl Rathmann to Mitchell Kip's office revealed little. After the most recent bail hearing for Luis Ayala had once again failed to gain his release, defense attorney Kip caught a night flight to San Francisco where he was lead counsel for a well-known celebrity in a bungled murder-for-hire case that had gained nationwide attention in the tabloids.

AUSA Rathmann left a message with Kip's secretary for him to call her as soon as he was out of court.

"This is extremely important!" she emphasized.

CHAPTER FIFTY-FOUR

Word of one dead police officer, another near death, two officers in serious condition, and two missing FBI agents spread quickly through the close-knit clans of the Palauan community.

As officers and families sat anxiously at the hospital awaiting condition updates, word arrived that a couple of local snitches had been asking questions the day before regarding where the agents were staying. With this information, two officers jumped up and rushed out of the hospital and into their patrol truck. It did not take long for them to come up with one of the names mentioned.

"You slimeball!" the senior patrol officer told the surprised snitch as he threw him up against the wall and pulled his arm up behind him into the small of his back.

Grimacing in pain, the snitch responded, "What's up?"

Continuing to put pressure on his arm, the officer now grabbed the snitch by the hair with his other hand and shoved his face further up against the wall. "Did somebody ask you to get the room numbers of two FBI agents?"

"Why man? Sure. They paid us two big ones apiece to come up with where those FBI agents were staying."

"You came up with what they wanted?"

"Yeah," he nodded as best he could. "A couple of calls, a stop here and there, and that was it. Easiest two hundred dollars I ever made."

"Who paid you?"

"I don't remember," smirked the snitch.

The officer gave him a knee and put more pressure on his arm as he pulled his head farther back.

The snitch cried out in pain.

"You had better start remembering, and quick," the officer told him. "We have a police officer dead and others fighting for their lives because of what you did and if you don't tell me what I want to know, well. . . ."

Before the officer could finish, the snitch frantically interrupted, "I don't know nothin' about any cops, I swear! I swear!"

"Who paid you?" the officer demanded.

"Some guy with Es, at his bar."

Jerking his head back further, "Who?"

"Just some guy. I don't know his name. He didn't say."

"Is he from around here?"

"Not that I know of. I never seen him before."

"Anybody else there other than you three guys?"

"Rena," the snitch answered.

"The one that's Es's girlfriend?"

"Yeah, that Rena."

The officer eased up a little on the pressure, "You'd better be telling me the truth, or I'll be back and finish the job."

"I swear, that's the truth," the terrified snitch responded. "I don't know who he is."

The officer slowly finished releasing his hold and the snitch dropped to his knees in relief.

"On to Es's," he told the other officer.

Returning to the patrol pickup the two police officers sped away to the small bar to follow-up on what they had just learned.

"Police, open up!" the senior officer yelled as he pounded on the locked door leading into the bar and the two rooms set aside in the back where Es lived with his girlfriend, Rena. Having broken up domestic fights there on more than one occasion, both officers were well acquainted with the pair.

When there was no response, the officer pounded even more forcefully and repeated his command again. This time, Rena slowly slid the latch to the side and opened the door.

"Where is he?" demanded the officer.

Rena gave them a wiseass look, before asking, "Who?"

"Es!" growled the patrol officer's partner. "Who do you think we're talking about?"

Noting their no bullshit attitude, Rena said, "I don't know. He didn't come back last night."

"Is he with that guy he was with yesterday afternoon?" asked the senior officer.

"I don't know," she scowled, and started walking away.

Reaching out and grabbing her by the shoulder, the officer spun Rena around.

"Listen to me very closely," he yelled, pointing his finger as he jumped into her face. "You had better start knowing something, or else. At this very moment, we have a police officer dead and others fighting for their lives in the hospital, and Es and this other guy are involved. Now, I want some answers and I want them quick! Do you understand?"

Stunned at the news, Rena nodded.

"Good. Now start talking. Who is that guy, anyway?"

Her tone suddenly changed and she began to cry, "All I know is that Es called him captain."

"Why did Es and this guy he called captain want to find out where the FBI agents were staying?"

"It was the captain that wanted to know. He said something about the FBI having his half-brother and if the lawyers could not do anything about it, he would. That's all I heard, I swear. I don't know anything more."

Repeating his earlier demand, the officer once again asked her, "Where is Es?"

"Like I told you before, I don't know," she cried. "After those men returned with information about where the FBI agents were staying, Es left with the captain and I haven't seen him since."

Putting his hands on her shoulders and straightening her up so he could look her squarely in the eyes, the officer told her, "As soon as Es returns, I want to know. Do you understand?"

Still sobbing, with her head dropping downward, she nodded, "Okay, okay. I will call you."

Both officers hurried out of the bar and back into the patrol pickup where AC Adze was called and told what had been learned regarding Es and the captain.

Since his days of patrolling the local watering holes and breaking up late night fights were long past, the assistant commissioner knew little about Es other than he owned a small bar by that same name in Koror.

As soon as he hung up with his patrol officer, Adze called the SIOC at FBI Headquarters, who, in turn, put him through to both the Honolulu Division, and Ty Wong at the Guam Resident Agency, so they could all receive his report simultaneously.

"I have just learned from one of our officers that a local bar owner named Es and a stranger identified only as the captain paid three snitches six hundred dollars for the location and room numbers of your two agents," Adze told all of those on the line.

"Do we know why he wanted to know where the agents were staying?" asked the SIOC supervisor.

"There was something about the FBI holding the half-brother of this man called captain, and that if the lawyers couldn't do anything about it, he would."

"Your officers talked with these three men?"

"Only one of them."

"Did the officers talk with Es?"

"No. They talked with his girlfriend, Rena. It was from her we learned about this guy they call captain, and that the FBI is holding his half-brother."

"Did she say where Es is now?"

"She didn't know. She said the last time she saw him he was leaving with the captain. That was when those two left the bar in his truck to go see where the agents were staying."

"Any sign of his truck?"

"None yet, since we've just learned about Es being involved, but my officers will find it."

"What about this guy they call captain. Any idea who he is?"

"None. I don't think he's from here, though," replied Adze. "The officers said that neither the girlfriend nor the snitch knew who he was, and no larger than our community is, if he came from Palau, chances are good that at least one of them would have seen him before."

"Please let us know as soon as any additional information comes to light," requested the assistant director. "We have the SIOC here at FBIHQ operating 24-7, so, should you need anything, and I sincerely mean anything, there will be people available for call out anytime of the day or night. We can respond from here, Honolulu, Guam, anywhere. You just let us know."

"I appreciate that and I will call," Adze assured everyone. "We're continuing our search of the islands for Laynie and Nick, and now we'll also be looking for any sign of Es and his truck, and this guy they call captain. We won't stop until we find them."

After Adze hung up, the Criminal Division AD had Ty Wong and SAC Lange remain on the line.

"Ty, have your agents arrived in Palau to assess the situation, yet?"

"Not yet. Their flight was delayed because of mechanical problems, but they should be in route, shortly," he answered. "Nothing goes straight through to there. I'll let you know as soon as they've had a chance to take a look."

"You do that, and Winston, is your SWAT Team in Guam?"

"Not yet. They are due to leave on a flight from Hickam within the hour and will be available for call out anywhere in the territory by the RA."

"I want you to also send your hostage negotiator to Guam in case calls should come into there," the AD told SAC Lange. "CIRG negotiators have been called out to assist in Manila."

"Our hostage negotiator is on his way there, as we speak," Lange told the AD.

In the meantime, Air Force C-17's were already on the ground at Andrews Air Force Base, just outside Washington, D.C., awaiting the arrival of Cole Dawson and his FBI Hostage Rescue Team.

Orders calling for the deployment of HRT arrived from the special agent-in-charge of the Critical Incident Response Group just as this section of the HRT was returning from a training exercise conducted aboard ships in mothball at the James River ghost fleet.

Because time was critical, these Quantico based FBI agent operators wasted no time in packing their weapons, ammunition, 75-pound equipment bags, and other essentials aboard the heavy-duty vehicles and moving out to Andrews. Cell phone calls to their families would have to suffice for now, as there was no time to return home before departure.

Also arriving at Andrews within the hour, would be the specially equipped HRT helicopters for use in the operation. These choppers, along with their agent pilots would soon be loaded onto arriving Air Force cargo aircraft for their transport to Andersen AFB, in Guam.

When everyone was onboard the aircraft and in the air, Commander Dawson, his HRT operators, and the chopper pilots would all try to get some sleep as they flew across the continental United States and much of the vast Pacific.

CHAPTER FIFTY-FIVE

Onboard the *Fantom*, rays of sunlight beamed through cracks and small holes in the rusting framework of the old metal container housing Nick Costigan and Laynie Steele. Slowly awakening to his surroundings, Nick caught a glimpse of Laynie's silhouette as he opened his eyes and gazed upward.

"Where am I?" Nick asked.

The sound of his voice brought both a sense of relief and an immediate smile to Laynie's face. "We're onboard a ship," she answered.

"A ship," Nick responded. "Why?"

"No idea," Laynie answered. "Do you remember anything about what happened in your room on Palau, Nick?"

He grimaced in pain as he tried shaking his head, "No, not much."

Taking a deep breath to help clear her mind before starting, Laynie said, "All I can tell you is what happened to me. Early in the morning, while I was on the phone with Clay, I heard a noise outside my room. Before I could get to my pistol, a group of guys wearing camouflage fatigues and carrying guns and knives busted into my room and threw me onto the bed. We fought, and just as it looked as though they were going to do me in, the leader told the others to stop. He said something about needing to keep me alive for now, anyway. When he said that, the others tied my hands and feet, put a blindfold over my eyes, and dragged me out of the room and onto the beach. From there they put me on some kind of speedboat, then onto this ship, and finally threw me into this box. You were already in here lying on the floor unconscious by that time."

"This makes no sense," Nick responded, and Laynie agreed.

"What's with this ship?" he asked.

"I only got a brief glimpse of it when they dragged me on, but almost everything I saw is painted black, and there seemed to be a dozen or more containers like this one onboard."

Suddenly, the agents heard a commotion outside. As the two of them listened more closely, they heard several men boisterously laughing and what sounded like the voice of a teenage girl or young woman crying out "No, No," and pleading with them.

"You thinking what I am?" whispered Nick to Laynie.

"That's sure what it sounds like," she answered. "I've been hearing cries like that since they locked us in here."

Shortly thereafter, they heard the sound of a metal door opening and closing. That was followed closely by a series of faint, fading muffled screams, and then there was nothing.

CHAPTER FIFTY-SIX

LEGAT Robinson's office went from a nighttime on-call status to a manned 24/7 mode the instant the caller hung up demanding Luis Ayala's release in exchange for Laynie and Nick.

First, he called the FBI SIOC and others to make initial notifications, and then called the FBI legal attachés assigned to Bangkok and Tokyo. Both of those LEGAT's immediately set aside what they were doing and made reservations to board the next available flights to Manila. They would arrive shortly.

Also answering the call for help was Robinson's good friend, Agent Ricardo Perez of the Philippine National Bureau of Investigation. Six months earlier, Perez and the LEGAT received commendations for the work they did in securing the successful release of a half dozen American tourists kidnapped by terrorists in the southern Philippines.

Within an hour of Robinson's call, Perez was in the FBI legal attaché's office offering any assistance he and the NBI could provide.

LEGAT Robinson identified several immediate needs, and Agent Perez immediately responded with additional agents and tech support.

With telephone tracing devices and additional recorders now hooked up, NBI Agents set out to put the squeeze on local informants and canvass the area around where the call originated.

Since there was only the one brief call, they had little to go on, other than the caller ID information showing it came from a pay telephone in one of central Makati's large shopping malls. Agents processed that phone for prints and searched for any other evidence, but being a pay phone in a busy mall with literally thousands of people walking around shopping, the chances for a positive hit would be slim. Besides, the person they were looking for probably wore latex gloves when he made the call, and then slipped his hands into his pockets and walked away when he was done.

CHAPTER FIFTY-SEVEN

Standing on the bridge aboard the *Fantom*, pirate Captain Buruk placed another call to Manila.

"Sam, I think it's time for us to find out when Luis will be arriving in Manila."

"Yeah, they've had time to get word to LA," Sam agreed. "I'll make the call and let you know what they say."

"I will be waiting," Buruk replied, and he clicked off the call.

Wary that the police might be watching the pay phone he used before, Sam set out in the opposite direction where he found a smaller shopping mall with pay phones.

When the telephone rang in the LEGAT office from a number he did not recognize, Bill Robinson told NBI Agent Ricardo Perez and the two of them sprung into action. They stood anxiously awaiting a signal from the tech agent assisting that both the recorder and the trace were ready, before picking up the receiver.

Robinson would have preferred that an FBI agent hostage negotiator handle the call, but since there were none available, as they were still en route to Manila, the LEGAT answered the phone.

"Legal Attaché. May I help you?"

Sam had already started the chronograph on his watch so he would know exactly how long the call was taking.

"When will Luis Ayala be arriving in Manila?" Sam demanded.

"I don't have that information, yet," Robinson answered. "I want to talk to our agents. Put them on the phone."

"They are not here with me."

"How do I know you have them and that they're alive?"

"You will see them once we have Luis," Sam curtly replied.

Wanting to keep the caller on the line as long as possible for NBI agents to respond, Robinson explained, "You have to understand, requests like this take time. With us being here in Manila and him in the United States, we have time changes to deal with when trying to get in touch with each other. There are attorneys involved in both Los Angeles and Washington. We have. . . ."

Before the LEGAT could say another word, Sam interrupted. "Stop! Enough of your bullshit! You tell them we want Luis in Manila and want him here now. Do you understand?"

There was a pause before Robinson calmly continued. "I understand what you are saying, but this will take time. As I was saying before, we have. . . ."

Again, before Robinson could say anything additional, Sam cut him off. "There is no more time. We will be calling again, and the next time you had better have Luis on a plane to Manila and telling us when he will be arriving, or else."

"Wait, wait," Robinson said. "I told you, I want to talk with our agents."

Seeing a uniformed mall security officer walking in his direction, Sam looked down at his chronograph. Noting the seconds ticking away, he feared that the police might already be responding and immediately hung up the pay phone receiver and quickly slipped away.

"Got a location on that trap and trace," Perez told Robinson. "It was made from a pay phone in a Makati mall, not far from where the first call was made. We're responding now. We'll process the phone and find out if security had one of the mall's surveillance cameras on it."

Safely back in his hotel room, Sam scrolled to Buruk's number on his cell phone and pressed the call button.

"Captain, the FBI is playing games with us. All they gave me was a line of bullshit."

"You told them we are serious and will kill these FBI agents if they do not do what we say, didn't you?"

"Yeah, I told 'em."

"And nothing?"

"Nothing but bullshit," Sam responded. "The call ended with him wanting to talk to the agents."

Buruk stood on the bridge of the *Fantom* seething.

"Give me the number for that bastard," the captain said.

Sam read it to him.

Buruk clicked off his call with Sam and immediately took an international "throwaway" cell phone that he used when wanting to remain anonymous, from a nearby drawer. After clicking it on, he dialed the American Embassy in Manila.

"Another call coming in this soon?" questioned Robinson. "What's going on?"

Agent Perez shrugged and gave LEGAT Robinson the signal to pick up the phone.

"Legal Attaché. May I help you?" Robinson answered.

"You bastards!" Buruk replied.

This being a voice Robinson had not heard before, he asked, "What?"

"You listen and you listen closely," Buruk yelled into the phone, "If Luis is not released, these FBI agents of yours can kiss their asses good-bye. I will kill both of them. The guy is almost dead already, and the bitch, well, she will be too, once we start doing her. When she can't take it anymore, we'll feed her to the sharks," he sadistically chuckled.

"You'll have to let me talk to them before I can do anything," the LEGAT responded.

Growing more indignant by the second, the enraged captain motioned for Tomy and two mates standing nearby to follow. The four of them rushed to where the two agents were confined. Once there, the mates threw open the heavy door and stood guard over Laynie and Nick as the two sat stunned in the darkened container.

Waving the cell phone in front of the agents, Buruk demanded, "Tell them who you are!"

Puzzled, Nick looked up at Buruk and asked, "What?"

Buruk screamed, "I said, tell them who you are!"

"Tell who?" Laynie questioned.

"The FBI!" answered Buruk, and stuck the phone in front of her face.

Laynie started talking very fast. "This is Laynie Steele and we're locked in one of about a dozen containers aboard a black ship."

Before she could say more, Buruk yanked the phone back. "Stop! Stop!" he yelled, and slapped her across the face. "I told you to tell them who you are. No more!"

"Okay, you heard them," Buruk told Robinson.

"I heard only one voice," Robinson replied.

"That's all you are getting for now," Buruk bellowed.

In an attempt to keep the caller on the line, LEGAT Robinson tried to respond, but before he could get more than a couple of words out, Buruk cut him off.

"Next time we call, you'd better have Luis on his way to Manila," Buruk ordered. "This is no bullshit!" he ranted, before clicking off the call and turning off the phone.

"Anything on this last call?" Robinson yelled back to Perez.

"We got a number, but no subscriber information. It was not from here," Perez replied. "The rest is going to have to come from your people in Washington."

Just as he had done with Perez in getting a location on the local call received less than an hour earlier, this time Robinson immediately called the SIOC, and asked, "Any luck on getting a fix on where the call we just received came from?"

The SIOC agent hesitated while he quickly reviewed data he received. "Got it!" he exclaimed. "The coordinates appear to be in an area of water bordering a group of small islands off the coast of Palau."

"Sounds like the Rock Islands," said Robinson. "There are about two hundred of them in a twenty-five mile stretch between Koror and Peleliu. Most are uninhabited, with heavy vegetation and some caves."

"Tough place to find people in, huh?"

"Can be," Robinson confirmed.

"Bill, we're requesting satellite coverage over that entire area and should start getting photos back before long. I'll be back with you as soon as they start coming in," the SIOC agent supervisor assured him.

Before hanging up, Robinson replayed the recordings from those two calls recently received from the agents' captors for all in the SIOC to hear.

CHAPTER FIFTY-EIGHT

With Clay Steele's flight from Honolulu arriving at Guam's Won Pat International Airport nearly thirty minutes early, he was able to make a quick transfer and board a much earlier scheduled connecting flight to Palau that was still on the ground due to an extended mechanical delay. That holdup had gone on for many hours, and with the new part finally received from Tokyo and the repair now completed, the flight would lift off shortly.

Dave Adams, one of the two senior agents from the Guam Resident Agency assisting in the crisis was surprised to see Clay rushing onto the plane. Dave first met Clay while in Honolulu for a month long trial earlier in the year. Laynie had invited him over to their condo for dinner on two Friday evenings in a row, and the three of them went diving off the coast of Oahu the following Saturday afternoons.

After their flight was in the air and the seat belt light went off, Dave walked forward to where Clay was sitting and tapped him on the shoulder.

Clay looked up and smiled, "Dave Adams, its been a while," he remarked and shook his hand.

Dave knelt down in the aisle beside Clay's seat. "I'm so sorry to hear about Laynie and Nick, but we'll get them back."

"Yes, we definitely will," Clay nodded, giving a strong, affirmative response.

"For your info, another agent from Guam is in the back with me and the guy across the aisle and a couple of rows behind you is out of Quantico."

Clay turned around toward the aisle and looked back. Dave motioned to Matt Kelly for him to come forward.

Matt extended his hand, and introduced himself.

"Good to meet you," Clay responded as the two shook hands.

Redirecting his attention first to Matt and then to Clay, Dave added, "Clay is Laynie's husband, and Matt and Nick Costigan are agents on the faculty at the Academy."

"I can't believe what has happened," Matt said, shaking his head.

"Yeah, this thing is unimaginable," replied Clay.

All of a sudden, their flight hit a series of turbulent air pockets, and when the seat belt light came on and an announcement came over the speaker from the pilot, Dave and Matt returned to their seats.

If Clay knew of Matt's engagement to Laynie and their stormy on and off relationship while assigned to the Chicago Division he didn't let on that he was aware of it, and as far as Matt was concerned that's the way it would remain. The last thing they needed now was for something like that to get in the way of their working together in any upcoming rescue attempt that might be in the offing.

After a brief stop en route on the island of Yap, their flight landed on Palau. After getting off the plane, Clay joined Matt and the two other agents on the tarmac. An officer sent by Assistant Police Commissioner Adze met their flight and got them expedited through Immigration and

Customs. From there they made the fastest ten-kilometer trip to Koror that the two Guam agents could ever remember.

From Palau police headquarters, Dave Adams called Ty Wong in Guam to get an update and let him know that the three of them and Clay Steele had at last arrived on island.

"We think Laynie and Nick are locked in a container aboard a ship somewhere in the Rock Islands," Ty told him. "We're still waiting to see photos from satellite coverage over that area."

"With this heavy cloud cover settling in over the islands, I sure hope they can see something," Dave replied.

"We all do," Ty agreed.

"In the meantime, we'll take a couple of the police boats out there and see if we can come up with anything. Adze already told us everything he has is ours to use."

With a Palau police officer piloting each patrol boat, the agent teams split up, sending the two Guam agents off one direction while Matt and Clay searched in another. Their task was going to be formidable. In addition to having the expansiveness of the Pacific Ocean and over 200 islands in the Palauan chain to deal with, visibility was poor with non-stop drizzle, overcast skies, and a dense fog that was gradually settling in. That heavy cloud cover and the thick mist had also created significant problems for those back in Washington tasked with gathering useful photos from the satellites.

Although both had spent time on Guam while in the military, Matt at Andersen and Clay with the Naval Forces Marianas, ironically neither had ever landed on nor been in close proximity of Yap and Palau. As their police runabout headed from Koror toward Peleliu and into the twenty-three mile stretch known as the Rock Islands, both were surprised to see the extent of dense, heavy vegetation and numerous caves dotting this group of islands.

Without useful satellite photos, the task of locating the ship holding Laynie and Nick now rested solely with those aboard the two patrol boats.

"Spot anything?" Matt called over the radio to Dave Adams.

"A tanker and a large container ship, but that's all."

"Nothing black with a dozen containers on it, huh?"

"Nope. What about you and Clay?"

"Nothing here, either, and it's getting harder to see with the fog getting thicker and all of this drizzle."

"Same here," Dave responded. "I'm sure both boats are also going to be near their fuel limit for making it back to Koror before long, too."

"You're right," Matt answered. Moments earlier, the police officer piloting their patrol boat had told Clay and him the same thing.

"See you back in Koror," Matt told them, and nodded to the police officer that it was time for them to return to port.

The officer pushed the throttle forward to full speed ahead. As the patrol boat rose and skimmed along the top of the water, the drizzle blew across the faces of all aboard and they continued keeping an eye out for any sign of a ship resembling the one described by Laynie.

Nearing Koror, Clay looked over to Matt and said, "Something's been bothering me."

"What's that?" Matt asked.

Swashbuckler

"I think we've met before, but can't remember where."

"I've thought the same thing," Matt agreed, shaking his head.

After thinking about it for several more minutes, Clay suddenly recalled, "I've got it. NCAA's. You swam for Air Force."

Matt nodded, "Good memory. That's right, and you for Navy."

"Yeah," Clay responded. "As I remember we even hung out some together at the meet."

"Yeah," Matt agreed. "I think we were the only swimmers to qualify for the NCAA's from the Service Academies that year."

Clay nodded that he thought that was correct.

"Glad you remembered," Matt replied. "I'd also been trying to recall where I knew you from since we first met on the plane."

Pointing to his left, the police officer turned his head and called to them over his shoulder, "Get ready. We should be docking shortly."

Matt and Clay acknowledged that they understood.

CHAPTER FIFTY-NINE

Aboard the *Fantom*, shrieks of pain and cries of despair had continued throughout the night as Tomy and his fellow swashbucklers yelled profanities and carried out sexual attacks on their young captives. Thoughts of resistance by any of the girls, however, had been quickly dispelled a few days before, when pirate Captain Buruk ordered everyone out on deck to observe as he cast one objecting teen overboard into shark-infested waters. They had all witnessed her screams and pleas for help, followed by evidence of swirling blood near the surface, and then nothing. The consequence for non-cooperation was clear and the message received by each was unmistakable.

Nick nudged Laynie, "Look. Sunlight," he told her, and pointed in the direction of the same rusting cracks and small holes through which rainwater dripped and ran down the metal walls less than an hour before. Welcome rays from the sun once again found their way into the leaky container.

"Get me Es and the three mates who will be going with him," Buruk ordered Tomy.

The first mate rushed down to the room Es now occupied near the mates' quarters and found him sandwiched between two naked girls on the bunk.

"Captain wants to see you on the bridge, now," Tomy told Es.

Es grunted and rolled over, pushing the girls off the bunk and onto the metal deck. One cried out in pain as she hurt her arm in the fall.

"Get up, you bitches, and bring your clothes," Tomy yelled, grabbing a handful of long dark hair from each and pulling them to their feet in the direction of the doorway.

"I'll take these whores back to their box," he told Es.

Es quickly threw on a pair of pants and a shirt and headed for the bridge where three of the *Fantom's* nastiest mates were already waiting.

"Time to make the move?" Es asked Buruk.

"It's time," the captain nodded, as he motioned for the three mates standing nearby to join him and Es. "The four of you will take two boats," Buruk told them.

"Okay," Es answered.

"You all know what to do."

"Aye, aye, Captain," responded the three pirate mates.

"I will be leaving here after I hear back from you," Buruk told them.

"When are we to return to the ship?" Es asked.

"I will call you," the captain replied.

CHAPTER SIXTY

"We're at Andersen and ready to proceed," Cole Dawson reported in by phone.

"You'll have to hang tight for now," responded his CIRG boss who was now sitting at his desk in the SIOC. "A heavy cloud cover has been hanging over the region and giving us fits. There are problems with the satellites getting any kind of good looks, but that condition appears to be lifting."

"Any idea how long before we should know anything?"

"Nothing for sure," the special agent-in-charge of CIRG answered, "but we've been trying to stiff a call into that number used by the last caller. The cell phone has been turned off, but we'll keep trying. If he turns it on and all goes as planned with the call that should give us a fix on where he is now."

"We'll be awaiting those coordinates," Dawson replied.

"It hopefully won't be too long," responded the SAC.

A little over two hours passed before Buruk again turned on the cell phone he had used to make the earlier call to the Embassy. He was bored and decided to check the minutes he had left.

Shortly thereafter, the SIOC tried making their call.

"Yeah," Buruk answered.

The female voice on the other end of the call started speaking in a language that sounded to him like Philippine

Tagalog, but since Buruk understood very little *Tagalog*, he grunted, "What are you saying?"

The female caller again repeated all of what she had said before.

Still not understanding most of what she was saying and by this time having become increasingly annoyed and frustrated, he yelled into the receiver, "Shut up you stupid bitch. I don't speak *Tagalog*, so don't call again!" He immediately clicked off the call and turned the phone off.

"Did we get it?" the SAC anxiously called out.

Still awaiting final word, the technician hesitated before answering.

"Got it!" he beamed.

The SAC gave a smile and thumbs up to a female agent standing across the room.

"Good job in keeping him on the line," he told her.

"We were lucky," she responded. "My guess is that he understands only enough *Tagalog* to recognize that was what I was speaking, but did not know exactly what I was saying. At least, though, by having a female speaking in *Tagalog*, I don't think he suspected that it was related to the kidnapping. Hopefully, he thought I was just some Philippine broad who doesn't understand a lot of English and was calling a wrong number."

The CIRG SAC nodded in agreement.

With satellite coverage now zooming in on the identified coordinates, a call would go out shortly for Cole Dawson and his HRT team to make final preparations for a rescue at sea.

CHAPTER SIXTY-ONE

"Cole, have you received the coordinates and the satellite photos?" the special agent-in-charge of the Critical Incident Response Group asked his Hostage Rescue Team commander.

"They just came in about an hour ago," advised Dawson. "The ship looks like a freighter with containers on the deck."

"That's the one. When do you plan to make the rescue?" asked the SAC.

"An hour or two before sunrise," the HRT commander answered. "There's supposed to be minimal moonlight and that should help in concealing our insertion."

"Are you planning to launch the raid from Palau?"

"No, we don't know if all of those involved are gone from Koror. If any are still hanging around, they could let the others out on the ship know we've arrived on island and alert them to any movements we make."

"I had similar thoughts," responded the SAC, asking, "So where did you decide on?"

"Yap would be better, I think. We've already secured approval for landing and launching our attack from there. The Yap police arranged for us to use a corner at the airport, near the end of the airstrip, to set up our operations' tent."

"Sounds good to me."

Swashbuckler

"We'll fly the team and equipment from Andersen to Yap this afternoon. Once we're there we'll get some rest and be ready to begin the operation sometime after midnight."

"What about additional support from Palau?"

"I've already sent Tank Moseby to Koror to coordinate the support for the team from that end."

"Any problems?"

"None that I know of. Matt Kelly has assured me that the Palau police will support us with officers, boats, anything we need. He said they told him anything they have or can get their hands on is ours."

"Okay. Be sure to let us know when you arrive on Yap."

"Will do," Dawson replied.

While Cole Dawson was coordinating with his CIRG boss at the SIOC, most of the remaining snipers and assault team members from this section of the HRT were already out on one of the Andersen Air Force Base ranges firing and checking out their weapons. Although hundreds of rounds pass through the chambers of these custom-made rifles, pistols, and MP-5 submachine guns on a regular basis back at Quantico, all knew that there was no room for error when it came to carrying out life saving operations.

Most of the agents had participated in rescues on land and conducted training exercises aboard the ghost fleet as it sat idly in port, but few, if any, of this group of operators had ever taken part in an actual at sea rescue aboard a ship, and certainly not one holding two of their own as hostages.

Cole Dawson completed his call to the SIOC and then went to the ranges where the team members were winding up their shooting.

"Time for everyone to saddle up and get ready to make the move," Dawson called out.

Since most of the equipment had remained loaded aboard the aircraft, their preparation for this movement off Guam would be quick. They planned to be in the air and on their way to Yap shortly after noon.

In the meantime, Tank Moseby had arrived on Palau. He, along with Matt Kelly, Clay Steele, and the two agents from the Guam Resident Agency were already working with Adze and his command staff in gathering the necessary support for the upcoming assault.

At Moseby's request, Adze's men secured two large commercial fishing vessels. Manned with crewmen, police, and emergency medical personnel, these boats would keep the *Fantom* in sight and be available for immediate dispatch when called upon to assist. It was believed that the use of fishing vessels rather than other boats, would keep any suspicions aroused by those aboard the pirate ship to a minimum.

During the rescue, Clay Steele, Matt Kelly, and the two agents from the Guam RA would stay with the police patrol boats they had been using since their arrival, and Tank Moseby would remain with the assistant commissioner aboard the Palau police SWAT team craft. Although remaining out of sight, these high-powered boats would be able to respond instantly when called upon.

While everyone awaited his or her departure, a hush remained over the entire operation. With the element of surprise being essential, any leaks would be inexcusable.

CHAPTER SIXTY-TWO

As the operators prepared to board the choppers, Cole Dawson could not help but notice similarities revealed on the faces of these FBI agents and those troops he had led on like perilous missions decades earlier in Vietnam. There was that silence, the stare, the solemn expression, all evidencing an uncertainty pervading each man's thoughts as he prepared to risk it all for his fellow agents in carrying out one of the most dangerous and daring rescues ever attempted by the Hostage Rescue Team.

Having already changed out of their standard HRT olive drab uniforms and into black wet suits, all of the men stood ready to move.

"Tanks, masks, fins, and other equipment secured in the IBS's?" Dawson asked.

Responses regarding the status and loading of essentials into the heavy-duty, black and gray, IBS inflatable rafts came back affirmative.

With the chopper blades pounding, Dawson yelled out, "Double check that you have everything, and let's load up."

Once all were aboard and Cole Dawson gave the word, the helicopters slowly lifted upward and headed out to sea. As they reached altitude and the flight progressed, the operators somberly gazed out into a moonless night that had proved to be even darker than originally forecast.

Nearing the drop site, Dawson placed one final call to Tank Moseby.

"Everything ready at your end, Tank?" he asked.

"We're set," Moseby answered. "The fishing vessels have made their passes, and both are standing by along with the police boats and our agents. I'm with the commissioner on the SWAT boat. We'll wait for your word to come in."

"One minute," Dawson announced to the team.

The operators readied the heavy-duty inflatable rafts and equipment for quick release as the helicopters approached the drop site. Shortly thereafter, the IBS's and gear were released and splashed into the Pacific.

With all that the operators needed now floating below, the agents followed one another onto the helicopter skids and into the ocean near the IBS's.

Once all of the team members were out of the water and in the IBS's, Dawson spoke into his head set.

"Night lenses working and everybody set?" he asked.

When all signaled that they were ready, Dawson told the pilots hovering in the choppers overhead that it was time for them to move out of the area. They were to standby at the Palau airport.

Having insured that their drop was executed far enough away, so as to be neither seen nor heard by anyone aboard the *Fantom*, the assault teams quickly set their direction and began paddling their dark IBS's toward the crew of swashbucklers. Fortunately for them, the pirate ship had remained in essentially the same location since the previous afternoon.

Once the agents spotted the *Fantom* in the distance, Cole Dawson and an operator from each IBS donned their tanks, masks, and fins. Slipping over the bulging sides of their inflatable boats and into the waters of the deep, dark Pacific, they started swimming toward the *Fantom*.

Special underwater lights allowed the agents to get a good look, first, at a large school of fish passing directly overhead, and then to their surprise a pair of sharks that were approaching in the distance.

Sharks had never been a problem for the team on any previous dives, and Cole assumed these were seeking the school of fish. As the sharks got closer, however, the agents sensed that something was not right. Dawson signaled for everyone to start swimming away, and when they did, the sharks followed.

Their closing in brought back memories to Cole of when he was vacationing in the Caribbean and went out on a dive boat destined for shark-infested waters. There, they took him and the other divers down to the bottom of a feeding area, where they remained while food was tossed out and the sharks encircled everyone. No one was attacked or hurt as the sharks swarmed around brushing by Cole and the others, but he certainly felt relieved when the feeding was finished, and all of the divers were able return to the surface unscathed.

For these agent operators, however, this situation was not the same. These sharks were different. One menacing move after another eventually caused one of the agents to aim his spear gun in the direction of a shark he believed was about to attack Dawson. That shot missed, but another hit its mark, and when that happened, the shark dropped away with the other one following close behind.

The agents continued their mission and upon reaching the *Fantom*, they surfaced from the depths only long enough to survey the situation from the bow, stern, and both sides, gathering any additional intelligence that might be of assistance in their final assault.

Near the bow, Dawson spotted a single crewmember standing post on the deck and heard what sounded like a man's voice yelling and a woman crying out in pain, but that was about all.

"Could that have been Laynie Steele, he heard?" Dawson asked himself. He certainly hoped not.

With there appearing to be little else for them to learn from where they were in the water, Dawson signaled for all of them to return to the IBS's.

When they joined their fellow team members back in the inflated boats, the divers shed their tanks, masks, and fins, and quickly strapped on the custom-made pistols and flash bang grenades. They wore black ballistic vests and protective helmets with goggles resting on the front. Night vision lenses allowed them to get a good view of what was ahead, and the small radio packs with earpieces and mikes kept them in constant contact with one another.

While the operators stealthily paddled the IBS's into the peaceful tranquility of the Pacific, Dawson could not help being reminded of the expression, "the calm before the storm," and how totally appropriate that seemed at this time. If everything went as expected, it would not be long before this quiet calm came to an end and all hell broke loose.

CHAPTER SIXTY-THREE

Other than a slight illumination emanating from the heavens, the only light observed by the teams of FBI agents as they closed in on their risky at sea rescue appeared to be coming from the kidnappers' black ship, and the only sounds heard were from the pounding waves.

Seeing no crewmembers, Cole Dawson motioned for his men to proceed to the stern of the ship. An agent operator launched a rope and grappling hook. It failed to hold and dropped back into the ISB. He tried again. This time it attached. Agents quickly put up more hooks and as the ropes now dangled down the side of the vessel, the operators prepared to board.

Strapping scoped MP-5 submachine guns over their shoulders; the HRT assault team operators gripped the ropes and pulled themselves up, silently slipping onto the deck.

The crewmember spotted earlier by the divers as he stood guard near the bow suddenly reappeared. He yelled out and fired rounds in their direction. An assault team operator returned fire and the crewmember slowly slumped to the deck.

With the element of surprise no longer an option, and not knowing exactly where Nick and Laynie remained confined onboard the ship, the operators now had to rely on speed and violence of action to carry them through the operation. Dawson raised his phone and pressed the number for Moseby.

"Tank, we're on and they know it. Bring everyone forward. The police can secure the main deck while our assault teams search the interior."

Moseby gave the word and the SWAT craft he was on with Assistant Commissioner Adze, the two police boats with Matt, Clay, and the two Guam RA agents aboard, and the large fishing vessels carrying the others all pressed full speed ahead toward the *Fantom*.

"We'll be arriving shortly," Tank reported.

Knowing the necessity of getting control of the ship, Dawson ordered one assault team to head up a stairway toward the bridge, while the others were told to cover all entrances leading onto the main deck.

Flash bang grenades were tossed onto the bridge, and as the noise resonated throughout the ship, the assault team operators busted through the door.

"Don't shoot! Don't shoot!" yelled two crewmen standing back and throwing their hands high into the air.

"Don't move," ordered a nearby agent.

The mates froze.

A former Navy officer turned FBI agent team member rushed to the ship's wheel and took control of the vessel.

"Where are the FBI agents?" another agent operator demanded of the two crewmen.

The pirates shrugged, and when pressed, insisted they did not know.

When the swashbucklers sleeping below heard the flash bang grenades explode on the bridge, they quickly threw two girls being passed among them out of their beds and onto the deck. These buccaneers then leaped from their bunks, grabbing any guns and knives within reach.

Since the *Fantom* crew was known for carrying out surprise raids rather than reacting to them, this attack on them and their ship was just the reverse of what they were used to encountering.

Tomy immediately banded together a handful of the pirates in preparation to launch a counter-assault against these unwelcome invaders. Several of the crew had, however, already rushed through stairwells leading to doors opening onto the main deck and were now firmly in the grasp of FBI agent team members who quickly put them onto the deck.

Tank and officers from the Palau Police secured the main deck and continued to board additional weapons, powerful lights and other equipment. Cole Dawson and another HRT assault team maneuvered through the doorways and corridors leading to rooms located on the upper and lower decks.

Recalling Laynie's comment that they were "locked in one of about a dozen containers aboard a black ship," Tank quickly assembled a team of Matt Kelly, Clay Steele, and the two agents from the Guam RA to begin searching through the long metal container boxes.

The agents approached a nearby interior container and positioned an intense flood light directly in front of the doors so that when thrown open by the two Guam agents, the bright lights would allow Matt and Clay to get a good look inside before anyone in there could react.

Matt motioned to his fellow agents.

They pulled the bars and immediately swung the doors open all of the way.

"This container is empty," Kelly yelled.

They quickly moved on to another, which was sitting near the edge of the deck. At first glance, this container appeared similar to the one just opened, but closer scrutiny showed it to be more of a shell than a traditional container. When they opened it, they found that it housed a sleek, black, open-hulled fastboat.

Suddenly, shots rang out below, with bullets ricocheting off the walls and deck as Tomy and his men opened fire on the approaching HRT assault team. The agents reacted instinctively. They dropped two of the pirates in their tracks, but only after Tomy and the others had slipped through a nearby passageway, locking the door behind them. The agents continued to pursue their attackers.

As they had practiced hundreds of times before during live fire exercises at Quantico's Tactical Firearms Training Center, the assault team breached the metal door. Tomy's men sprayed barrages of fire, with one of the ricocheting rounds finding a lone operator. The agents peered into their red dot laser scopes and began squeezing off rounds. The pirates started dropping one after another.

Out of the corner of his eye, Tomy spotted one of the teenage girls who ran and hid in the corridor after being thrown out of a bed.

"Come here, you bitch," Tomy yelled to her.

The young girl submissively crawled toward him. Tomy grabbed a handful of her hair and pulled her up. He held her out in front of him as a shield. With the weapon selector switch already on fully automatic, he rested the barrel on her shoulder and fired a burst at the agents.

Another agent was hit, and he fell to the deck. Cole Dawson rushed to the wounded agent and pulled him back into a small side room where a paramedic trained operator was treating the leg of the agent wounded by a stray round only moments before.

Tomy fired another burst. While reloading, he lost his grip. The girl pulled away and lunged forward. Tripping over a dead pirate, she fell to the deck.

With his human shield now gone, Tomy pulled the trigger back and held it on full automatic, spraying a final burst. He was stopped by a succession of rounds fired by the operators. Tomy dropped to his knees, and then slumped onto the girl.

As blood-spattered bodies lay strewn along the lower deck corridor, the FBI agent operators carefully approached. The only sign of life they heard came from the girl that had been held as a shield during the shootout. As she cried out and struggled to free herself from the blood-covered bodies, the agents cautiously rushed forward to help.

On the main deck, Clay and Matt continued their frantic search for the kidnapped agents, but so far they had come up empty. In addition to the sleek, high-speed fastboats found sitting on their cradles in the specially constructed metal containers, there were also three other like shells that held only empty cradles. What had happened to the fastboats in those containers remained unknown.

Approaching another container, Clay motioned to Matt and the others to come over. "I hear voices," he silently mouthed and pointed.

With the floodlight now positioned, the doors were yanked open. A group of bloodied and beaten young women were huddled toward the rear.

"Come out," Matt told them.

Their heads lowered and bodies trembling, the girls slowly moved toward him.

Matt and Clay caught glimpses of puffy faces, and cuts and bruises running down their uncovered arms and legs as they shuffled out.

"Is there a woman and a man in one of these?" Clay anxiously asked one girl as he pointed at the container.

She gave him a questioning look, indicating she did not know what he was talking about.

Spotting two young teens struggling to help a young woman who was barely alive get out of the container; Matt quickly went to their aid and carried her onto the deck. "Are there others like you?" he asked the teens.

They nodded their heads and one pointed in the direction of two nearby containers.

Several Palau police officers and a medic rushed over to assist and watch over these girls while the Guam agents hurried to center the flood light on the closest container. With everyone in position, the doors were swung wide open. Fewer girls were in this one than in the first. When ordered to come forward, one teen did not respond. Matt again called for her to get up and come forward. There was still no response.

"I'm going in to get her," Matt told the others.

It was too dark to tell much, but her face looked like it has been used for a punching bag. He took her wrist. There was no pulse. He called for a Koror hospital nurse who had accompanied the rescue team to come in and check her.

"She's dead," the nurse solemnly reported.

As he had done previously, Clay asked the girls standing outside this container if they had seen a man and a woman being held against their will onboard the ship.

These girls gave the same puzzled response he had received from those in the other container box.

Moving on to the next container and opening the doors, they found more girls crammed into these disgusting conditions. Fortunately, when told to come forward, all of these were able to respond. The girls found in these last two containers, along with the teenage girl held up as a human shield by Tomy and the other girl from below, now joined those from the first group in the custody of the police on the main deck.

Except for what appeared to be a large cache of spare parts and some scuba gear, there was little else found in the remaining containers. There were no kidnapped FBI agents, no more young women, and thankfully no more bodies.

Being a former Navy officer and somewhat familiar with ship operations, Clay ran up to the bridge to see if he could be of some help there. The HRT operators appeared to have things well under control.

"Anything from these two on Laynie and Nick?" Clay asked the agents, as he looked over to the side at the two cuffed crewmembers.

"Nothing so far," answered the now captain FBI agent. "We haven't been able to spend a lot of time talking to them, though. We've been pretty busy trying to get on top of things here."

"Mind if I have a try?" Clay asked.

"No problem," came back the response.

Clay grabbed one of the mates by the arm and yanked him into a side room just off the bridge. After closing the door and throwing him up against the wall, Clay got up close and personal.

"That's my wife you bastards kidnapped and if I don't get her back, well. . . . I don't really care whether you live or die."

There was no response.

Reacting instinctively, Clay carefully placed his fingers on the mate's throat and began slowly applying deadly pressure.

The pirate started to gag, and then panicked when he tried to catch a breath.

"Do you understand?" Clay whispered into his ear.

The mate nodded.

"Now that we understand each other," Clay told him, as he slowly released some of the pressure, "if you tell me what I want to know, you live, and if you don't, you die. It is as simple as that."

"They left with Es," replied the panicked mate.

"When?"

"Yesterday morning."

"Where did they go?"

"I do not know."

Clay increased the pressure to the man's throat.

Chocking and gasping for air, he cried out, "I swear, I do not know. They left in boats with Es."

"The black fastboats?"

"Yeah, two of them."

"And who are the 'they'?" demanded Clay.

"Es and three mates."

"What about the captain?"

"Captain Buruk?"

"Yeah, Captain Buruk," Clay responded, hearing the name of the renegade pirate captain for the first time.

"The captain received a call yesterday afternoon and then left in another one of the boats."

"Who was the call from?"

"I think it was Es."

"Where was the captain going?"

He shrugged.

Clay once again increased pressure to the mate's throat.

The pirate mate gagged. "I do not know. I do not know where the captain went."

"Who would know?" asked Clay.

Gasping for air, the mate answered, "Tomy. He would know."

Slowly releasing the pressure, Clay glared coldly into the mate's eyes. "You'd better be telling me the truth or I'll be back, and I promise you that I will finish the job next time."

Having just survived this near death experience, the unnerved mate responded emphatically, "That is the truth. I swear! I swear!"

Clay led the mate back into the room and down the stairway onto the main deck where others from the pirate crew were kneeling with their hands cuffed behind their backs.

"Which one of you is Tomy?" Clay yelled out.

One of the crewmembers grumbled something that sounded like, "He is dead. You bastards killed him."

Clay turned to the girls and asked, "Is the one they call Tomy here?"

"No," responded the girl held as a human shield by Tomy during the firefight. "Tomy is dead!" she yelled, and a giant cheer of relief rose from the group of them huddled nearby. There was no question about how these girls felt about him.

Although they remained uncertain about their rescuers, these girls were visibly relieved knowing that, at least for now, they had escaped the throes of brutality handed down by this crew of vicious swashbucklers.

CHAPTER SIXTY-FOUR

"The assault has been successfully completed, and the ship is now under our control," Cole Dawson reported to the SIOC.

"Casualties?" the FBI deputy director asked.

"Two agent operators have been shot, but neither appears to be in a life-threatening situation. Choppers are taking them and the wounded crewmen from the ship to the hospital at Koror."

"Any sign of Laynie Steele or Nick Costigan?"

"None. It appears they were taken off the ship by four men aboard two fastboats."

"When?"

"Sometime yesterday morning."

"To where?"

"We don't know, and the first mate that supposedly had the answer was killed in the shootout with us."

"What about the captain, and do we know who he is?"

"We believe he is called Buruk and we have a description. As best we can tell, he left in a separate fastboat yesterday afternoon."

"Alone?"

"That's what we've been told. And to where, we don't know. Assistant Police Commissioner Adze has already called and told his officers to check with Customs and the airlines at Palau International to see if anyone matching the description of our Captain Buruk has boarded a flight in the last twelve hours."

"Anything else?"

"You mean other than the fact that this ship is being used for sex slave trafficking."

"What!" exclaimed the deputy director.

"Yeah. These guys are the worst kind of scumbags. We found containers filled with teens and young women who have been sexually attacked, brutally beaten, and terrorized."

"Where are the girls from?"

"Jakarta," Cole responded, adding, "One is dead and several others are barely alive. Some look like they've been used for punching bags and from what we've been able to get out of them so far, all were frequently attacked and raped by the animals aboard this ship."

"Are they talking?"

"Not much," Dawson answered. "I don't think they have much trust in us or anyone else out here at this point. Maybe after we get them to Palau and into the hospital for check-ups, they'll better understand that we're here to help."

"I can see them not trusting anybody at this point," the deputy director replied. "Let me know if there is anything you need or anything additional we can do."

"Just a minute, before you hang up," Dawson said, "I think the commissioner has some new info." Cole paused as he listened to Adze's update. "The commissioner has just received word back from his officers at the Palau airport. It looks like our man boarded a flight to Manila last evening," Dawson told the DD.

"So he's already there," confirmed the FBI deputy director.

"That's what his men have been told. The flight was to have arrived in Manila early this morning."

"I guess that means no chance to intercept him at the airport, huh."

"Doesn't sound like it."

"Call me when you reach the port at Koror, Cole," the DD instructed Dawson, adding, "and in the meantime, I'll give Robinson the word on this Captain Buruk and find out if he knows anything about him. I'll also have him check with the Philippine officials at the airport to learn if they have any information from that end that might help us."

"10-4," replied the HRT commander.

Cole Dawson had earlier requested those aboard the large fishing vessels used in the operation to take control of the girls and return to their craft. There, the nurses would be available to provide any immediate emergency treatment required prior to their reaching the hospital. Dawson had also asked Adze, Tank, and the SWAT officers to board onto their boat any prisoners not assisting the "FBI captain and agent crew" now in control of the *Fantom* in getting the freighter underway and into port. All of these boats would return to Koror together.

"Any problem if the four of us and these two officers take another route back to Koror? Matt asked. "I'd like to make another run through the area they call the Rock Island Gardens where Clay and I searched earlier."

"Go ahead," Dawson agreed, "but be careful and make sure you keep both boats in sight of one another."

CHAPTER SIXTY-FIVE

When LEGAT Manila received the call from the FBI deputy director, identifying the now missing pirate Captain Buruk as the one responsible for the agent kidnappings, Bill Robinson quickly brought the DD up to date on what he knew about the notorious swashbuckler.

Robinson relayed Captain Cruz's shocking account of Buruk's recent attack on the *Hafa Adai*, and how the pirate captain had set the Guam based cargo ship to sea without guidance, and as a result nearly created an international disaster.

"Sounds like this guy Buruk needs to be put on our 'Ten Most Wanted,' " the DD said.

"He certainly should," Robinson agreed.

"Well, I'll see what we can do," the deputy director told the LEGAT. "In the meantime, let me know what you learn from that airport lead."

"Will do," Robinson assured the FBI's number two man before hanging up.

Bill Robinson and NBI Agent Ricardo Perez left immediately for the Manila airport where the two of them examined required forms submitted by arriving passengers and showed copies of the artist's sketch of Captain Buruk to Philippine Immigration and Customs officers.

The arrival form submitted by the person that they believed to be Buruk had the family name "Santos" printed on it. That was also the name shown on the airline manifest and the passport he used. The form indicated he would be staying at a hotel near the bay, but a subsequent check at that hotel revealed what Robinson and Perez had expected. There was no lodger matching his description registered there. When shown the sketch of Buruk, one desk clerk vaguely remembered having seen a man that looked like him having stayed there in the past, but could not recall a name or any particular dates.

The legal attachés from Bangkok and Tokyo were now in Manila, and the two of them along with the tech agent and another NBI agent had remained behind at the American Embassy to answer and trace any demand calls that might come in. They would also pass along to the SIOC any messages or information received while Robinson and Perez were away.

"There were no calls or messages," Robinson learned upon his return to the office.

"Any more word from the CIRG hostage negotiators?" he asked.

"None. As far as we know they're still sitting in an airport somewhere between here and there trying to get out." So far, two of their connecting flights had been cancelled after long delays, and now, the third one they had been rebooked on was again delayed. It was beginning to look like they might never get there in time.

Perez asked Robinson, "Can you pull up that interview you did with the *Hafa Adai* Captain for us to take a look at? And, I'm also going to need more copies of that artist's sketch of Captain Buruk so I can get them out to my guys," he added.

Robinson opened the interview doc on his computer for them to read, and asked his assistant to runoff additional copies of the Buruk sketch.

While they waited for the copies to be made, the phone rang. As soon as the tech agent gave him the signal that everything was ready for a trap and trace, Robinson picked up the phone.

"Where is Luis?" demanded Buruk.

"I will have to check," LEGAT Robinson calmly answered.

"You lying bastards! If Luis is not here by tomorrow, one of your FBI agents will be dead! Do you hear me, D-E-A-D!"

"Let me talk with the agents," replied Robinson.

"You talked with them before."

"Just one of them," Robinson responded. "Let me hear both of their voices."

"I'm hanging up," Buruk threatened.

"No, no, wait," Robinson insisted. "How can I contact you?"

"You can't. I will contact you," Buruk shot back. "Remember, if Luis is not here by tomorrow, the throat of one of your agents will be slit. This is no bullshit!"

"How will you know when Luis arrives?"

"He has my number," Buruk replied. "You just make sure Luis gets here!" and he slammed down the receiver.

Robinson looked to Ricardo Perez who was standing next to the NBI tech agent.

"Got it!" announced Perez.

The LEGAT gave them a thumbs up.

Taking a moment to review the trap and trace, Ricardo added, "It came from a pay phone near where the first call was made."

"In Makati, huh?" clarified Robinson.

"Right," Perez nodded.

"Well, there's one thing we now know for sure," concluded Robinson. "That damned pirate captain is still in Manila and probably with the guy who made those first calls."

Perez agreed. "And, now that we know it is Buruk we are looking for and have the artist's sketch to spread around the city, we'll see what our agents can come up with on him and his whereabouts from their informants."

CHAPTER SIXTY-SIX

Searching for any coves or caves that might conceal a black fastboat, Clay, Matt, and the two Guam FBI agents all had their binoculars up and squinted into the lenses as they passed through this large cluster of islands, locally known as the Rock Island Gardens.

The early morning's brilliant sun was intense, and the glare reflecting off these pristine Pacific waters made it difficult for them and the pair of marine police officers piloting the high-speed police boats to see. They all knew, however, that this was just a temporary condition and visibility would improve significantly as soon as the sun got a little higher on the horizon.

"Over there!" Matt yelled, pointing in the direction of what appeared to be a cave surrounded by heavy green undergrowth.

There was no sign of a fastboat, but they decided that any opening needed to be checked out.

The boat with Matt and Clay aboard slowed as the patrol officer steered it toward the side of the opening. The pair put on masks and fins, and with the two Guam agents backing them up topside in the other boat, Clay and Matt dropped into the water and snorkeled toward the cave. Stopping first at the entrance and seeing nothing of note, they slipped underwater into the cavity. Surfacing in its dimness, they caught brief glimpses of stalactites hanging down here and there, but heard no noise nor saw any sign of a boat, pirates, or their captives.

Continuing the search, the patrol officers slowly guided the boats through a narrow passageway and passed a half dozen more islands that look like furry, green mushrooms.

Dave Adams focused his binoculars after he spotted what looked like an outboard motor tucked into the entrance of a cave. He signaled to the others and pointed ahead and to the left.

The patrol boats slowed, and as they closed in on this limestone island, the police officers shut down the outboard engines about an eighth of a mile from the near shore. From there, everyone paddled toward a narrow, sandy beach that extended to the entrance of the cave.

The two police officers remained on their patrol boats as back-up, while the three agents and Clay Steele edged their way along the beach toward the opening. They could now see the back of a boat that looked similar to the fastboats discovered aboard the *Fantom*.

Approaching the entrance, Matt and Clay signaled the Guam agents that they would climb up through some dense vegetation overhead and down the other side of the mouth. This way, both sides of the cave's opening would be covered when they were ready to make their move.

With the exception of the black fastboat tied near the entrance, the opening to the cave remained unobstructed.

Clay peered around the corner while the three agents remained concealed in their positions. Until his eyes had a chance to adjust from the bright sun reflecting off the water, it was difficult for him to see much or very far into the cave's darkness.

As things inside the cave became gradually clearer, Clay spotted what appeared to be a lone figure lying motionless on a sand bar near a large chunk of driftwood against the back wall of the cave. Reaching back and grabbing Matt's binoculars, he focused the lens. Could that be Laynie, he asked himself. If it were Laynie, her hands and feet were bound and there was a gag tied around her mouth and head. Also, since there was no movement, he couldn't tell whether she was dead or alive.

Clay quickly continued his scan of the darkened area for any signs of her captors or anyone else for that matter. Spotting no one, and convinced that it was his wife who was lying motionless on that sandbar, Clay's emotions took control.

Throwing caution and restraint aside, he whispered back over his shoulder to Matt, "Cover me. I'm going in."

Before Matt could say or do anything, Clay quietly slipped into the still waters and started swimming underwater toward her.

Matt motioned to the other agents, and as their eyes continued to adjust, the three of them gripped their .40 caliber pistols tightly, searching for signs of any movement in the darkness.

Clay surfaced to take a breath, and two shots rang out.

The muzzle flashes revealed the bullets coming from someone concealed amid the stalactites and kneeling on a hanging ledge that extended high over the pool.

Clay's body slumped in the water.

Matt dove into the pool and raced to his rescue.

With fifteen rounds in the magazine and one round chambered in their pistols, the two Guam agents immediately returned fire. They watched as the assailant dropped into the deepest part of the pool.

The gunfire roused Laynie and she quickly spotted two men in the water. The voice of one sounded like Matt Kelly as it resonated in the cave.

"Hang on Clay, I'm on my way!" he yelled.

More muzzle flashes appeared with rounds splashing in the water around Matt. These flashes originated from the gun of someone hiding in a crevice behind a large chunk of driftwood. As Matt closed in and reached Clay, he grabbed him under his arms and pulled him toward the sandbar. The second shooter quickly moved out from behind the cover of the crevice and driftwood, and fired more rounds in their direction.

Matt quickly pulled the two of them under.

This second swashbuckler now turned in a rage and approached Laynie, firing rounds in her direction, and yelled, "You bitch! I'll show the FBI!"

Laynie's hands and feet were still bound, but she countered by rolling over repeatedly until she was able to get off the sand bar and sink into the pool. The pirate continued his tirade and fired shots into the water, before finally being silenced by a burst of rounds sent his way by the Guam agents.

When the police officers heard the intense exchange of gunfire, they started the engines on their patrol boats and raced to the mouth of the cave.

"I think we've found at least one of the kidnapped agents and two of the bad guys are down," Dave Adams yelled out to the officers.

Matt dragged Clay to the edge of the sandbar, and then turned his attention to Laynie. He dove back into the pool toward her. Since she rolled into the water, she had been holding her breath and struggling to free her bleeding hands and feet from the taut ropes. Pulling his knife from its sheath, Matt quickly cut the gag from her mouth and began feverishly cutting the ties as the two of them ascended together.

Once they surfaced, Matt quickly asked her, "Are Nick, or any other shooters here?"

Gasping for air, Laynie shook her head.

When they reached her husband, he was conscious and breathing, but losing blood.

"Clay!" Laynie cried out and leaned over to give him a kiss on the forehead.

"Bring a boat forward," Matt called out to one of the police officers.

When the patrol boat ran up to the sandbar, Matt leaned in under the bow and after grabbing the emergency first aid kit, immediately started to work. He told everyone that as soon as he could get the bleeding stopped, they would load Clay and Laynie onto the closed-bow runabout and see how fast that 225 horsepower outboard motor could carry them to the hospital in Koror.

At the same time, the two Guam agents had jumped aboard the other patrol boat and were heading for the sandbar. On the edge of the bar lay the lifeless body of the second shooter, his blood pooling around the half dozen entrance and exit bullet holes from the agents' pistols.

"This one's dead," Dave Adams yelled over to Matt.

"What about the other guy?" asked Matt.

"He's lying at the bottom of the pool."

"Call Commissioner Adze on the radio and tell him we're bringing Clay and Laynie in and to alert the hospital that Clay's been shot."

Dave picked up the mike and pressed the button, "Commissioner, this is Dave Adams. There's been a shootout here in the Gardens. Two of the bad guys are dead and there's no sign of Nick Costigan, but we do have Laynie Steele. Her husband, Clay, has been shot and we're bringing the two of them in."

"What is his condition?" asked Adze.

"He's been losing blood and we need to get him into the hospital as soon as possible. Can you notify them that we're on our way?"

"Will do," Adze responded. "In the meantime, we'll get a chopper in the air to intercept you and pick them up."

"I just hope it will be soon enough," Adams mumbled to himself as he released the button and handed the microphone to the police officer so he could tell Adze exactly where they were.

"Time to go," Matt told Laynie. "We'll get you into the boat first and then carry Clay over."

Laynie nodded her head and reluctantly let go of Clay's head, resting it gently on the sandbar. With one arm around Matt's neck, she limped over to the boat and stepped in.

Matt hurried back to Clay. "You get on that side and I'll stay here," Matt told the police officer. "We'll lift at the same time and then lay him down beside Laynie."

"Are you set?" Matt asked Laynie.

"Set," she responded, and they carefully lifted Clay into the boat, laying his head to the side in her lap. Holding back tears as she tried to comfort Clay, Laynie gave him a kiss on the cheek and whispered in his ear that Ashley was waiting for the two of them back in Honolulu.

He smiled.

With Clay and Laynie now onboard, Matt pushed the runabout off the sandbar and jumped in. The police officer started the engine and their boat fell in behind the one carrying the two Guam agents as they headed toward the mouth of the cave.

Once both patrol boats cleared the entrance, Matt yelled out, "Let's hit it as fast as we can!"

The officers pushed the controls to full throttle and the engines roared. As the bows slowly lifted and both patrol boats started streaking toward Koror, Matt raised a convertible top to shield Laynie and Clay from the blistering sun.

"Any idea where Nick is?" Matt asked Laynie.

"None," she answered. "Nick and I were both tied up and thrown into separate boats with two crewmen from the ship in each. Both boats stayed together until we all got to that cave. When we got inside, a guy who seemed to know his way around these islands and was in Nick's boat told the guys in my boat to keep me there and that he would call them later."

"What happened, then?"

"They left, and that was the last time I saw Nick."

"We'll find him, too," Matt assured her.

As Laynie continued holding Clay's head in her lap, caressing the side of his forehead and temples, and running her fingers through his hair, Clay reminded her to call his CIA bosses at Langley and let them know what had happened.

"We'll make sure they know," she assured him.

Suddenly she felt him slipping away, and screamed, "Clay! Clay!"

Matt turned, "What is it, Laynie?"

"I feel him fading," she panicked.

"Check for a pulse," Matt told her.

She grabbed his wrist. "I can feel one," she responded.

"How's his breathing?"

"He seems to be having some trouble!" she anxiously exclaimed, "Where's that chopper!"

The police officer steering the boat responded by radioing for an estimated time of arrival.

"We have you in sight," the pilot replied.

A sigh of relief went out from Laynie, as the police officer slowed the patrol boat and brought it to a stop.

With the whirling blades from the helicopter whipping overhead, a water spray rose from the surface around the boat. Two EMT officers jumped into the water and a stretcher was lowered onto the patrol boat.

The EMT's quickly checked Clay's vitals before carefully strapping him onto the stretcher. Everyone watched anxiously as the rope lifted Clay into the chopper and returned the stretcher to the runabout. This time, Laynie gingerly eased herself onto the stretcher. The officers signaled to take her up. The EMT's followed her up on ropes with harnesses. When all of the crew were onboard the helicopter, the pilot wasted no time in heading for the hospital in Koror.

In the interim, the *Fantom* and its escorts had arrived back in Koror. Medical personnel were assisting in getting all of those requiring treatment to the hospital and the police were beefing up security at the jail as they processed the influx of swashbucklers.

"We'll meet you and the other agents and officers at the cave," Cole Dawson radioed to Matt. "A couple of the police officers coming with me can bring the fastboat and bodies of the pirates back to Koror while the rest of us continue the search for Nick."

"See you there." Matt responded, and relayed the message from the HRT commander to those in the other patrol boat.

CHAPTER SIXTY-SEVEN

"We've all arrived at the cave," Cole Dawson reported to Adze and those listening in at the SIOC on the conference line. "Any word from the hospital on the condition of our two agents, and Clay and Laynie Steele?" he asked.

"The agents are doing fine," the commissioner reported. "The doctor said he expects both of them to fully recover, and without any adverse consequences."

"That's good news," Cole replied, "Anything on the Steeles?"

"Laynie is doing as well as can be expected, but Clay is critical," Adze answered. "They are doing what they can for him here, but he needs to get to the hospital on Guam."

"When will that be?"

"Shortly. There's an Air Force medical plane and team already in the air from Andersen to get all of them."

"Any sign of Nick Costigan?" The deputy director asked from his desk in the SIOC.

"Nothing so far, but with the satellites hopefully getting a good view now, and our choppers up and boats scouring the area, we should come up with something soon," Dawson answered.

"We'll let you know about anything that shows up from the satellites," the deputy director assured Cole.

"10-4," answered Dawson, and he clicked off the call.

CHAPTER SIXTY-EIGHT

"What have you come up with on Captain Buruk?" Ricardo Perez asked his team of fellow agents assembled around a large mahogany table in their NBI Headquarters conference room.

"One of my snitches says Buruk was spotted with a guy they call Sam at a local strip club," reported one of the agents.

"In Makati?" questioned Perez.

"Right," confirmed the agent.

"Word on the street is that he is mobbed-up in that syndicate running a half dozen or more of those clubs," added another.

"Sounds like it might be a good idea for us to start paying them some visits," concluded Perez.

Everyone sitting at the table nodded in agreement.

"I see it's unanimous," Perez told the group. "Since they were seen at the club in Makati, we'll hit it first, and go on from there. See you in front of that club in an hour."

The team of NBI Agents wasted no time in getting to the Makati address. Shortly after entering the club, Ricardo Perez and the other agents moved among the patrons, making general nuisances of themselves as they checked ID's and nosed around, creating as uncomfortable a feeling as possible for everyone inside about being there. When approached by the club manager regarding what was going on, Perez made very clear what he wanted.

Opening a folder and taking out a copy of the artist's sketch of Buruk, he said, pointing, "I want him and a guy named Sam."

"Who?" the manager questioned.

"Buruk and Sam," repeated Perez, and again showed him the sketch.

"Never seen him before. No idea who you are talking about," the manager sarcastically replied.

Grabbing him by the front of his silk shirt, Perez responded, "You're a lying sack of shit, and we both know it. Now you listen closely. These guys kidnapped two American FBI agents and the heat is on. We know they were here and if you want to stay in business, it's up to you and your bosses to get them to us. Understand?"

The manager acknowledged that he did.

"Now you be sure and pass that on up the food chain," Perez told him, as he slowly released his grip on the manager's crumpled shirt. "Next time we will have licensing inspectors with us, and who knows, they might decide to revoke your license for this place on the spot, and poof, your business is closed."

Pondering those ramifications, the manager looked up, his eyes darting from side to side, as he nodded.

"So, the sooner you get us Buruk and Sam, the better it will be for everyone."

Still nodding, he indicated that he understood.

"We are not going away," Perez assured him as they walked out the door.

At the next club, the team of NBI Agents repeated their actions carried out an hour earlier at the first club.

Once again, checking ID's and wandering through the crowd making the patrons feel as uncomfortable as possible about being there was all part of the routine. When shown the artist's sketch and asked about Buruk, this club manager appeared to have no idea what Perez was talking about; however, the same could not be said regarding his reaction at the mention of the name Sam.

Having been busted by Perez a few years before for running a prostitution ring and having served hard time as a result, this guy knew Ricardo meant business when he told him that they would be back if Buruk and Sam were not handed over, and shortly.

Ricardo's team followed up those first two stops with drop-ins on the remaining syndicate-controlled strip clubs. At the conclusion of each visit, the club managers called the mob bosses to report what had transpired.

Threats of harassment and prosecution were not something new to the mob bosses, but receiving them for kidnappings they neither authorized nor knew anything about were unusual. As a result, their responses might have surprised some, but for those close to the operation the reaction was just what might have been expected.

CHAPTER SIXTY-NINE

The noise from the chopper blades was making it difficult for Cole Dawson to hear the supervisor in the SIOC.

"Say again," the HRT commander yelled into his cell phone.

Raising his voice as he spoke, the HQ supervisor repeated, "I said, the satellite has given us a fix on a fastboat like the one you're looking for."

"Where?"

"It looks like it's in a protected cove on the island of Peleliu."

"Any live bodies spotted around it?"

"None that I see, but there's a lot of thick vegetation on the land nearby."

"We can be over Peleliu in a matter of minutes. I'll have the boats start heading that way and call you back when I get there."

The skies were clear and the waters calm as Dawson and his HRT assault teams approached the island of Peleliu. None of the small boats floating in the surf along a nearby beach matched the black fastboats they found aboard the *Fantom* and at the cave, but this search starting at the southern tip of Palau's barrier reef was just beginning.

Dawson called the SIOC back and reported, "We're now over the island."

"You should be seeing the boat before long," the SIOC supervisor told him.

"There's a cove surrounded by heavy vegetation coming up on the right. We'll take it down a little and get a closer look."

"See anything?" asked the supervisor.

"Nothing yet," Dawson responded, "Wait, I see what might be the back of a boat sticking out from under some heavy vegetation."

As the chopper moved in closer and around to the side, Dawson peered through his binoculars.

"No question about it," he reported, "That's a black fastboat just like the one we found at the entrance to the cave."

"Let us know when you learn more," the SIOC supervisor replied.

"I will, but first I need to let the others know what we've found." Cole switched off his cell phone and called over the radio to Matt and the others who were moving toward them in the police patrol boats. "Looks like we have the black fastboat in a cove off Peleliu," he told them.

"Where do you want us to meet you?" Matt asked.

"We'll be putting down to the north on Ngebad Island," Cole responded.

Matt glanced at the police officer piloting the police boat. He gave a thumbs up that he knew where the chopper would be landing.

"Okay. We'll see you there, shortly," answered Matt.

Next, Dawson leaned over and asked the police SWAT leader to contact the substation on Peleliu and ask for an officer from there to join the team on Ngebad Island.

The officer nodded and gave Cole a thumbs-up.

Within thirty minutes of Dawson's helicopter setting down, all of those in the patrol boats and an officer from Peleliu substation were assembled.

Cole Dawson started the briefing by bringing the substation police officer up to date regarding their interest in Peleliu. Discussed were the agent kidnappings, the HRT's assault on the *Fantom*, the rescue of Laynie from the cave, and now the sighting in a nearby cove of the black fastboat believed to have carried Nick Costigan, Es, and another mate away from the pirate ship.

"I know who Es is," the substation police officer told them. "I have seen him at his bar in Koror."

"Do you have any idea where Es and the other mate might be holding Nick Costigan on the island?" Dawson asked.

He shook he head and answered, "None. No one has reported anything, and I have not seen them, but my guess would be that they are with Smuuch."

"Smuuch?" questioned Dawson.

"Yeah, '*smuuch*,' it is what we call stonefish."

"Like those deadly scorpion fish?"

"The very same."

"Why do you think they might be with him?"

"Smuuch lives near that cove. We don't know as much as we would like about him or what goes on around his property, and most of the locals tend to keep their distance," the officer responded. "He is not like the others living on this island. I think I would have heard if strangers were seen somewhere else, but not on his place."

"Anything else?"

"Nothing, other than Smuuch is a big, mean, nasty grower who is believed to have organized crime ties in Manila."

Pointing toward where Matt and two of the HRT operators were sitting, Cole told the officer, "I would like you to take those three agents with you into this area where you think they might have Nick and see what you can learn. In the meantime, I will contact the SIOC and have more satellite photos collected and forwarded."

CHAPTER SEVENTY

The ambulances were waiting on the tarmac when the Air Force medical evacuation flight from Andersen set down at Palau International Airport. Medical personnel rushed off the plane to get Clay Steele's stretcher and very carefully moved it and the IV's onto the aircraft. Laynie and the two HRT agents were pushed on in their wheelchairs.

With everyone now onboard, and Clay's condition necessitating that no time be lost, the engines churned, and the crew chief secured the door as the air-evac transport rumbled off the tarmac and onto the runway.

Laynie moved up beside Clay's bed and sat holding his hand tightly in hers, and praying. He was once again not responding to her touch. It had been shortly after the cave rescue that Clay started falling in and out of consciousness, and that had continued for much of the time since their arrival at the hospital in Koror.

As the flight progressed, the Air Force medical evacuation team continued monitoring the vitals of all four patients and did what they could to keep everyone as comfortable as possible throughout their flight back to Andersen.

One of the wounded HRT agents who had been an Air Force F-15C Eagle fighter pilot before joining the Bureau slipped out of his seat and limped up to the cockpit to talk with the pilots about flying.

During their conversation, the agent recalled a temporary duty assignment he had at Andersen and life on the island as he remembered it. The dive trips off Guam and Saipan, parties at the hotels around Tumon Bay, and nights spent at the Navy Officer's Club were all topics of conversation. The agent also recalled visitors commenting to him about the eerie feeling that came over them when they looked at the intimidating heavy B-52's sitting dauntingly along side the airstrip.

Nearing Guam, one of the nurses stopped and knelt beside Laynie, "I've just received a message that a surgical team is standing by to operate as soon as we land and can get your husband to the hospital."

Her eyes welling up, Laynie acknowledged that she understood, and thanked the nurse for all the crew had done.

In the meantime, the Andersen tower had given the medical flight priority for landing and the co-pilot alerted the crew.

Their landing was smooth, and after the plane pulled to a stop, the doors opened. The medical team acted quickly removing Clay and the three FBI agents from the plane. As they moved toward the ambulances, Laynie spotted Ty Wong and the local CIA station chief. Both rushed over to assure her and the two HRT agents that everything was ready at the hospital for the four of them and that they would meet them there.

CHAPTER SEVENTY-ONE

In Manila, Ricardo Perez and the NBI Agents were preparing to go back into the strip clubs. This time, however, in addition to checking ID's and making the patrons feel as uncomfortable as possible, the agents had also made good on their promise to bring along the licensing authorities.

When they were met by the manager at the door of the club in Makati, Ricardo asked him, "Do you have Buruk and Sam for me?"

"I told you I never heard of them," he responded.

"Okay," Ricardo answered, pointing in the direction of the licensing men, "These men are here to check your books."

"Wait, you can't do this," objected the manager.

"They can and they will," Ricardo told him, "and, we are here to make sure that no one gets in their way."

Grudgingly, the manager led them through the crowd and into his office where he pulled a CD from a box sitting on the credenza behind his desk and tossed it onto a nearby table.

One of the licensing examiners put the CD into his computer and started running it against tax revenues submitted by the club to date.

"Is this correct?" questioned the surprised examiner.

Without looking first, the manager indicated it was. He then walked over to look at the laptop screen. His face flushed and he exclaimed, "Something is wrong!"

It was obvious to the examiner that the club kept at least two sets of books and the manager had mistakenly given the examiner the data with the real numbers prepared for his bosses and not those altered and used in paying the club's taxes.

"This club is closed!" announced the examiner.

"You heard it men, time to clear the building," Ricardo told the agents, as they headed out the door of the office and back into the crowded club.

"Can't we do something to take care of this?" the manager pleaded with Perez.

"Nothing now," he answered, "And remind your bosses that we still do not have Buruk and Sam. Until we do, I can promise them there will be more visits to the other clubs like the one made here."

CHAPTER SEVENTY-TWO

Satellite shots showed Smuuch's compound to be located in the center of very thick foliage. Unfortunately, about all Cole Dawson and the others could identify from this series of photos was an empty pickup truck sitting beside a couple of cinderblock buildings with rusting metal roofs, and numerous bales of suspected *udel*. There were no occupants spotted.

Information gathered by the three agents and the local police officer during the reconnaissance they had now returned from, however, proved much more helpful. One of those single-storied cinderblock structures spotted in the satellite photos appeared to those carrying out the recon to be a residence. It had three doors, and several windows, both covered and uncovered.

The other building appeared to be a large garage or warehouse. It had a regular-sized door on the side, and a large, closed overhead garage door centered in the front. There were also two small windows on the sides, but they were dirty and located too high up on the structure for the agents to be able to see anything inside through their binoculars.

Although there was no sign of Nick Costigan, the police officer was able to identify both Smuuch and Es as they walked beside another man between the two cinderblock buildings. They assumed that the other man was most likely the mate from the *Fantom*.

Dawson's plan of attack called for a security perimeter to be initially set up around the compound. Matt Kelly was assigned to coordinate this phase, and he, along with the two FBI agents from the Guam RA, and the Palau police officers, would man it.

The HRT snipers would set up in positions identified by the sniper who joined Matt and the others when they went in on the initial look and see, and the two HRT assault teams would simultaneously hit the cinderblock buildings when Dawson gave the word.

The police officer from the Peleliu substation would remain with Cole Dawson and help in identifying the subjects and any others they might encounter. In order to maintain the essential elements of stealth and surprise, they would not employ any helicopter support overhead until "all hell" broke loose during the final assault on the compound buildings. Thus, everyone would be shuttled by boat from Ngebad Island to the cove, and move inland from there on foot.

"Communications check," Dawson yelled out.

Everyone put on and adjusted their earpieces and microphones.

"Can you hear me?" One by one, they all gave thumbs-up, and each checked his mike by responding individually.

"Sounds like we're set," Dawson replied. "Let's hit it!"

The men quickly gathered their weapons and equipment, and headed for the boats.

Upon reaching the cove, they discovered that the black fastboat was missing. Had someone borrowed it? Did they just move it to another nearby location? Had Es and the mate taken Nick somewhere else? None of them knew the answers to any of these questions.

"We'll continue the assault on the compound as planned," Cole Dawson told everyone.

Once on shore, the police officer from the Peleliu substation took the lead through the dense vegetation and heavy undergrowth leading onto Smuuch's compound.

Matt moved around the perimeter with the officers and agents, establishing a security net designed to keep anyone from the outside from coming in, while at the same time precluding Smuuch, Es, and the pirate mate from escaping.

Next, the snipers moved quietly forward, camouflaging, and strategically positioning themselves.

With the perimeter secured and the snipers now set and waiting, Cole Dawson moved forward with the two assault teams. Carrying scoped MP-5 submachine guns, and dressed in olive drab uniforms, helmets with goggles, boots, and black ballistic protective vests, the agent operators settled into position for the final assault. They had practiced operations similar to this hundreds of times back at the FBI Academy.

During those intense Quantico training sessions, there would occasionally be a fellow agent operator sitting in a chair, acting as a hostage, while they carried out live-fire training rescues with bullets from the operators guns hitting their mark on mock assailants positioned throughout the room and near the live hostage.

Still, this was not just another training exercise they were about to engage in, but rather the real thing. All one needed to do was take a look around into the piercing eyes and the intensity on the faces of each of the agent operators to get a sense of their mindset and a feel for what they suspected might lie ahead.

"Is the perimeter secured?" Cole asked Matt.

"Ready," Matt replied.

"Snipers in place?" questioned Dawson.

"Set," responded each, individually.

Not seeing anyone, but hearing what sounded like two bellowing voices coming from the inside the cinderblock structure that looked like the residence, Dawson told the two assault teams, "Hit 'em!"

That was also the signal for the chopper support to move in overhead and monitor action on the ground.

Out of the thick, dense, vegetation the FBI agent operators emerged, silently making their way under the rusting metal roofs and toward the entrances leading into both buildings.

Suddenly, tactics employing speed, shock, and violence of action quickly replaced the weapons of stealth and surprise. As the assault teams prepared to enter the two buildings simultaneously, operators tossed flash bang grenades through the doorways. The sound was deafening.

The assault team entering the warehouse found one large, dark, musty room containing knives, tools, a chair and worktables, and remains of *udel* cuttings spread across the floor.

Next door, in the house, Smuuch and the mate made their escape into a nearby safe room, slamming and locking the metal door behind them.

The operators quickly followed, breaching the door and entering the room.

The two hostage takers started firing automatic weapons in the direction of the assault team as Nick sat gagged and helplessly tied to a nearby chair.

The agent operators responded firing their red dot focused MP-5 submachine guns at the two kidnappers. The pirate mate dropped almost immediately, but Smuuch continued spraying rounds randomly around the room and toward the ceiling before finally falling to the floor.

When the building was secured, the operators rushed over to Nick and after cutting the ropes, assisted him up and through the doors to where Cole Dawson was located.

In the meantime, the other assault team had declared the warehouse cleared, and members were already in the process of entering the house to continue the room-to-room search.

"No sign of the other guy in here," the team leader reported over the radio to Dawson.

Gritting his teeth in pain as he spoke, Nick added, "I haven't heard or seen him for a while."

Cole nodded that he understood.

The two agent operators who had helped Nick out of the house lifted his arms around their necks and stretched their arms around his waist so that they could make their way to the waiting chopper.

"Let me know as soon as you arrive at the hospital," Cole told the agents.

"We will," they answered.

Next, Dawson motioned to the Peleliu substation officer. "Let's see who we have here," he said, and the police officer and Dawson headed into the house.

Pointing his finger at the big guy lying face up on the floor, the officer told Dawson, "This one is Smuuch and this other guy must be the mate from the ship. It looks like Es is not here."

"Anyone spotted trying to break through the perimeter?" Dawson asked over the radio.

"No one," replied Kelly.

"Two are dead, and we're missing one."

"We'll keep watching for him," Matt assured the HRT commander.

Scrolling down his cell phone to the number for the SIOC, Dawson clicked onto it and reported, "Both agents are safe," he told the supervisor.

"Let me put you on the speaker," the supervisor told him. "Now, say that again, Cole."

"I said, both agents are now safe."

A loud cheer went up from those inside the SIOC.

"What about the kidnappers?"

"Two are dead, but the one they call Es somehow managed to get away. I'm calling Adze as soon as we finish talking and asking him to have his men start checking around Koror for both the missing fastboat and our man."

"Let us know as soon as you learn anything," the SIOC supervisor responded.

"I will," Dawson assured him. "As soon as we finish here, we'll be heading back to Koror."

"What about Nick?"

"He's on his way back, by chopper, to the hospital there."

"In the meantime, I'll pass along the good news of your successful rescues to those here at HQ and Quantico, and call Bill Robinson in Manila," the supervisor told him.

CHAPTER SEVENTY-THREE

The moment the ambulance carrying Clay and Laynie Steele arrived at the emergency room entrance, attendants rushed the two away to radiology where x-rays of Clay would be taken.

"I'm his wife," Laynie said. "Please let me know as soon as you learn anything," she asked the doctor.

"I will," the radiologist assured her, and the attendant wheeled Clay away.

As Laynie remained in an adjacent room, anxiously awaiting the results, she was soon joined by the two wounded HRT agents, Ty Wong, and the CIA station chief.

"How's he doing?" Ty asked.

"He seems to be in a lot of pain and drops in and out consciousness," she answered. "That's about all I can tell."

The four continued to talk with her for a while longer, and when it was time for them to leave, Ty told Laynie, "We'll be in the waiting room, so if there is anything you need or anything we can do, you just let us know."

Trying to maintain her composure and hold back any tears, Laynie didn't say anything, but nodded that she understood and appreciated them being there. She would be joining them later.

In the meantime, the series of x-rays had been taken and the doctor was slipping the large sheets of film into the channel in front of the white light.

After concentrating his attention on an area near the spinal cord for several minutes, the radiologist asked the technician, "Please bring Mrs. Steele in here."

Although Laynie could manage to limp along on her own, the hospital policy required that she remain in a wheelchair for now. As the staff continued to observe her condition, however, it was anticipated that this restriction would soon be lifted.

When pushed into the room, Laynie sensed that the news might not be encouraging, and fearfully asked the radiologist, "What did you find, doctor?"

The expression on his face conveyed a message of concern and uncertainty. "The bullet is lodged in a location near the spine, creating a possibility that your husband might never walk again."

"That can't be!" Laynie cried out.

"I hope and pray you are right," the doctor responded solemnly, "but I have to let you know of that possibility. You have the finest surgeon on Guam performing the operation and I can assure you that he will do whatever he can to successfully repair the damage."

"May I see Clay now?" she asked.

"Sure. He'll start being prepped shortly, but you can stay with him until then."

Laynie took a deep breath before moving next to Clay. She didn't want him to sense how upset she was after being told what she had by the radiologist. Taking his hand in hers and giving him a kiss on the cheek, she whispered, "Ashley and I love you very much."

Clay sensed her presence and squeezed her fingers.

"Time to go," the orderlies quietly announced.

Laynie gave Clay one last kiss before she was pushed away in one direction and he in the other.

On her way to join the others in the waiting area, Laynie noticed a door marked "Chapel," and asked the attendant to stop. Inside she found a quiet and dimly lit room with religious symbols hanging on the walls, a small stained-glass window, several chairs, a table, rugs, and three rows of pews with kneelers. Since there was no one else in there, Laynie asked the attendant to move her to the front. He did, and told her that when she was finished to press a button hanging from an arm on the chair and he would take her to the waiting area. Laynie nodded she would, and he departed.

Closing her eyes in prayerful meditation, Laynie quietly repeated the "Lords Prayer." She and Clay did not make a practice of "going around preaching to others," but it was obvious to anyone who knew them and observed their actions and the way they lived that a strong belief in God and a love of family were the most important parts of their lives. Laynie was consoled by her faith and although in times like these one is often heard asking, "why us," she was comforted and realized a sense of lasting relief because of her and Clay's belief.

Moments later, a small group came into the chapel and Laynie pressed the button to leave.

Joining Ty and the others in the waiting area, Laynie tried to remain strong and unemotional. She initially resisted revealing what the radiologist had told her, but as time wore on and the pressures built, she buried her face in her hands and began to sob.

"Those bastards!" she cried out. "All he was trying to do was save me, and they shot him. Now, the doctor tells me he might never walk again."

Not knowing exactly what to say, or how to say it, the four men surrounding Laynie looked at one another and shook their heads in disbelief as they tried to console her.

This revelation that Clay might be crippled for life had never entered their minds.

CHAPTER SEVENTY-FOUR

"We found a black fastboat near the port. It wasn't here earlier today," the Palau police officer reported over the radio.

"Any sign of Es?" asked Adze.

"None, but we're still searching."

"You continue checking the port area and we'll have our SWAT guys check out Es's bar," he told the officer.

"Are they already back from Peleliu?" the officer asked.

"Yeah. With the exception of a couple of officers remaining behind to finish securing everything and be there with the coroner, everyone else has returned to Koror," Adze told him before hanging up.

Cole Dawson and Matt were standing less than twenty yards away from Adze when Cole saw Adze raise his arm and motion for the three of them to meet.

"A black fastboat has been found near the port, but there is no sign of Es," he said. "I have men still checking over there, but we also need to go to his bar. Can you and your men back us up?"

"No problem," Dawson answered.

"I'm in on this, too," Matt told them both.

Before approaching the bar, the police officers fanned out and talked to those in the immediate area to learn if anyone had seen Es. When every inquiry came up empty, those in charge made a decision that the closed bar must be approached. Since all of the police officers would likely be recognized, it was agreed that Agent Dave Adams from the Guam RA would pose as a visitor looking for an old friend who, he believed, owned a bar in Koror. If Rena answered the door, he would attempt to get her outside, where the police officers could pull her aside and learn if Es is in the bar. If Es answered, Dave would obviously take him down at the time.

As the Guam FBI agent prepared to approach the door, the Palau police SWAT officers moved up into position. Matt joined Cole and the other HRT agents as they secured a perimeter.

The high sign was now given, indicating everyone was set, and Agent Adams knocked on the door.

There was no response.

He knocked again, and this time heard a woman yell, "What do you want?"

"I'm looking for a friend," he responded.

The door creaked slowly open and Dave Adams moved to the side, making it difficult for her to see him without opening the door all the way and looking out around the frame.

First, she peered through the gap left in the side, and when she couldn't see him, continued her search, gradually opening the door wider and wider, before finally opening it all the way and stepping outside. When she did, Agent Adams pulled her aside and into the arms of the waiting SWAT officers.

Rena screamed, "Run, Es, run! They are here!"

Es leaped from where he was hiding inside the bar and ran out the back door.

"He's mine," Matt yelled, as he and several others took chase.

Reaching out, Matt dove, and caught Es by the foot. Es fell to the ground, and immediately pushed himself up to his knees. Matt lunged forward. Es pulled a switchblade knife from his pocket and clicked it open. The two struggled furiously, as Es attempted to plunge the cold steel blade into Matt's chest. Matt resisted with all the strength he could muster, twisting the tip of the knife back in the direction of his opponent. Their struggle continued to rage until Es suddenly slipped, forcing the forward momentum of his body to drive the switchblade squarely into his chest.

The other agents immediately rushed to protect Matt, and pull Es away in the opposite direction.

"Are you okay, Matt?" one of them asked.

"Yeah, I'll make it," he answered, while wiping some of the blood off his hands and onto his shirt. "What about him?"

"It looks like he's dead," responded the agent standing over Es.

CHAPTER SEVENTY-FIVE

"Is the boss still there?" Cole Dawson asked.

"Just a minute, I'll tell him you're on the line," the supervisor for the SIOC responded.

"Cole," the FBI deputy director answered. "Where are you now?"

"Koror," Dawson replied. "We just finished taking down the guy they called Es."

"Past tense?" the DD responded.

"Yeah, he's dead."

"What happened?"

"We went with the police to the bar Es owns. Dave Adams from the Guam RA knocked on the door and the girlfriend answered. She alerted Es and he tried to make a break for it. Matt Kelly chased him down. They fought. Es pulled a knife, and Matt turned the tables on him."

"How's Kelly?" asked the DD.

"A few scrapes and bruises, but he'll be okay."

"That's good to hear. I guess that leaves us with just the two in Manila," surmised the deputy director.

"As far as I know that's correct," Dawson agreed.

"How are the girls doing?"

"They're all undergoing examinations by the medical staff at the Palau hospital as we speak. After what they've been through I imagine it's going to take months for some of them to get back physically and probably years for most to recover mentally."

"If they ever do," the deputy director solemnly remarked. "Have you heard anything from the Indonesian authorities?"

"They've been contacted by Assistant Commissioner Adze and a team is expected to arrive here sometime next week to escort all of the girls and the Komodo dragon back to Jakarta."

"What Komodo dragon?" The surprised deputy director asked.

"Oh, I guess I forgot to tell you. We found a giant Komodo dragon onboard the ship. He was in a cage so large that they had it built on rollers."

"Any idea why he was there?"

"One of the crew told us he was the captain's pet and that his name is Besar."

"Sounds like this might be the first time the FBI's ever taken custody of a Komodo dragon," the deputy director remarked. "What did Buruk do with him?"

"I think he kept him around mostly for intimidation. One of the girls said the captain threatened to put any of them into one of those dark, empty steel containers alone with the giant dragon if they didn't do what they were told."

"Did he ever follow through on the threat?"

"I don't think so, at least not with any of these girls, but who knows what ever happened with others."

"Or to crew members on ships raided and taken captive by those renegades," responded the DD. "Robinson told me, reports he has received indicated that this guy Buruk and his pirates were some of the most sadistic, vicious bastards out there."

"No question they're bad asses," Dawson agreed. "In the meantime, our agents and investigators from the Palau police will have an opportunity to interview all of the girls before they leave and we'll hopefully find out much more about what happened."

"What about the pirate crew?"

"They're now being held in a makeshift facility here in Koror until we can get them flown to Guam."

"When will that be?"

"Supposedly tomorrow."

"Those should be some pretty heavy interview sessions conducted there, considering everyone will be looking at both the kidnapping of our agents and the killing and wounding of the Palau police officers."

Dawson responded, "Yeah, and remember the girls, too."

"That's right. Speaking of the girls, what is being said about the Indonesian authorities place at the table?" asked the deputy director.

"From what I understand, they plan to eventually request the extradition of the crew members aboard the *Fantom* for the kidnappings and sex crimes carried out against the girls, but that will have to come after we have finished with them, and who knows when that might be."

"Before you hang up, Cole, tell Nick there is one other note of interest. It's a message from Ty Wong that appears to be related to a murder he and Laynie discovered on Pohnpei. A lone crewmember was brought into Ty's office after being rescued at sea by a passing freighter. The seaman reported that their ship, its captain, and he believed all of the remaining crewmembers, were lost during a typhoon. Included in their cargo was the marijuana boarded on Pohnpei that was to be exchanged for some girls being held on another ship at Palau."

"Okay, I'll be sure and pass that along to him," Dawson assured the deputy director.

CHAPTER SEVENTY-SIX

Exhausted after having spent endless hours assisting LEGAT Bill Robinson on the FBI agent kidnappings, Agent Ricardo Perez had at last returned to his office at NBI Headquarters to sign off on several pressing matters before heading home for some well-deserved sleep.

Just as he was getting up from his desk and preparing to leave, the phone rang. "Agent Perez," he answered.

"There is a present for you inside the large trash bin behind your building," the caller told him.

"What is it?" Ricardo asked.

There was no reply.

"Who is this?" he demanded.

The caller again failed to respond, as the line went dead.

Was this just a crank call? Had the trash bin been booby trapped by terrorists? Or, was there something else in there awaiting him?

Although several secured NBI-only trash bins were located on the sides of the building, there was only one bin in the back, and that one belonged to the occupants of a building across the alleyway.

Ricardo immediately reported the call to the hierarchy who decided that everyone should be moved out of the NBI building and any buildings in close proximity until the bin could be checked out. Agents and technicians from the explosives unit rushed to the scene to conduct a preliminary screening.

Although the detection devices identified no explosives in or around the container, the explosives team still opted to remain back, utilizing a remote-controlled robotic track unit with mechanical arms to approach and open the trash bin.

Watching from what they hoped would be a safe distance; the team guided the tracked unit toward the bin. Once in position, the mechanical arms extended to the edge of the cover and flipped it open. Cameras mounted near the tips of the arms transmitted photos of the contents located inside the bin back to those controlling the robot.

"It looks like paper, trash, and mummies!" the understandably surprised technician reported to the NBI personnel monitoring the radio.

"Mummies?" questioned Ricardo.

"That is what it looks like."

"No detection of powders or explosives?" a senior NBI official asked.

"None," the technician answered.

"Then, it's safe to re-enter the area?"

"Yes, as far as we can tell," came the response.

"Give the 'All Clear,' " announced the NBI official.

Once NBI personnel and others from the evacuated buildings had safely returned to their offices, Ricardo, and the team of agents and technicians conducting this operation made their way into the cordoned off area securing the dumpster.

When the contents were carefully removed from the bin, the agents discovered the remains of two semi-wrapped bodies. Their pulverized faces were disfigured nearly beyond recognition, and on the exposed hands of both men were no thumbs and the finger tips had been lopped off, leaving a series of bloodied end joints.

Tied to an uncovered big toe on each was a paper tag. "Sam" was printed in bold black letters on one tag and "Buruk" was clearly lettered on the other.

Although Perez could not tell how long the bodies had been there, it did appear that the crime syndicate had at last given their answer.

CHAPTER SEVENTY-SEVEN

Although the surgeon had skillfully removed the bullet without further damage, the question as to whether Clay Steele might be paralyzed for the rest of his life continued to remain unanswered.

As his eyes opened and Laynie gradually came into focus, a smile spread across her husband's face.

No longer in the wheelchair, Laynie leaned down and gave him a tender kiss.

"Where are we?" Clay asked.

"The hospital in Guam," she told him.

"Why? What happened?"

"You were shot in that cave in Palau and brought here for surgery."

"Huh, I guess I don't remember much," Clay responded.

Laynie gave him a loving smile and nodded. "That's certainly understandable, honey. How do you feel?" she asked.

"A little groggy," he said. "How are you doing?"

"I'll be fine," she answered.

Before Laynie could add anything more, there was a tap on the door and in walked the surgeon. After introducing himself to Clay and telling him a little about the surgery he had gone through, the doctor lowered the railing and started his post surgery examination. Laynie moved back to give the doctor more room.

Waiting anxiously, Laynie agonized over in her mind, what she would say, and how she would react, if the news were bad. She closed her eyes and said a silent prayer.

When he finished with his initial examination, the doctor looked first to Clay and then toward Laynie, as she waited nervously.

A broad smile came across his face when he told them, "It's going to be a while before we know for sure, but as of now, everything looks good."

Overjoyed with the news, Laynie gave the surgeon a hug.

She then leaned down to Clay and closed her eyes as she touched his lips to hers. Lingering there as long as she dare, Laynie gave him a passionate, and loving kiss she hoped he would long remember.

A surprised look came across her husband's face, as he caught a breath. "What was that all about?" Clay responded with a big smile.

"That's for how much I love you," beamed Laynie, as she grinned and gave him an amorous wink.

CHAPTER SEVENTY-EIGHT

Assistant United States Attorney Cheryl Rathmann was now ready to move forward with their case. Although she knew there was no way the FBI was going to bow to the demands of the kidnappers, she had been unwilling to pursue any kind of legal action that could possibly further jeopardize the agents well-being until their safe return was assured. With their rescue no longer in question, it was time to resume the Federal Grand Jury (FGJ) proceedings. She would immediately begin eliciting testimony from witnesses and presenting the evidence necessary for the issuance of a True Bill.

In connection with these FGJ proceedings, Rathmann hoped that the man known to them only as Luis Ayala would finally see the light and be more forthcoming with information about both him and the organization he worked for. So far, though, he had been totally uncooperative, and with no criminal record and no fingerprints on file, there remained little additional for them to go on regarding confirmation of his true identity and background.

In addition to working with Rathmann in preparing witnesses and gathering evidence for presentation to the FGJ, Jack Stacy would also be assisting a Los Angeles district attorney investigator in his attempt to tie this case with theirs by identifying the driver who ran down the LA health inspector in the as of yet unsolved hit and run murder.

Meanwhile, after successfully defending his San Francisco celebrity client in the bungled murder-for-hire plot, Mitchell Kip returned to Los Angeles nearly half-a-million dollars richer. While gone, Kip did return the call Cheryl Rathmann left for him after she received word of the agents' kidnappings and ransom demands. His client's mocking response to the agents' fate, coupled with a refusal on Ayala's part to cooperate in any way with Jack Stacy, however, had put Rathmann in no mood to offer up any kind of deal to Kip and his client. As far as she was concerned, their subject should receive the maximum sentence allowed under the Federal Sentencing Guidelines and forfeit anything and everything they could identify as being derived from the illegal activity.

To that end, special agents and forfeiture specialists of the FBI continued to identify assets, while attorneys from both the Bureau and the United States Attorney's Office moved forward with the seizure actions. Already identified for forfeiture were ships, apartment buildings, strip malls, several small grocery stores, restaurants, movie theaters, strip clubs, video arcades, a large precious metals business, an international jewelry operation, and numerous bank accounts located both in the U.S. and around the world.

IRS-CID agents had also now joined the investigation, and in addition to working up criminal tax cases against all of those involved, these financial investigators would continue searching for additional leads as they sorted through those "hawala" folders found in the file cabinet at the West LA apartment building.

CHAPTER SEVENTY-NINE

What had started out with a new bank teller reporting "something kind of funny going on," when a mysterious man made suspicious cash deposits three days in a row, had turned into a high profile international organized crime investigation with tentacles that spanned across the Pacific.

This combination of OC sex slave trafficking syndicates, sadistic modern-day pirates, kidnappings, and a myriad of money laundering schemes had provided Assistant United States Attorney Cheryl Rathmann and FBI Special Agent Jack Stacy with a career case.

Case Title: **SWASHBUCKLER**

EPILOG

Jack Stacy continues to work and play as hard as ever in LA as an FBI street special agent. He vows never to move into FBI management and divides most of his off-duty time between the horse race track and the golf links.

Harold Moore decided that while still in good health and able to enjoy travel with his wife and a life with his grandchildren, he would stop chasing the bank's money. He told friends he had enough money to live on, and decided it was time to retire – retire.

Teri Lee received a promotion she had been seeking to the Bureau of Immigration and Customs Enforcement Headquarters, and has since made the move to WDC.

Jim Cassidy retired from the LAPD and relocated to Idaho where he built a house overlooking the Snake River and now spends his days kayaking, hunting, and fishing.

Winston Lange III remains assigned as the FBI special agent-in-charge for the Honolulu Division where he will likely stay after having received word that he should not expect to receive further advancement.

Adze was confirmed and received his promotion from assistant commissioner to commissioner of police in Palau.

Ty Wong retired from his position as FBI supervisory special agent for the Guam Resident Agency and is now in business with **Eric Costigan** operating dive shops on Guam and Chuuk.

Bill Robinson returned from his LEGAT position in Manila to FBI Headquarters in Washington, where he is serving as an inspector on the Inspection Staff.

Cole Dawson received another extension exempting him from the mandatory FBI special agent age retirement provisions, and shortly thereafter moved from commander of the Hostage Rescue Team to the special agent-in-charge of the Critical Incident Response Group.

Laynie Steele has since been re-assigned from her duties as the FBI's liaison agent to the Pacific Island nations. She is currently the White Collar Crimes / Terrorist Financing program manager and field supervisory special agent for the FBI's Honolulu Division. She nominated **Matt Kelly** to receive the FBI heroism award for saving her and Clay's lives.

Clay Steele fully recovered from his surgery with no ill effects. Continuing to write novels, volunteer as a youth swim team coach, and carryout intermittent assignments for the Agency, he remains a busy stay at home dad for Ashley.

Cheryl Rathmann was recently promoted to chief of the Criminal Division in the Office of the United States Attorney for the Central District of California. While successfully prosecuting the LA portion of the SWASHBUCKLER case, she learned the true identity of the man using the alias "Luis Ayala," and secured a long prison sentence for him, as well as all of the others involved. Maximum forfeiture of those assets derived from the criminal activity was also obtained.

Nick Costigan and **Matt Kelly** returned to Guam and Palau where they joined **Laynie Steele** in testifying at the pirate trials. Both continue to work internationally and remain assigned as supervisory special agents on the faculty of the FBI Academy at Quantico.

ABOUT THE AUTHOR

Ron Cleaver served more than twenty years as an FBI Special Agent and he is currently a writer and international advisor. During his FBI career, he investigated and supervised complex criminal investigations and was a member of the faculty of the FBI Academy at Quantico. His international assignments with both the FBI and as an advisor / consultant have taken him to over forty countries around the world.